CREATURES OF THE ID

CREATURES OF THE ID

Richard Cain

4-CAIN

Copyright © 2000 by Richard Cain.

Library of Congress Number: 00-192009
ISBN #: Softcover 0-7388-3534-X

All rights reserved. No part of this book may be reproduced or transmitted in any form or by any means, electronic or mechanical, including photocopying, recording, or by any information storage and retrieval system, without permission in writing from the copyright owner.

This is a work of fiction. Names, characters, places and incidents either are the product of the author's imagination or are used fictitiously, and any resemblance to any actual persons, living or dead, events, or locales is entirely coincidental.

This book was printed in the United States of America.

To order additional copies of this book, contact:
Xlibris Corporation
1-888-7-XLIBRIS
www.Xlibris.com
Orders@Xlibris.com

CONTENTS

TO MY PARENTS AND MY WIFE, SHARRON,
FOR THEIR LOVE AND SUPPORT

ACKNOWLEDGMENTS

I am indebted to John Malcom Brinnin for his kind permission to quote lines from his poem, "Architect, Logician." The sonnet, "I know a hundred poems . . . ," is my own, as is the poetry attributed to the protagonist's college friend, Dick.

Much of the Sahaptin language used in the story was adapted from Professor Eugene S. Hunn's excellent reference on mid-Columbia Indians, *Nch'I—wana—The Big River*, published by the University of Washington Press, Seattle (1990). Other background material came from another fine reference, *A Guide to the Indian Tribes of the Pacific Northwest*, by Robert H. Ruby and John A Brown (University of Oklahoma Press, 1992). Any distortions, errors, or misinterpretations of historical, linguistic, or cultural facts are mine.

Disclaimer:

This novel is a work of fiction. Events, characters, and names are used fictitiously. Descriptions of the traits, opinions, and actions of characters representing or named after real public figures are purely fictitious. Any other resemblance to actual persons or events is coincidental.

Richard E. Cain

PROLOGUE

As soon as it was light enough to see on that fall morning in 1958, Dad and I crawled stiffly out of our tent into the wet chill of the fog. We shivered down our cold biscuits and hot tea quickly and quietly and we were soon shouldering our packs to head farther up the mountain.

In places, the fog seemed as thick as freshly sheared wool. In those places we could barely see the trail at our feet. Then it would swirl away, and fifty yards farther up the hillside the vine maples, their burgundy leaves muted in the gray light, would come into view for a minute before fading again into the mist.

Dad led in his usual professorial gait, deep in thought, his blackthorn walking stick measuring our progress in even-metered prods.

Thinking of nothing in particular except the regularity of my heavy pulse and the placement of my feet on the rocky path, I nearly ran into Dad when he stopped abruptly. He was staring into the wall of mist that separated us from the hillside above.

He froze like a setter pointing a covey of quail, and I followed the jut of his jaw to a point about thirty yards up the hillside.

At first, I saw only a cloudy swirl against an indistinct background. Then, after a few seconds, the mist thinned momentarily and I saw a weathered snag protruding from a jumble of moss-covered lava rocks. I wondered what Dad saw that I didn't.

As I studied the hillside through the shifting mist, I began to see that the snag resembled an animal, a bear perhaps, but different.

I started to comment but Dad waved his hand slightly to stop me. When I glanced back at the stump, its shape and position had changed. Then the mist began to close in again.

Must be the light and the mist, I thought. Everything on the hillside seemed to run together like objects in my watercolor paintings.

Even at ten years old, I knew the silence and the fog stimulated the imagination and that one must never let the imagination get loose. For once out of its cage of common sense, it would create monsters real enough to make you pee your pants.

As I tried to focus my eyes on the depthless fog, I began to feel a hot surge of excitement. There was something wild out there, something big and furtive, something I had never seen before. And judging from Dad's catlike intensity, it was something he had never seen before either.

We stood there motionless for a very long time, straining to see and hear. But the fog hovered over us and the only sounds were the sounds of our breathing, now amplified a hundred times it seemed in our attempts to hear beyond ourselves.

What was it? Did my father know? I was bursting with questions.

The adrenaline surging through my body kept me from feeling the packstraps biting my shoulders, the cold air gnawing at my fingertips, the ache chewing its way through my foot from a sharp rock I was standing on.

At last the cold air stirred and the hillside materialized out of the fog. Nothing. There was no stump. The whatever-it-was was gone.

And then the stirring became a steady breeze and a patch of blue opened up overhead. Gradually the fog dissipated and the mountain stood naked in the morning brightness.

Dad took out his binoculars and searched every inch of the hillside. Nothing out of the ordinary was to be seen. Finally, leaving our packs on the trail, we climbed to the spot where the thing had been standing. With agonizing meticulousness, Dad scrutinized every stone, every tuft of moss in our path as we approached the spot.

It's true Dad was sometimes a little absent-minded, forgetting where he left his keys or his battered briefcase. When he was thinking about something else, which was most of the time, he would drive right past our driveway and not realize it until he got to the stop sign at the bottom of the hill. But when he was looking for something, nothing escaped his keen observation.

Indirect evidence was as telling to my Dad as if he had witnessed the entire event. A smudge, a broken twig, a twisted leaf might tell him as much as a ten-page report. You could never be sure whether he was paying attention or not when he was walking or driving, but when he was really paying attention it was as if his whole being were concentrated in his eyes, like he had x-ray vision or something. It was awesome to behold.

He began working his way around the spot in a decreasing spiral, searching for any signs the creature might have left: footprints, hair, feces. Everything was dripping with mist. Our own movements left a clear path through the tiny pearls of moisture huddling on every surface.

On the high side of the spot, Dad found a broken spider web from which the mercurial droplets had been shaken off. And a short distance from the spot on a pristine pad of moss, pointing away from the broken web, was stamped the partial imprint of a huge, human-like foot. Nothing more.

Dad looked at me with a broad grin. I hadn't seen him so excited since he had found some small errors in Owen Chamberlain's calculations in a paper on antiprotons.

Sometimes Dad would cry when he read a novel or listened to music—at least tears would run down his face. He didn't seem to be ashamed of it. Nobody ever said anything about it so maybe I was the only one who noticed. The tears were running now, trickling down the creases made by his grin, scintillating red and blue and green in the sunlight as they danced on his square chin.

The first word he spoke was "Sasquatch."

"Son, we have just seen a Sasquatch. My God, I didn't think it was possible. I can't wait to see the look on Sid's face when I tell him about this." Dr. Sidney Cunningham, professor of psychology and Renaissance man, was my Dad's best friend. Dad always said he was the smartest man he had ever known.

Dad noted the approximate dimensions of the footprint in the dog-eared notebook he always carried. He made his own footprint beside it and compared the indentations in the moss. The creature's foot had crushed the moss much flatter than Dad's foot had and it was evident even to me the creature had weighed much more than my Dad's 195 pounds.

There were many unanswered questions. Actually, there were no answers to any of the questions. What was the creature doing there? There was no evidence it had been bedded there, and there didn't seem to be anything in the area to eat. And how had it vanished so quickly without a sound or hardly a trace?

It took no time at all for my feverish questions and Dad's reasoned responses to propel us up the mountain another two miles to a vantage point overlooking the Lewis River drainage area. To the east 12,000 foot Mt. Adams gleamed like an enormous tooth protruding out of a dark, dense forest of silver spruce. To the south, partially obscured by haze, 11,000 foot Mt. Hood dominated the purple horizon beyond the Columbia River. Below us thick, white fog still blanketed the valleys.

I decided there was enough country out there to hold a myriad of mysteries, conceal a thousand secrets, and hide all the exceptions to the rules. Out there one might find the unexpected and the implausible, the improbable and the impossible. All of which were a lot easier to believe while shrouded by creepy mist and circumferenced by prehistoric wilderness. Maybe it was too easy.

But Dad was certain. That was all I knew for sure and all I needed to know then. Still, I couldn't help wondering how it would all seem when I got back to Seattle, back to school, back to civilization.

CHAPTER 1

Noble Savage

By the third week of January 1971, the northeast monsoon was beginning to blow itself out, its rumbling low clouds and sniffling showers lingering like the last sobs and whimpers of an infant's tantrum. Weather for low-level air operations would be marginal, probably allowing flights in the afternoon only, when the lower clouds tended to break up for a few hours to release the pent-up gray light filtering through the upper strata. In three months the southwest monsoon would crawl in and throw its own tantrum.

A broken, muddy track euphemistically designated "Highway 9" followed the north side of the swollen Xe Pon River about twenty-five miles through the rugged terrain from Khe Sanh in South Vietnam to Tchepone, the NVA's logistical hub in Laos. On the other side of the river valley ran a sheer sandstone escarpment leading steeply into mountains that here and there snagged the ragged ceiling of clouds moving across them. Snarls of dense undergrowth matted much of the area, and a dripping double-canopy jungle stood knee-deep in muddy swirls along the river.

In a few days American troops along the DMZ would begin sweeping the area along the Laotian border and reestablish Khe Sanh as a base of operations. ARVN airborne, armored, and infantry units were supposed to launch an assault along Highway 9 and destroy the logistic installations and supplies in and around Tchepone.

At the time I didn't know the details, just that an operation into Laos was imminent, and intelligence on NVA movements was needed. I did know it would be an ARVN operation and that its success would most likely depend on the information provided to American air support and artillery by the dozens of American-led reconnaissance teams that had infiltrated southern Laos to gather intelligence. As I studied the area from my observation point on a hill overlooking the valley, I shook my head.

The low clouds obscuring the higher parts of the hilly Laotian terrain would channel helicopters and low-level air operations into a few corridors where enemy antiaircraft units could concentrate. The one-lane road, flanked by ridges, begged for ambushes, and the destruction of any vehicle on the narrow road would stall the entire column. It didn't seem to require much imagination to envision the potential for a debacle of the first order. But then, as Second Lieutenant Huddlestone was fond of pointing out, "Soldja, you don't have the big pickchah"—which I soon came to understand as that sorry scheme of things entire by which all ostensible anomalies of logic and common sense were accommodated and molded closer to the heart's desire of the powers that were.

After all, who was I to say anything about anything? I had entered the University of Washington in the fall of 1966 with an ambition to become an anthropologist—American Indian culture having been an interest of mine, fostered and encouraged by my adoptive father since I was ten years old. Many of my friends from high school were facing the possibility of military service. Some of the kids who graduated from high school before me had been sent to Vietnam. Several had died there already. Whether or not our involvement in Vietnam was necessary or just, I was deeply disturbed that there were those who denied their obligation to share the risk and responsibility of military service. It was just not right for some to bear the burden of war while others shirked. Not that I was eager to die for my country—it just violated my sense of honor and ethics to allow someone else to die for my country in my stead. So, feeling guilty about my college deferment and angry at the abusive protesters who harassed the military recruiters at the Student Union Building, I dispatched my hundred and eighty credits in slightly less than three years. On a wet, blustery morning two weeks before Easter, 1969, I callously ignored my parents' pleadings and reported to the Armed Forces Induction Center in north Seattle for my induction physical.

And now here I was in Laos, where the Cooper-Church Amendment said I was not supposed to be, trying not to think about why I was here. An E-5 LRP on special operations assignment with MACV/SOG, I talked the talk and walked the walk with the best and worst of them, acting out the unlikely persona of a bad-assed warrior that I could not have invented even in my dreams a scant two years earlier. But to anyone who cared enough to reflect on the matter, I was nothing more than an expendable, disposable tool. All I wanted to think about was doing my job without getting any asses shot off, especially mine. There were only three rules: get in, get the information, and for Christ's sake whatever you do, don't get caught doing it.

The overwhelming majority of the spec ops (special operations) team leaders came from special forces units—Green Berets, Recon Marines, Rangers, Navy Seals. They were tough, professional soldiers who had been hardened and honed to razor sharpness by years of experience and endless training. The fact that I was out here with them was a fluke, the result of the kinds of improbable errors, oversights, and vacuousness that have made "military intelligence" a definitive example of the term "oxymoron."

The story of how I found myself in a Long Range Reconnaissance (LRP) unit my first month "in country" and working with Special Operations in less than a year has never failed to get me a free beer or two when narrated to any bar patron who has ever worn a sleeve with a stripe on it.

When I first came to Vietnam in August of 1969, after a week of processing in Dha Nang I was sent out on a helicopter that dropped me off at the camp of Bravo Company, 1st Brigade, 9th Infantry, somewhere up by the DMZ. I stumbled around the camp with my gear asking directions to the 2nd Platoon until I finally found it and reported to the platoon leader, Second Lieutenant Rufus Huddlestone, a gung ho, red-haired, stiff-necked product of Officer's Candidate School and, as I soon suspected, of some anachronistic military school in Georgia.

I stood at attention while the lieutenant looked me over.

"What's yowa name, private?" he asked. His Georgian accent was as thick as I had ever come across.

"Sir! Brockman, John T., Sir!" I was determined not to let that scowl fringed with carrot-colored hair and overlapping freckles find fault with my military manners.

He raised his orange eyebrows and smiled slightly.

"You look like an Indian," he drawled. "Brockman is a funny name for an Indian. Don't chew have some tribal name you go by?"

"Sir?" I couldn't believe he was serious.

"Yowa Indian name, what is it?" he asked impatiently. Jesus, he was serious! I blurted out the first thing that came into my head.

"Sir! Trotting Fox, Sir!" The lieutenant beamed with satisfaction.

"Ah knew it! Trotting Fox! A real honest-to-goodness noble savage raht heah in mah platoon." He grabbed my hand and shook it vigorously. "Welcome, Trotting Fox," he said, saluting, "Ah welcome you as a brother warrior. Yes suh, those Sioux braves are the fahnest lahht cavalry in the wuld!"

In spite of my shock I managed to mumble a "Thank you, sir. Yes they are, sir." Where had this guy been for the last hundred years?

The lieutenant turned to the sergeant standing nearby whose barely concealed look of disgust seemed to escape the lieutenant.

"Sergeant Hines, you see this heah warrior gets settled in proppah now, you heah?

"Yes sir," the sergeant responded wearily and led me out of the lieutenant's bunker. We looked at each other and there was no need for either of us to say anything.

It got even more interesting.

After a few weeks and a few patrols, the lieutenant, convinced I was a natural-born scout, decided to send me out with a LRP team assigned to our company, despite their vehement protests. I could understand why they didn't want an FNG (fucking new guy) tagging along, but I was naive and eager to go. For some reason both the company commander and the executive officer were gone that day so the LRPs had no recourse but to take me along. The LRPs didn't hide the fact they were plenty pissed, and I should have known what was coming, but that was before I learned how things were done.

At dusk they led me into the bush. For four hours I stumbled and fell in the dark, as they led me on a tortuous route through fields of elephant grass that sliced my hands and face, and across sucking-mud swamps swarming with bloodthirsty mosquitoes.

We finally stopped, and having been rudely threatened at the outset not to talk or make any noise whatsoever, I sat up the rest of the night as silent as a tombstone, thinking the other four guys were doing the same thing. As soon as it got light, I discovered I was by myself. The other guys had disappeared sometime during the night. I waited around for a couple hours before I realized they weren't coming back for me and then I got really panicky. They had done the navigating and I didn't have a clue as to where I was or how to get back. I knew Rufus was going to be sadly disappointed in his noble savage.

I had heard the stories about the mines, the booby traps, the VC snipers, and the distinct possibility of being shot by another American. Moving in any direction seemed like a bad idea, but so did just sitting there. The land appeared to rise slightly to the west, and I thought maybe I could find a high place from which I might be able to see something. Following the rise, I came to the high place: a grassy knoll about fifty yards in diameter, surrounded by trees, and all of fifteen or twenty feet higher than the ground I had come from. There was nothing else to do but sit at the edge of the clearing and get heavily into feeling sorry for myself.

I sat there for half an hour before I heard them. A few seconds later three Hueys appeared over the clearing. One of them was smoking badly and dropped into the clearing like a rock while the other two circled. The gunner, carrying his M-60, jumped out of the smoke-filled helicopter, the pilot right behind him. One of the circling Hueys descended steeply to pick them up. I ran toward them waving and yelling at the top of my lungs. As I approached, the gunner must have heard me above the noise of the descending chopper because he whirled and pointed his M-60 at me as if to fire. I slid to a halt and the gunner, apparently seeing I wasn't worth shooting, motioned for me to come on over. God was I glad to see those guys! Ten minutes later they had dropped me off back at camp and had continued on toward their own base to the south.

When the four LRPs filed into the lieutenant's bunker later that afternoon and saw the two of us drinking coffee and talking about Indian stuff, they simultaneously moaned and gave each other that oh-shit-we're-in-for-it-now look. The lieutenant got up and, to their amazement, greeted the LRPs cordially.

"Glad to see y'all made it back safely, gentlemen. Trotting Fox has told me all about how y'all ran into that NVA patrol and got separated during the naht. Lucky thing y'all had this fahn warrior along. He didn't want to say much about it, but ah did get him to tell how he held off the NVA so y'all could get away. Ah told you he was a natural-born scout and fahter." The LRPs just looked at me sheepishly and grinned.

"Yes, sir," they all said, and one of them added, "He's got some pretty good moves and that's a fact."

I don't know whether he was taken in by the lieutenant's fantasy or if he just wanted to rescue me from it, but shortly thereafter the company commander learned of my "natural-born" talents and sent me off to Recondo (Reconnaissance/Commando) school and I became an official LRP.

All of the Special Operations work was carried out by volunteers and there was a long waiting list of Special Forces personnel who were eager for that assignment. I was assigned to a Ranger company in the reactivated 75th Infantry, designated as the parent unit of all LRP companies. Of course, in a Ranger company, LRPs like me, who had not undergone Ranger training, were not allowed to wear the Ranger arc, i.e., we weren't Rangers; we were just LRPs attached to a Ranger company.

Three months before my tour of duty was up, the CIA approached me with an offer of a five-thousand-dollar reenlistment bonus and a promotion to E-5 to work in Special Operations. Apparently, a report of a well-educated American Indian Ranger with "uncanny natural abilities" as a recon scout had been picked up by someone in the CIA and "verified" by my meteoric rise from FNG to LRP in a matter of mere weeks. The CIA had decided I was bad and they wanted me. It was an offer I couldn't refuse.

* * *

AGE OF INNOCENCE SEATTLE, WASHINGTON 1958

I don't really know how sure I was of what I had seen on Mt. St. Helens. That eerie glimpse of something through the swirling mist became less and less distinct the more I tried to revisualize it. Mostly it was my father's certainty that bolstered my acceptance of the incident as fact. I wanted to believe in Sasquatches—what ten-year-old wouldn't?—but I would not have had the conviction or self-confidence to believe my own eyes if it hadn't been for my father's enthusiasm and my complete faith in him.

I knew the event was momentous without being able to understand its implications or to imagine what might come of it. I sensed my father and I had been made different somehow by the event—different from the man and boy who had set out to hike up the mountain; different from other people. During the next fifteen years I was to learn what that difference would mean to my father and to me.

Any underlying uncertainties I may have harbored did nothing to dampen my excitement about the event. I could hardly wait to tell somebody about our encounter.

When we got back to Seattle, I burst into the house yelling and jumping up and down.

"Mom! Mom! We saw a Sasquatch! We saw it! It was the neatest thing ever!"

"Johnny, you wouldn't be trying to tease me, now would you?" she asked suspiciously.

"Mom," I moaned, "we really saw one—a real Bigfoot, a big hairy thing that looks like a gorilla!"

She looked at Dad, still not certain we weren't joking around.

"Ted? What's this about a Sasquatch?"

"He's right. We really saw one. It was the most extraordinary thing." The way he said it and the way he looked when he said it convinced Mom we weren't kidding. As always, she was immediately concerned about any risks to which we might have been exposed.

"You didn't get too close to it did you?"

By this time Dad was chuckling at Mom's predictable consternation.

"Louise, we were never in any danger. We just caught a glimpse of it at a distance and then it disappeared. If it hadn't been for the footprint, I wouldn't have been completely sure we saw anything at all."

"For goodness sake, Ted, what kind of thing is it? I mean, is it some kind of ape?" She had suddenly become as excited about it as we were.

"It must be, but none I've ever seen before or even heard of. I took Sir Edmund Hillary's accounts of the yeti with a grain of salt, and the stories about Bigfoot sightings all seemed so conveniently insubstantial. Boy, when I saw that thing it really took me by surprise."

"What are you going to do now that you've seen this thing, this Sasquatch?" Mom was always thinking ahead.

"Well, for one thing, I'm going to start taking a camera with me when I go hiking. I think I'll look into this, Louise. I'd like to find out more about these Sasquatches. I'm intrigued as to how they've managed to stay so well hidden—not to mention that they're actually out there at all."

Dad put his huge arm tightly around Mom's petite shoulders and kissed her forehead. Even with her hair stacked pertly on the top of her head she was still nearly half a foot shorter than Dad, who stood four inches over six feet.

As long as I could remember, she had worn her waist-long auburn hair pulled back into a braid and stacked on top of her head. Sometimes in the evening when Dad was away, the two of us would talk as she brushed her hair; and I would marvel at the straight, coppery strands that fell in glowing cascades over her shoulders and down to her tiny waist. Her oval face and delicate features would have reminded me of a china doll except for the lambent expressiveness that animated her every feature. According to her mood, her large, luminous eyes became a bluer or greener shade of turquoise. The smallness of her mouth combined with the fullness of her lips to create a slightly pursed, sultry expression, which Dad always told her put Gloria Graham to shame. Mom was a beauty and I was proud of her.

"You know I worry about you boys out there in the woods and mountains," she complained good-naturedly. "And now I find out there are big, hairy apes out there, too.

"Come in and tell me all about it while I fix dinner," she said as she gathered Dad and me to her and hugged us tightly. "I didn't know when you would be back so we're not having much, just fishsticks and potatoes. Is that all right?"

"Sounds good to me," Dad said hungrily. "How about you, Bigfoot tracker?"

"Me, too. I could eat a whale. How long before dinner?"

"About half an hour, now don't run off."

"I just want to run over and tell Sonny. I'll be back in a flash, ok?"

"Ok, but be back in half an hour." She gave me a swat on my butt as I stampeded toward the door.

Sonny Larson's family had moved into the neighborhood at the beginning of August that same year. I had met him one day down at the park while I was riding my bike. He was my age and had a Schwinn exactly like mine and we got to talking and seemed to hit it off pretty well. Not many kids lived in our neighborhood, and they were either older or younger. Sonny and I were drawn together immediately as each other's antidote for long summer days without much to do.

Sonny was brash and pugnacious, almost getting us into a fight with some kids at the local movie house over practically nothing the first Saturday after we met. But he treated me ok and I was intrigued by his aggressiveness, which by contrast made me seem timid. By the time school started, I had come to regard Sonny as my best friend and I assumed that he felt the same way about me.

The route to Sonny's house demanded that eight major moves be performed in the proper sequence and as rapidly as possible: sprint to corner, crawl under fence, cut through yard, vault over gate, race up alley, slew around house, scramble up stairs, and lean on doorbell. Flushed and panting I leaned on the doorbell button as I waited for someone to appear on the other side of the polished panes of the French doors.

In less than a minute Sonny's mom opened the door. She was wearing an apron, and the house emanated the delicious smells of fried chicken and fresh-baked bread.

"Hi, Mrs. Larson, my dad and I saw a Sasquatch on Mount St. Helens today. Is Sonny here?"

"That's amazing, Johnny. I thought Bigfoot was only a myth. What does your father say about it?"

I could see Mrs. Larson was intrigued and I was flattered by her interest even though I was anxious to talk to Sonny.

"My dad's real excited about it. He's going to read everything he can find about Sasquatches, and we're going to try to find another one and take some pictures of it."

"That sounds very exciting, Johnny. What did this Sasquatch look like?"

"Well, it was big and hairy like a tall man in a gorilla suit. It was kind of reddish brown. We only saw it for a minute and then it sort of vanished. But we did find a big footprint on a mossy rock where it had been standing."

"How close were you and your father to it?"

"We saw it up on the hillside just above us. Dad said it was about thirty yards from us. It was kind of spooky."

As I described the event to Mrs. Larson, I could not quite bring an image of the creature into sharp focus. But I could feel with startling clarity the swirl of cold mountain mist on my sweaty face and hear the thud of my heart as it had pounded twelve hours earlier.

"That's absolutely fascinating, Johnny. Tell your father I'd like to talk to him sometime about this Sasquatch. It's just so interesting."

I nodded with a big grin on my face.

"Run on up to Sonny's room and tell him about it."

I liked Sonny's mother. She was tall and blond and had a really friendly smile and an attentive manner that always made me feel like she was genuinely pleased to see me and interested in what I had to say. Even when she got after Sonny and me for wrestling in the living room or tracking mud on the carpet, there was never any unpleasantness about her.

I never saw Sonny's father very often because he was gone a lot on trips for the Boeing Company. When I did see him, he never had much to say to me, not as much as Mrs. Larson anyway.

"Smells wonderful," I said as I darted toward the stairs leading up to Sonny's room at the end of the hall on the second floor.

"Thank you, Johnny, a compliment like that could get you invited to dinner."

"I'd like to eat with you, but my mom's expecting me back home in a few minutes. Thanks a lot anyway, Mrs. Larson." I felt a slight tug of misgiving followed by a trace of guilt. I was passing

-CAIN

up fried chicken and fresh bread for frozen fish sticks and shoestring potatoes.

She gave me that wonderful radiant smile of hers as she turned toward the kitchen. I bounded up the stairs two at a time. Sonny was going to be amazed and envious as all get out.

* * *

"You're crazy! There ain't no Sasquatches!"

Instead of the awe and admiration I expected, Sonny was bitterly incredulous.

I had entertained a fantasy about the notoriety and prestige my experience would bring me. Sonny's reaction shattered the fantasy into smithereens, like the old vase Sonny and I had accidentally knocked off the stand in his hallway only a week earlier.

"But we saw it—my dad saw it, too. There was a footprint and everything. Don't you see? It means there really are Sasquatches."

"My dad says you might as well believe in Santa Claus and the tooth fairy as in flying saucers and Bigfoot. He says the people who say they've seen things like that are either crazy or trying to pull a trick on somebody. He's an engineer for Boeing; he knows. You and your dad must have seen something else."

If I could have agreed that my dad and I might have been mistaken in what we thought we saw, everything would have been fine. But I was not about to do that. It rankled me that Sonny could suggest his dad was smarter and wiser than my dad. I couldn't let that pass.

"My dad has a Ph.D. in physics and he's a professor at the University of Washington," I retaliated. "Do you think he's crazy or doesn't know what he sees?"

And then we were at that point in adolescent dialectic where anything remotely relevant or rational had already been used and the "at least" had been drawn, not to be resheathed until it had tasted blood.

Sonny transfixed me with his ice-blue eyes as he apparently sought out my most vulnerable spot; then he made his thrust.

"At least I'm not adopted. My dad is my real dad."

At first I was confused. I knew I had been born to Umpqua Indian parents, who had died soon after in a car accident that miraculously I had survived. I had known it since I was five years old. I knew I had been adopted as a baby. I was the one who had told Sonny and I assumed everybody else knew it, too. But my dad was my real dad. He had always been my real dad and he would always be my real dad. No one had ever suggested otherwise, until now. What sort of reply was this? Was this the best rebuttal Sonny could muster?

Then it finally sank in that Sonny was trying to hurt me and that he had been successful in a way he probably hadn't planned. I had been deeply wounded, but not by the business about being adopted. I didn't care about that. What hurt was that Sonny would say something that was calculated to hurt me.

Sonny's disdain and spitefulness were overwhelming and I wilted in the frost of his disfavor. It had never occurred to me how important it was for us to agree about things. Up until that time, I had thought we were in agreement about everything in the universe. I believed we were best friends because we agreed on everything, and because we were best friends, we could not help but agree on everything. Foolishly, I also believed that because we were best friends we could never deliberately hurt each other.

Now a gaping chasm of disagreement and hurt had abruptly opened between us, and the empty ache in the pit of my stomach told me the chasm would be hard to bridge.

The person who I had thought was my best friend was spiteful and would not believe me. What kind of friend would do that? And what good was the truth if I couldn't even get my best friend to accept it? Is this how it was going to be? Could any truth, any belief be worth this awful feeling? At that moment I wished I had never seen the Sasquatch.

I didn't know what else to say to Sonny and if I had thought of something I probably wouldn't have been able to say it without blubbering. So I just turned my back on him and stumbled away, leaving a trail of angry, confused tears all the way home.

I heard Mom and Dad talking in the kitchen when I came sniffing and dripping back from Sonny's. I went straight up to my room and flopped facedown on my bed. My Mickey Mouse alarm clock ticked indifferently at eye level on the shelf next to my bed, its four-fingered hands pointing imprecisely at five-forty something. It seemed impossible so much could have changed in less than half an hour.

Mom's voice echoed into my room from the foot of the stairs.

"Johnny, dinner's ready. Don't forget to wash your hands."

My hunger had been displaced by more acute pangs, and I didn't feel like presenting myself at the dinner table. On the other hand, I didn't want to have to explain why I didn't feel like eating. Reluctantly, I slid off my bed and moped into the bathroom, where I tried to quench my red eyes with splashes of cold water.

Dad sat at the yellow Formica dinette, a steaming mug of coffee in one hand and a folded section of the *Sunday Post Intelligencer* in the other. Mom hovered over the oven with her back to us. I quietly pulled my chair up between the gleaming chromed legs of the table and stared into the street through the kitchen alcove's bay window.

Where the last rays of the setting sun still caught the tops of the big maple trees lining our street, the yellow leaves incandesced against the deep blue sky. The streets, sidewalks, and yards were all spread with fallen yellow leaves. Here and there leaves separated from the branches, wafting and gently fluttering to the ground like enormous xanthic snowflakes. As beautiful as those trees were, they also seemed a little sad and lonely. The frost will come tonight, I thought, and they will be cold.

"Johnny. Johnny? Yoo-hoo. Anybody home?"

I realized Mom was offering me a bowl of green beans and both she and Dad were looking at me quizzically.

"My!" Mom exclaimed, "you were really way out there!" "Do you feel all right?"

Mom always suspected I was on the verge of coming down with something.

"Yeah, I was just thinking about something, that's all."

"Something you'd like to share with us maybe?" Dad asked a little too casually. I just knew he knew.

"Naw, it's not anything important," I said, being careful not to look into his eyes.

He pushed the platter of fishsticks and the ketchup bottle toward me and smiled.

"Ok, but you'd better dig into this before it gets cold."

My appetite came back with my feeling of relief that I wasn't going to have to talk about things I didn't want to talk about. I had two helpings of everything and volunteered to clear the table and dry the dishes. Dad finished the paper and another cup of coffee at the table while Mom and I made small talk over the dishes. When Mom and I had finished putting everything away, I announced I was going up to my room to read some more of *The Adventures of Huckleberry Finn* and I headed for my room with a glass of milk and a handful of peanut butter cookies.

The next day at school Sonny and I didn't speak and I didn't look at him. I don't know if he looked at me or not. I didn't mention seeing the Sasquatch to anyone else at school and, as far as I know, neither did Sonny. That's how it was for the entire week.

4-CAIN

CHAPTER 2

The Lair

Sergeant Chun tapped my shoulder lightly, touched his ear, and pointed down one of the steep draws eroded into the south flank of Hill 836 (designated by its elevation in meters) from which we were observing the river valley below. Chun's keen hearing had picked up the telltale sounds of an NVA patrol ascending the difficult hillside to carry out their own observations and to deny the use of the vantage point to anyone else. It was time to move to another location.

A sinewy wraith barely five and a half feet tall, Sergeant Chun was as loyal and dependable as he was seemingly ageless and indestructible. Completely without fear, indefatigable, and possessed of extraordinary senses and survival skills, Chun was the ultimate scout. He had been among the Nung tribesmen recruited early in the war by Special Forces teams implementing the Civilian Irregular Defense Group project in Laos. Chun had distinguished himself in a Nung Mobil Strike Force unit under Special Forces command and had eventually been given the supervision of Nung recon teams dressed as VC operating along the VC/NVA trail networks.

Whether by intent or by accident, as far I as was concerned Military Assistance Command Vietnam/Studies and Observation Group in all its clandestine wisdom could not have teamed me with a better partner. Whatever Chun's deficiency in spoken English, he more than made up for it with his fluency in Vietnamese, Lao, and several obscure dialects. Chun acquired skills and knowledge easily and displayed great cleverness in solving problems. These attributes, combined with a natural good-nature and a subtle sense of humor, made Chun the ideal recon partner, in whom reliability and compatibility were attributes as crucial as skill and daring.

And how did Chun feel about me? I think the first time he saw me he knew my pathetic experience and skill did not amount to a small pimple on his left buttock. Yet, regardless of the disapproval he must have felt and should have felt, he showed no resentment at being placed under my nominal leadership. Perhaps he was satisfied I didn't pretend to know anything I didn't know and that I deferred to his expertise. Maybe he liked the fact that I wasn't tall, white, and hairy—thanks to my Athapascan-speaking biological parents, whose ancestry I had traced back as far as the Upper Umpqua Miwaletas, "the small long-time-ago people." If Edward Sapir were right about the link between Sino-Tibetan and Nadene (the North American Indian languages, Athapascan, Tlingit, and Haida), perhaps Chun and I shared ancestors 30,000 years ago or so. Of course, Chun did not know anything about the linguistic theories of Edward Sapir. But even putatively ancient blood is thicker than water. For whatever reasons, Chun quickly took on the role of mentor, tutoring me in all things with a paternal interest and patience, seeming pleased and at times surprised at my progress.

I imitated Chun's movements as he carefully stepped along an exposed vein of concrete-like sandstone running around the brow of Hill 836. The NVA patrol would find no tracks, no trace of our having been there. Although the greater part of our invisibility depended on stealth, our faded tiger stripe utilities and olive drab scarves tied around our heads helped us blend into the surrounding foliage. Slung Over our Maguire/Stabo harnesses we carried NVA canvas bags for our rations and magpouches for our AK-47s. We did not much resemble NVA regulars, but in theory, from a distance the outlines of the captured equipment might cause some uncertainty as to who we were, allowing us an extra margin of opportunity to escape. We carried nothing that would serve to

-CAIN

identify us conclusively—no tags, no serial numbers. If we were killed or captured, the NVA would surmise our identity and purpose, but they couldn't prove anything. We would simply disappear without a trace, like the many already missing on covert operations. We had each started with nine canteens of water, which we carefully buried as we emptied them. This was supposed to be the last day of our three-day patrol and we were down to two canteens apiece.

Descending into a brushy saddle between Hill 836 and Hill 1079 to the west, Chun and I moved slowly but steadily, painstakingly untangling the brush in order to move through it quietly. I watched as he moved; he watched as I moved. The plan was to circle the much larger Hill 1079 from behind to avoid being spotted from the valley or from adjacent hills. We could observe from a point two thirds of the way up the far side of Hill 1079 without being in view of the NVA who would soon be settling in where we had just vacated. A straight line between them and our new destination was roughly a click (kilometer). The travel distance by way of the backside of the bigger hill was more than five clicks.

Sandstone bluffs terraced the backside of Hill 1079 and terminated at the bottom in a steep gorge. Colorless morning light barely seeped through the multiple layers of gray clouds, turning the landscape into a grisaille—a watercolor rendering in shades of damp gray unrelieved by shadows except for the velvety depths of the caverns and holes honeycombing the bluffs. Sound, too, seemed deprived of color. The crunch and click of our gray boots through the gray scree languished in a monotone of muffled murmurs, indistinct, as if we had stuffed our ears with gray cotton.

In near perfect silence, Chun and I moved through the pallid gloom in surreal fashion. As I concentrated on my footing and little else, a feeling of familiarity, deja vu, overtook me. I was back on Mt. St. Helens half a lifetime ago in the swirling mist, my heart pounding, my eyes straining in the grayness.

Chun knelt abruptly, silently, his telescopic eyes scanning a point more than a thousand yards ahead of us, where our present course was leading us across the slope of the hill. There were patches of brush behind us and below us, but at that moment we were in the open. We had a clear view of the figures moving toward us, even at that great range—and they of us, if they had looked hard enough.

I had caught sight of the two men for only an instant as they briefly appeared on the hillside and then dropped out of sight again into a ravine. Deliberately and without expression, Chun pointed to a large cave in the bluff about fifty feet up the slope almost directly above us and motioned me to go. Without hesitation, I scrambled up to the ten-foot-high mouth of the cave, although Chun's decision to take refuge in the cave puzzled me.

Stair-like shelves of sandy shale layered the hillside, making possible a virtually trackless ascent to the cave. We could defend the cave easily enough if necessary, at least until we ran out of water or ammunition, but in the end it wouldn't matter because we would be trapped. The golden rule of recon was to avoid being discovered; if discovered, to flee; and to fight as a last resort only. If we had scurried back to the nearest brush patch about fifty yards behind us, we would at least have had the option to flee. But Chun could not have made a mistake. I knew he had a reason for choosing the cave.

The men were still out of sight in the ravine when I got to the cave and I motioned Chun to come up. Goat-like, Chun hopped from ledge to ledge up to the cave. He found a position from which to observe without being seen while I took out my flashlight to have a look into the darkness of what appeared to be a deep, multichambered cavern.

I could stand upright in the largest passage that veered sharply to the right about thirty feet in. The rubescent illumination of my red-lensed flashlight allowed me to see little beyond the closest contours of the cave and its nearly flat floor. But there was no time to explore. In a few minutes, the two men approaching us would be close enough to throw rocks at, and we couldn't be sure they hadn't spotted us.

-CAIN

I turned the flashlight off before starting back to the entrance, a precaution against its being seen from outside. In so doing I fumbled and dropped it. As I bent over to pick it up, the slightly cooler air of the cave flowing outward along the floor gave me a whiff of a stench as repulsively pungent as a litter box that hadn't been emptied since the cat died of diarrhea. Cat?

"Shit! a tiger's lair!" I exclaimed under my breath as I graphically visualized a great saber-toothed cat about to reprise its ancestral vendetta against troglodytic hominoids.

I felt somewhat comforted by the weight of the Chinese-made Kalashnikov cradled in my right arm. Its .30 caliber rounds killed men effectively, but its punch was only about the same as that of a 30-30 Winchester. It was not a big game gun by any stretch of the imagination. I made certain the selector lever was set on full automatic. Backing out of the passage, I tried to convince myself the smell must have come from something else—anything else.

Chun glanced at me inquiringly as I knelt behind him at the mouth of the cave. He saw in my face that I had found something. It was not a good time for us to talk, even in whispers. Besides, I wasn't sure Chun even knew the English word "tiger." Digging a small notebook out of my breast pocket, I hurriedly penciled a bad outline of a tiger and held it up for Chun. He pointed to his eye and I shook my head. "No, I hadn't actually seen it." I held my nose as if smelling something awful. "I smelled it!"

A broad grin spread across his normally expressionless face and he shook his head from side to side slightly as if I had told him a lame joke. Either he discounted the idea of a tiger living in the cave, or the possibility didn't bother him, I couldn't tell which. Whatever the source of the smell, there was no time to worry about it. The men were in sight again.

* * *

THE LAST SUPPER. SEATTLE 1958

A week after the falling-out between Sonny and me, Mom cornered me when I came home from school.

"Sonny's mother called me today. We had a long talk. She was concerned because she hadn't seen you for a week and Sonny didn't have much to say about it. She wanted to know if you had said anything about having an argument with Sonny. We started comparing notes and we both decided you and Sonny have been acting a little strangely since last weekend. Want to tell me about it?"

My mom sometimes gave the impression of being a flibbertigibbet, but she usually knew more than she let on. And whenever she got a whiff of anything that smelled like it might be trouble for Dad or me, she was as relentless as a bloodhound. Once she was on your trail, it was futile to attempt evasion. So the whole thing came out as we sat together on the sofa.

After I had told her what had happened and how I felt about it, she just sat for a minute and looked at me with the sort of pouting frown she always wore when she was contemplating something difficult. Then she moved over a little closer and draped her arm around my neck.

"Sweety, I know how much words can hurt and the closer you are to someone, the more pain that person's words can give you. But people sometimes say things they don't really mean—especially to those who are closest to them—things they later would give anything to take back. I'm sure Sonny is terribly sorry for the things he said. You two have been such good friends. You need to give him a chance to apologize; you need to accept his apology; and the two of you need to get back to being friends.

"It's part of growing up I'm afraid," she continued. "Goodness, I'm surprised the two of you haven't had a knockdown-dragout disagreement about once a week. It's perfectly natural between

-CAIN

friends, and when they work out their differences, it can make their friendship even stronger.

"Come on," she coaxed, "it's been a week. Don't you miss all those things you and Sonny do together? Swallow a little bit of that stubborn pride you men have so much of and let things work themselves out. Ok?"

I wasn't completely persuaded, but I agreed to meet Sonny halfway. I did miss him and I had been thoroughly depressed by the state of affairs all week. However, I still had a problem with the concept of hurting most the ones you like most. It just didn't seem right.

Mom and I had barely finished talking when the phone rang. Mom answered and said it was for me. I had an uncomfortable feeling I knew who it was.

"Hello?"

"Uh, hi, John, it's Sonny."

"Hi, Sonny," I said absently. I wasn't going to make it easy for him.

"Well uh, you know about last week?"

"Yeah, what about it?"

"Well uh I kinda wanted to uh, you know, to say uh I'm sorry. I'm sorry we had an argument, ok?"

I could hear Sonny take a deep breath and then sigh heavily into the phone.

"Yeah, it's ok, Sonny. I mean, I understand. Thanks for telling me you're sorry." I'm sure Sonny heard my sigh as well.

"John, my mother says I should invite you to dinner. You want to come over? I got a new bridge kit for my Erector set, maybe we could put it together."

I suspected Mrs. Larson would be happier to see me than Sonny would be, but I figured it was hard enough for him to have to apologize.

"I'd like that, Sonny," I said, not quite sure it was a lie. Regular time?"

"Yup, six o'clock on the nose just like always."

"Ok, see you then. Bye."

"Bye."

I could see the grandfather's clock through the French doors as I leaned on the Larsons' doorbell: five minutes to six.

Mrs. Larson, beaming as usual, opened the door and surprised me by giving me a hug.

"Come in, Johnny, I'm so glad you could come over for dinner. Nils and Sonny are in the dining room already and dinner will be ready in a few minutes. You know where to hang your coat."

Her teal skirt matched her eyes, and her white blouse and string of pearls made her look pretty fancy for a Monday night dinner. I thought she looked beautiful.

"You look very nice, Mrs. Larson," I stated with the air of an experienced observer.

"Why thank you, Johnny." She looked pleased that I had noticed.

I entered the dining room with trepidation, not having looked directly at Sonny for a week and not having seen Mr. Larson for nearly a month while, according to Sonny, he was in Washington D.C. doing business with the Defense Department. I had never felt too much at ease around Mr. Larson anyway.

There was an awkward exchange of greetings between Sonny and me, and Mr. Larson seemed reluctant to set his wineglass down so I could shake his hand.

I remember Nils Larson as a tall, slender man with piercing gray eyes beneath bushy eyebrows and a thick shock of sandy hair cut close on the sides. From my perspective, he seemed to have a very long face, but his angular features were handsome enough and he had big, even teeth that were nearly as white and shiny as my mom's kitchen sink.

I had shaken hands with Mr. Larson before and I was always impressed by the length of his fingers. Even my mom, who had met him several times, had commented that it was a shame he didn't know how to play the piano.

Mercifully, Mrs. Larson seated us at the table and served dinner right away. More accurately, she served a sumptuous feast: gorgeous china and crystal goblets, a silver chafing dish heaped and sizzling astride a dancing blue alcohol flame, tall white candles in silver candlesticks, and starched linen napkins—the whole fancy shebang.

Mr. Larson talked about his trip to Washington D.C. and drank nearly a whole bottle of red wine during the first part of dinner, his delicate glass cradled loosely between fingers Horowitz would have envied. Mostly, he complained about the restaurants, the hotel, the traffic, the taxis, the flights to and from, and the stupidity of the people with whom he had to do business.

Mrs. Larson was attentive and seemed interested as she interjected questions and made appropriately sympathetic exclamations at all the right junctures. I noticed, however, she gave Mr. Larson a disapproving look when he left the table and returned with a second bottle of wine.

Sonny and I didn't have much to say and we were not called on to say much. I, for one, was happy to occupy myself with eating, although I did tell Mrs. Larson I thought the dinner was one of the best I'd ever had.

As soon as Mrs. Larson's chocolate cheesecake appeared, Mr. Larson directed his attention to Sonny and asked him questions about his activities during the past few weeks. Sonny related an anecdote about Mr. Johnson, our 5th grade teacher, who had conducted class all morning until recess one day with his pants unzipped.

I thought Sonny's gossip was tasteless enough, but Mr. Larson thought it was hilarious and carried on for several minutes, joking about show-and-tell and learning about flies for a science project and some other stupid stuff like that. I was embarrassed for myself and for Mrs. Larson.

Mrs. Larson poured coffee for Nils and curtly placed the cup and saucer on the table directly in front of him. Nils pushed the coffee to one side and set his wineglass there instead. Then came my turn to answer some questions.

"Well then, Johnny, I hear you and your father had a run-in with a monster up on Mount Rainier, was it?" He smiled but it seemed more out of amusement than friendliness and I suddenly felt extremely reticent.

"It was Mount St. Helens, but I don't think it was a run-in exactly," I said hesitantly.

"Ah!" Mr. Larson exclaimed appreciatively, "Mount St. Helens is such a beautiful mountain—and mysterious, too. Just the place to find monsters. Wouldn't you agree, Johnny?"

I wasn't sure how to answer.

"I suppose so," I stammered after a long pause.

Furtively lifting my eyes off my plate, I could see Sonny was watching me intently with more than a hint of a smirk. I guessed he was enjoying immensely watching me squirm.

Glancing at Mrs. Larson, I was startled to see her glowering darkly at her husband. I had never seen her glower before. Becoming aware I was watching her, she quickly looked away and busied herself cutting several more pieces from the cake.

Mr. Larson ignored her and lifted his glass to make a toast.

"Let's drink to all the mm-mysterious mm-monsters on mm-Mount St. Helens." From the way he laughed I assumed he must have meant the exaggerated alliteration to be funny. But he and Sonny were the only ones to laugh.

By now, Mrs. Larson was visibly agitated and trying unsuccessfully to hide it.

"Please have more dessert, everyone," she said nervously. "I'll never be able to get all of this into the refrigerator. Johnny, you'll have another piece, won't you? Nils, wouldn't you like more coffee?"

Mr. Larson didn't reply. He had not touched his coffee yet and I wondered why she was asking him if he wanted more. I accepted another piece of cake, even though I was uncomfortably stuffed. A piece of cake on my plate was something to hide behind.

Meanwhile, Sonny was laughing and really getting into the spirit of the thing. He thrust his water goblet into the air and offered his own toast:

"Let's drink to all the mm-morons and mm-maniacs
who think they see mm-monsters on mm-Mount St Helens!"

Sonny and Mr. Larson began to guffaw uncontrollably. Mr. Larson barely managed to squeak out a "Here! Here!" as he thrust out his brim-full wineglass to touch Sonny's water glass.

A sharp, melodic shatter was followed by Burgundy and water and tinkling shards of glass showering everyone and everything as the two fragile goblets collided above the elegant table.

I sat shocked into saucer-eyed silence as Mrs. Larson screamed and began to sob, and Sonny and his father broke into raucous howls of laughter like two hyenas from Hell.

They were still laughing as I slipped off my chair and, not knowing what else to do, grabbed my coat and hightailed it for home.

I remember feeling sorry for Mrs. Larson because her efforts to reconcile Sonny and me had turned into such a disaster. I also remember how upset I was at seeing her pretty face all terrible and teary. Not counting movies, it was the first time I had ever seen a woman cry. I was sure my mother had never had occasion to cry like that and I hoped she never would.

Mom was furious when I came home wine-splattered and wide-eyed and I recounted the details of my evening's adventure. Fortunately, Dad hadn't come home yet or she probably would have wanted him to go over and punch Mr. Larson's long face. Not that he would have. My father was a kind, gentle, contemplative man, hard to anger. It would have been a grave mistake for Mr. Larson to act untowardly in our house, but it would have required far direr circumstances to move my father to violence.

After picking a piece of glass out of my hair and checking me all over as if I'd been hit by a car, she hugged and kissed me and told she was really sorry about what had happened at dinner and she sent me upstairs to take a bath.

When I came downstairs after my bath, Mom told me Mrs. Larson had called to apologize and to make sure I was all right. Mom said Mrs. Larson sounded like she was having a nervous breakdown.

That was the last time I visited the Larsons' house. Sonny and I got back on speaking terms before Thanksgiving weekend and maintained a cool but civil acquaintanceship for the remainder of the school year. We tacitly acknowledged that our ill-fated friendship had run aground on irreconcilable shoals, never to float again.

Maybe we could have worked it out. I don't know. But because of pride or resentment or something, neither of us could approach the other and finally we just drifted too far apart.

Shortly after school let out for the summer, Sonny and his mother moved to Wichita, Kansas to join Mr. Larson, who had been transferred there several months earlier. It would be a long time before I saw Sonny again, but I did know of his progress from the sad, rambling letters Mrs. Larson would send me sporadically during the next ten years.

It was the first time I had become aware of the terrible human capacity for making final, irrevocable choices. How many times since have I seen human lives and relationships tragically terminated by this perverse ability of stubborn mortals to make eternal decisions.

CHAPTER 3

Troglodytes

We could see now the man in front was an Asian of about the same stature as Chun. The second man was clearly an American, whose bulky six-foot-plus frame would have been impossible to disguise. They were obviously in a hurry, and because they took turns running and covering each other toward the rear, I surmised they were being hotly pursued.

Taking out my binoculars, I glassed the slope behind the two running men. Half a dozen NVA regulars swarmed into view on the far side of the ravine and began firing ineffectively at the two running men, who were at least six hundred meters ahead of them. The distant sound of the enemy's shots seemed almost innocuous and reminded me of popcorn popping in my mom's big aluminum popper. Much closer and far more sinister were the whines and whirs and pings of rounds ricocheting off the slope, some of them rattling against the bluff all around our cave.

I hadn't picked up on the size of the American or how fast they were moving during the few seconds when I had initially observed them, but Chun had, and he had known instantly what was going on. That is why he chose the cave. It was a place to stay out of the action. The two men had enough of a lead to evade their pursuers as soon as they got to the brushy area. While the patrol was busy searching the brush we would slip out and continue on our merry way around the mountain.

No other teams were supposed to be operating in our area, but it was SOP for Command Control to keep all operations and missions secret, even if it involved lying to its own agents and giving them misinformation. If captured, team members could not be forced to give up information they didn't have. The standing order was for all recon teams to avoid deliberate contact with each other.

I thought the two men would run past us and we would never know their names or their mission, or ever see them again. Yet, I felt I did know them somehow. They were like Chun and me, members of the same track team: running to win, running to finish the race, running to survive. I wanted to stand out on the slope above them and cheer them on as they ran by—sweat flying, hearts thumping, lungs burning, muscles screaming—far ahead of the pack.

I had been ahead when I ran in the state cross-country meet my senior year in high school—the first time our team had made it to state in ten years. It had been us against them and we had beaten them; nothing else had mattered.

Now neither wars nor battles nor missions mattered. Only this particular race mattered. Run, goddamnit! Run!

As soon as the bullets had begun to pepper the hillside and the two men knew exactly where their pursuers were, they stopped covering each other and just ran as hard as they could, slipping and stumbling across the loose slope toward the brush patch. The first runner, who appeared to be a Nung, was now at least forty meters ahead of the American and almost directly below the cave. At that moment the pursuers fired one last volley en masse at the runners and disappeared into the ravine to continue the chase.

About two seconds later the rounds they had aimed high above the heads of the distant runners hailed down in a steep arc directly on top of the Nung. At the end of their long flight, the 150 gr. jacketed bullets had slowed to the velocity of a subsonic pistol bullet—slow but lethal. As the bullets splatted, skipped, and whirred all around him, the Nung grunted once, broke his stride, and crumpled into the hillside, rolling and sliding until he came to rest limply against a solitary bush a dozen meters down the slope.

"Fuck!" The bitter expletive hissed involuntarily between my clenched teeth as I watched helplessly. I looked at Chun. The runner was possibly a tribesman of his, maybe even a relative or friend. I felt guilty, ashamed of having sat in the safety of the cave and watched the man die. I wanted to apologize to Chun and I expected to see anger, blame, anguish—something—in his eyes. But there was nothing, not a sign of what he might be feeling.

For all his external impassiveness, I knew Chun was not an unfeeling man and I could not imagine at what cost he maintained his stoic armor against the emotional onslaught from within. I wanted to pity him for his hardness, but I realized that if I should fall, Chun's heart would most certainly weep, even if his eyes did not. I decided I could settle for that.

The American stopped when he reached the place where the Nung had fallen and looked back across the slope. Seeing the patrol had not yet emerged from the ravine, he bent over and gasped for air, steadying himself with the sound-suppressed Swedish K submachine gun in his right hand. He wore tiger strips and a matching boonie hat. His face and neck from his collar to his hat were blackened with camouflage paint. His web gear bristled with half a dozen 36-round mags for the Swedish K.

"I've had enough of this shit, Chun," I said matter-of-factly, and I walked outside the cave where the American could see me. "Hey, buddy, get your ass up here ASAP!"

Before I could say anything else the startled American dropped, rolled, and came up with the submachine gun pointed at me, his white eyes wild in his blackened face. I thought he was going to fire, but then I saw the flash of his big white teeth signaling recognition. Not seeing the patrol yet, he hustled his big frame up the slope and into the cave.

"Jesus, what a fucking dump!" he managed to gasp as he surveyed the cave. There was close-cropped blond hair under his boonie hat when he pulled it off and with his hat off I got a better look at his long face. He seemed to be about my age. I thought I saw something familiar in his penetrating blue eyes.

"I'm John and this is Chun," I said and he crushed my hand and then Chun's in the long fingers of his big dirty paw.

"Thanks for inviting me in. Everybody calls me Sonny."

It seemed an impossible coincidence, but I had to ask.

"Sonny Larson?"

"That's right, do I know you?" He looked at me quizzically.

"If you're the Sonny Larson who went to the fifth grade at University Heights elementary school with Johnny Brockman you do." I could see the wheels turning, but he was drawing a blank. As vividly as I remembered him, I was surprised he didn't remember me. Finally it came to him.

"Oh yeah, now I remember. You're the Indian kid who used to come over to my house all the time. Shit, man, that was a long time ago. Talk about your small fucking world!"

Chun had been watching for the patrol and he motioned us to stop talking. Six North Vietnamese soldiers in dark green uniforms and pith helmets trotted toward us in single file, their canvas packs bouncing on their backs.

They should have left an observer to keep the runners in sight while the rest of the patrol crossed the ravine. The patrol leader must have assumed the runners would continue straight across the slope to the cover of the brush. Apparently, they were as green as their uniforms. With any luck they would continue the chase into the brush and give us a chance to didi out the other way.

I quickly presented my assessment of the situation with a few gestures and both Sonny and Chun nodded in agreement. If the patrol decided to investigate the cave, we'd have to play it by ear.

The patrol stopped where their distant shots had rained death upon the fleeing Nung. The leader greeted the Nung's body by firing a dozen rounds into it without bothering to descend the slope to check it. He was interested in the American only. Looking around suspiciously, the patrol leader began to study the bluff above him. Maybe he wasn't quite as green as I had thought. Picking three men, the patrol leader barked some instructions and pointed to the several caves above him that were accessible and large enough to accommodate a man—including the cave we occupied. He then trotted off toward the brush patch with the other two soldiers.

After discussing it for a minute, two of the three men assigned to check the caves produced Russian-made grenades from their packs and began climbing toward the base of the bluff. The third lagged behind to provide cover with his AK-47.

One of the men climbed obliquely up the slope in the direction of another large cave fifty meters to our left. The other one moved up the hillside toward us with a grenade in his hand.

The three of us pulled back from the mouth of the cave so we wouldn't be seen. We could take these guys out, but the other three would be back as soon as they heard shots and we'd have to start all over again. I had a hunch these guys were going to toss a grenade into the likeliest caves and have a peek when the smoke cleared. If they didn't see anything, they were going to tell the patrol leader the caves were clear.

I looked around the cave. The sandstone was hard and thick. One grenade was not going to cause it to collapse. We could still hide. There was that stinking black tunnel at the back of the cave. It was a variation on the Lady-or-the-Tiger dilemma, only there was no lady and I was deliberately choosing the door I thought the tiger was behind. Time was up. I had to decide right then.

I motioned for Chun and Sonny to follow and scurried toward the back of the cave on all fours. They hesitated and I frantically pointed to the passage. Chun moved first, followed reluctantly by Sonny. As soon as we rounded the bend in the passage on our hands and knees, I turned on my flashlight. We jumped to our feet and careened down the dark, irregular tunnel, oblivious to everything except the imminent expectation of a grenade exploding behind us.

The passage descended steeply. Suddenly we were tumbling into a large cavern, large enough that I could not make out the opposite wall in the dim redness of my flashlight beam. The smell was staggering. Then a jarring thump shook the cave, followed by the concussion and deafening noise reverberating through the chamber. Sand and pebbles showered down from the cavern ceiling and a cloud of dust boiled out of the passage. My eardrums ached and it sounded as if I had a phone ringing in each ear.

I turned the flashlight off and the three of us crouched in the dark with our weapons pointing into the dust-filled passage, waiting.

Ten minutes passed, then another ten minutes. The dust had mostly settled except for flour-like particles still floating in the foul air of the cavern. The ringing in my ears had become a hissing roar that reminded me of the sound of a seashell held to my ear. Not being able to hear well bothered me and I wondered how long the effect would last.

It turned out that my hearing was still adequate to detect a sound I would rather not have heard. From somewhere in the darkness a low, menacing growl emanated, releasing a jolt of adrenaline into my blood and pumping up my pulse by a dozen throbs a minute. Had Chun and Sonny heard it? Had I actually heard it, or was it just another complaint from my battered eardrums? There it was again, and it was no more imaginary than the fetid air I was reluctantly breathing. I was scared into atavistic shitlessness—Homo erectus cringing in the dark, hoping the beast wouldn't find him.

The white beam of Sonny's flashlight playing on the interior of the cavern re-evolved me into Homo sapiens and I began to follow the beam with the sights of my rifle, just as Chun was doing. As the light moved over the ledges and pockets of the catacomb-like chamber, I expected at any second to see the reflection of yellow eyes, a roaring blur of orange and black bursting upon us.

Right there! The light found something and stopped. I almost squeezed the trigger before I fully absorbed what the light revealed.

Huddled together on a ledge half way up the wall of the cavern, not more than fifty feet away, were what appeared at first to be a man and a woman. But they were not fully human.

The male was somewhat larger than the female, maybe as tall as Sonny, it was hard to tell. Enhanced by my adrenaline, the long shadows of the creatures against the wall made them look like giants. Both were thinly covered with reddish-gray hair about two inches long, with matted hair on their heads perhaps a foot in length. Their eyes, set deeply in narrow faces beneath jutting brows, rolled fearfully. Their flat-nosed nostrils flared and both had large, protuberant lips snarled back beneath prominent cheekbones to expose their broad, yellow teeth. Long, pink nipples tipped the female's pendulant breasts. The light blinded them and they held up their hairless hands to shield their eyes, all the while growling in unison. All about them in the limited purview of the flashlight were indiscriminant piles of feces, and urine stains ran down the wall from the ledge.

Breathless, amazed, I could not imagine how these creatures could be here or even what species they might represent. Chun was fond of spinning a yarn in his broken English about the "wild men" who came down from the mountain caves to steal food from the villagers. But I knew his Buddhist religion to be deeply colored by the animistic beliefs of his ancestors and I had never taken his stories to be anything but folktales. It was unbelievable. Dad, if only you could see these creatures.

"Chun, what are these things?" I had to know. I could not live without knowing.

"No kill! No kill!" Chun shouted. He was agitated as I had never seen him before. "No kill wild people!" he repeated.

At the sound of our voices the creatures yelped and suddenly bolted along the ledge and leaped to the cavern floor, trying to escape deeper into the cavern. Sonny's flashlight lost them momentarily and then they reappeared just as they hit the floor and turned to flee, standing upright. They were definitely bipedal.

Overlapping reports no louder than gloved handclaps mingled with the rattle of the Swedish K's reciprocating bolt. I watched in horror as the 9mm slugs stitched rows of dark red buttons up the creatures' hairy backs.

Screaming something in his own language, Chun lunged at Sonny and pushed the short barrel of the still-firing submachine gun into the air, knocking the flashlight to the floor and causing it go out. For a few seconds rounds ricocheted off the ceiling and walls in the darkness, buzzing by my face like angry hornets.

My flashlight was on before the echoes faded. Neither of the creatures was dead. The female alternately whimpered and yipped, and appeared to be paralyzed. The male, bleeding profusely and limping, was dragging her by one arm deeper into the cave. I had to force myself to take the light off them. I could do nothing for them. Sickened and outraged, I turned the light on Sonny. I wanted desperately to smash his big face into the wall again and again.

"You sonofabitch! Why the fuck did you do that!" My head throbbed and I screamed so loud my voice cracked.

Chun lay on the floor on his side. Sonny was kneeling over him applying a compress to the bloody hole in his throat just below his Adam's apple where one of the ricocheting bullets had caught him. Chun's eyes rolled back as he choked and gurgled.

Seeing Chun down and bleeding doubled my rage. Sonny was trying to help Chun. He hadn't meant for a bullet to ricochet off two walls and wind up in Chun's throat. But Chun was badly hurt, nevertheless, and Sonny's wanton act had doomed two near-human creatures to a slow death in some dark recess of the cave. Goddamnit, it was his fault, the bastard. Savagely, I grabbed Sonny's shoulder to pull him away from Chun.

The next second I was flat on my back with Sonny straddling me, crushing the hot Swedish K across my throat. I could neither breathe nor move. His words spat out of his painted face like cobra venom.

"You listen up, motherfucker. It's too bad about the Nung, but it's his own goddamned fault. The fucker shouldn't have touched my gun. And don't go apeshit over those two stinking gorillas because they're nothing, understand? And don't ever jump me again 'cause I'll cap your ass sure as shit . . . you got that?" He took the gun away from my throat, stood up, and stepping over Chun, disappeared into the darkness.

I tried to get up and couldn't. I had nearly blacked out from the pressure on my larynx and I felt dizzy, nauseated. It hurt to swallow and my breath came in wheezes. My throat throbbed and burned. Sonny had come close to killing me.

Finally able to roll over, I reached for my flashlight lying at the end of a pool of red light. Crawling over to Chun I felt futilely for a pulse.

I don't know exactly how long I lay on my back next to Chun's body, the rasp of my breath and the rush in my ears swallowed by the absolute silence of the empty cavern as I tried to pull myself together.

Modern man had won the evolutionary competition because he could adapt to changing conditions. He mastered fire, made tools, developed language, and utilized the strength of others for mutual support and protection. But Homo sapiens was not simply smarter and more aggressive than his less-well-endowed cousins who shared his domain, he was also imbued with the mutant attributes of ruthlessness and cruelty. Fear and hunger as motivations for animals to kill were expanded by modern man to include hate, greed, pleasure, and killing for any reason and for no reason at all. I had shuddered for an instant in the throes of archetypal fear, imagining myself the prey of a tiger. I wondered how many generations of the creatures we had found had shuddered in fear of a beast more terrifying than any other—Man.

When I finally forced myself to get up, I bashed Chun's rifle against the side of the cave until it was no longer functional, removed his extra magazines from his pack, took his canteen, covered his face with his headcloth, and left. I had to leave Chun in the cave, just as I had to walk away from the anachronistic creatures who fittingly shared Chun's sepulcher, their destinies seemingly predetermined to converge at that time and place.

I wanted to go look for the creatures, to confirm that they were what I had taken them to be, to perform some penitent act out of guilt and shame for their molestation. But if they were still alive, they could be dangerous and almost certainly would not let me approach them. Besides, there was no guarantee I could find them in the labyrinth of the cave, or find my way back, for that matter. There was no time. There were too many reasons . . . No, they weren't reasons, they were excuses—rationalizations to hide the fact I was really too cowardly and ashamed to look at the creatures again, to see them dead or dying and to violate them a second time by my gawking, helpless presence.

I would not be able to provide any evidence of having seen them when I got back. No one was going to believe me. Maybe it would be better if no one did. It certainly would be better for any remaining evolutionary relics if people like Sonny didn't take their existence seriously.

What about Sonny? Would he report what he had seen? Did he even understand what he had seen? Probably not. But I understood, even if my proof consisted solely of the sights and sounds and smells infused immutably into my memory.

Twenty feet inside the cave where the grenade had exploded the smell of the explosive still hung in the air. Aside from the pockmarks blasted into the walls by the radiating fragments, and a small amount of ceiling rubble littering the floor, the grenade had damaged the cave very little.

Only Sonny's outbound tracks marked the new layer of dust created by the explosion. The NVA soldier had not bothered to walk into the cave to check it. My footprints in the dust would not matter. I would be far away before anyone might discover them, if anyone ever did.

It was raining hard when I emerged from the cave. The black clouds had dropped even lower since I had entered the cave little more than an hour ago. Their somber wisps hung in loose shreds among the blue-gray stanchions of driving rain.

Good. There would be less chance anyone would see me. The NVA cave blasters would have rejoined their comrades by now, reporting the caves were empty. That meant they would still be looking for Sonny, although they were probably taking refuge from the rain right now, smoking and talking.

I wasn't sure which direction Sonny might have taken, but I had a feeling I wasn't going to run into him again before I got back. The mission was over as far as I was concerned. The NVA obviously were suspecting something in this area or they would not have had patrols out.

I would cross the slope and make a long loop to the north around the next series of hills, a twenty-kilometer hump that would take all night to complete. When I crossed the border, I would use my emergency radio to call for an extraction.

* * *

A chopper flew me from the Command and Control site at Quang Tri to Dha Nang, where I underwent a mission debriefing. A special forces intelligence officer, Lt. Col. Brown, and a wrinkle-suited CIA agent who introduced himself as Mr. Smith asked questions as I pinpointed on the big map the gun placements, vehicle movements, and troops Chun and I had noted.

The next phase of the debriefing was more difficult. I had never met either the colonel or Mr. Smith. Colonel Brown was tall, tan, fiftyish, his receding gray hair clipped short in the de rigueur special forces style. He had a lean, hard look about him and a manner to match. Mr. Smith, sloppy and paunchy, seemed pleasant enough at first—maybe a little too pleasant, like a spider charming a fly to dinner.

Mr. Smith offered me a glass of ice water from the pitcher standing on Colonel Brown's battered metal desk. My throat was feeling the effects of talking for an hour after four days of almost no talking, not to mention the soreness from Sonny's assault on it. That and the dryness in my mouth from dreading what lay ahead in the debriefing gave the ice water a soothing sweetness. I drained the glass quickly and set it back on the colonel's desk.

The colonel sat across the desk from me, his square jaw set, his humorless eyes working me over as if he were trying to decide where to start skinning me. Mr. Smith leaned on another desk to my left and behind me.

"I want the details on Sgt. Chun's death," the colonel said abruptly. "What exactly happened out there? And don't leave anything out." The debriefing was beginning to feel more like an interrogation.

Starting with Chun's hearing the NVA patrol coming up Hill 836, I described how Chun, Sonny, and I came to be in the cave, our retreat into the interior of the cave to escape the grenade, and the wounding of Sgt. Chun.

"We were waiting for the smoke and dust to clear and to find out if the NVA were going to search the cave after throwing in the grenade. We heard something behind us we thought might be a tiger. Sonny shined his light around, thought he saw something, and opened up with his K. One of the rounds ricocheted off the walls and hit Sergeant Chun in the throat. He died within a few minutes. Sonny and I split up, leaving Chun's body in the cave, and I returned by looping north of Hill 1079 to the border, where I was extracted." It was done. I had chosen to omit the part about the creatures and about Chun's attempt to keep Sonny from shooting them. If Sonny's report contradicted mine, one of us was going to be in deep shit.

"And was it a tiger?" I was relieved to hear what seemed to be genuine curiosity in Mr. Smith's question. I turned in my seat to look at him as I answered.

"I didn't see one. The noise we heard could have just been some debris shaken off the ceiling by the grenade. I don't know what it was—maybe the blast in the cave affected our hearing. I don't know."

I had never been a good liar and I wondered if Mr. Smith and the colonel suspected I was withholding information.

"What made you think it might be a tiger in the first place? They're pretty rare around here now. There hasn't been one reported in this sector since before the French left in 1954." Smith's voice was matter-of-fact, not accusatory. There was no need to panic—yet.

"I just assumed there were a few around. The cave smelled like cat litter. I suppose the NVA could have been using it for a latrine." Careful, don't get too cute, John. These guys are pros and this is their game.

"So you're the one who suggested it might be a tiger?" I had to twist around in my chair to look at Smith when I answered and I could feel the colonel's eyes smoldering into the back of my head. It was becoming clear to me just how tactically effective it was for Mr. Smith to have placed himself behind me.

"That's the first thing I thought of. I don't know about the others." I was trying not to sound defensive. Smith didn't respond.

Then it was the colonel's turn and I twisted around to face him again.

"In your estimation, Sergeant, was Sergeant Larson negligent in firing his weapon?"

"Neither Sergeant Chun nor I saw anything at which to fire. I have no idea what Sergeant Larson thought he saw, but he should have had a better reason to risk spraying dozens of rounds into that confined area." Judging by the colonel's expression, the correct answer must have been "No, sir, he wasn't negligent."

The colonel pushed his chair back and stood up, placing his hands on the desk and leaning over it toward me. Apparently, he had finally decided which part of my anatomy to begin flaying. That I was sitting on the part inconvenienced him not in the least.

"In your humble opinion Sergeant Larson exercised poor judgment, is that what I hear you saying, Sergeant?" He continued before I could reply. "Sergeant Brockman, you are entitled to a humble opinion because you have the most humble qualifications of any man working out of CCN. Frankly, I don't know how the fuck they let you into this unit. Just because some shit-headed second lieutenant recommended you for meritorious promotion, it does not mean you are qualified to evaluate, criticize, critique, question, or comment on the performance of any soldier attached to this unit, including the indigs, in any way, shape, or form whatsoever. Are you starting to catch my drift, Sergeant?" He paused. His angular jaw jutted across the desk threateningly, the high voltage of practiced indignation arcing between his eyes and mine.

"Yes, sir. I meant to say that the incident was an unavoidable mishap with no culpability on anyone's part." The colonel kept glaring at me for several seconds as if I might suddenly alter my humble opinion again. Straightening up, the colonel exchanged coded glances with the CIA representative, who still lounged against the desk across the room.

"Do you have any further questions for the sergeant, Mr. Smith?" the colonel asked brusquely.

"Not at this time, Colonel. Thank you for your cooperation, Sergeant." There was something implied and sinister in the way Mr. Smith looked at me.

Colonel Brown reseated himself at his desk and began writing in the file folder that lay open before him. Without looking up he grunted "That will be all, Sergeant, see Lieutenant Wilkes outside for your new orders," and continued to write. I stood up, coming to attention. As I turned to leave, the colonel put down his pen and looked up at me.

"By the way, Sergeant, there never were any 'ape men' in that cave, isn't that right?"

I was stunned. Sonny had actually reported the creatures in the cave. They knew about the relic hominids, or hominoids, or whatever they were. And because they knew about them, the information would be irretrievably lost in an orderly and military fashion.

"Uh no, sir, I mean, yes, sir," I stammered.

"Well? What are you waiting for? Get the fuck out!"

4-CAIN

CHAPTER 4

Intermezzo

The phone rang three times before a familiar voice answered.

"This is Sid Cunningham, may I help you?" The kindly patience and genuine pleasantness of his voice made me smile, as it always did. I knew that whatever Dr. Cunningham had been doing when the phone rang, he was immediately prepared to give his full attention to the caller—whether it was a student, a colleague, or a textbook salesman. During the past eight years of having been growled at over the phone by supercilious officers and officious corporals, every one of the dozens of calls I had made to the Cunninghams had seemed like a psychological oasis: sanctuarial, restorative.

"Dr. Cunningham, sir, it's John Brockman. I just got into Sea Tac. I apologize for calling you at your office, but no one answered at your home. I hope I didn't interrupt anything."

"Goodness no, John. I'm delighted you called. Maxine and I are so pleased you decided to work on your doctorate here. Is there anything I can do for you, John?"

"You've helped me so much already, sir, I'm not about to impose on you further, but I did want to see if you and Mrs. Cunningham would be available this evening to let me take you to dinner. I realize it's short notice."

"I can't think of anything nicer, John, and I know Maxine will be ecstatic to see you again. She thinks the world of you. Your timing is impeccable, too. I know for a fact Maxine and I were going to do nothing but read all evening. We've let it be known that Tuesday is our reading night in order to give us an evening to ourselves, or to share with someone like you." He chuckled mischievously at his disclosure. How refreshing to have an invitation accepted so graciously, I thought.

"I'll have a rental car for the next few days. May I pick you up at 1900 hours?"

"Seven is fine, John. We'll be looking for you."

We said goodbye and it occurred to me I had used military time, which usually elicited either mystification and embarrassment or mystification and annoyance among the many civilians who viewed it as an arcane artifact of military gobbledygook. Dr. Cunningham responded as if he used the twenty-four-hour system all the time. But then, I suspected he probably was just as conversant with rock music, batting averages, and the names of all the Marx brothers. Let's see: Groucho, Harpo, Chico . . . Firpo? Zippo? Alpo? . . . Damn!

Some of my friends thought it was strange I still addressed someone I had known practically all my life as "Dr. Cunningham." But it was precisely because I had known and addressed him as Dr. Cunningham all my life that no other form of address seemed appropriate or possible. Once, when I was about twelve, Dr. Cunningham told me I could call him Sid if I liked. I remember I thanked him and asked him if it would be all right if I continued to address him as Dr. Cunningham. He just smiled wryly and said, "That which we call a rose by any other word would smell as sweet. 'Dr. Cunningham' I am to thee."

* * *

As wise and wonderful as Sid Cunningham was, a trace element of stubborn, almost foolish pride marked his character. Although well closeted as a rule, this element revealed itself often to his wife—by her own report—and occasionally to the inner circle of his closest friends.

Exemplifying this trait is an anecdote my mother first pieced together from comments, snatches of conversation, significant sighs, revealing glances, and more than likely a good deal of conjecture.

Isolde Cunningham was a few years older than I and I didn't really get to know her until we became good friends many years after the incident described in the anecdote, the telling of which seems to lend itself to the form of a parable:

Isolde was lithe and vivacious. Like a Thoroughbred filly, she was a little skittish, a little temperamental, and she had more energy than good sense. But she had a loving heart, a boundless capacity for empathy, and a mortal dread of hurting anyone's feelings.

Her father, Dr. Sidney Cunningham, linguist and romantic, was reading Gottfried Von Strassburg's version of Tristan and Isolde during the latter months of his daughter's fetal quest for nativity. Maxine Cunningham could see the lyricism and logic of "Isolde" or "Tristan" and made the mistake of saying so. Thereafter, "Kathleen" or "William"—Maxine's earlier suggestions—deferred to antiquity.

In addition to being a gifted linguist and inveterate romantic, Sid Cunningham played the violin. Not brilliantly, but well enough to perform some pieces beautifully.

For example, his rendition of the "Romance" movement of the *Wieniawski Concerto in D minor* was liltingly subtle and sonorous and conveyed an intensity of passion that would have surprised most of Sid's acquaintances and colleagues.

But he declined to perform the first and last movements of the Wieniawski. He practiced them. He had been practicing them in the bathroom since he was in high school. The acoustics of the small, hard-surfaced room enhanced the already excellent sound of his old violin until he could imagine it resonating with the brilliance of a Guarnerius, the sweetness of an Amati, the sonority of a Stradivarius.

Sid had played solos during high school. His music teacher was pleased to arrange engagements with the Ladies' Aid Society,

The Sons of Finland, etc. He played in the high school orchestra, in the community orchestra, in the college orchestra. But as he grew older, his time and attention were diverted from practice and performance so that by the time Isolde set her wedding date few outside the family even knew Sid could play.

He had not always assumed that he would play at Isolde's wedding. It was only when he was forced to acknowledge the fact that his little Isolde was old enough to marry that he began to envision himself in St. Mathew's choir loft, sanctifying the ceremony with heavenly strains.

Isolde, however, was swept away by the pandemonium of preparation during the twelve months preceding the wedding: the bride's gown, the bridesmaids' dresses, the flowers, the reception, the honeymoon, the music.

Isolde made it clear she wanted music that was modern, upbeat, different. She did not mention a violin solo.

Sid was troubled. He wanted desperately to play, but he did not want to ask Isolde. Once asked and realizing how much it meant to him, she would not want to hurt his feelings. Sid wanted to play only if Isolde really wanted him to. For some inexplicable reason he could not bring himself simply to ask her. She would have to approach him. Actually, it was not the playing but Isolde's wanting him to play that meant so much to Sid.

What would he play? The Romance movement? Too long, too heavy. What then? A Fritz Chrysler piece, maybe?

Meditation from *Thais*. Yes. Simple, beautiful, not too long. Perfect!

But did she want him to play? Did she think him too old fashioned, too sentimental, too out-of-practice? Was she worried he would mar her perfect wedding?

Months sped by and the wedding loomed closer. Still she did not ask. He began to feel that she would not ask.

A month after the wedding Sid said something to Maxine, either inadvertently or subconsciously on purpose, that revealed

-CAIN

to her his disappointment in not being asked to play. She began to cry.

"Isolde wanted you to play," Maxine sobbed. "She thought because you didn't say anything you didn't want to play and she didn't want to say anything to you for fear of making you feel pressured."

There are certain important things that happen only once in a given lifetime and there is consequently but one opportunity to experience them in the ideal way that fulfills our heart's desire. Once past, seldom does another opportunity occur that allows us to make it up. And even if such a rare opportunity were to present itself, it could never quite be the same. Like lost youth and lost love, a lost opportunity to do that which means the most to us remains an empty and painful niche in our psyche until we die.

Overcome with guilt and regret, Sid made Maxine promise upon the loss of her soul she would never disclose his feelings to Isolde, who long after would recall with disappointment that her father had not wished to play at her wedding.

* * *

DO NOT GO GENTLE

I had come home only once before in the past eight years. That was in the fall of 1971, three weeks after my father had been buried. My mother had exhausted herself trying to get word of his death to me, but I was on an assignment in the boondocks of Thailand and I wasn't notified until I got back to Bangkok.

I caught a military flight in Bangkok that eventually brought me to McChord Airforce Base in Tacoma. After another forty miles by Greyhound and fifteen minutes by Graytop, I was surveying the khaki September yards lining the street I had played on as a kid, yards already half covered with leaves of curled brown and translucent yellow shed by the burly old maples.

The afternoon breeze awakened and found the treetops. Leaves rustled and fell, turning in the wind, turning as the colors turned, inexorably as the season itself turned; life turning implacably like the leaves themselves turning in the wind.

Why were these thoughts so familiar? It was that piece by Wallace Stevens, "Domination in Black." I hadn't thought of his poetry for years and then his imagery pops into my head. I wondered how much of my thinking was destined to be colored by the imagery of others. Indeed, was there any original imagery left to create, or had everything already been said about everything in every possible way?

The seemingly deserted neighborhood broiled under the afternoon sun and I stood on the sidewalk for several minutes, sweating and reflecting on the sere-ness of things present, the verdancy of the past.

I pushed the doorbell button and heard the familiar "ding-dong" chimes inside. The oak door opened slowly, tentatively. Mom's face lit up instantly when she saw me and as quickly clouded over and began to rain tears.

"Oh Johnny, Johnny, you're here!" She pressed her pale, wet cheek against my chest and embraced me with all her strength, shuddering uncontrollably in a paroxysm of affection and anguish.

I held her, gently rubbing and patting her back, struggling—I don't know why—to hold back my own tears until my eyes ached and I thought the roof of my mouth was going to collapse.

"Tears from the depth of some divine despair . . ." Tennyson, you magnificently maudlin alliteralist! These are not idle tears and we do know what they mean.

After a few minutes she brushed at her wet face with her hand and tried to smile. Taking my arm in hers, she led me into her spotless kitchen redolent with a mingling of perked coffee, floor wax, and the sweet, cinnamon scent of freshly baked apple pie. For the next hour we sat at the shiny yellow table and talked ebulliently over mugs of strong brew about little things that seemed to mean so much.

-CAIN

The late September sun slanted through the spotless glass of the bay window, and the sharp-edged shadows stole imperceptibly across the effulgent floor. Finally, when we had said everything except the things that mattered the most but which were too painful to utter, we drifted into silence, staring absently at our big-handled cups.

"Goodness, Johnny, I didn't realize how late it's getting. I have to get my meatloaf in the oven." She jumped up from the table, slipped on a starched print apron and began bustling around the kitchen like her old self. As she worked she began to hum. Watching her, I began to understand. Cleaning and cooking—that's how she was coping.

Mom had always seemed so tough and together. I had never heard her complain about anything, I seldom had seen her lose her temper, and I had never seen her cry before. She had studied English at the University of Michigan, where she met Dad. A dedicated and proficient learner, her broad interests, meticulous study, and judicious comments made her a popular conversationalist among my dad's academic friends and associates. She could discuss history, psychology, and literature with the same degree of knowledge and enthusiasm that informed her discussions of cooking, sewing, and gardening. Dad had helped me sort out high school algebra, but it had been Mom who had critiqued my English themes, and who, above all, had introduced me to poetry.

"Mom, do you remember that poem by G. M. Hopkins that has the line about the 'dearest freshness lives deep down things?' How does that part go?"

She stopped kneading the onions, green peppers, and dried bread into the ground beef and smiled wistfully at me over her shoulder with a kind of metaphysical radiance that seemed to emanate from her whenever she recited poetry.

The last five lines of "God's Grandeur"rose from her heart and rolled off her pouty lips with more grace, authority, and meaning than most English professors would have been able to read into the evocative words and sprung rhythm of the sonnet.

When she had finished, she started kneading again, but her motions did not disguise her silent sobs.

"I love that part, Mom," I said, cursing myself for so thoughtlessly having brought up a painful association.

"So did your father, Johnny, so did your father." She went on kneading and sniffling.

The next morning I drove the family Ford sedately up Aurora Avenue to the Evergreen-Washelli cemetery. Of all the things Mom did well, driving a car was not one of them. She didn't like to drive and she was always happy to let someone else take the wheel. She directed me to go past the main entrance and turn off at 115th street, which bordered the north side of the cemetery. I turned right at the second gate and followed the winding drive to the east end of the cemetery, where stands a granite and marble necropolis of large and small markers. All of the markers I could read from the car were inscribed with Japanese names.

"Over there, Johnny, by the big cedar." Mom was pointing to a solitary cedar tree on the west side of the drive. In contrast to the miniature skyline on the other side of the drive, there were no standing markers in the several acres sentineled by the great cedar. Even rows of various-sized slabs dimpled the dewy lawn, and sprinkles of red and white flowers decorated the recumbent green landscape.

I stopped at the edge of the drive and we walked gingerly through the wet grass toward a bright new granite slab just inside the drooping canopy of the cedar. It was a double marker that bore Mom's name as well as Dad's. Seeing her name there was disturbing, as if it were waiting for her, beckoning to her. But for some reason neither of us said anything about it.

Mom fussed with the arrangement of the flowers she had brought and then was quiet while I stood awkwardly at the foot of the grave, unable to focus my thoughts but acutely aware that Dad was gone forever and that my memories of him, as vivid and precious as they were at that moment, did not preserve more than a fraction of his essence.

-CAIN

I couldn't comprehend all that the man was while he was still alive. How could I now enshrine in my memory the whole man when I knew only the part of him that was my father?

"I don't want to forget anything about him." At first I spoke more to myself than to my mother, but I realized I needed her reassurance that Dad would not be forgotten. "Mom, how can I hang on to everything he was when I didn't even know everything he was?"

She looked at me with shimmering eyes but her voice was steady.

"You can't, Johnny, nor can I. No one knew everything about him. He didn't even know everything about himself. None of us does. Each person who knew him will remember him from a special and different perspective, but even the collective memories and impressions of his friends and relatives and acquaintances will not add up to what he was.

"The important thing, Johnny, is that you never forget what he was to you—his strength, his kindness and patience, his wisdom, his idiosyncrasies—always remember the things about him that made you love him and respect him, the things that made him your father and your friend. I know you will remember because those are the things you will miss the most. Johnny, just hang on to the part of him you loved. That's all you need to do."

I knew she loved me very much, but it was Dad who gave her life meaning. I admired and respected her for her devotion to Dad, but part of me kept thinking it was foolish to love anyone as much as she loved him. Perhaps reality was beginning to rust through the shining armor of my romanticism, or maybe I was just worried about her. Only the most jaded cynic could find fault in that kind of virtue, and I hoped I had not yet become a cynic.

Mom was strong and healthy and she would deal with her loss and go on with her life. Judging by the emptiness I felt, I couldn't imagine how she was going to manage it, but I knew she would.

By the time we left, I was completely enervated. I caught myself sighing heavily and I had to brush away a few hot tears that would not be repressed. I reached over and took Mom's hand and she gripped it tightly. Her chin was up and determination pursed her pouty lips.

I didn't want to leave her, but I strongly believed she would be ok. Besides, I had to go back. I wanted to go back. I wanted to go back and finish my contract and put the mindless violence and stupidity of war behind me. I wanted to come home and take care of Mom, maybe go back to school, and maybe, if I were extraordinarily fortunate, find a girl who was half the woman my mom was. It was only fair. I figured I would be lucky to amount to half the man my dad had been.

* * *

Back in South Vietnam in November of 1971 things were unraveling. The Marines were gone. Of the seven Army divisions that had served in Vietnam, only the 101st Airborne remained and it would be gone by December. The 196th Infantry Brigade and the 3rd Brigade of the 1st Cavalry Division were the last large combat units left. They were scheduled to leave by the following June. The Vietnamese were taking over some of the American installations and weapons. The monsoons, the heat, and the scavengers were taking over the rest. The scroungers who teemed out of the countryside like ants after sugar were undoubtedly delighted and perhaps also disgusted by the wealth of a society t that could abandon such opulent refuse. The Americans were going, but the changes they had brought would not go away. Neither the Vietnamese, nor the Americans would ever be the same.

It was nearly a month before Mom's letter caught up with me. Her handwriting, like everything else about her, was neat and distinctly feminine. The letter was postmarked only a week after I had left her.

October 27, 1971
My Dearest Johnny,

It was so wonderful having you home again, Johnny. I wish your father could have seen you. He talked about you all the time, you know. He loved you very much and he was so proud of you, as am I.

You'll be happy to know I finally got tired of cleaning the house and carting my baked goods to charity bake sales. Mrs. Peterson, the principal at the elementary school, called me right after you left and asked if I might be interested in volunteering some time as a tutor. I wasn't sure at first, but I agreed and now I couldn't be more excited about it. The children are so responsive to individual instruction. Johnny, it's one of the most rewarding things I've ever done. I love it! Mrs. Peterson has encouraged me to apply for a full-time job as an educational assistant and I'm going to do it. The income would be modest but welcome, and I do so love working with the children.

You don't have to worry about me, Johnny. I'm fine. I'll always miss your father; it's an empty place that can never be filled, but I know he always believed I could handle just about anything (except a car, of course) and I won't let him down. I won't let you down either.

Please be careful, Son. I want you back. There is so much of life met to experience, so much love and joy, and wonder—enough for a thousand lifetimes. I am counting on there being time for us. I trust you haven't forgotten your T.S. Eliot? Goodbye for now, Johnny. Remember that I love you and I think of you constantly. I'll write again soon.

With all my love,
Mom

Right on, Mom! I knew she would be ok. I was relieved and pleased—hell, I wasn't pleased, I was ecstatic! She had found a new and compelling interest in her life. She had not stopped hurting, but she had set the pain aside and stepped bravely into the beginning of the rest of her life. I was damned proud of her and I missed her. And I did remember *The Love Song of J. Alfred Prufrock.* Yes, there would be time for all those indecisions, visions, and revisions.

The Thursday after I got Mom's letter was Thanksgiving Day. A tired and disgruntled corporal escorted by an ARVN scout limped into our temporary observation base west of Pleiku near the Laotian border and handed me an official envelope, explaining he had been dispatched to deliver it to me personally in the field. He also let me know I was not an easy person to find and that he was not happy about what he had had to go through to deliver the envelope to me.

Curious as hell, I invited the corporal and the scout to have some coffee and took the envelope aside to open it. Inside was an ominous-looking telegram stamped "Urgent," and a handwritten note which read:

> John Buddy,
>
> The telegram was sent to MACV/SOG HQ. It got to me and I looked at it and used up a few favors to get it to you ASAP. It's real bad news Buddy. I'm real sorry. Hang in there.
>
> M.Sgt. Ed. Dereaux

My hands trembled as I unfolded the telegram and read it:

> Sgt. John T. Brockman. MACV/SOG-SA119. Dha Nang Republic of South Vietnam. 21 Nov 71. 945 AM PST. Regret to inform your mother killed in car accident 6 PM 20 Nov. Services 10 AM 26 Nov. Everything taken care of. Letter with details to follow. Deepest sympathy. Sid Cunningham.

CAIN

CHAPTER 5

Nobler in the Mind

After Mom died I, was able to return to Seattle briefly to settle her affairs. My parents had paid off the mortgage on the house and there were few outstanding debts and bills to be paid. The bonus I had received from the CIA took care of those and the taxes, but not the reimbursement to the Cunninghams, who had taken care of the funeral arrangements and expenses. Dr. Cunningham agreed and I gladly gave him power of attorney to sell or rent the house as he saw fit in order to recover the funeral expenses, which had come to just over $3000.

I knew I wasn't going to need the house for myself. It held too many memories, too many associations. I didn't want to lose the memories, the reminders, but they kept the wound of loss open and bleeding. It hurt too much. A gnawing grief ached beneath my breastbone like a throbbing tumor. Objectless anger flooded my emotions between attacks of senseless guilt. I tried to force myself to sort through my parent's personal belongings, but I couldn't decide what to keep and what to part with.

Only when I had found all of Dad's things exactly as he had left them had I understood something about the dilemma posed by the effects of the dead. Mom had been unable or unwilling to dispose of Dad's things or even to move them. I realized how she must have been torn between preserving the only tangible remainder of Dad's existence and suffering the acute reminders of his death. For me, the smallest items took on painful, imponderable meaning: Mom's hairpins on her dresser, a pencil stub in Dad's tweed coat. In the end I boxed everything—books, dishes, pictures, hairbrushes, my dad's favorite chair, even their clothes—and sent it all into storage to be pondered after time had softened the trauma of associations.

After talking to his daughter, Isolde, and her husband, who were living in an apartment at that time, Dr. Cunningham proposed renting the house to them. When they came to look the place over, Isolde asked if I would mind leaving the rest of the furniture. I was happy to oblige because it allowed me to avoid making a decision about what to do with it. I suggested a token rent in return for their stewardship of the house: paying the property tax, insurance, utilities, and maintenance. Although they didn't have the resources at the time, they thought they might eventually like to buy the house. I arranged with Dr. Cunningham to have a portion of the rent placed in escrow until Isolde and her husband decided whether to buy the place, at which time they would have the option to buy the house using the accumulated rent as a down payment. I sold them my parents' ten-year-old Ford for $500, which was how much it was going to cost me to store the stuff I couldn't deal with.

From the time I got back to Vietnam after Mom's death until I left the army six years later, I stopped thinking about having a life. It was easier to let the army structure my existence. After a year the CIA gave me back to the army and I returned to the States, to Ft. Bragg, where I transferred into the special forces and was gradually absorbed into the peacetime army's cycle of training and boredom.

Finally, when there was little to do and no place to go as training instructor, I had enrolled in an extension program of the University of North Carolina and worked on a master's degree in anthropology. It had been more to kill time than to achieve any other goal, but slowly I began to climb out of my emotional lethargy and see the potential for a life outside the army. Gradually the desire to justify my parent's pride in me returned. I began to

CAIN

feel I might even be able to vindicate what had become nearly an obsession for my dad just before his death: finding a Sasquatch.

When I returned to Seattle, the Cunninghams had practically begged me to stay with them. They had an extra room they had planned to rent to a student and they wanted me to use it, at least for a while. I agreed, on the condition they let me pay them whatever they had planned to charge someone else. They had partitioned their basement into a studio apartment with a separate entrance. The apartment was self-contained and I was able to fix myself modest meals. Maxine had wanted me to share meals with them, but it seemed an imposition in view of her busy schedule of interests and activities. Not to be thwarted, she managed to invite me to dinner at least three times a week anyway. I reciprocated by helping her and Dr. Cunningham from time to time around the house.

The first weekend after I began classes at the University of Washington, Professor Thomas Danner, my doctoral advisor, invited all of his doctoral advisees to his home for a barbecue.

Professor Danner's home was in the exclusive Broadmoor district, a gated community protected by an elderly security guard with a clipboard listing authorized guests. My name was on the list and he waved me through. Professor Danner's home was manorial. Not bad on a professor's salary, I thought, as I parked my Volkswagen behind the motley assortment of vehicles belonging to Danner's advisees—four other cars. The Danner family cars were evidently in the garages. I assumed he wouldn't have more than five advisees, but I didn't know.

The house, a tile-roofed, sprawling rambler with a three-car attached garage, sat behind a spacious landscaped front yard forested with exotic shrubs and plants. Ornate drapes covered the low, wide windows from which yellow light spread out onto the carpet-like grass. Landscape lights ringed the perimeter and outlined the walkway curving up to the double-doored entrance.

Somehow I had managed to be the last to arrive, even though the invitation said six and my watch said five to. I pushed the doorbell button and was greeted by a big Ben chime. I could hear talking and laughter inside. Soon a tall, red-haired lady wearing expensive-looking casual clothes came to the door. Definitely not the maid, I decided.

An attractive woman in her forties, she smiled with the polished graciousness of an experienced hostess as she greeted me. "You must be John. I'm Joanna," she said, offering her hand. I shook her hand politely. It was warm, but not as soft or as smooth as I would have imagined. "I'm so glad you could come, everyone just got here and we're having some hors d'oeuvres and wine before dinner. Tom is out on the patio slaving over the barbecue."

I thanked her and she led me through the knee-deep shag carpet of the living room into the dining room.

The table was decked out with a buffet befitting royalty, and the four people gathered around the table were wasting no time consuming cheeses, crackers, raw vegetables, dip, and nuts, and helping themselves to the half dozen open bottles of wine sitting on the table. They turned toward me as I entered the room behind Mrs. Danner, who introduced me to everyone.

"Everyone, this is John. John, the young man on the left across the table is Eric, next to him is Janice, and then Roberta, and this is Max—actually Maximillian, but he said we could call him Max. There was a ragged smattering of "hi's" and Max, being closest, stuck out his hand.

"Nice to meet you, John," he said with a Hispanic accent. "Better grab a glass. We're about two snorts ahead of you."

I poured myself a glass of white wine and nibbled a piece of very good Swiss cheese while exchanging small talk with Max. He was about my size and height, with an abundance of dark wavy hair on a head that seemed slightly too big for his lean body, with its swarthy skin, and curly black chest hair pushing out of the neck of his knit polo shirt. I guessed he was European and I decided his accent was Castilian Spanish. I asked him in Spanish how long he had been living in the United States. He was surprised and responded cautiously, obviously used to people trying

CAIN

out their Spanish who spoke little and understood less. He quickly saw that I was reasonably fluent, and appearing relieved, began to talk more rapidly and naturally in Spanish. When the others began to notice, we changed back to English.

"Your Spanish is excellent, John, not Castilian, but very understandable. Where did you pick it up?"

"Army language school, Monterey, California, and a year in Panama."

"I see. It's a pleasure to converse with you, John."

"Thanks, Max, the feeling is mutual, but I think your English is better than my Spanish."

Roberta had been grazing along the table and had tuned in our conversation. Tall and heavy set, she carried a napkin heaped with green olives in one hand and a rapidly draining wineglass in the other. She entered the conversation like a dentist examining our teeth by force while asking us questions with her hands in our mouths.

"You guys Mexican? I heard you jabbering in Spanish but you talk too fast for me. I took high school Spanish but I've forgotten most of it. You guys from around here? I'm from Idaho. Went to Idaho State, you know? in Pocatello? This is a real feast, isn't it. Try some of that soft cheese, it's sooo good. I think I'll have some more wine."

Roberta didn't pause for a response to her questions. She just continued to talk as she wandered off.

Across the table Eric was listening and ogling while Janice talked. Eric was tall and thin with a scraggly beard. Janice was a curvy cutie who moved like a stripper and dressed like a streetwalker. She posed with various parts of her anatomy thrust out seductively, pursing her big red lips as if begging for someone to kiss them. Like Max, I had a hard time pretending not to stare at her. Eric didn't even bother to pretend as his eyes caressed every inch of her body from top to bottom in cycles of ten seconds or less. Janice seemed unaware of the attention she attracted, but she had to know, and I was pretty sure she would have been disappointed had she failed to get it.

I feasted my tongue on Joanna's appetizers and my eyes on Janice's attributes for about ten minutes before Professor Danner came in from the patio. Dr. Thomas Danner was five-ten or eleven, of medium build, in his mid forties. His dark, handsome features reminded me a little of the actor, John Gavin. There was a neatness about him—his appearance, his clothes, his behavior, his surroundings—that fell short of affectation and yet seemed almost mythical to a messy mortal like me. His urbanity bespoke wealth and breeding, but his likeable familiarity with people and lack of any trace of stodginess suggested roots of a more common origin. I suppose the impression he made upon me was that of an accomplished actor who had just come from makeup and wardrobe with his lines, mannerisms, and persona polished to the point of utter naturalness.

He had already greeted the others and he immediately moved to welcome me.

"John, glad you could make it. You met Joanna I presume, how about the others?"

"Yes, your wife introduced us. You have an elegant home, Professor. I like it very much."

"Thank you, John. Actually, we moved in only last year and we're still trying to get things sorted out, but Joanna has done a magnificent job with the place. Let's eat first and then I'll show you around if you like."

"I'd like that."

He clapped his hands. "Ladies and gentlemen. The ribs are ready. But before you are transported by culinary ecstasy and experience the rapture of the ribs, hear this: eating with the fingers is mandatory; slurping and belching are optional. Now then, procure your plates and bibs and I will serve the *pièce de résistance*. Please forgive the absence of fanfare. It's the herald's night off." He bowed with an extravagant flourish and made his exit to the patio, returning with a large platter bounteously laden with sumptuous ribs. Joanna followed him with a second, equally impressive platter of ribs. More food appeared manna-like from the kitchen: casseroles, corn on the cob, and warm bread.

Everyone dug in. For an hour we ate, drank, talked, and laughed, faces and hands smeared with butter and barbecue sauce, plates piled with the remains of vanquished ribs and decorned cobs. Eric consumed steadily without flare, whereas Max put away his portions with gusto and frequent appreciative salutes to his hosts. Roberta talked incessantly as she ate, and ate, and ate. Licking sensually at her food, Janice ate less than anyone else, but confirmed conclusively the suspected link between eating ribs and eroticism. Even Mrs. Danner, as refined and tasteful as she was, got caught up in the gluttony and began feeding in a kind of fastidious frenzy. Professor Danner, like an officer rallying his command in the chaos of battle, cheered us on, exhorting us to even greater heights of voracity.

In the aftermath, when the repast had been waged and won, we fell away from the table with eyes glazed and bellies distended grotesquely.

As Professor Danner's impressive stereo system massaged us with Mozart in the living room, I noticed Mrs. Danner had dutifully addressed the task of clearing the table, and I realized no one had offered to help her. Excusing myself from the assembly of bloated slugs in the living room, I went to assist her.

Mrs. Danner's back was to me as I came into the kitchen. "The herald and the maid have the same night off?" I asked.

She turned and looked at me strangely for a second and then smiled. "Yes, I'm afraid so," she replied. "May I get you something?"

"Actually I came in to offer my assistance. I'd like to help if I may."

At first she insisted she didn't need any help, but she was appreciative and seeing that my offer was sincere, relented. She had regained her equanimity after the debacle of dinner and the two of us were able to talk as we worked.

"Do you and Professor Danner have any children?"

She smiled as she put the remnants of the casseroles into smaller containers and set them into the refrigerator. "Two girls. Angela is a sophomore in high school. She's staying with some friends this weekend. Michelle is in New York. She just started her second year at Vassar."

"Family tradition?"

She looked surprised. "Why yes, I suppose it is. Now how in the world did you guess that?"

"It wasn't entirely a guess. It would be hard to mistake that Vasser quality in her mother."

"Mr. Brockman, you certainly are a gracious flatterer. Thank you for the compliment."

"My pleasure. But I think it's more fact than flattery. While I'm at it, I want to thank you for the wonderful meal. I am so stuffed I won't be able to eat again for a week."

"You are very welcome, John. It's so refreshing to see people actually enjoy the act of eating. I attend so many teas and luncheons and banquets where prissy old ladies nibble and sip, quibble and snip. Sometimes I feel like Alice in Wonderland." She had gone further than she had intended and she was embarrassed. "I'm sorry, I didn't mean to get carried away. It's been rather a hectic week."

"No need to apologize, Mrs. Danner."

Professor Danner came into the kitchen as we were finishing up.

"Aha! What's this? Trying to seduce the Professor's wife, eh?" He laughed and so did I, but I suddenly felt very uncomfortable. Mrs. Danner didn't see any humor in it at all.

"Tom, that was rude."

"Sorry, John. But come with me. I want to show you my den. Joanna will finish up here. Joanna, we'll be ready for coffee and dessert in about fifteen minutes." For an instant I thought I had heard a note of imperiousness in Professor Danner's voice, but I wasn't sure and my attention was diverted by Mrs. Danner smiling at me and motioning for me to go with her husband.

"Thanks for your help, John. I'd give you the biggest piece of pie, but that would just make Tom even more jealous."

"Are the others coming, too?" I asked, looking around for them.

"No, I've got them out in the garage trying to reassemble a piece of pottery from fragments. I thought seeing my den might be more interesting for you."

Curious, I followed Professor Danner down the hall into an open hexagonal room featuring a grand piano in the center of the room beneath a large skylight. Books lined four of the room's walls from floor to ceiling. The drapes were pulled back and the glass wall on the front looked out into the landscaped front yard. An illuminated swimming pool filled the view through the glass wall to the rear of the house.

"This is the library," Professor Danner said, stopping for a moment to let me take it in.

At the end of the hall past two bedrooms, we came to an impressive old oak door.

"I like this door," I said. "It looks like the doors in the old university library."

"Very perceptive, John. It is one of the doors from the old library. Faculty members had first crack at bidding on it. It cost me five hundred dollars. I thought that was quite a bit until a contractor charged me a thousand dollars to place it here. You see how they had to widen the hallway and raise the ceiling in order to accommodate it. When they finally got it hung and I saw it, I knew it was worth every penny. It weighs nearly three hundred pounds with the hinges."

"Do you hunt, John?," Professor Danner asked, opening the door and turning on the lights.

"A little," I replied. It was a long story.

A large room with a high ceiling, the den had only one large picture window on the front side of the house. A billiards table occupied the space in front of the window. Commanding all of the attention on the wall across from the door was a magnificent, massive stone fireplace. Large basalt boulders formed the central support for the end of the building as well as providing the structure for the fireplace. In front of the fireplace, just off the edge of the hearth, lay a gigantic brown bear skin. I walked over to the fireplace to get a closer look at the flintlock hanging above the monolithic mantel. The piece appeared to be an authentic .36 caliber, octagonal-barreled, Kentucky squirrel rifle, an antique, not a replica.

I could see that Professor Danner was pleased by my obvious interest. "Unfortunately, not all of my students and colleagues would approve of my passion for hunting. There are those who are offended by the killing of animals for sport. That's why I didn't invite the others to see this particular room. I was pretty sure a man of your background might be able to appreciate it, however."

"Thank you, Professor, I do find it fascinating."

The abundant wall space around the room was covered with photographs and trophy heads: deer, antelope, elk, bison, bears, moose, mountain goats, bighorn sheep—every North American big game animal was represented several times over. Professor Danner remained by the door, smiling as I moved in awe around the oak-paneled room. I examined the heads and the engraved brass plates beneath them carefully. These were genuine Boone and Crockett certified trophies, many of them record holders.

On the wall by the door, stood a glass case containing hunting rifles. Professor Danner opened the case, unlocked the rack and handed me a beautiful .300 Weatherby magnum. The oil-finished stock was finely checkered, with the ebony fore-end tip and grip cap set off by ivory spacers.

"Got that bison over there in the corner with this one," he said proudly. "I paced it off at a little over 400 yards. How do you say it in the military? One shot, one kill?"

I opened the smooth-as-silk bolt and checked the chamber. Satisfied it was empty, I brought the rifle up to my shoulder, sighting through the variable-powered scope at the bison head in the far corner of the room. The stock with its thick rubber butt pad was slightly too long for me and I had to stretch to get a full field of view in the scope. The high-recoil rifle required plenty of eye relief to avoid having the scope kick back and gouge a bloody crescent into the shooter's eyebrow.

Admiringly I handed the rifle back to him. He snapped the trigger and returned the rifle to the rack, taking down another for me to examine. It was an open-sighted .458 Winchester magnum Model 70—just shy of being adequate for elephants, but sufficient to stop a charging Kodiak bear, or at least piss him off considerably.

"I had to put three bullets from this .458 into that bear whose skin is on the floor by the fireplace. I had the taxidermist leave the holes in the hide. The bear was standing upwind in the open and he didn't see us. My first shot from a hundred yards unfortunately just made him jump. He ran off into some brush and we were faced with the unpleasant prospect of having to go in there after him. The bear didn't wait for us to come after him, however. He circled around, got our scent, and came after us instead. We heard him crashing through the willows before we could see him. Fortunately for us, he had to cross about fifty yards of open ground to get to us. He charged out of the willows and my second shot broke his shoulder, knocking him down, but he got up and kept coming on three legs. I hit him again and he continued another ten yards with half of his heart blown away. They're smart animals, John. Very tough and very determined."

"That's what I've heard." I said. "Sounds pretty exciting."

"Exciting? More on the order of thrilling, John. There is nothing to compare with it. Sex, perhaps—sometimes."

I gave the Winchester back to Professor Danner. The story, the weight of the heavy rifle in his hands, the lingering perfume of gun oil and Hoppe's No. 9 must have rekindled the fever of the kill in him. Breathing faster and bright-eyed with excitement, he smiled to himself as he lovingly stroked the walnut stock of the Winchester.

We spent a few more minutes looking at his other rifles: a Browning BAR .30-06 deer rifle with an engraved receiver; a heavy-barreled .220 Swift varmint rifle with a custom curly maple stock made by Anthony Guymon across the Sound in Bremerton; a Model 700 Remington .257 Roberts Danner hunted antelope with; a Model 1895 Winchester chambered for .30-40 Krag cartridges, and an old Marlin .22. The latter two had belonged to his father.

I browsed through the photos on the walls while Professor Danner locked up the rifles. In one picture Danner and another man, his hunting guide presumably, posed with their rifles while sitting on the mountainous carcass of a Kodiak bear. The guide was fair-haired and husky . . . and familiar.

"Who is the guy in this picture with you? I have the feeling I've seen him somewhere."

"Oh, he's the guide I've been hunting with in Alaska for the past five years. Really a topnotch guide. We've become good friends over the years. He's a former Green Beret, too, maybe you met him in the army. His name is Sonny Larson."

The sound of Sonny's name slapped me in the face, stunned and angered me. Sharp-edged, bitter memories cut into my consciousness. "Sonny Larson. So that's where you went." I thought it without realizing I had said it out loud.

Professor Danner could not have missed the rancor in my words or in my expression.

"Do you know Sonny?"

"I met him once in Vietnam. But that was a long time ago." Sonny's blackened, bellicose face flashed into my mind. It passed and I changed the subject. "I suppose the others will be wondering where we went."

I could tell Danner was still curious about Sonny and me, but he restrained himself.

"You're right, John. Time to go check on the coffee and dessert. After you." He switched out the lights in the den, closed the gothic oak door, and we walked the long hallway back toward the dining room.

* * *

Tuesday 15 May 1979. Professor Danner was adding his final remarks to the graduate seminar in anthropology:

> "We conclude that the primitive mind is childlike in its cosmology. It encompasses reality and imagination in a sphere of possibilities in which dreams, beliefs, and intuitions are no less real than pain, hunger, and desire; where anything that can be imagined can also be experienced by the senses and the emotions; where anything physical—animal, mineral, or vegetable—can become animated by spirits."

He paused eloquently and looked at each of the dozen graduate students sitting around the long table.

"A primitive does not make the distinction between real and imaginary that you and I make. At least I make a distinction, I'm not too sure about some of you." He flashed his perfect teeth to a round of titters and chuckles.

"To the primitive understanding," he continued, "the physical universe is merely a substance to be occupied and used by the hierarchy of spirits who created the world and who control it."

He brought his hands together as if reverently closing a large *Bible* and turned his lean, handsome face casually toward the wall clock. His students dwelled on his every movement as raptly as the twelve apostles at the Last Supper.

I could see no one else was going to ask so I put it to him.

"Dr. Danner," I queried innocently. "Does that mean primitives didn't know the difference between real and imaginary?"

"Good question, John. I'm glad you brought that up." I assumed Danner looked mildly amused because he knew I hadn't asked the question for myself. Everyone else looked at me as if I had just farted during communion.

"We don't have enough time to do justice to John's question. Let me answer with another question and we'll take this up next time. Was Don Quixote crazy, or did he just have a different perspective? Or, as W.B. Yeats asked, 'How can we know the dancer from the dance?"

Two students nodded in profound affirmation"—transfers from the English department I surmised. Three others scribbled intensely in their notebooks—psychology majors? The rest smiled with expressions of vacuous bemusement—obviously anthropology majors.

Danner was smooth. He was knowledgeable, articulate, persuasive . . . too persuasive to suit me. I had become suspicious of anyone who had everything figured out and could explain it so it seemed to make sense: salesmen, politicians, preachers, and professors. Sure, I usually listened, but I had to swallow an impulse to shout "bullshit!" when it started sounding too good. As Sam Clemens once said (or maybe it was Dan Smoot), "I don't believe a word of it, especially if it's true."

Fortunately, my dad taught me to control the bullshit response and to convey it with more subtlety. Regardless of their perspicacity, unabashed bullshit bellowers too often make the accusation before they have marshaled their facts and thought out their case. Consequently, they wind up stigmatized with reputations as retarded, redneck naysayers, and their cries of "bullshit!" go unheeded. That is why articulateness and cleverness nearly always sustain orthodoxy (embodying the truth or otherwise) against righteous but rustic iconoclasm.

After the seminar I jammed my notebook into my bag and headed for the door. I was ready for some coffee and space-out time before grading my section's tests in *Introduction to Anthropology*.

Danner broke away from the huddle of after-class groupies and flagged me down.

"John, could you walk back to my office with me? I'd like talk with you about your research."

"Yes sir," I said reflexively.

I had been in the army only eight years. I had been out for two. And I was still possessed by a plethora of army acronyms and the compulsion to address people as "sir," and "ma'am." Fortunately, however, I was able to control the invidious and pervasive four-lettered tongue infection that plagued some vets.

True, my language had become a good deal coarser—or should I say, more colorful—in the past ten years. But I never unintentionally affirmed with "fucking-A!" or inadvertently asked my host to pass the fucking pâtè de foie gras.

We walked down the hall to Danner's tiny office. It was stuffed with books and papers until there was hardly enough room for the two chairs. Danner was married and had children, but there were no pictures of this family to be seen. The clutter in his office always seemed to me to be out of character for a neat, methodical man like Danner. It even occurred to me that Danner kept it that way just to create a classic academic ambiance.

"How's the Sasquatch research coming, John?" he asked pleasantly. Professor Danner had the gift of being personable. Moreover, he had the gift of making you feel that he was completely ingenuous. He would have made a hell of a car salesman. "Been able to find enough similarities in the Sasquatch myths of the Pacific Northwest Indians to support a thesis?"

"Yes and no," I said cautiously. "As you might suspect, the similarities correspond to the degree of similarity in the cultural practices and cosmographies of the various groups. Each group assimilates reality into its own unique set of beliefs and cultural milieu. Most of the more closely related Salish groups share a common core of beliefs and practices, although there are many variations. Even though the Sasquatch figure appears in some form almost universally among them, I have found no way to form a composite understanding of the figure."

"So you're still trying to establish the Sasquatch as a natural phenomenon. Too bad, John. I think you're on the wrong track. I think you'd be better off trying to explain the evolution and function of the Sasquatch as a mythical creature. You don't really think they ever existed do you?"

I squirmed a bit because I was thinking "Yes I do because I've seen them myself, asshole, but I'm not dumb enough to tell you what I really think."

What I replied was, "There is certainly no tangible evidence to support that view."

Danner laughed. "John, John, you are a mystic. You want to believe that somewhere out in the woods an eight-foot-tall hominoid is still walking around, miraculously avoiding detection.

"John, I'd hate to see you make the same mistake your father made."

I tried to speak without rancor, despite my rising ire.

"With all due respect, Dr. Danner, I think my father's biggest mistake was about people, not about Sasquatches. He made no claims except about what he saw. The footprint he found was no hallucination."

Danner made an apologetic gesture.

"You know, John, someone brought up the possibility the footprint might actually have been created by a foot-shaped piece of rock that rolled down the slope and left an impression there. Of course, there was no way for your father to preserve the footprint for others to analyze. I'm not criticizing your father, John. I'm just saying he made the mistake of trying to defend an untenable position and his life and career suffered as a result. It always happens. Look at Alexis Carrel, Immanuel Velikovsky, Timothy Leary . . ."

"And Galileo? And Copernicus?" I threw back at him. "It's amazing how often heresy and truth seem to coincide. I thought ridicule and ostracism were supposed to be the defense mechanisms of dogmatists, not scientists."

"In any event," I added quickly, "You can be certain I won't make the same mistake my father made about people. My personal views and those of my father will not affect the objectivity of my dissertation."

"I'm relieved to hear that, John," Danner said, smiling benignly. Jesus, I thought, the man is absolutely insidious. "From what I have seen, John, I believe you're a good writer and a good thinker. I'm looking forward to reading your first draft."

"No more than I am, I assure you, but it will be a while before there's a draft for anyone to read." I stood up to leave.

"No hurry, John," Danner said as he reached for a book among those stacked on his desk. "You're already further along than most of the doctoral students who started a year ahead of you. Keep up the good work."

"Thank you, sir, I'll try."

Forty-five minutes and three cups of coffee later I was still embroiled in the ongoing debate with myself as to whether I should like Danner or garrote him.

* * *

Wednesday 3 October 1979. I left the Cunningham's house about seven thirty to attend Richard Leakey's eight o'clock slide talk at Seattle University. I took the Montlake Bridge over the ship canal to 23rd Avenue N.E., turned west up Madison Street toward Capitol Hill and found a parking space just off Madison about two blocks from Seattle U's campus.

I zipped my light jacket up to my chin against the chill when I got out of my car. The October air had already dropped below the dewpoint and the streetlights illuminated the evanescent puffs of my breath as I exhaled into the coolness. By the time I returned to the car the dew would be dripping off everything like light rain, and the windows inside my Volkswagen would be fogged up. I'd be home before its air-cooled engine got hot enough to defog the windows or warm up my feet. If the skies remained clear, I'd be scraping frost off the windows before the end of the week.

I entered the old auditorium a few minutes before eight. Finding it nearly filled, I had to take a seat on the side and considerably farther from the lectern than I would have liked. The only advantage of having almost the entire audience in front of me was that I could look it over without having to turn around. Beth Hansen caught my eye in the tenth row of the center section. She was sitting with one of the other female students from Danner's seminar. Several other members of the seminar were sprinkled around the auditorium.

I got a glimpse of Danner in the front row, accompanied by a teaching assistant, Janice Rawlings, the sultry brunette whose considerable charms always appeared to be on the verge of busting out her oh-so-tight jeans and way-too-small T-shirts. While the rest of us teaching assistants were referred to as "TA's," Janice was affectionately known in certain circles as "T and A." Janice also was well known for her ambition and well rumored to have round heels for some of the faculty. Although it was not a rumor I had to strain to believe, I suspected it probably had been concocted by one or more of the dozen other applicants she had edged out of the teaching assistantship. Whether the rumor was true or not, her presence in the classroom undeniably lent a certain touch of drama to the learning environment.

The evening's presentation also might also have benefited from the presence of Janice Rawling's pulchritude on or near the speaker's podium. A thoroughly competent scientist and a fascinating individual, Richard Leaky turned out to be a less than rousing speaker. His unassuming and painfully matter-of-fact comments about his work and the fossil discoveries at Olduvai had an immediate soporific effect on me and I spent an uncomfortable hour and a half trying not to nod off. Among the first to exit the auditorium after Leaky concluded, I decided to walk over to Broadway and try to find someplace to get a piece of pie and some coffee.

Waiting for the light to change at the intersection of Broadway and Madison, I noticed an obese young man among the several people standing on the corner across the street from me. A heavy-looking bookbag kept trying to slide off his round shoulder, and he was puffing from the exertion of walking. I sucked in my stomach and stood there pinching my haunches to reassure myself

-CAIN

I also hadn't turned completely into flab. The ritual of early morning calisthenics and two-mile runs in fatigues and boots with a 50 lb. rucksack had kept me in top physical condition at Ft. Bragg. For a while after I became a civilian I had tried to maintain a regimen of morning exercise, but it had become increasingly harder and decreasingly important. Now, as irregularly as I exercised, I could barely do fifty push-ups or run two miles in shorts and running shoes. It was high time I cut out the late-night desserts and started working out more often. I vowed to rise early the next morning and get back into a rigorous routine of conditioning.

The light changed and the fat young man puffed and waddled past me as we crossed the street. Two blocks up Broadway a small cafe sign glowed and I started thinking about cheesecake instead of apple pie.

I returned to my car half an hour later, my stomach heavy with cheesecake and my conscience heavy with annoyance at myself for being so weak-willed. When I pulled out on Madison to head home, I got a good look at Danner and Janice Rawlings as his blue Buick came up behind me and passed. Apparently, they were just leaving after having stayed to talk with Leakey. Janice sat close to Danner with her arm around his neck and her head on his shoulder.

So . . . the rumors were not without substance. But why would Danner, the head and darling of the Anthropology Department, so carelessly risk his reputation and, presumably, his marriage by fooling around with a teaching assistant? I had never seen him do anything that suggested he was an out-and-out lecher. There was the matter of the curious absence of any pictures of his family in his office, the significance of which, if any, was not clear, but nothing else on which to predicate prurience came to mind. It was not hard to suspect Danner's glossy veneer of concealing a devious and sophisticated alter ego, but I would never have guessed him to be just another horny old reprobate.

Maybe there was more to it than I could see from a fogged-up Volkswagen. Maybe he wasn't just a petty philanderer, but the victim of an unhappy marriage. Maybe he and Janice Rawlings had some sort of meaningful relationship underway.

In the end I decided maybe I should just mind my own business, but it was with some difficulty I shook off an impulse to follow Danner's car.

* * *

TO SQUEAK OR NOT TO SQUEAK

My first platoon sergeant, who was given to reminiscing about his sexual exploits, once commented: "You know the worst blow job I ever got? . . . It was wonderful!"

Many of the men I knew in the army, like the sergeant, were preoccupied with sex, as if erectile tissue comprised some significant portion of their neocortex. They joked about sex, bragged about it, dreamed about it. Their language was replete with sexual analogies, epithets, innuendoes, and double entendres. Of those men preoccupied with the subject of sex, perhaps half—not counting the ones who kept switching categories—were vicarious participants, sublimators who seemed successfully to substitute bawdy banter and photos of nude cuties for indiscriminant intercourse. The rest were resolute practitioners undaunted by the prospect of disease, indignity, difficulty, cost, or consequence in the pursuit of pussy. Humping was their hope and ejaculation their joy. Not to mention the thrill of the chase and the satisfaction of conquest, which were undoubtedly more important to some than to others, but probably lurking somewhere in the motivations of every one of them.

I came to Vietnam an arrant neophyte in naughty matters and received my initiation in keeping with the proud and noble tradition of soldiering.

My very first night of R & R in Vietnam, I wound up sick, semi-comatose, and stark naked in a Saigon alley behind a brothel; a drunken marine reeling over me, pissing and puking. I had lost

CAIN

my ID; even my dogtags had been stolen—a consummation devoutly to be eschewed, as the ensuing ass-chewing by my CO convinced me.

I had let my new buddies talk me into getting drunk and getting laid. I remembered going to a couple of bars with them and vaguely I remembered swilling beer with the girls at the boom-boom parlor, but I had no memory of having had sex with any of them. My only mementos of the event were a horrific hangover the following day and a painful, embarrassing case of gonorrhea the following week. After that edifying experience, I stuck strictly to soft drinks, soccer games, and sightseeing. I have no doubt my abstinence thenceforth caused some of my friends to wonder about my manhood, but I didn't care.

Besides, it wasn't as if I had sworn myself to celibacy forever. I dated a half dozen or so women while I was at Ft. Bragg and, properly condomized, slept with a few of them. True, casual sex was better than no sex, but I never became comfortable with the idea of it. I almost always had a more convivial, enjoyable time with the women with whom I did not expect to have sex and who did not expect me to have sex with them.

Needless to say, such a confession would have been tantamount to an admission of deviancy. As a member of the army's elite, I was expected—make that "required"—to have a big swinging libido as a measure of my manhood. Over time I came to feel isolated by my different perspectives on many things and I knew I did not belong in a society of priapic titans, military or otherwise.

As Wallace Stevens—successful executive, poet, and titan in his own right—intimated in "Le Monocle Mon Oncle," sex, whether as an idea in the platonic sense or as an itch in the phallic sense, is neither everything nor is it enough:

"But not every trembling hand can, does, will, or should make us squeak."

CHAPTER 6

The Waking

The Hub cafeteria on campus was a good place to talk because it had the right amount of background noise to create the illusion of privacy—the hum and rumble of conversation, laughter, scraping chairs. But it wasn't just the background noise that created the illusion of privacy. The students paid little attention to what others were doing or saying. Everybody was engrossed in whatever he or she was doing—arguing, studying, conversing, staring, reading, strumming a guitar, playing cards, sleeping. Whether active or passive, each table was insulated by a cocoon of white noise and by a myopic sphere of involvement, social or otherwise.

From mid morning until mid afternoon the cafeteria bussers couldn't keep up with the mounting litter of empty hamburger baskets, chili bowls, coffee cups, and assorted trash inundating the tables. The folded cardboard signs on the tables asking patrons to please bus their own dishes were excellent for doodles and graffiti, for impromptu notes, as flightworthy airplanes, and as convenient booger wipes. Generally, however, the request conveyed by the cards went unheeded except by some visitors and a few students who were either conscientious or compulsive.

I had observed the situation closely enough to note that those who removed their own dishes were disinclined to prop their feet up on the tables or to place on the tables their bookbags or briefcases, which only minutes earlier had sat on the wet restroom floor next to a urinal or a splattered crapper (I had actually followed some of them from the men's restroom to the cafeteria). Maybe I

CAIN

was the only one who noticed these things or was bothered by them. I suppose I was also the only one who observed that no more than one person in five or six washed his hands before leaving the restroom. I often wondered if any greater concern about sanitary behavior might be observed in the women's restroom. Although I had never been in the women's restroom, I pondered whether the lack of urinals there might contribute to some de facto cleanliness advantage over the men's facilities. I hoped so.

I had never thought of myself as being such a prissy bastard, having eventually become inured to picknose privates, crotchscratch corporals, and all the rest of the loogyhawking NCO's in the army. "Inured?" Hell, the reason I stopped paying attention was that I had become one of them. I guess I mistakenly expected something better from privileged civilians attending a public university. My recollection of life as an undergraduate no doubt had been reshaped by selective memory and eight years of army life—eight years in a different universe. Now I hardly knew the person I had been then. These students seemed so young, and I felt as out of place and anachronistic in their presence as Rip Van Winkle must have felt after waking from a drunken, dreamless night that had lasted twenty years. In Rip's case, however, it had been the world that had changed, not he.

The bussers, outnumbered and overwhelmed, squeezed through the disarray of sprawling student bodies and stumbled over bookbags lying around the tables, valiantly but futilely endeavoring to clear away the mess. Like the heads of the Hydra, each dirty dish removed would be replaced by two more. Only a Hercules could have dealt with the problem, presumably either with a fire hose or a flame thrower. Every few minutes the din and drone would be punctuated by the crash and clatter of trays and dishes falling off the heaped bus carts. Flying saucers and other flying objects were frequently sighted in the cafeteria as bussers tripped over chairs, bags, and feet, or slipped on someone's trampled tuna sandwich, launching dishes like clay pigeons over the crowded tables.

The solipsistic illusion of privacy amidst the clamor did not necessarily preclude eavesdropping on nearby tables or having to tolerate their raucous inanities. Study groups drove me crazy: a bunch of students sitting around asking each other questions they could have asked themselves, interspersed with shit-shooting and tomfoolery. I don't know if it really helped, or if they just needed the socialization to soften the boredom of study. Speculation on the possibility there might exist study groups that were actually an aid to study rather than a diversion from it always led me into the domain of statistical improbability.

For me, study was an individual, solitary pursuit. I read, reflected, and analyzed. I summarized, synthesized, and memorized. I paraphrased, condensed, outlined, and diagrammed. I found information, took notes, answered questions, and wrote papers. What I didn't know, I looked up. That was how I studied. That was how I learned.

My dad had once explained to me that going to school was like having a job. Some of the time it would be interesting, even rewarding, but for the most part it would just be work.

"John," he said, "you'll be better off if you don't try to turn work into play. The two things are not very often compatible. You don't have to like work, you just have to discipline yourself to get it done. When you work, work toward an objective. Set a goal for each work period and accomplish that goal as efficiently as you can. Then forget about work and go play. There is more pleasure in play when you have done your work for the day."

The Hub cafeteria, a seemingly appropriate place to do almost anything, was where Beth Hansen and I emptied many cups of coffee and exhausted more than a few topics of conversation—most of them amicably.

Beth Hansen thought the sun rose and set in Gloria Steinem's derriere. Or, as I think about it, it might be more accurate to say she thought the sun rose in Steinem's butt and set in Bella Abzug's ample ass. Not that I ever would have confronted Beth with my synopsis and analysis of her politics. On the contrary, our cafeteria

CAIN

discussions delved into more substantive issues, ranging from the university's mandate against sexist language in theses and dissertations to the ups and downs of toilet seat etiquette.

Beth was about five-six with short, shiny, honey-colored hair that hung in bangs across her wide forehead and curled in around the smooth curves of her face. The ineffable prettiness about her came as much from her expressions and movements as from her comely features. Her pleasingly full lips framed a nice set of teeth and an easy, engaging smile that was as natural as it was warm. When she smiled every thing about her smiled. I suppose it was her naturalness, her wholesomeness that I found to be almost as attractive as her good looks. She wore little if any makeup most of the time, but then she didn't need to. Her face and looks had the charm and depth and luster of natural beauty that a woman can't paint, powder, or rub on—the kind a woman either has or doesn't.

Her hazel eyes were warm and wide open, giving her an expression of innocence and intelligence, reinforced by her broad forehead and a tendency to focus her attention quickly and intently. Not the least among the attributes of her appearance were her well-defined breasts, the contrast of a narrow waist above round hips, and a posterior shaped like an inverted heart. Her movements were quick, but not nervous, and she exuded natural grace in her posture and demeanor. She stood straight and sat straight while appearing relaxed and supple. Her walk was poised yet subtly emphasized her flexibility and athletic qualities. And all of this was supported by long, tan, shapely legs.

Short, unpainted fingernails on her ringless fingers did not disguise the gender of her graceful hands. When she wasn't wearing shorts and sandals, she wore loose- fitting slacks that did not quite hide the tight curves of her buttocks. Her untucked shirt, sleeves rolled up to the elbows, enhanced rather than hid the pleasing orbs of her firm bust. She didn't wear the look or the clothes that would land her on the cover of *Cosmopolitan* or *Mademoiselle*, but she stood out in a crowd and turned heads when she walked by a crowded table in the Hub.

She contrasted sharply in every respect with her long-haired, sloppy, big-breasted friend, who usually went bra-less in a baggy, benippled T-shirt. Beth's friend was an ascerbic, foul-mouthed bitch named Anna Milosevic, whom I nicknamed "Muff." I gave her the handle because her acned skin reminded me of a blueberry muffin—and because I wanted to irritate her.

I know it was cruel, but after five minutes in her company even the most gentlemanly man would have understood and approved my otherwise reprehensible behavior. Muff predictably interpreted the nickname as a crude, sexist label and despised me for it. Of course, she hated my guts on general principles anyway, so the nickname didn't really hurt our relationship. At every opportunity, I baited her with any blatantly sexist comment I could come up with, such as the one about female editors thinking a monthly magazine was supposed to come out every 28 days. That would set her off on one of her scurrilous tirades against men. So imaginatively obscene was her invective, I'm sure George Patton would have blushed at it and Sam Clemens would have taken notes and applauded.

At first I suspected Muff of being a dyke. I even had passing doubts about Beth at first because I couldn't understand how she could tolerate sitting at the same table with Muff, yet alone call her a friend. After a while, when I decided they didn't have that kind of relationship, I figured Muff must have had some redeeming qualities in order for Beth to like her, although it took me a long time to discover any. Beth didn't have any sapphic tendencies, of that I became certain, much to my relief. I never quite made up my mind about Muff. I did decide, however, if not a lesbian she sure as hell had to be a repressed nymphomaniac. Otherwise, how could she possibly have accused me of being a chauvinist?

Beth, on the other hand, was something of an enigma. Despite her passionate biases regarding women's liberation, she had a good head on her shoulders. That her head and shoulders and everything else about her were damned attractive is beside the

CAIN

point. I attributed to her youth her getting carried away from time to time by the rush of radical feminism. Feeling like an old man at thirty, I could allow the twenty-two-year-old Beth a reasonable degree of youthful excess. As attractive and engaging as I found her, I also assumed she was too young for me, at least in experience if not in years. Of course, when I say "experience," I mean life experience in general—not experience with the opposite sex, of which I had had little. She certainly was smart enough, an academic whiz, intellectually formidable enough to discourage and demoralize most of the jocks who hit on her, or wanted to, and able to hold her own in any discussion.

She had more maturity about her, though, than many of the other young women her age—at least from my viewpoint: no adolescent flirting, teasing, vacillation, or petulance. Nor was she androgynous and nasty enough to be a true feminist, no matter how hard she tried.

When I finally stopped being annoyed at her feminist attitude long enough to actually listen, I reluctantly began to respect her, then admire her. After a while we became friends, but not the kind of heterosexual friends between whom every conversation became a thinly disguised form of foreplay. There was simply no underlying sexual agenda to get in the way of our friendship. As I said, she was too young for me. I figured it would be only a matter of time before she became involved with someone nearer her own age, someone who hadn't fallen into a stupor and awakened to find himself a stranger to the world. I liked her; I liked to be around her; I even had more than a few erotic dreams about her, but I treated her like my best friend's daughter and she seemed to reciprocate in kind. Except for the small matter of her feminism and my chauvinism, no man-woman tension existed between us that I was aware of—or would admit to—not in the beginning anyway.

The first time Beth Hansen and I crossed swords was shortly after we became aware of each other's existence. We showed up along with nine other graduate students at the beginning of fall quarter 1979 for Professor Danner's seminar on human evolution.

Thanks to Danner's insistence that we introduce ourselves with a brief autobiography, Beth learned that I was a little over a year into a doctoral program in cultural anthropology, and I discovered she had just started her graduate work in physical anthropology. I found out she had come from Eastern Washington State University with a B.S. in zoology and she found out I was studying northwest Indian cultures. I think I also must have mentioned doing my undergraduate work at the University of Washington and getting a master's in anthropology from the University of North Carolina while I was stationed at Ft. Bragg.

In that first session, Danner used most of the time outlining the topics and assignments for the seminar. After answering questions, he turned to me and asked me what I considered the most important evolutionary force in the ascent of Homo sapiens. Danner had been my advisor for over a year and I had taken several of his classes, so he knew what I would say and I knew what he thought I would say.

"A number of theories have come into vogue at various times, but I'm partial to the 'Man as Hunter' explanation. Individual hunting skills and the kinds of organizational and communication skills required for group hunting seem to have favored and fostered the evolution of abstract thinking and language development."

As I talked, I knew I might have picked any of a half dozen other explanations of equal or greater plausibility. There was one disturbing theory, however, I had confirmed emotionally, if not intellectually, deep in a Laotian cave during a previous life. Raymond Dart's dark thesis of Man's descent from the killer ape was more compelling to me for personal reasons than because of the evidence supporting it. In 1949 Dart had shocked the scientific community with his pronouncement that the four-foot tall Australopithecus africanus killed baboons with the leg bone of an antelope. Four years later Dart published "The Predatory Transition from Ape to Man" *in The International Anthropological and Linguistic Review*. In that paper, he concluded that the transition from anthropoid to humanoid took place as a result of the de-

CAIN

mands of a predatory existence. According to Dart, as the necessities of the hunting life forced our ancestors to stand erect, the newfound freedom of their hands allowed them to compensate for their lack of effective jaws and claws by learning to use weapons. Using weapons stimulated the development of a bigger brain to coordinate hands and eyes and to fabricate better and better weapons. Because of a bigger brain and better weapons, Homo not only acquired a survival advantage in hunting, but acquired the means and the taste for annihilating his more primitive competitors and neighbors.

At some point evolution had transformed the non-aggressive ape into the killer ape. Modern Man, with his ability to design catastrophic weapons and his capacity for killing, was the inevitable result. But Dart's assertions were not popular, and more acceptable theories of the influence upon evolution of tool-making and of hunting-gathering prevailed.

Dart's theory of Man the Killer was too disturbing to discuss rationally, and I substituted a more benign speculation about Man the Hunter, a proposal in which I had no emotional investment—unlike Beth Hansen.

"So, Mr. Brockman . . ." She pounced on me somewhere between my last word and the period at the end of the sentence. I parried by immediately interrupting her.

"Call me John," I said, smiling. She was concentrating on what she was going to say and ignored the interruption.

"You're saying the development of collaborative hunting skills—planning, language, etc.—was the driving force behind the evolution toward our present state of humanness?"

"Not the only factor, but most likely an important one." I responded cautiously. I wasn't sure on what grounds she was going to challenge what I took to be a widely accepted, inoffensive deduction. I did have an inkling, however, that she had mauling on her mind. It would be interesting to see whether her tactics were based on long clauses or on long claws.

Danner was sitting on the edge of the desk enjoying himself like someone who already knew the punch line listening to a good joke.

"And the males were the hunters, right?" The hint of sarcasm in her voice was becoming trenchant. Still smiling, I maintained eye contact with her as I replied. I could see where she was heading and I all I needed to do was to make her lose her cool.

"Of course," I said, "they were bigger and stronger than the females." Before she could say anything, I quickly added, "And probably smarter." That brought a mixed murmur from the gallery and I thought I had put Miz Hansen on the defensive. To my surprise she responded not angrily, but with beguiling mockery.

"So poor, little, stupid Lucy just hung around the cave barefoot and pregnant while big Mr. Erectus and his hunting buddies increased the cranial capacity of the species by wandering around until they found a dead animal to drag home?

Then she closed in for the kill. "That certainly explains why the mother-child bond is the foundation of society, why most of the domestic technology was created by inventive females, and why food-gathering by the females formed the basis for complex social structures. Thank you for clarifying that for me, John." Beth Hansen smiled at me sweetly and then looked innocently at Prof. Danner. I was barely able to keep the smart-assed reply I had ready from falling out of my open mouth as I realized she had almost suckered me into my own trap. *Touché*!

Danner laughed and said, "As you can see, folks, there is more to the study of evolution than gluing pieces of old bones together. Yes, we have some facts, but much of what we know is putative and the rest is based on conjecture, pet peeves, personal prejudice, and the art of persuasion. Each of you will be presenting one of the topics from the list I have given you. I want you to be able not only to justify your explanations, but to evaluate them in terms of their scientific merit. Anticipate every possible criticism and objection on logical and scientific grounds. This will not be an exercise in oratory or rhetoric. It will be an exercise in objective analysis. Thank you, ladies and gentlemen . . . and John." He grinned at me as he added that. It sounds as if we are going to have an interesting and lively dialogue in this seminar."

Everyone rose to leave and I approached Beth, who eyed me warily.

"I'm surprised you're in anthro," I said in my friendliest voice. "You'd make a helluva courtroom lawyer." She smiled at me, but not too warmly.

"Thank you, John. I think you'd make a helluva nightclub comedian." I must have had a silly look on my face because she broke into a nervous laugh.

"I'm sorry," she said, grasping my arm. "That was a terrible thing to say. I just hate nightclub comedians." She could hardly speak for laughing. Her remark hadn't offended me, but I wasn't used to not having the last word, rejoinders being my specialty. Maybe that was why Danner seemed so amused.

"And I just hate lawyers," I said, still smiling. We looked at each other for a moment and then both of us began to laugh. How about that! A feminist with a sense of humor!

As Danner walked past us toward the door, he said jokingly, "Now, don't you two get too friendly. I'm counting on you to put some sparks into this seminar."

Two weeks later as I walked north past Suzzallo Library on my way to Denny Hall, I saw Beth by one of the columns at the main entrance to the library. She was cornered by a beefy no-neck wearing UW sweats. I recognized him as one of the starting senior linebackers for the Huskies. I wasn't close enough to make out their words, but it seemed pretty obvious he was trying to make a move on her and she was not having much luck getting rid of him. I guessed she probably knew him, but not as well as he wanted her to.

He was big—too big for a guy my size to antagonize without having a compelling reason backed up by a baseball bat. Judging by the size of his crotch bulge, he had just come from the deli over on University Avenue where he must have stuffed a five-pound Gouda cheese and a foot-long salami down the front of his tight sweatpants. It seemed obvious the poor guy couldn't help himself, so, as daunting an undertaking as it appeared, I reluctantly decided it had been given to me to counsel him.

I walked up the steps to the library entrance and stopped five or six feet away from them. Mr. Woody had Beth pressed up against the column, holding her around the waist with one hand and messaging her butt with the other. I couldn't see her face, but there was more than just annoyance in the tone of her demands and I could see she was beginning to struggle. I was surprised she hadn't already treated Mr. Woody to a knee in the Gouda. Maybe he would listen to a devoted fan.

"Hey, aren't you Brent Woody? You guys really kicked some butt Saturday. That one play just at the end of the third quarter was . . ."

"Yeah, yeah, I'm busy, OK?" He turned and scowled at me without loosening his hold on Beth. The droplets glistening on his forehead looked like perspiration, but I knew it was actually excess testosterone oozing out. Thinking he had dismissed me, he turned back to Beth, and I kept on talking.

"Man, that one play, you know the one? right at the end of the third quarter? That was the damnedest thing I've ever seen! Hey, how about giving me an autograph right here on this book? What do you say?" I held out my copy of Julian Jaynes's *The Origin of Consciousness in the Breakdown of the Bicameral Mind.* This time Mr. Woody brought both hands with him when he turned around. As soon as he let go of her, Beth slipped away from him. Apparently Mr. Woody was used to intimidating people, and he was annoyed by people who were slow to realize they were being intimidated.

"What the fuck is your problem? Take a hike before I kick your ass." The moment of truth was shaping up nicely. It seemed Mr. Woody was now ready to accept counseling.

"Ah, come on, please? Just your name, right here on the title page, see? If you don't know how to write, you can just make a little scribble, and I promise to tell everyone who made it, OK?"

CAIN

Mr. Woody took the two steps that separated us and grabbed me by the front of my jacket. His breath reeked of pepperoni pizza. I was a little disappointed because I had hoped he would lunge at me so I could throw him hard on his big ass. But life is full of little disappointments, as Mr. Woody was about to discover.

I let go of the 467-page hardcover book, and its bold hypothesis of the bicameral mind came as quite an intellectual shock to Mr. Woody's left big toe. Before he could sum up his critical analysis of the book with an insightful "Shit!" the fingers of my left hand clamped around the lower part of his right, my other hand moved to assist and I stepped into him, thumbs pressing hard into the back of his big hand, twisting and bending his palm down toward his arm, my right elbow coming rudely into contact with his adam's apple as he dropped to his knees in excruciating pain.

Beth started to hop around us in a frenzy shouting "Stop it! Stop it you two! What are you doing? Are you crazy?"

Two students coming out of the library stopped to stare and several others on their way up the steps gathered around our little one act play. Fortunately for me, none of Brent Woody's teammates showed up among the spectators. I leaned forward to whisper into Mr. Woody's ear, sending an additional bolt of agony up his big arm.

"Brent, I really think Miss Hansen deserves her personal space, don't you?" His eyes rolled and I took that for an affirmative since all he could do was moan with my elbow pressing against his throat.

"Perhaps this is an awkward time for you. I'll tell you what, why don't I get that autograph some other day." I gave his hand a final thrust before giving it back to him and leaned heavily on my elbow. Despite his pain Mr. Woody wasn't injured, but he wouldn't be getting an "A" in his calligraphy class that afternoon. Nor would he be inclined to kick anyone's ass with his left foot for a day or two.

As soon as I let him go he did manage to thank me for setting him straight.

"I'll get you, motherfucker," he croaked hoarsely.

Picking up my book, I pushed through the circle of onlookers and went into the library, down the stairs to the south entrance, and back outside again. There was no point in having to make explanations to the campus police.

The next day Beth cornered me in the hall as I was going to Danner's seminar. For some reason, I thought she was going to thank me.

"What were you doing yesterday?" she demanded, hotter than hell. "Who asked you to butt in, anyway?" She was not pretty when she was mad.

"I'm sorry, you looked as if you could use some help with that creep. Don't tell me he's your boyfriend."

"That's none of your business and you don't have the right to go around deciding what I need help with! I could have handled it myself without resorting to violence."

"I see. You'll have to forgive me. I have this urge to pick on big guys who are bothering women. I guess I'm nothing but a bully. Shame on me." I stepped around her and went into the classroom.

Danner got no sparks from either of us that period—not even a comment.

A few days later she walked by me with a cup of coffee in her hand as I sat by myself in the Hub.

"Beth. Would you come and sit with me for a minute?" I said it without really knowing why. She turned and looked around as if trying to think of some reason not to accept my invitation. Finally she came over and sat down.

"What do you want, John?" she asked sullenly. I enjoyed pushing her buttons during our debates in Danner's seminar, but for some reason having her put out with me over the Woody thing bothered me, and I wanted to get it sorted out.

"I just wanted to tell you I'm sorry if I was out of line the other day with you and Woody. I thought I was doing the right thing."

She seemed a little uncomfortable with my apology, as if she felt she owed me one instead and hated to admit it. She sighed and looked away.

Still not looking straight at me, she said, "Ok, maybe I overreacted . . . a little. It's just that men don't give women credit for being able to take care of themselves. It's bad enough to have a man think he can put his hands all over me, but it's almost as bad to have another one assume he needs to jump in and save me. Can you understand that at all?"

"Not very well, but I'm trying."

She finally looked directly at me. "It's not that I don't appreciate your motives. You took a pretty big risk doing that. Brent's a big boy and he has a reputation for being a tough guy. I'm glad you didn't get hurt. I'm surprised you were able to do that to him."

"Thank you . . . just lucky I guess. Next time I'll ask if you want any help, ok?"

She smiled and shook her head slowly from side to side.

"Ok, John. I guess that's a beginning anyway." She finished off her coffee and got up. "I'll see you in Danner's seminar this afternoon."

"Oh yes, I'll be there. See you." As I watched her walk away I felt a lot better—a whole lot better.

CHAPTER 7

Where Nature Guides

A pale sun had broken up Saturday morning's fog. By ten-thirty, when I arrived in Woodland, a lukewarm light scattered through a bronze haze, warming little except the autumnal reds and yellows splashed around the surrounding hillsides. I stopped for gas and used the restroom, thinking about Ernie Wells' effluvial, fly-infested outhouse, which five cups of his boiled coffee grounds and eggshells had forced me to visit several times on my last visit.

I drove east up the Lewis river road, crossed the bridge and continued up the river on the south side. Just past Merwin dam I turned onto an obscure gravel road leading steeply into the hills south of the river.

A decade earlier I might have encountered logging trucks snaking down the narrow road, headed toward the mill in Woodland or farther on toward the freighters waiting to load logs on the Columbia river at Kalama. I might have risked meeting a Peterbuilt, a Kenworth, or an Autocar on one of the many narrow curves between the infrequent turnouts. Airhorn booming, it could have loomed large and fast just ahead of me on a blind turn, an eighteen-wheeled juggernaut bearing down with forty tons of unstoppable momentum barely restrained by a snorting exhaust brake and the drag of hot asbestos against the steaming steel of water-cooled brakedrums. But now the area was logged out and the road was quiet, seldom used by anyone except the old Indian who lived at the top of the hill. The once well-maintained road was now partially overgrown and pockmarked with potholes. Reluctantly, my Volkswagen scraped, jolted, and ground its way up the steep switchbacks in second gear.

Ernie Wells, ex-logger and self-proclaimed shaman, lived in a moldering log cabin he had built by himself as a young man in the 1920's. The BIA considered him a member of the Cowlitz tribe, although he steadfastly asserted he was the last living descendant of the mysterious Taitnapams, who had dwelt among the headwaters of the Lewis river and who had fallen into obscurity and apparent extinction by the mid 1800's.

I had known his grandson, Wally Wells, in Vietnam, and one of the first things I had taken care of when I finally returned to the Pacific Northwest was to look the old man up. Wally hadn't talked much about his family, except occasionally to express a sad and bitter contempt for his alcoholic parents. But during the short time I had known him before he was killed, Wally had talked incessantly about his grandfather, the shaman. I think Wally couldn't decide whether to be proud of his Indian heritage or ashamed of it. Although ashamed of his family's poverty, alcoholism, and purposeless existence, he saw his grandfather as a hero: an Indian who had prevailed against the paradox of living in the white world while at the same time preserving the old ways.

I had felt sorry for Wally because he didn't know who he was, and because he seemed to feel no love for his parents. At the same time, I was embarrassed that I could not identify with Wally's unhappy rootlessness. I could not imagine not having the support and comfort of a loving family. I could not imagine being ashamed of my parents. I could not imagine being poor. I could not imagine being Indian. And not being able to imagine those states of being made me feel guilty. Was my adoption by the Brockmans the only thing that made me different from Wally? There but for the grace of the Brockmans and the accident that killed my Indian parents go I.

Ernie Wells, Wally's grandfather, had no doubts about who he was and no compunctions about telling me.

"I am Sings-To-Man-Bear," he said. "But you may call me Ernie."

His eagerness to share his astounding knowledge of Indian lore provided me with the kinds of cultural and linguistic insights for which any serious anthropologist would have died and for which some, perhaps, might have killed.

Wally had told me his grandfather knew all about Sasquatches. It didn't take long for Ernie to make me think maybe he did know all about them. It was as if he had found in me a repository where the knowledge he had accumulated over a lifetime could be preserved and passed on, even as he himself had become a repository. Ernie knew he was one of the few, if not the last, of the oral historians of his people.

When Ernie asked me to record the stories, ceremonies, and spoken language of a people that were supposed to have disappeared more than a century before, I was concerned about the authenticity of his sources, the accuracy of his memory, and, frankly, his motives for sharing what he knew with me. I found it difficult to believe he could have acquired, organized, and memorized such a large volume of material in a language presumably extinct. How was he able to translate the language so easily? If indeed it turned out to be authentic, from whom had he learned it, and to what degree had the original language been corrupted by the long succession of teachers and learners so far removed from the culture that had used the language?

Our first and subsequent meetings had convinced me Ernie Wells was an extraordinary man whose consuming interest in his people's history was supported by a source of vast mental and physical energy and the most phenomenal natural memory I had ever come across. As an undergraduate I had learned a smattering of nouns and verbs in the Duwamish dialect of Salish—the names of body parts, numerals, the words for water and fire, for running and singing—but I did not have much training in linguistics. Ernie also spoke the Cowlitz dialect fluently, and the similarities between the Duwamish words I knew and the Cowlitz names for them were quite clear. But the other native language Ernie spoke with such ostensible fluency was one I had never heard. When I

CAIN

asked him the names of body parts and numerals, the sounds seemed to have no connection with the Salishan family of languages. After the first visit, I had come prepared with tape recorder, camera, notebook, and a good deal of research under my belt. I now knew that the Taitnapams had spoken a dialect of Sahaptin similar to those of the Klickitats and Yakimas.

At the top of the hill I turned off the narrow gravel road onto an overgrown, rutted lane that took me another quarter mile along the ridge to a dense stand of hemlock. A rusty Jeep pickup that was old enough to vote languished along with Ernie's log cabin in a small clearing at the end of the lane.

The log cabin was about ten by fifteen feet with walls about six feet high. The low walls necessitated a low doorway no more than five feet in height. A single small window about two feet square next to the cabin door looked out through an opening in the trees and provided a view of Merwin and Yale lakes behind the small dams in the river valley below. Mt. St. Helens loomed large and symmetrically beautiful to the north, and the perennial white cone of Mt. Adams gleamed to the east. The bottom logs, sitting directly on the ground had long since succumbed to rot and carpenter ants, and one corner sagged, giving the cabin a serious rake. The roof was covered with corrugated steel panels caked with decades of needles from the surrounding trees and tarped over with a lumpy mat of thick, velvet moss. A rusty stovepipe protruded at an oblique angle from one end of the cabin.

Split wood reposed in surprisingly neat stacks against most of the outside wall area under the dubious protection of overhanging eves. On the remainder of the wall hung a galvanized tub, a bucket, a bucksaw, and a shovel. The badly fitted plywood door failed to cover a two-inch gap around the greater part of its perimeter.

A well-worn path led from the cabin eastward along the brow of the ridge about forty yards to a small stream that rushed down the steep slope through a tangle of fallen logs and boulders. An equally well-used path angled off to the west about the same distance toward Ernie's infamous outhouse.

The dark interior of the cabin was even more Spartan than the exterior. The old plywood floor was spongy and uneven, having been patched and reinforced with a variety of plywood scraps, boards, and flattened tin cans. The furniture consisted of a small folding table, three rickety chairs, a cot built against the wall, a cupboard, and a potbellied stove. An enameled bucket of water with a dipper in it sat in a corner. A double-bitted axe and an ancient Winchester Model 1894, .30-30 lever action rifle hung on nails next to the door. A big blue coffeepot with chipped enamel sat on the iron stove, which served both for cooking and for heating. In the space under the cot sat a steamer trunk, and a kerosene lantern hung from a nail in one of the three horizontal logs that connected and braced the tops of the low walls.

I mused on the number of times the old man must have forgotten to duck his head as he walked beneath the pole or used the door because he was two or three inches taller than I and stood very erect. Aside from a plaid wool coat and yellow rain gear hanging on the walls, a fishing pole and tackle box, miscellaneous cans, bottles, and boxes stacked on the floor or sitting on boards placed between the support poles, the old man had no other possessions.

Ernie's clothes reflected the same simple utility. He wore a frayed and faded green flannel shirt beneath wide suspenders, which prevented his loose denims from slipping off his spare frame. In vogue with the time-honored tradition of loggers, the ragged bottoms of his pantlegs barely reached the top laces of his twelve-inch leather boots.

His thick, gray hair hung to the middle of his back in a ponytail cinched by a leather strap. Like old brown paper, his weathered face and strong hands were finely creased and heavily wrinkled. Large pores cratered the skin of his broad nose, and his wide teeth were as chipped and discolored as old ivory piano keys. Yet, he was still a handsome man with intense black eyes flashing beneath shaggy gray eyebrows and with an easy sense of humor that played his furrowed face and transformed his craggy features into an engaging, quizzical grin.

We spent all day recording his stories in Taitnapam and in English. The stories charmed and fascinated and Ernie narrated with the enthusiasm and skill of a consummate story teller. In what seemed like no time at all, dusk began to draw its dark drapes around the little clearing, and Ernie announced it was time to stop for the day and prepare dinner.

I was not all that anxious to eat with Ernie, but I couldn't very well insult him by refusing. He sent me out to build a fire in the rock-ringed pit he used for cooking outside the cabin when it was too warm to cook inside. For Ernie, that was anytime the temperature climbed into the mid forties and it wasn't raining or blowing too hard. While I was working on the fire, Ernie lit the lantern.

He carried the lantern over to the stream and retrieved a plastic bag containing a skinned rabbit. He said he had taken the rabbit from a snare that morning. Having dressed it, he had placed it in a bag and hung it in the stream to keep it cool during the day.

When the fire was ready, Ernie skewered the salted rabbit with a steel rod and set it across the rocks of the pit to roast. Trimming the sprouts off two wrinkled potatoes, he punctured them and set them in the coals. A can of peas, its top opened but not removed, also went into the coals. After smoking and sizzling twenty minutes on each side, Ernie pronounced the rabbit done. He fished the potatoes out of the coals with a forked stick, used his folded handkerchief to handle the hot can while he divided the peas on our plates, and we were ready to eat.

Ernie and I sat on a log and watched coffee boil in the fire as we ate. The fatless rabbit was tough but tasty and the mixture of peas mashed into the mealy potatoes was surprisingly good. I hadn't realized how hungry I was until I started to eat. We picked the rabbit carcass apart and gnawed on it until nothing was left of the two-pound cottontail but a pile of bones. When everything else was gone, Ernie brought out a can of peaches for dessert. Cleanup consisted of rinsing the food off the forks and enameled plates with a few dippers of water and setting them by the fire to steam dry.

The chill of the clean night air penetrated my jeans and sweatshirt, and I fetched my jacket from the car. The fire felt good and so did Ernie's company.

"Damned fine meal, Ernie, thanks."

"I'm glad you liked it, John. I like to have company for dinner once in a while."

"Don't you get lonely up here by yourself, Ernie?"

"Sometimes, but I keep busy, and the mountains and the trees are good companions. Besides, I can go down to Cougar anytime I want and find someone to talk to. I go to Kelso to visit my son once in a while, and I go to the Native American Conference in Seattle or Puyallup, or wherever it might be held. I also have friends in Toppenish and Umatilla."

"I guess I'm not much of an Indian, Ernie. I like this place, but I wouldn't be able to stay here even though I'm sort of a loner myself."

Maybe sitting around the fire had triggered some sort of primitive bond between Ernie and me, or maybe it was just that Ernie was easy to talk to, but I felt as if I had known the old man all my life.

Gazing into the fire, Ernie spoke thoughtfully. "You know, John, you should have an Indian name."

I laughed. "I told a second lieutenant in Vietnam I was called Running Fox. It was a name I made up on the spur of the moment because he thought I ought to have one, too."

"Running Fox? That's a yuppy name, John. You need a name that has spiritual meaning. It would have to come from a vision."

"How did you acquire your Indian name, Ernie?"

"The old-fashioned way: I had a dream vision."

"I've had some of those recently myself, but they weren't exactly spiritual in nature and I can't say I would care to be known publicly for what I was doing in them. It might be a little embarrassing."

Ernie got up, poured some of the bubbling black gumbo into two chipped mugs that had been collecting fly ash by the edge of

CAIN

the fire, and set the pot back on the coals. "You look too old to have wet dreams, John. Do you dream of someone in particular?"

"Yes."

"Does she dream about you?"

"How would I know that, Ernie?"

"Ask her, John. Then you will know for sure. It's best for people who dream of each other to share their dreams."

"You're probably right about that, Ernie, but I think this person might be a little upset if I told her what she and I had been doing in my dreams."

"She might be, but even so, if you plant the idea in her mind, it will grow like a flower. In time the roots will touch her heart and soften it. The bloom will open and fill her head with loving thoughts. Even if she didn't dream of you before, the flower of love in her head will bring dreams of you to her."

The smoke from the fire wafted towards us and I tried to fan it away from my burning eyes. Ernie merely squinted another notch and went on watching the yellow tongues lick at the sooty pot.

"The power of suggestion, huh, Ernie? You may be on to something. I'll have to think about it, though."

"Don't think about it too long, John. Other men will dream of her. The best flowers are planted early."

"Yeah, if the frost doesn't get them."

"Life makes many promises, John, but the death of our bodies is the only one it always keeps."

"Thanks for reminding me, Ernie." I tried sipping the molten coffee and burned my lip.

"It is the same advice my father gave to me," Ernie said."

"Did it work?"

"It sounded good, John, but it didn't work worth a shit. Once, when I was seventeen, I had a dream about a good-looking whore who had flirted with me in Vancouver. The next time I saw her, I told her I had made love to her in a dream. She said I wasn't entitled to any freebies and demanded ten dollars for every time I had sex with her in my dreams."

"No kidding? What did you do?"

"I gave her the ten dollars and twenty more on account."

"You couldn't see she was taking advantage of you?"

Ernie shook his head solemnly and gulped from his scalding cup without flinching. "No, she didn't cheat me. I had only one more dream of her. When I saw her again after several months and told her, she gave me a refund of ten dollars."

"Did you learn anything from that transaction?"

"I may have been inexperienced, John, but I was no fool. After that, whenever I made dream love to a whore, I always remembered to pay her in the dream." Ernie looked over at me in all seriousness. In a few seconds a waggish grin began to pry up the corner of his mouth and both of us laughed.

CHAPTER 8

The Leech's Kiss

After I saw Danner with Janice Rawlings, I began to look at him differently, trying to discover any behavioral clues to his real character that I might have overlooked. I was a pretty good judge of character, by my reckoning at least, and there had always been something about Danner that bothered me, something I couldn't quite put my finger on. Because I couldn't decide what exactly it was about him that bothered me, I attributed my feeling to the resentment of authority I had acquired in the army.

There was nothing complicated about my attitude. I hadn't felt that way before I got into the army. It was simply a side effect of constantly having to accept orders from someone of higher rank—or worse, from someone of the same rank with more seniority—who usually didn't know anymore than you did and often knew even less. I don't know why, but it seemed as if the surest, quickest way to turn private Jekyll into that prick, Hyde, was to pin an extra stripe or two on his sleeve.

Most privates would whine their asses off if their squad leaders put them on report for having wax in their ears. But as soon as they became squad leaders themselves, some of them would write up their best buddies for inadvertently farting in formation. Lord Acton's observation that power corrupts and absolute power corrupts absolutely was ostensibly no less true for the chain of military command than for the hierarchy of civilian politicians and potentates. Although to be fair, I have to acknowledge the many good men and women who remain uncorrupted by the power of their authority, officers and NCO's capable of intelligently exercising the kind of responsible, humane leadership respected by both the people under them and the people above them. As for the rest, they create a pervasive atmosphere of resentment and mistrust of authority in the rank and file, resentment and mistrust that become suspicion of and hostility toward anyone in a supervisory or evaluative position in the civilian afterlife. For me it was one more prejudice I had to constantly monitor in myself and slap down from time to time.

Nonetheless, I kept watching Danner for some telltale sign of perversion that never manifested itself. I could neither shake nor substantiate the niggling notion that Danner was, somehow, something other than he appeared.

On a Wednesday afternoon during the last week of fall quarter, before finals week and winter break, Beth found me hard at work grading papers in the Hub. Even before I looked up from the student paper I was reading, I knew she was agitated.

"Hey, what's up?" I asked, finishing my comments on the unfortunate junior's paper: "Unfocused, Undocumented, Unsatisfactory." When I did look up, I saw Beth was more than just agitated—she was seething, absolutely livid. I put down the paper, drained the last swallow of tepid coffee from my cup, and studied her as I waited for her to say something.

Beth dropped her bookbag heavily into the empty captain's chair next to her and slammed her trembling, brim-full cup down on the table, sloshing coffee on the stack of student papers I had placed there.

"Dammit! Sorry, John." She dabbed at the spots on the papers and the puddle on the table with a napkin. Something was definitely amiss.

"Don't worry about it, Beth. I always splash a little coffee on the papers—fools the little SOB's into believing I might actually have spent some time thinking about what they wrote." I grinned but she was too preoccupied to respond to my attempt at humor.

-CAIN

"John, I am so upset I just feel like screaming! The arrogance of that bastard!

"Yes, I can see you are upset. That asshole Woody hasn't been after you again has he?"

"No, he's not the problem. John, I . . . oh, you're not going to believe me!" Tears flooded her eyes and splatted on the table. She covered her face with her hands and blubbered big time.

This was not the Beth I knew and I was worried about her and empathizing, anger rising in me against whoever was responsible for . . . for what?" I leaned across the table to pat her on the arm and to offer her a napkin.

"Here, blow your nose on this and you'll feel better." She took the napkin and wiped her eyes and nose.

"Now then, what makes you think I wouldn't believe you, anyway? What's the matter?" Her wet hazel eyes locked onto mine, her uncertainty fading.

"It's Professor Danner, John. That breast-fondling bastard is trying force me into bed with him."

"Jesus! Danner? Are you sure? I mean it wasn't some kind of misunderstanding or something was it? He really did proposition you? He actually touched you?" The hurt and disappointment in her eyes told me instantly I had reacted stupidly. Of course she was sure. She wanted reassurance, not cross-examination. John, you asshole!

Beth shrank away from me, tears gushing anew.

"I knew you wouldn't believe me," she sobbed, getting up to leave. I sprang out of my chair and darted around the table to intercept her.

"Beth, I believe you, I believe you. I'm sorry. I'm an insensitive shithead, ok? Just sit down and tell me what happened. Please?" She took a minute to decide, but finally she sat down again and took a sip of her coffee. Sniffing and wiping, she began to talk.

"You know there is going to be another TA job available next quarter?"

"Yes, somebody mentioned it last week. Beverly Watson started the job at the beginning of this quarter and she just up and quit with no explanation last week. Rumor has it she's pregnant."

"If she is, I bet I know who did the honors."

"Danner?"

"Exactly. I went to Danner to talk to him about the job. Lisa, my sister, entered Eastern this fall and my father just found out he's going to have to accept early retirement now or face termination next year. I told you his company had merged with a company from back east? Now my parents won't to be able to finance schooling for both Lisa and me. That's why I really need this TA job."

"What about your part time job with the veterinarian?"

"I work ten or twelve hours a week and he pays me $3.75 an hour."

"I see. And what did Danner say?"

"At first he was very understanding and sympathetic. He told me how impressed he was with my background and with how well I had been doing. You know him, he's smoother than talcum powder on a baby's behind. He told me he would be delighted to see me get the assistantship, but that it was a committee decision and all he could do was recommend me. Then he modestly confessed that his recommendation carried a good deal of influence. He really caught me off guard. He was saying all these things and I was thinking he really wanted me to have the job, and I was feeling relieved and grateful to him, and . . ."

She trailed off into silence and I guessed she was replaying the event in her mind, trying to make sense of it, perhaps looking for something she might have said or done that had given Danner the wrong impression.

"Is that when he touched you?"

"Yes, but it was way more than just touching. You know when you're sitting in his office how your chair faces his so your knees are almost against his?"

"Yeah, I've always thought it was a bit too cozy myself."

-CAIN

"Well, we were talking and he leaned over and put his hand on my shoulder and I didn't really think too much about it, and then he was all over me. He had one hand up my sweater, the other hand between my legs, and he was slobbering on my neck. I was completely shocked for a second; but then I came totally unglued, hitting and kicking and yelling at him to quit, tipping my chair over backward in the process. While I was getting up from the floor, Danner went over and stood in front of the door as cool as you please. I remember exactly what he said: 'Calm down and listen to what I have to say. Quid pro quo: I get some of that tight ass of yours, and you get the assistantship. It doesn't have to be right now. I'll give you a week to think it over. If you don't want to cooperate, ok, but don't be foolish enough to think you can cause me any trouble over this. What happened here is that you came to me and offered to screw me in exchange for the assistantship. I guarantee my version is the viable one, especially since I have already informed the Dean that you have made passes at me on other occasions. Any questions?' Then he just walked over and picked up the chair with a smirk on his face and let me leave."

"Christ, what an evil, cunning bastard! I knew there was something malignant about that man!"

Other than promising Beth that Danner was going to get his comeuppance, I could offer no immediate suggestions as to how that might come about. But even though I wasn't sure yet who was going to throw it, I thought I could predict a monkey wrench was about to land in Danner's machinations and that the event was imminent and inevitable.

I had crossed paths with a few evil schemers and discovered them to be formidably cunning and ruthless. They possessed the advantage of an amoral perspective on life that freed them from having to play by anyone else's rules. Being masters of their own game, they were generally very successful in their endeavors, often for a very long time. Despite their cunning, however, they were driven by forces that were at the same time the source of their shared vulnerability.

They were addicted to and driven by an all-consuming need to serve and satisfy themselves only, and that meant they were motivated by greed, lust, and power. It meant winning by any means, gratifying the self without regard for the consequences to others—unleashing the conscienceless creatures of the Id. But, as is the case with addicts and overreachers, at some point their needs become greater than their ability to satisfy those needs, and they are brought down by their own mistakes, no matter how clever they believe themselves to be, or actually are. Sooner or later, they will begin to overestimate their own cleverness and get careless. They will disdain the ability of anyone else to interfere, they will take too many risks, they will take a fall; or they'll piss somebody off who sees to it the fall comes sooner rather than later.

There was only one person on campus whose counsel in this matter could be trusted: Sid Cunningham. Although Beth was initially hesitant, I finally got her to agree to talk with Dr. Cunningham. I left her staring into her coffee while I went to call his office. I would be seeing him that evening, but Beth really needed to take some kind of action right away—and so did I.

Dr. Cunningham wasn't in his office in Guthrie Hall. The Psych Department secretary said she thought he might be in the main library, but that he had a seminar in Johnson Annex at four. I looked at my watch: in twenty minutes he had a two-hour seminar.

When I came back, Beth was still frowning thoughtfully into her cup.

"Sorry, Beth, I couldn't get a hold of Dr. Cunningham, and he has a class from four until six. Let's go over to Guthrie a little before six and catch him after his class. Are you hungry?"

"No, not really. I think I'll go back to the dorm and lie down. I can meet you at Guthrie, all right?"

"Do you want me to walk over to the dorm with you?"

"I'll be fine, John, really. Thanks anyway." She gathered her stuff together and rose to leave. "I'll see you a few minutes before six, right?"

-CAIN

I nodded. "Sure you don't want company?"

She shook her head and managed a half-hearted but pretty smile in response. "John, I'm ok. See you later."

I watched her as she left the cafeteria, and then through the glass wall for a few seconds as she turned up the hallway toward the stairs at the north end of the Hub. When I could no longer see her, I turned back to the papers I had been reading, absently thumbed through one, and tossed it back onto the table.

I was flattered Beth had come to me with her problem. She might have chosen to tell Muff, instead. Good thing she hadn't. I had no doubt Muff would have marched over to Danner's office and, excoriating him with obscenities, proceeded to kick the holy shit out of him—getting herself and Beth into big trouble and probably expelled from the university in the process. Meanwhile, Danner would wind up with nothing more than scorched ears, a black eye, and Muff's pointy little boot prints all over his aching crotch. Not that I wouldn't have liked to use his pretty face for a punching bag myself. Unfortunately, dealing with Danner was going to require rationality, not rashness.

Thinking about Danner's hands on Beth disgusted and infuriated me, even more so than Brent Woody's behavior had. I had been able to keep my objectivity about that—for the most part, anyway. But now my reaction included much more than simple anger and outrage at the abuse to which Beth had been subjected. Danner's mistreatment of Beth had opened a well of hidden emotions deep inside me, intense, disturbing feelings of possessiveness and protectiveness that surprised and even frightened me a little. What the hell was going on with me, anyway? I had thought I knew how I felt about Beth: we were friends. Period. I liked her and I would stand up for her—that was all.

Or was it? As I sat there in the cafeteria looking at the Rorschachian coffee stains on the paper in front of me, I suddenly realized I had been fooling myself, maybe from the very beginning. Lord! As if things weren't complicated enough already. Right there in the public privacy of the noisy cafeteria, with a stack of coffee-stained student papers still to consider and wild, wonderful fantasies welling up inside me, I realized I wanted more from Beth than her friendship—infinitely more. I realized I loved her and I needed her love in return.

For all my protestations of neutrality, I had been hooked from that first encounter in Danner's seminar. If I hadn't been, I wouldn't have bothered to swim the foaming moat of feminist cowshit she surrounded herself with, and to scale the daunting wall of our differences just to get a glimpse of the fair maiden who dwelt within. I didn't know when I had crossed the threshold of enthrallment, and I didn't care.

Twenty cups of espresso couldn't have pumped me as high as that self-revelation. It pasted a silly grin on my face and intoxicated me with a joyful delirium. I couldn't remember ever feeling so buoyant, so alive, so damned good. The feeling was too wonderful to last long.

Abruptly, like an iceberg looming out of the fog, a cold, terrible question took form, chilling my ecstasy into numb despair. What if she didn't feel the same way about me? Why should she?

At a quarter to six, I gulped a last swallow of coffee and stuffed into my briefcase the papers I had painfully finished grading during the last two hours. A hue and cry would arise in class the next day when I handed those papers back. Nearly half of them bore the dreaded "Unsatisfactory—Redo" that the students in my quiz section had come to loathe me for. A short paper every other week—that's what I required, and not a single student had escaped having to redo at least one of them. I had critiqued a few of the papers in class each time, pointing out and explaining how to correct or avoid some of the common problems I found, and citing positive examples to be emulated. I also had stiffened the criteria for each succeeding assignment, and a majority of the papers had improved each time. Even the unsatisfactory papers from the last assignment were better organized, better documented, and better written than most of the papers from the first assignment eight weeks ago. I wondered when some of them were going to catch on that coming

-CAIN

to class occasionally was not enough; they actually were expected to learn something.

I thought of the hawk-nosed, somewhat eccentric associate professor of English who always wore a battered fedora and carried a bulging old leather briefcase—Dr. Garland O. Ethel. Ethel had preached the holy trinity of writing to me as an undergraduate: "Unity, coherence, and emphasis," he would repeat like a mantra. I recalled he also had told me I used too many big words.

I walked out of the Hub into an early darkness. A fine mist was descending on the nearly deserted campus, and the city's nocturnal aura revealed a low, sullen overcast. Soft lavender orbs hovered around the mercury street lamps. Down the glistening crowns of wet brick walkways shimmered long, slick lines of reflected building lights. In the square between Guggenheim and Bagley Halls, Drumheller Fountain lay dark and dormant. Rainier Vista, its broad walkway deserted along its lamp-dotted length, led away from the fountain in the direction of Mt. Rainier, sixty miles to the southeast. Now obscured by darkness and clouds, on a clear day Mt. Rainier thrust magnificently above the low hills on the horizon, between the Husky stadium and the University Hospital on the southern edge of the campus. For all I knew, at that murky moment blizzards might be blasting the mountain's glaciers, or starlight might be scintillating in silence on new snow, against a black sky above Seattle's overcast.

Still undecided between blizzard and starlight, I crossed Stevens Way and approached Guthrie Hall. It was about five minutes before six, and Beth, wearing her familiar knit hat, was standing by the front door with her hands jammed into her long, dark coat. As soon as I saw her, I began to feel awkward, nervous, excited.

That was exactly how I had felt the first time I asked a girl to dance. Fraught with a thirteen-year-old's fear of humiliation, I had felt vast relief when she hadn't said no. We danced and I held the girl politely at arm's length, my right hand trembling lightly against the electric softness of her waist, my left hand swooning in the embrace of her hot, sweaty fingers. I don't know whether it was the heat or the hormones that made me heady, but I started feeling immensely satisfied with myself and boldly confident—until she told me I was a terrible dancer and that I really needed to take lessons. Mortified, I spent the remainder of the two-hour school dance talking to the chaperones, drinking punch, and going to the bathroom. It took me the better part of a year and a score of top secret, terpsichorean tutoring sessions with my mom before I regained the courage to ask another girl to dance.

Beth's expression was serious until she saw me coming and smiled at me. I must have been looking at her rather intently as I walked up.

"Anything wrong, John?"

"Huh? Oh, no, everything's fine. Why do you ask?" I tried to smile but my damned lips suddenly became self-conscious, and I couldn't tell what sort of face I was making.

Puzzled, Beth studied me closely. "I don't know, exactly. You have sort of a strange look."

"Must be those papers I was reading. Some of them are enough to give anyone a vacant stare."

My response didn't appear to satisfy her, but she dropped it anyway. "I've been standing here about five minutes and I haven't seen anyone fitting Dr. Cunningham's description go into the building."

I had described him to Beth as tall, white-haired, and wearing a white turtleneck sweater and a dark blazer. Dr. Cunningham always wore a white turtleneck sweater and a dark blazer.

"Let's go up to his office and wait for him," I suggested, and we entered the building.

On the other side of the vestibule, the Psych Department office was dark and empty. We took the stairs up to the third floor and followed the concentric hallway from the elevator around to a door with the number 338 on it and a plastic nameplate that read "Sid Cunningham." He was a full professor with a Ph.D. from Stanford and his was the only nameplate along the hall untitled by "Dr." or "Prof." Both of us leaned against the wall to wait. Dr. Cunningham would be along any minute.

As we waited I looked at the floor, afraid to make eye contact with Beth lest she discover how I had changed in the two hours since she had last seen me. I didn't want her to know how I felt until somehow I could figure out how she felt about me. Indirectly, Danner's lechery had forced me to recognize my true feelings about Beth, but that didn't mean I was going to send him a thank-you card. After an experience like that, Beth could not possibly be in the mood to learn that her coffee buddy and sparring partner, good old Uncle John, was, after all, just another horny suitor. I couldn't stand the idea of my newly recognized feelings about Beth being misunderstood in that way. But how else could she understand it. Men just have one thing on their minds, right? Hell, I could wind up being the one with the scorched ears and sore crotch instead of Danner.

We heard the elevator bell ding, and then Dr. Cunningham came around the corner carrying a heavy briefcase and fishing for his keys in the pocket of his dark blue blazer. He saw us right away and approached us smiling broadly.

"Hope you haven't been waiting long, John. I got cornered after class. You know how it is, somebody always has a problem." He laughed while Beth and I glanced at each other somewhat guiltily.

"Dr. Cunningham, I'd like you to meet a friend of mine, Beth Hansen. She's a grad student in anthro."

Beth extended her hand and Dr. Cunningham shook it warmly. "I get to meet you at last, Beth, it's a real pleasure. Now I see why John would rather have coffee with you instead of me."

The comment caught Beth off guard and I thought I could detect a faint blush on her cheeks as she glanced over at me with surprise. "It's nice to meet you, too, Dr. Cunningham. John has told me so much about you I feel I almost know you already."

"In that case, my dear, for heaven's sake please call me Sid. Don't pay any attention to John, he's such a hopeless formalist."

Beth looked at me with a hint of coyness. "Yes, I've noticed that about him."

Dr. Cunningham found Beth's reply amusing and he laughed again as he unlocked the door, flipped on the lights, and ushered us into his office. "Have a seat," he said, gesturing toward the two Queen Anne chairs in front of his antique desk. All of his books and papers were carefully arranged in glass-doored cases, and several umbrellas with carved handles rested in an ornate brass and marble umbrella stand near the door. Gold-framed pictures of Maxine, Isolde and her husband, and Dr. Cunningham's three grandchildren populated the otherwise uncluttered room.

Dr. Cunningham noticed Beth eyeing the furniture and taking in the well-organized neatness of the small cubicle. "My Aunt Ruth left me her furniture about ten years ago. We didn't have room for all of it and I couldn't bear to sell it, so I redecorated my office. Do you like it?"

Beth was obviously impressed as she ran her hand over the delicate chairs. "I think it's beautiful! It's so elegant! I'm surprised you don't have antique dealers lined up trying to buy these things. These pieces appear to be very old, yet they're in such perfect condition."

"I always admired Aunt Ruth's furniture. I guess that's why she left it to me." As he spoke, he rubbed the graceful curves of the cherrywood desk reminiscently with his fingers.

The office lay on the outside perimeter of the building, which entitled it to a small window overlooking the roof of Guthrie Annex sitting in a clump of maple trees. Beth moved over to the window ledge and smiled at the trio of small faces beaming out of one of the gold picture frames. "These little guys are really cute. Grandchildren?"

"Oh yes, the three musketeers: Andy, Billy, and Bart. Andy's as strong as Porthos, Billy's as clever as Aramis, and Bart is moody enough to be Athos. No d'Artagnan yet, but we're still hopeful."

I sat and watched the two of them talk. I could tell they liked each other right off. Beth seemed to be at ease when she finally sat

-CAIN

down next to me across the desk from Dr. Cunningham and looked to me to explain why we were there.

I had to clear my throat before speaking. "Dr. Cunningham, Beth had an upsetting experience today involving the unwanted advances of a faculty member. I brought her here because I know she can trust you. I'm hoping you will be able to advise her about how to proceed against this man, how she can seek redress."

Dr. Cunningham had been sitting back in his chair. He leaned forward, placed his elbows on his desk, and rubbed his palms together, looking at Beth, then at me, and then back at Beth again as he addressed her. "This must be very difficult for you," he said sympathetically.

Beth looked down at her hands folded in her lap. "Yes. Yes it is."

"Could you tell me what happened?"

Beth looked over to me for reassurance. I nodded and said, "It's ok, Beth, just tell him what you told me."

Beth turned back to Dr. Cunningham and began relating the incident as she had related it to me. Dr. Cunningham was attentive, his expression clearly revealing the anger and disgust he felt toward Danner's behavior. When she had finished, he sat back in his chair again, frowning and rubbing his chin with his right hand.

After a few minutes, he leaned forward again with his elbows on the desk. "First, Beth, I want you to know how deeply ashamed and sorry I am on behalf of this university. No apology can be adequate, of course, but you deserve one anyway from Danner, from the dean of this college, from the regents, and, by God, from the president of this institution." He brought his fist down on the table hard enough to cause a picture of Maxine on his desk to fall over and to make Beth and me jump. His vehemence startled me. He was not given to using oaths, and certainly not to pounding on desks.

Appearing somewhat surprised and abashed at his own display of emotion, he carefully reset Maxine's picture, recomposed himself, and continued. "I've met Tom Danner only a few times, but I have heard some things that make me suspect this isn't the first time he has done this sort of thing. Apparently, no one else has had the courage to accuse him, but I can understand that. Danner is well-liked and respected, brilliant, even powerful in a sense. He has taken full advantage of the University's self-serving inertia in these matters and its reluctance to prosecute the moral and ethical transgressions of its faculty unless forced to do so by public scandal.

"But, I'm sorry, I didn't mean to go off on a tirade. Beth, I believe this is the reality of the situation:

"First, unless a strong case is established against Danner—probably requiring other victims to come forward—it is unlikely the University will take any action against him. He could even succeed in turning your accusations against you as he threatened, although I doubt if he wants to draw attention to your accusations unless he has to.

"Second, even if the University takes action against Danner, there will be no public condemnation. At best, he will be asked to resign, or if he refuses, he will be quietly dismissed. It is more probable he would be privately censured, perhaps placed on some sort of informal probation. But even if he is forced to leave, the reason will be repressed or falsified so that he won't have any trouble finding a new position with another university. Regrettably, I've seen it happen quite a few times.

"The bottom line is that unless you can raise a clamor either convincing enough or embarrassing enough to the University, nothing is going to happen. You could hire a lawyer and file a civil lawsuit against Danner, but I suspect his is the position of advantage. Quite frankly, without rape or physical injury, I think your suit would be hard to win. Without a good prospect of winning, you may not be able to find a lawyer who will work for a contingency fee. Also, the litigation would likely drag on for several years and not be resolved until after you have already taken your degree.

"You could also try getting the ear of the press and creating a public scandal, but before most newspaper editors would print an accusation, they would require a case against Danner as strong or stronger than would the University. Maybe some good investigative reporter could get the goods on Danner, but I wouldn't hold out much hope for that approach, either."

Dr. Cunningham gestured in exasperation. "I am truly, truly sorry, Beth, that I can't be more helpful, but there you have it."

An oppressive silence held dominion around the desk for a long minute while Beth dejectedly returned to contemplating her hands in her lap and I stared angrily at the ceiling.

"*Semper pravus.*" Dr. Cunningham incanted the phrase more to himself than to anyone else.

"Eternally corrupt?" I echoed bitterly. "How about *Tenebrae sint*? 'Let there be darkness.' I think either one would make a more appropriate motto for this university than *Lux sit.*"

He shook his head sadly. "Too often, John. Far, far too often."

I stood up and so did Beth and Dr. Cunningham. Beth reached awkwardly across the desk to grasp his hand. "Dr. Cunningham, thank you for your kindness, and your frankness. I wasn't sure who to talk to besides John. At least now I know where I stand."

He walked around the desk and accompanied us to the door. "You have every right to be disappointed. All I've done is give you bad news and tell you there is no good news. Some advice! Beth, I can't make any promises about the outcome, but I can promise to make some discreet inquiries. Maybe there is a way to see justice served."

Beth perked up. "Another way? What do you mean?"

"I have to check on some things before I can answer that and I certainly wouldn't want to get your hopes up. Give me a little time. In the meanwhile, let me know if there is anything I can do for you, anything at all."

He looked at Beth and me as if trying to decide whether or not to say something. "I'm probably not supposed to say this, but I'll say it anyway. Beth, you are lucky to have a friend like John, if you don't know that already. And you, John, from what I can see—and these old eyes see more than either one of you would guess—you're even luckier to have her."

Flustered by Dr. Cunningham's statements, Beth weakly attempted to clarify to him what kind of relationship we had, as I stood by, unable to say anything. "Well, we really aren't, uh, I mean yes, we're friends, but just friends—so far anyway."

Dr. Cunningham smiled. "Neither of you owes me an explanation. It's none of my business. I just wanted you to know that I think John has good taste in friends."

Beth got organized again and smiled back at him. "I've noticed that about him, too."

When we left Guthrie Hall, I walked with Beth back to her dorm. The mist had attenuated to little more than soggy air, but it was cooler, and I flipped up the collar on my mackinaw. Beth looked over at me several times while we were walking as if to say something, but didn't. I wanted to say many things, but didn't. We walked on, each turned inward.

I kept hearing her say "just friends—so far anyway." Did that mean what I wanted it to mean? Maybe she was just rattled and it didn't mean anything at all. Should I ask her? Should I? Do I dare? John, you abject wimp, ask her and get it over with. But do I dare disturb the universe? And how should I presume? And how should I begin? John, John, John. You aren't Prufrock. Shit! Why do I always wind up living in someone else's poem? Why his lovesong and not mine?

CHAPTER 9

The Mythos

Ernie Wells' repertoire of legends and folktales seemed endless. By now I had more than twenty hours worth of them stored on tape and he continued to think of more. They covered the gamut of themes concerning creation, of how certain geological features came to be, of the exploits of the culture hero, Coyote, common to all of the interior tribes. The legends dealt with the time before humans populated the earth, a time when animals and mountains talked and behaved like people.

I was struck by the similarity between these stories and the themes and events of Greek mythology. The formal distinction between legends and myths notwithstanding, there were parallels to the stories of Orpheus and Euridice, of Leda and the Swan, of the adventures of Perseus, Theseus, Icarus and Daedalus. There were also themes similar to those in the stories of the Old Testament: of Job, Lot, Jonah, Cain and Abel, of Solomon, of David and Goliath, of Sodom and Gomorrah, the Battle of Jericho, the Exodus, the Deluge. The folktales told of human heroes and moral lessons, of quests for guardian spirits, of punishment for evildoing. In these stories were the religion, philosophy, humor, and tragedy no less devout, no less wise, no less flawed than that of the Greeks, the Hebrews, the Egyptians, the Persians, the Sumerians, the Chinese, the Arabs, the Norse, the Celts.

The stories were of human beings with hopes, fears, loves, hates, hardships, and triumphs—the same as the stories of all cultures. I felt a great sense of loss in the imminent and certain disappearance of the languages and life of the American Indian. Suffering, uncertainty, disappointment—these were no less a part of Stone Age culture than of New Age culture. But the American Indians, the Australian Aborigines, the Papuans of New Guinea, the Jivaros of the Amazon, the Bushmen of the Kalahari—these primitive cultures and thousands more like them once lived closer to Paradise than any culture on this earth is likely ever to live again.

The human race has not evolved toward a higher plane of existence in the millions of years since it first acquired self consciousness. We have known all we need to know about living as humans for millenia. We have known for so long we have already begun to forget. Only technology has evolved. Unfortunately, the part of our intelligence that creates technology, depends upon it, even worships it, is not the best attribute of humankind. For all their wisdom acquired so long ago, some cultures never learned to appreciate when they were well off. I suppose even without the encroachment of European civilization, it was only a matter of time before the primitive societies strayed from the old ways and dreamed up the wheel and the computer. But in the primitive cosmos, where all change was absorbed into the eternal sameness of the cycles of things, time moved infinitely more slowly. If we could have remained primitives a while longer, perhaps we could have realized the perfection of letting the universe change us, instead of succumbing to our hubristic compulsion to change the universe.

One of Ernie's stories was different. It connected a tradition begun seven generations earlier to Ernie himself. Part legend and part folktale, the story, although interesting in itself, was equally interesting because of its mention of the dwelling place of the Tahtah kle'-ah, the Taitnapam term for the creatures called "Sasquatch," from the name given them by the Kwakiutls of British Columbia.

This is the story in Ernie's words.

This story is of the time before my people knew the white man, but after the migration of the Taitnapam to the new land

-CAIN

between the great mountains, Klickitat and Pahto, which you know as Adams and St. Helens, at the headwaters of the Lewis River.

We were always few. Half our original people had chosen to live to the north on the headwaters of the Cowlitz. There were fewer mouths to feed, but also fewer hands to feed them. In the new home game was plentiful. Salmon swam up the river. Berries and roots grew in abundance. We had horses and could pack the game we killed many miles, but because of our horses, we also had to avoid the densest timber and the fields of broken rock that spread out from the mountains.

The father of my great, great grandfather's grandfather, Wa-pan-thla, which means "Paws the Ground" and is my people's name for the grizzly bear, lived then. He had never seen a white man, although he had heard stories of them as a child. One day he was hunting and he saw a large creature drinking at the edge of the river. At first he thought the creature was a bear, but when the creature stood up and walked away on two legs Wa-pan-thla believed the creature to be a spirit. Frightened, but also curious, he said, "Am I not a warrior and a mighty hunter?" Does not the spirit of the great silver-backed bear protect me? I shall follow the spirit who appears as a man-bear and learn its secrets."

Wa-pan-thla followed the man-bear for several miles on horseback, but the creature reached the river of stone, which had once flowed from the mountain, and he was forced to continue on foot. Tired and thirsty, he could barely keep pace with the creature over the broken rock. But he was a skilled hunter, and the creature did not discover it was being followed.

Suddenly the creature vanished into the rocks and Wa-pan-thla was worried that it had become invisible and might be waiting to ambush him. Gathering all his courage and clutching his bearclaw charm, he walked on toward the place where the creature had vanished. When he reached the spot, he found a hole descending into the rocks. Dropping a pebble into the hole, he heard it echo against the bottom and decided he had discovered the cavern in which the creature lived.

Not having materials for a torch or a means of lowering himself into the cavern, Wa-pan-thla paced three small stones near the entrance to mark the spot and retraced his difficult steps back to his horse, and from there back to the camp.

That night Wa-pan-thla dreamed of coming face to face with the man-bear in the cavern. He looked into the creature's glowing red eyes and the creature, exhaling his foul breath upon him, turned him into stone.

Wa-pan-thla awoke in great fear and startled his wife, Mups-mups—Little Fawn—who lay beside him. Mups-mups, the wise and beautiful daughter of a Pshwanwapam chieftain, loved Wa-pan-thla very much and seeing her brave husband afraid, she comforted him.

"You have been dreaming, my husband, but all is well. Do not fear. You are a good man and your guardian spirit will watch over your sleep."

Reassured by his wife's words, he fell asleep again. Soon he began to dream once more.

This time his guardian spirit appeared to him in the familiar form of the great hump-backed bear and spoke to him:

"Wa-pan-thla, my namesake, you have seen the spirit of the underground, which no human was meant to see. For having laid eyes upon the spirit you must take an offering of meat, roots, and berries to the creature's dwelling on each of the next three full moons. If you see the creature, you must not look into its eyes lest you be turned into stone. You must never speak of this creature to anyone, for whoever hears of it from your lips shall also be turned into stone. I cannot protect you if you heed not my words."

The next morning Wa-pan-thla was troubled when he awoke. He no longer wished to learn the creature's secrets and he was angry with himself for having been so prideful and presumptuous. Now he would have to return to the cavern three times with an offering, and the moon would soon be round and bright.

That morning he spoke to his wife and asked her for her help. "My guardian spirit commands me to make an offering in two days' time," he told her. "Can you fill a basket with roots and berries while I hunt?"

Mups-mups was pleased that her husband had asked for her help. "I shall start right away and not stop to rest until the basket is filled. It shall await you when you return from hunting."

Wa-pan-thla hunted all day and finally returned late in the evening with a deer slung across his horse's back. Mups-mups and his two older children ran to greet him. As promised, a basket of roots and berries sat by the entrance to the mat lodge.

"The children helped, my husband. We worked very hard," she proudly told him.

"I thank the spirits for such a good wife. With such a family a man need take pride in nothing else."

Early the next morning he set out to make an offering to the spirit of the underground with two deer haunches hanging across his horse, and the basket of roots balanced in front of him.

He reached the river of stone and continued on foot as before, carrying the basket in one arm and balancing the heavy haunches hung on the ends of a pole across his shoulder.

Wa-pan-thla traveled the route he had carefully memorized. He came to the rock shaped like a giant frog, and farther on, the dead tree with a forked trunk stood as he remembered. The creature's dwelling was but a short distance ahead. Arriving at the place where he expected to find the hole into the cavern, he saw only the expanse of the river of stone. He searched and searched, but he could not find the hole or the three stones he had left as a marker. He went back to the forked tree trunk and tried again, but still he could not find the hole. Exhausted and defeated, he sat down upon a rock and cried out to the spirit of the underground.

"Man-bear, spirit of the underworld, I have brought an offering on the first full moon. Where am I to leave it? Why do you disguise the offering place and prevent me from making the offering?"

But the spirit did not reply. Dejected and fearful of what might happen if the spirit rejected the offering, Wa-pan-thla left the offering in the middle of the stone river and sadly returned home, believing he had failed in his duty.

Mups-mups saw her husband's dejection and she, too, became fearful. "Did the spirit reject the offering, my husband?" she asked.

"I do not know," he replied with much guilt. "I could not find the offering place. I fear for us all."

After a restless night, Wa-pan-thla was awakened by the shrieks and wails of his wife. Rushing to her side, he saw to his great horror that in the place where their eldest child had lain the night before, now lay only a piece of stone.

Mups-mups, hysterical with grief, cursed her husband for his failure to appease the spirit, and she cursed the spirit as a heartless trickster. Fortunately, she did not know the spirit's name and her curses did not reach the ears of the man-bear, in whose shape the spirit roamed the earth.

For a whole moon, Wa-pan-thla became an outcast and was despised not only by his grieving wife, but by everyone in the band. On the night before the second full moon after he had first seen the man-bear, Wa-pan-thla lay shivering in his sleep outside the camp when his guardian spirit appeared to him and spoke.

"Do not lose heart, namesake. You have two more offerings to make. Heed my words."

Wa-pan-thla woke up and could not go back to sleep. He spent the rest of the night thinking about what he should do. By first light he had made his decision and with great determination he undertook the task he had set for himself.

Late that evening he returned from a second unsuccessful attempt to find the man-bear's dwelling and make an offering. Fearing what a second failure might bring, he kept a vigil all night outside the camp.

The following morning a terrible cry awakened the camp, just as it had one moon earlier.

"My middle child has been turned to stone!" a woman screamed. In great despair he recognized the voice of Mups-mups

-CAIN

and knew that for a second, terrible time he was responsible for the loss of his own child. Soon he heard the twati chanting and the angry voices of men calling for Wa-pan-thla to be hunted down and killed for the curse he had brought upon the camp.

During the next journey of the moon, his clansmen hunted Wa-pan-thla like an animal. Only by his great skill as a hunter himself was he able to evade them. He was forced to live without fire and to move about constantly. As a result, he was always cold and hungry, for he also had little time to find food or to eat. Risking death, as often as he could he would sneak to the edge of the camp with the hope of glimpsing his wife and his remaining child. The mixture of joy and sadness he felt upon seeing them was the only thing that gave him hope.

By the eve of the end of the moon's third journey since his sighting of the man-bear, Wa-pan-thla was a broken man. He was starving, lonely, and filled with despair. He prayed one last time to his guardian spirit to remove him from his suffering and take him into the spirit world.

"Spirit of the Great Bear, have I not followed your commands?" Have I not done all that is within my power to serve you? Have I not suffered enough? I beg you to take me into the spirit world, for this world of flesh is finished with me and I with it."

The rain began to fall. Lightning flashed from the sky and thunder shook the ground. Suddenly the Great Bear appeared to Wa-pan-thla and stood before him, not in a dream, but in the flesh. Wa-pa-thla was certain his prayer had been answered, that the Great Bear had come to take him into the spirit world at last.

"Wa-pan-thla," the Great Bear growled, "you must make the final offering to the spirit of the underworld. Heed my words."

The Great Bear's words stunned Wa-pan-thla and filled him with bitterness. "I am despised by my wife; two of my children are turned to stone; my people hunt me. I am dying, Great Bear. How much more can I give?"

"Wa-pan-thla," said the Great Bear, "search one last time for the offering place. Take no food. Your offering is your life. Go now.

Heed my words." The Great Bear turned and slowly walked away into the rain and darkness.

Wa-pan-thla lay on the cold, wet ground, ready to give up except for one small spark of hope that still glowed in spite of his ordeal. Painfully, he pulled himself up. His weak legs barely able to support him, he staggered off into the night to fulfill his final obligation.

The morning sun found him crawling toward the offering place, bruised and bleeding, more dead than alive. At last, he could pull himself no farther.

"Even in this I have failed," he said, and gave himself over to death.

As the last breath left his body, he felt himself being lifted up. Strength flowed back into his ravaged body and his sight returned to reveal the glowing red eyes of the man-bear burning into his own.

"You have suffered much on my account, Wa-pan-thla," the spirit said. "Yet you never failed to follow the guidance of your guardian spirit. You have been tested, Wa-pan-thla, and I find you worthy to serve me. Henceforth, you and the chosen ones who come after you shall be the keepers of my secret, and in return I, too, shall become your guardian spirit along with the Great Bear."

"But my children, my poor children!" lamented Wa-pan-thla.

Return to your people, Wa-pan-thla. Your trial is over." The man-bear then jumped into a hole in the river of stone and vanished, as did the hole itself.

The man-bear had given Wa-pan-thla enough strength to walk back to the camp, but as he approached, he began to feel weak again. What would he say? Perhaps they would kill him before he could say anything. Still, he walked into the camp, not knowing.

"Father! Father!" Wa-pan-thla looked around and saw his two lost children running toward him. "Father! Father" they cried joyfully, "We have come back!"

He was filled with joy and thankfulness as he gathered his children to him with all his remaining strength. Looking up, he

-CAIN

saw Mups-mups holding the youngest child, crying and laughing at the same time.

"My husband, my husband, forgive me. I did not have your faith," she said. "Can you forgive me?"

All of the people of the camp gathered round and they, too, asked Wa-pan-thla to forgive them, saying "Forgive us, for we were weak and foolish."

Wa-pan-thla forgave them, for he knew only too well how hardship can test one's belief in the goodness of the guiding spirits.

Since that time the secret of the man-bear has been passed down, and each keeper of the secret has led a long and happy life.

CHAPTER 10

A Sea of Troubles

The quarter was over for Beth and me. We wouldn't have to have any contact with Danner for nearly three weeks. Maybe by January I'd be able to look at him without wanting to inflict serious injury upon him. Maybe not. Maybe by then I would still want to injure him, but somehow manage to control myself. Maybe not.

Continuing as Danner's advisee was impossible now. Changing advisors would raise a lot of questions, but none I'd have to answer if I didn't want to. I decided I would send Danner a written request to change advisors. Avoiding a confrontation seemed the wisest course of action.

Beth left with some friends that Friday afternoon to return to Cheney for the Christmas break. On my way home I dropped some books off at the reserve desk in Suzzallo and saw Max there using a copy machine. I waved and he motioned me over. I guess the emptiness I was feeling knowing I wouldn't see Beth for another two and a half weeks showed.

"John, my friend, don't look so glum. The quarter is over. No more quiz sections. No more *estudiantes estupidos. No es verdad*?"

I had to smile. "*Si, y tanto*! You enjoyed your quiz section, too, huh?"

"Someone must lead them down the path of knowledge, John. If only it were someone else besides me!" He threw up his hands in exasperation. "Hey, John, come over to the Northlake tavern with me for beer and pizza this evening. I'm buying. What do you say?"

"Sounds good, Max. How about if I meet you over there? What time?"

"*Siete*?"

"Seven it is, Max. *Hasta luego.*"

"*Hasta luego*, John."

* * *

The Northlake tavern sits at the north end of Lake Union between the old University drawbridge on Roosevelt Avenue a block and a half to the east, and the double-decker I-5 freeway bridge half a block to the west. Resting on rectangular concrete columns fifteen feet square at the base and more than sixty feet high, the freeway bridge spans the northeast corner of the lake where it funnels into the Montlake Cut, a man-made channel connecting Lake Union to Lake Washington.

The tavern occupies the narrow center space between two other connected, concrete block buildings on the north side of NE Northlake Way. The tavern had been there as far back as I could remember and probably dated back to the twenties or thirties.

The street in front and the small lot on the west side of the building were parked full, and by the time I found a parking place farther east on Northlake, it was a few minutes past seven. Fifties' rock and roll jarred the old building, and since it was Friday night the place was crowded.

The dark room was layered with cigarette smoke and permeated with the aroma of half a century or more of foaming beer, fuming pizzas, and sweating patrons. Squeezing through the people milling about the floor, I found Max sitting at a small table next to the juke box, contemplating a pitcher of beer that was already half empty. He saw me and smiled, a bit wistfully I thought. I sat down and poured some beer into the extra glass by the pitcher.

"How did you get a table, Max? The place is packed."

Max cupped his hand behind his ear and leaned toward me. "*Que*? Speak up, I can't hear you," he shouted.

"Never mind," I shouted back. I sipped my beer and began to absorb some of the atmosphere—not that my clothes and hair weren't already tainted by the spicy smoke and musky milieu of the place. I'd have to hang my clothes outside when I got home.

The crowd was mixed. Gray hair and shiny pates bobbed among the flopping locks of the younger revelers. T-shirts and jeans predominated, but the patrons were garbed in everything from blue blazers to black leather jackets; from baggy slacks and long dresses to skin-tight leotards and thigh-high miniskirts.

A harried barmaid slid a deep-dish pizza onto our table and wiped the perspiration off her forehead with the corner of her apron as she waited for Max to peel off several bills from the folded wad he took out of his shirt pocket.

A break in the music a few minutes later made conversation possible. "You were looking a little homesick, there, Max, when I first came in. Holiday depression setting in already?"

"You won't believe this, John, but I saw a girl here who is the spitting image of someone I used to be serious about in Madrid. It brought back some sad memories I'm afraid. See, there she is, over by the bar, the one with the red dress and the long, dark hair." Max pointed toward a group behind me and I turned to catch a glimpse through the crowd of an attractive young woman wearing a clinging red dress and red shoes.

"Good-looking girl. I'm surprised you left Madrid."

"She was most beautiful, John, but too aristocratic. Although my parents are well off, my family and I were simply not good enough for her. It is just as well, I suppose. Her family would not have permitted her to marry me even if she had wanted to."

"So you came to America for a little egalitarian aegis against the inequities of *el amor*, right?"Max looked puzzled for a second, then laughed. "I think I understood that, John, and I think the answer is yes, although I had never thought of it in just those terms. 'Egalitarian aegis?' 'Inequities of *el amor*?' John, my friend, you are a walking, talking dictionary. Not only do you cheer me up, you build my vocabulary in the process. Bravo!"

-CAIN

"Thanks a lot, Max. You are not the first person to call me a sesquipedalian son-of-a-bitch.""Such a gift, John. I love polysyllables with my pizza." Trailing strings of cheese and dribbling grease across the table, Max attacked a substantial wedge of pizza with gusto. I joined him.

The music blared forth again and the gal with the red dress danced by, wiggling her butt delightfully.

Another pitcher of beer later I thanked Max for showing me a good time and departed with a good bloat in my belly and a pleasant buzz in my head. The air was brisk , but I was flushed from the beer and I got halfway to my car before I realized I had left my jacket hanging on the back of my chair. I turned around and started walking back toward the tavern just as a gold Firebird chirped to a stop beside me and four big guys bailed out. The only one I recognized was the driver, Brent Woody.

They came at me fast, all business and no banter. The guy on the passenger's side got to me first and grabbed at me.

He's easy. Roll with him; pull him through, foot on his ankle.

Down he goes. No time to hurt him, second guy on me.

Spin around, elbow high. Hard crunch against his face.

Blindside jolt . . . lights bursting in my head.

On my knees.

Shoe bouncing off my ribs.

Down, everything dim.

That rushing sound in my ears.

Shake it off.

Somebody shouting.

Another kick in my side.

Max jumping, kicking.

One down.

Max kicking high.

Another one down.

Got to get up.

Got to . . .

"John, my friend, are you all right? John? Can you hear me, John?" I felt as if I had fallen into a deep well and somebody was calling down to me.

Only one of my eyes wanted to open as I tried to bring into focus the face looking down on me. "Max?"

"*Si amigo, estoy aqui*. You scared the shit out of me, John. I thought they had killed you."

"Nope, they just made me wish I was dead. Jesus, I hurt all over. Good thing for me you followed me out."

"You left your jacket, John. I ran out to give it to you and saw these guys jump out of the car and come after you. You threw one to the ground and knocked out another, but one of them hit you and you went down. The one you threw to the ground got up and started kicking you. That's when I got here."

"Max, did I see you jump up and kick two of those guys? What was that?"

"Savate—French foot fighting. The two years I spent studying at the Sorbonne were not wasted, *n'est-ce pas, mon ami*?"

"*Certainement*! *C'est formidable*!"

"Don't tell me, John. Army language school?"

"Nope, high school French."

The police officer who had been talking to the four assailants came over to talk with Max and me.

"How are you doing? Are you ok?"

"Yes, I think so."

"Look, I've got a shitpot full of paperwork to do on this. If you and your friend want, you can come into the Wallingford station tomorrow morning and give your statements. We're hauling these guys in for booking. Personally, I'd like to see their butts in a wringer, but that's up to the prosecutor."

"I have to agree, officer. Four on one is a butt-wringing offense. We'll be in first thing tomorrow to make statements."

"Good enough. Sure you don't need an ambulance?"

"No sir, thanks to Max I'll be able to walk away from this one. Thanks anyway."

-CAIN

The officer went back over and said something to the other three officers who had converged on the fracas, and the four ball players drew a penalty for unnecessary roughness.

Max helped me up. My jaw felt as if it had been dislocated. My right eye was swollen shut, and I couldn't take a normal breath because my ribs hurt like hell. Other than that and the headache trying to hammer out my eyeballs from the inside, I felt great.

I didn't think I was ever going to convince Max I wasn't seriously hurt. I finally got him to let me go home by agreeing to let him pick me up the next morning and take me over to the Wallingford station to make our statements.

I got back to the Cunningham's about nine thirty. Having pretty much persuaded Max that I wouldn't die before morning, I examined myself, hoping I hadn't lied to him.

Once I got my swollen eye pried open, I could see in the mirror that my pupils were equal and responsive. My headache continued to throb, but I didn't appear to be suffering from anything worse than a mild concussion. My jaw seemed to work all right, although it hurt to move it. Let's see, what was that checklist for a fractured/dislocated mandible? trismus, crepitus, asymmetry . . . naw, it's ok.

The ribs were a different story. One was probably cracked, maybe two. A rummage through my dresser drawers turned up an elastic bandage that I wound tightly around the bottom half of my rib cage. I flushed a couple of acetaminophen tablets down my gullet with a glass of milk and propped myself up in a chair. It was my intention to stay awake, at least for a few hours. I made a mental note for future reference to avoid drinking half a pitcher of beer just before getting knocked unconscious. That was the last thing I remembered thinking when I woke up the next morning stiff-necked, aching all over, reeking of stale cigarette smoke and pepperoni.

I put on some coffee and took a long, hot shower. As I shaved the few scraggly black hairs off my chin and the shadow off my upper lip, a battered face with a black eye and a bruised jaw stared back at me through the smeared condensation on the mirror. Dark, deep-set eyes looked back at me under heavy black brows separated by the beginnings of a chronic furrow. It was a handsome enough face by white standards, I guess. I didn't have any objections to it. My cheekbones were prominent, my cheeks slightly hollow, my nose straight and not too broad. My short, thick black hair combed over well enough from a left-hand part, and my skin was not much darker than a Dutch farmer's summer tan. It was too good a face to let anyone pound on.

I had spent enough time in army barracks to disdain the Friday-night flow of miserable bastards returning from an evening of fun and relaxation in the bars. They had come staggering and limping in, black-eyed, broken-nosed, fat-lipped, bloody-knuckled, smelling of smoke, beer, and vomit.

Seeing the same people dragging in every week in the same condition gave me a sense of arrogant superiority. I was too smart to hang around the bars and fraternize with the big-balled, bibulous brawlers who did. So what happens? Mr. Smart-ass becomes a civilian and gets his clock serviced outside a tavern by four college kids who probably aren't even legally old enough to drink. Ironic, huh, John? "Pride goeth before destruction, and an haughty spirit before a fall." The Olympians were hell on hubris, too. Better watch it, John.

While I dressed I discounted the likelihood the gods might have any interest in punishing my arrogance. However, I was a little apprehensive about being hauled away for psychiatric evaluation for talking to my mirror.

Max came by at nine and seemed pleasantly surprised to find me among the living. We finished off my pot of coffee and then he drove me over to the Wallingford station in his Fiat 850. A tall sergeant with a thick shock of gray hair and a long scar on one cheek gave us some forms, and we spent about twenty minutes filling them out. When we handed the forms back to the sergeant, I asked him about the four football heroes who had been brought in the night before.

-CAIN

"Don't know anything about it," he replied indifferently. "They would've been booked into King County jail downtown. You'd have to check with them." He looked over the forms, stamped the date and time on them, and pushed them into a basket on his desk. "You'll be notified if you have to appear in court on this matter. Any questions?"

"I guess not," I said, seeing Max raise his eyebrows and shake his head. The sergeant turned away and Max and I walked out.

"I liked the officer we talked to last night better," Max said, looking over his shoulder. "This man is not very friendly."

"You noticed that, too? Well, Max, I guess civil servants are not always civil. Maybe he's a Husky fan."

Max was indignant. "Surely he has no sympathy for those *brutos*."

"You never know, Max. You just never know."

After I bought Max breakfast at a McDonald's, he dropped me off at the Cunninghams'and I worked into the evening reading and taking notes on the stack of books I was soon going to have to return to the library. The Cunninghams had left early Friday to drive down to Portland to visit friends. They wouldn't be back until Wednesday. Without any distractions or obligations, I could get a lot of work done.

About five I got hungry and fixed myself a ham sandwich and a bowl of tomato soup. By the time I finished the soup and sandwich, the sun was setting. Needing exercise, I painfully pulled on a warm sweater, donned a watch cap and lined leather gloves, and went for a walk.

Sometime during the afternoon the clouds had broken up to expose a cold blue sky. A few copper-bottomed puffs of gray wool hung over the horizon. The thermometer was dropping toward the freezing point about as fast as the sun was sliding down the far side of the Olympics.

As I walked along the quiet residential street, I wondered what Beth was doing at that moment. I wondered if she would have any thoughts of me during the holidays. It got darker and colder as I walked. When the sun had disappeared completely behind the mountains, the stars began to appear, scintillating like ice crystals growing on blue glass. The deserted street stretched out mutely in both directions. I was alone.

Solitude had never bothered me. I enjoyed it. I sought it out. But thinking of Beth surrounded by the warmth and love of her family filled me with a longing and a loneliness to which I was unaccustomed and for which I was unprepared. The loss of my parents had created in me a great emptiness that friends and work and denial had never begun to fill—couldn't fill. Somehow I had managed to seal off the emptiness, but it had lingered like a disease in temporary remission. Now it seemed that the emptiness had become acute. I needed someone. That someone was Beth.

I turned and walked rapidly back toward the Cunningham's house and the cocoon-like sanctuary of my room, my books. I knew the emptiness, the loneliness, the longing would still be there, but I tried not to think about it. Not thinking about it was going to be hard.

During the next three days I immersed myself in reading and writing and transcribing the tapes of my sessions with Ernie. I lost track of hours and days. Time ceased to be a "clock prying the hours apart with its bare hands," as ascending UW English professor David Wagoner had described it in a reading I had attended. Time instead became cups of coffee consumed, sandwiches half eaten, bowls of cereal slurped down, trips made to the bathroom, chapters read, note cards filed, and note books filled. I worked steadily and napped only when I couldn't keep my eyes open any longer. By the following Tuesday I had all but escaped the diurnal cycle and had entered a dissociative dimension without past or future—a continuous present extended into infinity.

Finally, rummy and disoriented, I began to realize that indeterminate periods were passing for which I had no recollection of any mental activity whatsoever. I would suddenly become aware that I was staring at nothing in particular and have no idea how long I had been doing it. The feeling was spooky, bringing to

-CAIN

mind reports of the effects of sensory deprivation experiments. It was time to return to earth before the hallucinations set in.

I hadn't shaved, showered, or brushed my teeth for three days. I hadn't seen a newspaper, listened to the radio, or even looked out the window. At three o'clock on Tuesday, the phone rang for the first time in three days.

"Hello?" My voice cracked and I had to clear my throat. As far as I knew it was the first word I had spoken in three days.

"May I please speak with John Brockman?"

"This is he."

"Mr. Brockman, my name is Eileen Duggins. I'm with the City Attorney's office. I'm calling in reference to a police report of an incident in which four men allegedly assaulted you. I would like to have you come in and see me, tomorrow if possible. Could you arrange that?"

"Yes I could. At what time should I come in?"

"Can you be here at ten tomorrow morning?"

"Yes."

"Excellent. Just take the elevator up to the fourth floor of the Municipal Building. The City Attorney's office is at the end of the hall. Tell the receptionist you have an appointment with me, ok?"

"I'll be there."

"Thank you, Mr. Brockman, I 'll see you then. Goodbye."

"Goodbye."

As soon as I hung up, I heard the Cunninghams' doorbell ringing. I went outside and around to the front of the house, where a man wearing an overcoat and carrying a briefcase impatiently punched the doorbell button.

"The Cunninghams are not home. May I help you?"

Startled, the man turned around. He was a thin-mouthed man in his mid thirties, balding and fidgety. His watery eyes peered superciliously over wire-framed glasses perched halfway down his aquiline nose. "Oh, yes. I'm looking for John Brockman. Is this the right address?"

"I'm John Brockman. I live downstairs."

The man stepped off the porch and hurried up the sidewalk toward me. "Mr. Brockman, I'm Allen Hirsch with the law firm, Blackwell and Associates." He held out his hand and I shook it perfunctorily. "I need to talk to you about the incident that took place last Friday."

"Let's go inside," I said, and motioned him to follow me. I opened the door and let Hirsch enter first. When I came in behind him, the messiness of the place hit me. Books and papers were scattered over the floor along with my dirty clothes. The table was buried beneath layers of books and dirty dishes. The blinds were closed, the bed unmade, and the room stank of bad breath, body odor, and a recently used toilet. I rubbed the stubble on my chin and surreptitiously checked my zipper. No wonder Hirsch was standing with his elbows tucked in as if he were afraid he might brush up against something. Repugnance was written all over him.

I went over and cleared off a chair for him. "Sorry about the mess. I've been studying." That sounded lame even to me.

Hirsch sat down cautiously, opened his briefcase on his lap, and removed some papers. "Mr. Brockman, you were involved in an altercation with Robert Briggs, Timothy Warren, Jesse Monk, and Brent Woody on the evening of Friday, December 14th. Is that correct?"

"If Briggs, Warren, and Monk were Woody's cohorts, yes. Woody was the only one I recognized."

Hirsch thumbed through the sheaf of papers he was holding. "I see," he said absentmindedly. Finding the paper he was looking for, Hirsch looked up at me. "You will be interested to know, Mr. Brockman, that my firm will be representing these four young men in a civil suit seeking damages from you and a Mr. Maximillian Alavedra."

"What! You have to be kidding! Take a close look. I'm the guy with the black eye, the sore jaw, and the cracked ribs." I moved over and thrust my face close to his and pulled up my shirt to show him the elastic bandage around my middle.

-CAIN

Recoiling from my behavior, or my breath, Hirsch turned away from me with obvious distaste. "I'm sorry about your injuries, Mr. Brockman, but my clients also sustained injuries." I went over and sat on the bed while Hirsch searched for another paper. "Hmm, yes . . . a broken nose, a dislodged tooth, a sprained wrist, a knee injury, various cuts and contusions. Of course, my clients are also seeking damages for potential adverse effects on their football-playing careers, and for the intentional infliction of emotional stress. Each of my clients will be asking compensation in the amount of fifty thousand dollars."

"That's ridiculous. I don't have two hundred thousand dollars even if you win this silly suit. Neither does Max."

Hirsch found yet another piece of paper. "We are aware of that, Mr. Brockman. However, you do own a private residence in this city, appraised at eighty thousand, you own a 1970 Volkswagon with a value of let's say one thousand, and your savings and checking accounts have a balance of, let me see, twelve thousand forty-eight dollars and sixty three cents. Of course, there is your future earning potential to be considered."

I took out my wallet and held it up for Hirsch to see. "You missed the seven dollars in my wallet and the change in my pocket. How the hell did you get that information? It's supposed to be confidential. For that matter, how the hell did you get it so quickly? What's going on here?"

"Blackwell and Associates is the largest, most prestigious law firm in this state, Mr. Brockman. It has a most impressive array of data-gathering resources.

"Actually, Mr. Brockman, we are not interested in acquiring your negligible assets. But even if my clients do not receive a favorable judgment down the road a few years from now, by then all of your assets will have gone into defending against the suit."

"So what do you want from me and Max?"

Hirsch's expression of mock innocence did not conceal the pleasure he was taking in holding a pat hand.

"Why, nothing, Mr. Brockman. Nothing at all. What ever made you think that?"

"Yeah, what ever made me think you wanted something. What I don't understand is if you don't expect to get any big money, who's paying you? Four college students don't just break open their piggy banks and come up with the kind of retainer you guys must ask for. So who's paying? Their parents? The University? Who?"

"Obviously, Mr. Brockman, I'm not at liberty to answer that. It's irrelevant anyway."

"You could have just sent me a letter. Why does a high-priced lawyer waste his time on an unnecessary house call?"

He ignored my questions. "The statute of limitations gives us two years in which to file a civil suit against you. Of course, if you were to convince the prosecutor the incident was simply an unfortunate misunderstanding, I wouldn't be surprised if my clients were inclined to abandon their suits."

"Oh, I get it. No assault charges, no civil suits."

"Why, Mr. Brockman, you make it sound as if I'm trying to coerce you in some way. I assure you Blackwell and Associates would never resort to any unethical or illegal maneuvering."

"Why, Mr. Hirsch, you make it sound as if I don't know you're full of shit."

"Really, Mr. Brockman, there is no call for crudity."

"Ok, suppose I try to talk the prosecutor out of bringing charges against your clients. What if Max doesn't want to cooperate?"

"Oh, I'm sure Mr. Alavedra will want to do the right thing. His student visa is in order I trust? It's funny how the INS gets picky about these matters from time to time and decides to make an example of some unfortunate individual."

I stood up, walked over to Hirsch, stuck my scowl two inches from his face, and gave him a good sniff of my rotten breath.

"I think this little pas de deux is finished, don't you? Maybe you had better leave before you have to sue me for one more intentional infliction of emotional stress."

CAIN

Hirsch nervously replaced the papers in his briefcase. He closed it and got up, brushing off the back of his overcoat and wiping his hands on a monogrammed handkerchief. He walked to the door and opened it; then turned around smugly for a final comment. "I was thinking, Mr. Brockman, you might want to take that seven dollars in your wallet and purchase some mouthwash and deodorant. You smell horrible."

Few people like being told what to do. Fewer yet enjoy having no recourse in the matter. The ultimate minority comprises those who love being forced into doing or not doing while at the same time being told they smell horrible. That I really did smell bad is beside the point.

The power over me that Blackwell and Associates had acquired practically out of thin air rankled me royally. Ironically, it wasn't important to me whether Brent Woody and his teammates were charged or not. I had already begun to think that filing a complaint against them might not be the best way to end the matter after all. Life is complicated enough without a vendetta.

I had to direct my ire toward something, so I cleaned up my apartment and myself, washed my clothes, and returned my library books. I tried to call Max from the library, but no one answered. He and some other Spanish-speaking graduate students from wealthy families rented a house on Lake Washington just south of the Sand Point Naval Station. Usually someone was there to answer the phone. I needed to talk with Max before I went to the prosecutor's office in the morning.

It might have been better if the police hadn't become involved, although it had been nice to see those four ugly bastards in handcuffs. Hirsch's insidious ultimatum stuck in my craw like a crossways fish bone, and I had a feeling it wasn't going to be any easier for Max to swallow. If only there were a way to flip off Blackwell and Associates with impunity.

Picking up a box of take-out pork chow mein on University Avenue, I went back to my apartment. Still no one answered at Max's place. I ate the chow mein and started reading an old paperback book of John Malcom Brinnin's poetry. Brinnin's ornate pithiness, murky metaphors, and mystical menagerie, in some ways like the poetry of Wallace Stevens, fascinated me. I could learn a lot from the snail in Brinnin's poem, "Architect, Logician":

Like those who temper opal for a house,
A wise man keeps the cosmos in his skull
Rimmed with a box of sound where every day
Repeats his wishing yet confirms him whole.

One thing I truly regretted about my life was not having written a single line of poetry—pretty, poignant, powerful, or otherwise. Not of the stature of Brinnin or Stevens by any means, but a published poet whose poetry I admired and whose talent I envied, a college friend of mine had written of "strident frogs ringed round with ruby warts." Unlike my friend, however, it seemed unlikely I would ever be able to write anything like the following:

I am come together for a while—
A vortex of ephemeral flesh,
Stalks of bone
Singing mutely
A song without an echo in the reeds.

Dick, my poet friend, was majoring in English when I was an undergraduate at the University of Washington. He had been writing poems since junior high school and he thought he was pretty good. After a long wait, he had finally gotten into Theodore Roethke's demanding verse-writing class. When Roethke read Dick's first assignment to the class, to my friend's humiliation and horror Roethke dismissed it as garbage. But then he added, "Except for one line," which he read again to the class. My friend was crushed. Roethke saw that he was mortified and said, "What's the matter with you? My God! do you know what it means to write one good line of poetry? Do you have any idea how many lines of garbage you have to throw away first? You're an amateur, kiddo. When you learn which lines to keep and which to throw away, you'll be a poet. Congratulations."

Dick did learn which lines to keep and which to throw away, and he did become a poet.

But one good line of poetry would not be enough. I knew that having written one good line I would want to write more lines, better lines. I would want to master a variety of verse forms, write a book of poems, a book of better poems, another book of better poems.

If I could write a decent poem, I'd write one to Beth. However, the prospect of that happening was about the same as my showing up at the front door of her parents' house naked. Better to stick to reading and quoting other people's poetry. If only I could book a passage on that inner voyage, as did my friend, Dick, who wrote about the inward bird:

Like a dove enamored of its whiteness,
My senses see a single quality.
My eye becomes a bird with inward wings;
Swirls and flutters as does the timid tern
Toward primeval perch;
Preens its misty plumage in a dream;
Streams incandescence at first light
At the edge of an inner world;
Flaps away with timeless beat;
Descends and disappears
Into the distant microcosm of itself.

It was after eleven before someone finally answered at Max's house and called him to the phone.

"Max, compadre, where have you been? I was beginning to think you had gone back to Spain without saying goodbye."

"All of us here were attending a dinner hosted by the deputy ambassador from Spain. It was part of a cultural relations program between some American and Spanish universities. It was a formal affair. Very nice."

"The deputy ambassador, hmm? Does this mean I have to start calling you *Señor* Alavedra?"

"You call me *señor* and I'll call you a *pendejo gringo.*"

"Whoa! You've been picking up some Tijuana trash-talk. What will the deputy ambassador think?"

"Screw him, John. He's just another politician."

"Spoken like a true American, Max."

"You must be very bored to call me for this conversation, my friend."

"Sorry, Max. I wanted to tell you about a visitor I had today. By the way, I got a call from the city attorney's office today, too. How about you?"

"No, no one has called me."

I gave Max the details of Hirsch's visit, leaving out the part about the mouthwash and deodorant. I told him I thought it might be prudent for me to try to talk the prosecutor into dropping the whole thing, assuming that was possible. Max reluctantly agreed. He steamed, but he recognized the folly of pointless defiance.

"Very well, my friend, the matter is closed. If I had known they were going to escape punishment, I would have kicked them harder. Next time, John, try to choose enemies who have some honor."

"If they had any honor, we wouldn't be enemies."

"Yes, I see what you mean. Let me know how your visit to the prosecutor turns out."

Thanks, Max. *Buenas nochas.*"

I got up early Wednesday intending to jog around Green Lake. The sharp pains in my ribs began stabbing into my chest before I had jogged a hundred yards along the frosty asphalt ribbon ringing the lake. Walking the remainder of the lake's circumference, I got back to my car just as the sun was beginning to climb over the white rooftops on its journey toward a pale blue zenith low in the southern sky.

-CAIN

Thick, opalescent frost blanketed the grass. A delicate, white crystalline lace rimed the bare branches of the deciduous trees. The evergreens, flocked with heavy frost, stood motionless in the frozen air. Everything sparkled in the long rays of the morning sun. Hooded figures walking or jogging faded in and out among the wisps of fog hovering low above the lake. Beauty was everywhere—the cold, indifferent, lonely beauty of winter; the kind of beauty that sends an ecstatic shiver up your spine and then goes on to make your teeth chatter and your fingers numb.

Back at the apartment, I warmed up with oatmeal and coffee. I then showered, dressed, read for a while, and drove downtown.

Ten minutes of touring finally produced a parking place about three blocks from the Municipal building. The expectation of Christmas was strewn over lamp posts and store fronts. All was tinseled, wreathed, belled, bowed, candled, starred, and stood twinkling inanely. Somewhere up the street a band played strident carols to the cacophonous counterpoint of honks, squeals, roars, and rattles of busy traffic.

A dozen or more people waited for an elevator on the first floor of the Municipal building so I took the stairs up to the fourth floor. Just inside the frosted glass door of the prosecutor's office, a disgruntled-looking, middle-aged woman manned a switchboard behind a high counter. She was busy with multiple incoming calls, and I waited patiently, ten minutes early and in no hurry.

After a few minutes she glared over her half-lens glasses at me. "May I help you," she asked sullenly.

"John Brockman to see Eileen Duggins at ten," I replied.

She was listening to a caller over her earphones and didn't acknowledge right away. After a succession of calls, she finally just motioned me to go over to the waiting area, where two older men sat looking bored and impatient. I sat and twiddled my thumbs for another fifteen minutes until a tall, attractive, professional-appearing woman in her late thirties or early forties came down the hall. She scrutinized me and the other two men seated in the waiting area.

"John Brockman?" she asked, looking at me.

I stood up. "Yes, I'm Brockman."

She held out her hand. "I'm Eileen Duggins." Her handshake was businesslike—terse and crisp. She wore a dark gray jacket and skirt, a white blouse, and low-heeled shoes. Her short, dark hair was carefully styled and very shiny. Dark, piercing eyes set in an expressive but mirthless countenance probed my face.

"Come back to my office, Mr. Brockman."

She led me down the hall past several doors to her office, which looked more like a greenhouse with potted plants standing and hanging everywhere. Long ferns draped over the filing cabinets, and vines grew up the bookcases. Big, spiny cactus plants sat on their haunches around her desk, guarding it like a pack of silent green bulldogs with spiked collars. She motioned toward one of the several chairs partially hidden among the foliage in front of her desk and I sat down. Vying for space with the files stacked on her desk amidst the fronds and tendrils was a picture of her, a man, and a small boy—presumably her family. Since that picture had been taken, she had apparently lost about twenty pounds. Diplomas from Central Washington University and Gonzaga Law School hung on the wall behind her desk.

She sat down, riffled through a stack of files before finding the one she wanted, and spent half a minute skimming through it before saying anything. She looked up at me with a frown.

"Mr. Brockman, I don't usually spend much time on something like this, but there is something very wrong with the picture I'm seeing here. The police report assumes you are the victim, but the four alleged assailants swear you were the aggressor and you have only the statement of your friend to corroborate your version. The thing that bothers me is this UW campus police report provided by Brent Woody's attorney. According to the report, you threatened and assaulted Mr. Woody in front of witnesses on October 23rd of this year. What do you have to say about that?"

"Well, I think a lot of things are wrong with this picture. To begin with, I did not threaten Woody and I did not assault him. I

-CAIN

objected to his harassment of a young woman, he grabbed me, and I restrained him for about a minute with a judo hold. The campus police did not show up during the incident and they never contacted me afterwards. And yes, there were witnesses. As for this latest incident, do you really think I would pick a fight with four big guys?"

"According to Woody's attorney you are an ex-green beret trained in hand-to-hand combat and martial arts. In view of that I don't find it hard to believe that you might confront four young college students."

"I suppose I should be flattered, but having been in the army special forces does not make me some kind of superman. I'm a college student, too, and I have to tell you those four fine fellows would have kicked out my brains if my friend hadn't come to my rescue. It's bad enough they are threatening to sue me without my having to sit here and listen to you accuse me of wantonly molesting a thousand pounds of muscle."

She tossed the file back onto the stack, glaring at me.

"I'm not filing any charges in this matter, it's just too muddled. I'm not sure what to make of you, Mr. Brockman, but don't let me find your name in another police report."

I got up, angry and eager to leave. Knowing full well I was better off to keep my mouth shut, I said it anyway.

"Ok, the next time I get busted for picking on half a football team I'll tell the police my name is Clark Kent. Will that do?"

"No that will not do. Don't give me any of your smart-assed remarks. Consider yourself lucky you're not facing charges."

I just shook my head in frustration and walked out, thinking how really clever I was to piss off people in positions of power.

CHAPTER 11

More Rhyme than Reason

The Cunninghams returned from Portland shortly before five. I was working on a lexicon of Taitnapam words based on the tapes and notes of my sessions with Ernie. Hearing the distinctive sound of their noisy diesel Olds, I walked around to the front of the house to greet them and help them with their luggage. Dr. Cunningham was behind the car with the trunk lid up. Mrs. Cunningham saw me first and had to give me a hug. Of course, she noticed my shiner right off. "Goodness sake, Johnny, you've hurt yourself!" My wincing when she gave me a squeeze did not escape her either. "Johnny, are you all right?"

"Yes, I'm fine. It's nothing, really. Just some bumps and bruises from being in the wrong place at the wrong time."

Dr. Cunningham stuck his head around the side of the car to see for himself. "Maxine, try not to smother him, Dear. He is a grown man after all. Hello, John. Nice shiner."

I laughed. "Ok, ok you two. I'm not going to get out of telling you how I got it, am I?"

"I don't believe he is, do you Maxine?" he asked in mock seriousness.

Maxine giggled. "Absolutely not!"

Dr. Cunningham glanced at his watch. "Let's let him tell us about it over dinner at Luigi's. You haven't eaten yet have you, John?"

"No sir, I haven't and it sounds good. I'd trade a story for a dinner any day." I walked over and lifted the two largest suitcases

-CAIN

out of the trunk, my ribs smarting sharply. "Let me help you with these."

He took out the smaller of the two remaining pieces of luggage and held it up. "This one's mine," he said with a grin. "Everything else is Maxine's. Isn't that so, Dear?"

"Oh, Sid, you're such an old fibber. If I hadn't packed another suitcase for you, you wouldn't have had anything to wear at all."

"Now Maxine, that's not exactly true." The banter continued into the house and all the way to Luigi's Fine Italian Restaurant in Bothell.

Over red wine and spaghetti, I described my initial encounter with Brent Woody, the sordid details of Friday night's sidewalk soiree, and my subsequent meetings with Hirsch and Duggins. The Cunninghams were duly flabbergasted and inflamed, as I knew they would be. Maxine was fit to be tied. She wanted to drive downtown right then and throw a brick through Blackwell and Associates' window.

Dr. Cunningham was more philosophical: "At times one has the feeling that Justice is not only blind, but deaf, mute, retarded, and flagrantly promiscuous as well; particularly in cases of ordinary people versus institutional juggernauts, political power, or ruthless wealth—not that those categories are mutually exclusive by any means. I hope you don't let this latest inequity and that frustrating business with Danner disillusion you."

I glanced over at Maxine when Dr. Cunningham mentioned Danner, wondering if she knew about him.

Reading my thoughts, Maxine reached over and put her hand on mine. "Sid told me about Danner, I hope you don't mind. I was so upset. That poor girl. How is she doing?"

"Beth is resilient. She's handling it very well . . . Probably better than I am," I added.

Maxine studied me for a long moment and then said knowingly, "You care for her, don't you?"

I looked uncomfortably at Dr. Cunningham. "Uh, yes, I do," I mumbled.

Maxine smiled reassuringly. "Good gracious, John, it's nothing to be ashamed of. I think it's wonderful. From what Sid tells me, I gather Beth is quite an extraordinary young woman. I'm happy for you, Johnny."

"Well, we aren't exactly an item . . . I mean, we aren't exactly going together. I don't know if she, uh . . . well, I don't that she has the same feelings for me."

My discomfort was beginning to affect Dr. Cunningham and he became inordinately preoccupied with examining his wineglass.

"Shame on you, Johnny," Maxine scolded, "you haven't told her how you feel, have you?" She threw up her hands and rolled her eyes. "I'll never understand why it's so hard for you men to express your feelings. It's so silly." She tossed an accusative glance at her husband, who was absorbed in holding his glass up to the light. "So much misunderstanding and heartache could be avoided by simple communication." She turned back to me apologetically. "Forgive me, you must think I'm a bossy old buttinsky."

Dr. Cunningham, still inspecting his glass, lifted an eyebrow, but said nothing.

"Not at all. I've often thought the same thing myself. It hasn't made it any easier to talk about my feelings, however. I guess it's just inherent in maleness."

"Johnny, let me say one more thing and then I promise I'll shut up."

Dr. Cunningham looked up at the ceiling as if to give a silent prayer of thanks.

"Tell her how you feel, Johnny. Tell her soon. Life is too short, too permanent, too unforgiving for you to wait."

Dr. Cunningham completed his inspection of the wineglass and set it on the table. "Amen!" He may or may not have meant the interjection as a retort, but he uttered it without a trace of sarcasm. Clearing his throat, he looked at Maxine and me a little self-consciously. "Are we ready for sherbet?" he asked.

The following Friday night I accompanied the Cunninghams to a performance by the Juilliard String Quartet at the newly re-

-CAIN

furbished Meany Hall. We parked in the underground garage and ascended the concrete stairwell up to the auditorium, emerging through a heavy firedoor into clumps of students, faculty, and miscellaneous music lovers thronging the covered entry area and ticket box.

As we shuffled along in the throng's movement toward the entrance, the boyish young woman collecting tickets and handing out programs made me think of how Beth objected to the demeaning sexism of the term "usherette." I smiled to myself, remembering how indignantly she had rejected my proposal to eliminate the demeaning aspects of the term while retaining the gender distinction, as in "usher/ushim." The feminists, of course, objected as much to the conceptual genderfication of the job title as to the denotation of femaleness by means of a diminutive suffix. "Usher/ushim" was about as acceptable as "usher *sans* penis/usher *avec*."

To tell the truth, I was not much in the mood for Mozart and Haydn. I often found their music buoyant and full of intellectual clarity. But sometimes the music seemed cloyed with an annoying presumption of orderliness and predictability in the universe that was almost mocking. I knew this was going to be one of those times. True, the nastiness in my universe was becoming altogether too predictable, but nowhere did things seem to be evolving with the balance, euphony, and general neatness of the classical sonata.

The Cunninghams, though, were enjoying themselves already, waving and calling out to friends, acquaintances, colleagues, and students in the crowd. It was easy to see they enjoyed being around people and having people around them. The responsive synergism of crowds and audiences stimulated them. They loved to share and to have others share with them.

I, on the other hand, felt indifferent at best to group experience. At worst, I felt almost threatened by it. A growing desire to avoid crowds influenced me more strongly with each passing year, and a crowd meant any group where my presence brought the number to three or more. I had always had something of a predilection for solitude, but having an out-and-out aversion to gatherings, assemblies, congregations, throngs, herds, masses, clusters, and huddles had come upon me so gradually I didn't know exactly when the transition had taken place. Henry David Thoreau would have been proud of me: not only didn't I want to march to the same drummer as everyone else, I didn't even want the damned drummer around. Some asocial, self-centered seed had sprouted in my psyche. The question now was if that sprout would eventually bear fruit and whether that fruit would be nourishing or noxious. No, I was not in a gregarious mood.

Shuffling my five-nine frame along in the press of the queue behind the Cunninghams, but in front of some Watusi-sized Mozart aficionado doused with killer aftershave, I was trying to come up with some plausible excuse for an early exit, possibly even a pre-entrance exit.

The line finally swelled into the lobby before I got up enough courage to break and run. The Cunninghams veered off to the right to talk to some people they saw there. Taking a last fix on the Cunninghams, I turned to head for our seats down close to the stage in the center section. One step and I literally ran into the last person in the world I wanted to run into. I started to apologize and looked up into the unruffled aplomb of Professor Tom Danner.

My only plan, if it could be called a plan, had been to avoid Danner. Knowing I would not be able to deal with him in a civilized manner and knowing better than to deal with him in any other way, I had decided not to deal with him at all. Now face to face with Danner, in a public place, with Mrs. Danner at his side and the Cunninghams within ear shot, what was I supposed to do? What was I going to do? I had no idea. The only thing that flashed into my mind was that whatever I did was going to surprise me more than anybody else.

"Hi, John. I'm a little surprised to see you here. Since you didn't come around last week, I thought you might have gone somewhere for the Christmas break."

"Nice to see you, John." Mrs. Danner added pleasantly.

-CAIN

Trying hard to create at least the illusion of composure, I ignored Danner and spoke to his wife. "It's nice to see you, too, Mrs. Danner." Despite an attempt to separate my response to her from my latent response to Danner, my words sounded wooden and surly. "All ready for Christmas?" It was an idle question, desperate and doltish.

"Is anyone ever ready for Christmas the week before?" she complained good-naturedly. She seemed not to take notice of the tenuously restrained and barely camouflaged rancor seething to have at her husband.

I didn't hate my feelings, but I really hated being controlled by them. What I needed at that moment was a block of ice in my chest and cold blood flowing into a detached intellect like chilled tomato juice into a crystal goblet. What I had to work with was a cardiac volcano and a beleaguered brain trying to keep its basal ganglia from dangling in a river of molten emotion.

I was aware of Danner's hand on my shoulder and he should have felt my hostility in the way I tensed up, but the charm continued to bubble out of him. "Why don't you come by the house this weekend and have some hot-buttered rum, John? You know you're welcome anytime."

I looked straight at him. Christ, didn't he know about Beth and me? But what was there to know? Not even Beth knew about Beth and me. Couldn't he read it in my eyes? The bolts of blue hatred I imagined flashing from my eyeballs should have scared him shitless, but he acted as if nothing had happened. The man had brass balls, or he deserved an Oscar for best performance by a guilty bastard.

Danner matched my stare and did not look away. I had to say something. He had to know that I knew about him.

"Beth Hansen wanted me to give you her regards," I heard myself say. He would react. He could not do otherwise. I waited.

Danner did not flinch. He did not blink.

He smiled.

The house lights dimmed, signaling the performance was about to begin, and, still smiling, Danner took his wife's hand and turned away from me. He stopped and looked back over his shoulder at me, this time with an almost imperceptible hint of derision in his smile.

"Give Beth my love when you see her, John," he said softly, confidently, and then he walked away.

Danner's malevolent sang froid stunned me. If he had so much as stuttered, coughed, shuffled, perspired, or even looked away, I might have taken a measure of satisfaction from the encounter. Instead, I stood there feeling as confused, thwarted, and unnecessary as a fly snubbed by a piece of dog shit. How the hell could Danner be so smug? I was the one filled with indignant ire and righteous passion. He was the one walking away with a smile on one or more of his several faces. Brent Woody wouldn't have thought about it. He simply would have punched each of Danner's faces—consequences be damned. But then, Brent Woody was all balls and biceps.

Hamlet and I—what a pair! "made cowards by conscience, our native hue of resolution sicklied o'er by the pale cast of thought."

The Cunninghams were hurrying over to get to their seats, apparently unaware of my encounter with Danner. I could do my John La Mouche thing and crawl down the aisle with bent antennae and a wounded look, or I could just buzz off.

Hardening myself against an hour and a half of Haydn and Mozart, I assumed a defiant smirk and swaggered to my seat. Dammit! Danner's watertower icicle of an ego didn't intimidate me. Besides, no self-respecting fly was about to take that kind of abuse from a piece of uppity dog shit.

So when was Danner going to get the comeuppance I had promised Beth?

I couldn't have felt more useless.

The remainder of Christmas break passed more or less uneventfully. The Cunninghams invited me to share Christmas dinner with their family at Isolde's house—my house technically, until

-CAIN

Isolde and her husband paid off the mortgage. Although the old house had been completely refurbished and much altered, memories of my parents and my childhood were everywhere. Like a dime that wouldn't stand on edge, I vacillated between pleasure and pain in those memories, unable to stay on the middle path of objectivity.

We exchanged gifts, we ate, and we sang carols. I played with the boys; we ate some more, sang some more, and played some more; and then Christmas was over. I returned to my room in the Cunninghams' basement with an unsettling mixture of warm feelings and loneliness.

Max invited me to go skiing with him at Snoqualmie Pass the day after Christmas. We got stuck in traffic for two hours on the way up because of an overturned semi blocking the highway. When we finally did arrive, we skied the crowded slopes in mixed rain and snow with poor visibility. On the way back, the left front tire on Max's Fiat picked up a broken tire chain link and went flat.

Surprisingly, we both enjoyed ourselves. We stopped in Issaquah for a leisurely dinner, and it was about eight o'clock when Max dropped me off at the Cunningham's house.

After a long shower, I began to work on something that had been taking shape in the back of my mind: a poem. It took three or four hours of feverish scribbling and frustrated head scratching, but when I had finished, I felt emotionally satisfied and comfortably exhausted. Sleep came easily, and I slept soundly, dreamlessly until nearly ten the next morning.

I know a hundred poems, a thousand lines.
I've learned the images of others but created none.
Yet, I must choose my own words if this is to be done.
The rambling of an inarticulate heart defines
Humbly, hopeless with inadequacy, a feeling that shines
Too brightly to be emulated by some poet's lesser sun;
Means too much to be cast in the glibness of anyone
Else's eloquence, or trusted to another's designs.

Shakespeare, Browning, Rossetti have said it better
Than I ever shall. But it was their profession.
Perhaps their feelings were as intense as mine for you;
It matters not. I make to you, Beth, not as debtor
To them, but from my own heart and soul this confession:
Infinitely, eternally, desperately, I love you; I love you.

Winter Quarter 1980 began on Monday, January 7. According to the Cunninghams' outside thermometer, the temperature was 35 degrees. Wind, wetted by showers of rain mixed with snow, gusted across the colorless campus. Remnants of the previous week's wet snowfall melted in dirty lumps along the curbs and sidewalks. A large, headless snowman slumped out the rest of its short existence on the gray grass in front of Miller Hall.

At a quarter to eight most of the students hurrying across the quad, leaning into the wind, trying to keep umbrellas from turning inside out, were undergrads. A majority of the graduate seminars had been scheduled for the more civilized hours of the afternoon by professors whose teaching loads in some cases did not exceed one or two classes per week.

The familiar smell of coffee and cinnamon rolls emanated from the cafeteria as I entered. Filling a cup too full with the dark brew, I sloshed over to the cashier, dug a wad of lint out of my pocket looking for change, and dripped into the eating area, eager to see if Beth had arrived yet.

I found her sitting alone by the window on the southeast side of the building. She had an open book on the table in front of her, but she stared pensively out across Stevens Way, past the austere brickwork of the Engineering Library, through the tall fir trees shaking their black-green manes and bucking in the wind.

As I looked at her I began to feel nervous, embarrassed, giddy. I reached into my coat and touched the hot piece of paper burning a hole in my breast pocket.

Should I presume?

How should I begin?

Swallowing my Prufrockian uncertainty with difficulty, I approached her table. I knew how I was going to tell her. I just didn't know whether I'd have the courage to do it. In a fleeting panic, I saw myself handing her the poem like a bashful dummy and running like hell. Maybe she was right: my social/emotional development had somehow been arrested at age twelve.

John, you simple son-of-a-bitch, get a grip.

Beth reeled in her consciousness from somewhere out in the middle of Lake Washington and looked up at me. A warm smile brightened her face.

"John, I'm glad to see you." She cocked her head slightly. "You're looking a little wild-eyed this morning. Is everything all right?"

I smoothed back my hair nervously and smiled. "Oh, yeah. I guess the wind ruffled me a bit. How about you? You looked as if you were having an out-of-body experience when I came up." She looked down with an uncharacteristic diffidence and grinned self-consciously.

"I was just thinking about some things, that's all." She sighed slightly and then after a few seconds looked at me again with her usual sparkle of self-assurance.

"So what have you been up to over the holidays?"

"I missed you . . . I mean us—you know, our coffee klatches."

"Yeah, so did I."

"You did? I mean, what with all of the Christmas activities and everything, I'm surprised you had time to think about it." My grin felt too big for my mouth and I involuntarily patted my breast pocket to reassure myself the poem was still in there and that it wasn't pulsating, smoking, or otherwise attracting attention.

"With my sister home and a house full of visiting relatives, it's pretty hectic around my house at Christmas, but there are always little quiet times here and there."

Beth seemed very outgoing, very receptive, very intimate just then. Was this the time? Should I do it now?

"I uh wrote something last week, Beth. I'd really like for you to take a look at it." My right hand almost lost its nerve as it reached for the poem smoldering in my pocket, but the bold declaration jumped into my fearful fingers and I held it out to her.

Beth accepted the folded paper with what appeared to be an equal mixture of curiosity and caution, unfolding it as if she expected a spider to jump out. Seeing that the mystery was couched in the form of a sonnet, she looked at me with her eyebrows arched in surprise and puzzlement and then began to read.

I sat on broken glass with cold sweat running down my spine, afraid to watch her expression as she read, yet unable to take my eyes off her face. I tried to sip my coffee and had to use both hands to keep from splashing it all over the table.

Beth's eyes widened as she read and she blushed. She glanced at me with astonishment and then re-read the poem, her lips moving, her blush blossoming into a bright crimson.

I was a mess. I must have been turning blue from holding my breath. My hands had no place to be. I felt suspended in that eternal millisecond between the click of the detonator and the explosion of the mine.

Then, after re-reading the sonnet several times; after I had decided for certain she despised me; long after my heart had pounded itself into oblivion; she looked at me.

Her look contained everything: joy, fear, compassion, relief, regret—I couldn't read it all and I wasn't sure what it meant.

She took my hand gently, searching for the right words. Tears shimmered in her eyes.

"It's the most wonderful poem I've ever read, John. Thank you. What I was thinking about so intently when you came up a little while ago was you . . . us. I was wondering if I would always be just a friend and nothing more. I was wondering if I should tell you how I feel about you. John, I love you, too."

And so the mine exploded and I stepped forth more whole than before—dazed and shaken, joyous beyond measure, jubilant beyond restraint. I loved someone and that someone loved me—what else could a person ask for?

CAIN

On second thought, maybe there were a couple of things a person could ask for, beyond loving and being loved. After the adrenaline drained out of my sinus cavities and the compulsion to dance on the table while howling like a wolf subsided somewhat, the situation got pretty awkward again. I suddenly realized I didn't know what to do next.

In the movies the pledge of undying love is always followed by the big embrace and the lip-splitting, tooth-chipping kiss on a windswept hilltop, with a spectacular sunset forming the background. No wonder so many tales of romance end with that scene—writers don't know what real people do next either.

During the four months I had known her, I had treated Beth like my niece, and I had all but deluded myself into thinking of her as such. Now we were mooning at each other and holding hands across a cafeteria table at eight in the morning, and she was late for a class. The physical aspects of this romantic revelation were going to have to evolve much more gradually.

Beth leaned across the table and touched my forehead with her warm lips just for a second. Throwing her book into her bag and grabbing her coat, she gave me an anguished look. "Oh, John, I'm sorry. I've got to go. See you here at two?"

I nodded dumbly. She started to hurry away, turned, and came back to the table. She squeezed my hand and kissed me again, this time on the mouth—softly, quickly—and then she rushed off, leaving me floating six inches above my chair with the sweetest taste on my lips.

Sometime during the next forty-five minutes gravity prevailed and I was able to feel the press of the chair against my rear end and the cold draft off the windows, swirling around my legs. I got up and headed for the library.

Making a detour over to Miller Hall, I found a small patch of snow, packed it into the size of a soccer-ball, scratched a happy face on it, and set it on the shrinking snowman.

The sky was brighter now and the wind seemed warmer. A greenish hue tempered the grayness of the grass. Jesus! It was going to be a fine day!

My study carrel in the Graduate Reading Room of Suzzallo Library was about as inviting to me on that first day of Winter Quarter 1980 as a cold window niche off the cloister of a Benedictine monastery would have been to a hyperactive rock musician.

The oldest part of the library, The Graduate Reading Room epitomized the nineteenth century tradition of High Gothic architecture. Approximately fifty feet wide and more than two hundred feet long, its vaulted ceiling ascended perhaps seventy-five feet to the crown. Harbored in its tapestried recesses above the twenty-two chandeliers, a pigeon that had found a way into the building cooed, fluttered, and, like the reincarnation of some malcontent professor, defecated indiscriminately upon the scholars hunched over their books below. Stained glass windows filtered the western light dimly through old reds, blues, yellows, and greens onto the massive stonework and onto what remained of the original carved oak bookcases lining the walls. Long oak tables stood in solemn ranks in the center of the vast room. Rows of study carrels filled the northern third of the rectangular floor, where a chilling draft roamed like some restless spirit in search of something. Chair-scrapes on the cork-tiled floor and coughs resounded and echoed with cathedral-like grandiloquence.

The monastic atmosphere of Suzzallo was right for plowing tomes and thinking deep thoughts, but my heart and mind had other priorities. After two hours of trying to confront a boring text with a head full of fantasies and an intellect reduced to a silly grin, I finally cast off my hooded robe and returned to the Hub to regroup over a cup of very secular coffee.

By two o'clock I still hadn't accomplished much, but I was eagerly waiting for Beth when she came into the cafeteria from her last class of the day. She was with Muff, who had been involved in some sort of internship for most of the month of December and hadn't been around campus much.

As hideous a bitch as Muff was, I had missed our little dog and cat skirmishes. Besides, I hadn't completely rejected the idea of siccing her on Danner as a last resort. I wondered if Muff knew about Beth and me, and if she did, what she thought of it.

It struck me as odd that I should care what Muff thought. Perhaps it was because Beth liked her, and in some way she was a part of Beth, like an annoying little habit or mannerism that I didn't mind overlooking.

The two of them sat down at the table I'd been saving for half an hour. Beth beamed broadly at me but said nothing and sat with Muff on the opposite side of the table. So, she hadn't told Muff after all. Muff set her book bag on the table just to annoy me and flopped down, peeling her coat off and letting it drape over the back of her chair.

"John, you little Native American prick, how have you been? She gave me her little half-mouthed, sneering smile I think she had developed just for me.

"Just fine, Muff, and you?"

"Well, except for this damned itch I'm doing really well." She made a point of conspicuously scratching her crotch, which grossed out even Beth, who was used to her crude antics.

"Anna, Jesus." Beth complained disgustedly. Since Muff did it mostly for my benefit, I ignored it.

"You're looking pretty trim, Muff. You haven't started wearing a girdle have you?"

"No I haven't, shithead, have you?"

"Not yet. But just in case you were wearing one I wanted to warn you not to trust anybody named Heracles."

Muff bristled. She naturally assumed she was being insulted, or was about to be insulted, when she wasn't sure where the conversation was leading. That made her even more suspicious and defensive than she was normally. "And what is that supposed to mean?" she said testily.

"If you will recall from the Greek myths, Heracles killed Hippolyta, Queen of the Amazons, and took her girdle. It's something to think about." I gave her an innocent look and scratched my chin philosophically.

"You mean 'Hercules' don't you?"

"'Heracles' was his Greek name. 'Hercules' is what the Romans called him," I replied.

"Whatever—I always knew that muscle-bound fartbreath was a transvestite. But don't worry. Just because I can kick your ass doesn't mean I'm an Amazon. Anyway, I can shoot a bow and arrow just fine with two tits." Beth rolled her eyes and shook her head.

Making a conciliatory gesture, I said, "In that case may your arrow always fly straight and your bowstring never touch a hair on your right breast."

"You watch your mouth you little shit-lizard!" Muff snapped back. I could hardly believe it when she broke into a grin. "You're an amusing little fart, I'll have to give you that. Hair on my breast? Shit, man, I shave those damned things twice a day."

Muff's comment caught Beth in the middle of a drink of coffee and caused her to snort all over me across the table and wind up coughing and laughing until I thought she was going to choke.

Beth's condition struck Muff as hilarious and she began to guffaw, too, until tears streamed down her ugly face. At first I was shocked to find out that Muff had a sense of humor, but then the absurdity of it all engulfed me, as well, and the three of us laughed uncontrollably until we could hardly squeak from exhaustion—much to the amazement and amusement of the people who walked over to our side of the cafeteria to check out the commotion.

"Beth," Anna said when she was finally able to talk again, "I think you could have done better, but that's your business. Mister, you're my business and you had better treat her right or these Slavic stompers of mine are going to do a war dance all over your skinny little red ass. You got that?"

CAIN

"How could I ignore such graciously offered advice?" I replied, grinning. Then I added in all earnestness, "I'll treat her right, Anna. You can count on it."

She gave me one last warning look and then clasped Beth's hand and patted her on the shoulder as she was leaving. Without turning around, as Anna walked away she said, "See you lovebirds later."

I took Beth's hand and watched Muff disappear around the corner. I had never imagined I could ever have a warm feeling of any kind for that woman, but there it was. Beth must have read my mind. When I looked back at Beth she said, "That's why I like her, John. She has a lot of flaws, but she's a loyal friend and, believe it or not, she has a good heart. She would do anything for me and I'd do the same for her."

"I guess I owe you both an apology," I said. "Friends like that are hard to find. I'm glad she's your friend. That doesn't mean I'll probably ever like her as much as you do, but I have the greatest respect for her as your friend."

"Are you sure, John?"

"Absolutely. Shall I walk you to your place? Maybe I could take you to dinner tonight."

"Oh yes, John. Do you realize that it will be our first date?"

"Don't remind me, Beth. I was never very good at first dates—second dates either."

"So you really get going on the third date, huh?" she asked coyly.

"Now, wait a minute. I'm not that kind of guy."

"But when you take me home you are going to kiss me goodnight aren't you?"

"Uh Yes, I think that might be appropriate under the circumstances." I felt a little foolish talking about kissing her and Beth laughed playfully, fondly at my backwardness.

"That a boy, John!" she said. "I'll make a lover out of you yet!"

Somehow, this was not what I had expected, but I wasn't altogether too disappointed.

CHAPTER 12

Something Old, Something New

In 1957, the year before my father and I had sighted the Sasquatch on Mt. St. Helens, we had explored Ape Cave, just a few miles northeast of Cougar. It wasn't a cave, actually, but a long tube formed by external cooling around a river of lava flowing from Mt. St. Helens about eight thousand years ago. After the exterior of the flow had cooled and solidified, new lava had remelted a pathway and pushed its way through the semi-molten interior of the flow. It had drained out, leaving a twenty-foot-diameter tube buried in the lava field like some giant wormhole. Over time, flaws in the crust making up the roof of the tube had allowed sections of the roof to collapse, forming skylights and providing access at several points along the length of the tube. It had been named after a group of local explorers known as The Apes, whose members had discovered the tube in 1951.

Even after twenty-two years, my impressions of exploring the lava tube with my dad were still vivid. Dad had borrowed a couple of Bakelite safety hats from the Physics Lab. Mine wobbled heavily on my nine-year-old head and kept falling down over my eyes. But the big white helmets with "Physics Lab" stenciled on the back and the University of Washington seal emblazoned on the front had lent an air of officialdom and a heightened sense of excitement to our activities. I remembered climbing down a long, rickety ladder into the chilly tube with our flashlights, and rucksacks stuffed with raincoats and lunches. I had marveled at the ridges marking the flow lines of the receding lava in the nearly symmetrical tube. Sandcastles formed by silt dribbling from the ceiling cast long, eerie shadows along the wet floor. Except for the occasional crunch and click of our footsteps and a background chorus of dripping water, the silence seemed almost as palpable as the cold, dark air in the tube. Rubble from the thirty-foot-thick ceiling littered the tube and in places half-filled it, forcing us to climb over the mounds of broken rock. It took us nearly two hours to reach a skylight at the upper end of the tube near its origin. Dad estimated we had traveled more than two miles up the tube.

Ernie's story about the man-bear disappearing into the lava field made me wonder if it might not be explained in terms of troglodytic Sasquatches having adapted to living in lava tubes. Surely there were more tubes radiating out from Mt. St. Helens and Mt. Adams. The tubes could provide a means of traveling unseen for miles from the bases of the mountains to the valleys, where food was abundant. Did Ernie know where any of these tubes were? Would he tell me if he knew?

The first week of February Ernie Wells was due back from his annual pilgrimage to the Warm Springs Reservation near Umatilla, Oregon, where there were still several elders at Warm Springs with whom Ernie could converse in his dialect of Sahaptin. I wanted to discuss the possibility of looking for the lava tube used by the Sasquatch in his story. I also wanted Beth and Ernie to meet each other. I sent Ernie a letter with a return card by which he could let me know when to come. A week later I got the card back with Ernie's neatly printed, cryptic note:

> Come on 9th or 10th John. I want to see your woman.
>
> E.W.

Beth agreed to accompany me to Woodland on Saturday the 9th. It was cold and rainy when I picked her up a few minutes past seven. We stopped for breakfast at Denny's on Aurora Avenue before getting on I-5 to head south.

Beth had fallen asleep in the fifteen minutes it took to get to Tukwila, and she didn't wake up until we passed Centralia an hour and twenty minutes later. I pulled into a rest area, where we used the restrooms, stretched our legs, and poured some hot coffee from my Thermos bottle. Beth wasn't sleepy after that, and we talked as we continued on toward Woodland.

"John, would you be interested in coming home with me during spring break and meeting my family? They've been hearing about you for quite a while now and they're anxious to meet you." She sounded a little apprehensive about asking me.

"Sure I would," I replied, without having to consider it, "I'm eager to meet them, too."

"I'm glad you feel that way. I was afraid you might be reluctant, you know, maybe it might not be the right time or whatever." I could see she was relieved.

"I didn't say I won't be a little nervous, but I'm looking forward to it. It's only right they should know the person you're keeping company with."0

"John, there is one thing. It's never come up before and I don't know exactly how to say it, but my dad is, well, 'old-fashioned' I guess is the expression I'm looking for. I've brought a number of male friends home since high school and, well, my dad can be very intimidating. I don't think anyone I ever brought home was very comfortable around him."

"I can understand that. I've met a few fathers myself. They can be pretty formidable. I can handle it, Beth, don't worry."

"I know you can, John, but there's something else."

"Oh yes? A skeleton in the closet? A two-headed brother chained in the basement perhaps?"

"No, no, nothing like that. Be serious for a minute."

"Sorry. What were you going to say?"

"I've told them so much about you, but . . ." She sighed heavily. "You see, I haven't told them you're Indian." I could tell she was holding her breath, waiting for my reaction.

I thought about it for a minute before responding. "Will it make a difference?" I asked.

"No, of course not, not after they get to know you and find out what an wonderful, intelligent person you are. It's just that they'll be surprised when they first see you, that's all. I hope you'll understand and be patient with them."

"You might be surprised to find out I've never run into that sort of thing much, and when I have it hasn't bothered me. Hell, I have a hard time thinking of myself as an Indian even when I'm looking in a mirror. I'm not the least bit self-conscious about who I am or who my biological parents were. If my race is a problem, it will be your family's problem, not mine. But there is one thing that bothers me a little."

"What's that?"

"Why you haven't told them. I can't help but wonder if you don't have a problem with it."

"Oh, no, John. That's not the reason I haven't told them. You're handsome, smart, kind—everything I've ever looked for in a man. I just didn't want to allow an opportunity for preconceptions and prejudice to creep in before they got to know you as a person. John, you must know how even good people can have stupid ideas about racial stereotypes, ideas they might not even be aware of. I truly believe my family would eventually accept any man I brought home—no matter what race, no matter how ugly, stupid, or obnoxious—as long as they believed I really loved him. John, you have too many wonderful qualities for them not to accept you as you are. I want them to accept you because I love you, but only after they have come to know you and like you for yourself. Does that make any sense at all?"

"It makes a lot of sense, Beth. It's the most thoughtful, sensible statement I've heard in quite a while. I don't know what to say. I just wanted to make certain we weren't keeping anything from each other. Don't worry. Your family and I will get along just fine. I'm not about to blow my chance with the smartest, sexiest, most beautiful, caring, wonderful woman I've ever met—and those are just her minor attributes."

Beth laughed and gave me a hug and a kiss on the cheek and nestled her head against my shoulder. "John, you're such a boyish charmer. How come some lucky gal hasn't claimed you already?"

I shrugged. "I don't know. Maybe I've been waiting for you all my life."

"Kismet?"

"Nope—it's a bloody miracle."

For the rest of the trip we talked about Ernie and how I had come to know him.

"Do you want to hear how I met Ernie's grandson in Vietnam?" I asked her.

"Yes I do. So that's how you came to meet Ernie? Through his grandson?"

"That's right. I was the only Indian in my unit when I first arrived in Nam until Wally transferred in. Naturally, since I was an Indian everyone called me 'Chief.' Wally reported to our unit with a spectacular case of diarrhea, and since he couldn't stop talking about his grandpa being a shaman, Sgt. Hines tagged him 'Shitting Bull.' Unfortunately, the name stuck. The nickname 'Chief' didn't seem quite as stupid after that.

Wally was obviously ill when he arrived. He bailed off the APC and made a beeline for the latrine. An hour later he stood weaving at attention, greenish-gray and sweating. Then the poor kid lost control of his bowels and fainted dead away. The smell was awful. The guy behind him in formation had just come back from a two-day drunken pass and he threw up at first whiff of the diarrhetic stench. Then two more guys threw up, too, and everybody else was either laughing or groaning. The LT was so furious he made all of us stand at attention for two hours."

Beth was properly disgusted and equally concerned about what happened to Wally. "That's horrible. The poor man—did they just let him lie there?"

-CAIN

"No, the LT actually let the medic drag Wally out of formation and work on him while the rest of us stood at attention, eyes forward. Doc—the medic—talked the LT into calling a Medevac copter, which showed up in a few minutes, and then Doc got back into formation with the rest of us. We didn't see Wally again for at least three weeks. It turned out he had a near-terminal case of dysentery.

"Anyway, when he got back nobody was glad to see him. I felt sorry for him and I guess I was about the only one who would talk to him for quite a while. I don't know that I ever actually thought of Wally as a friend, but I liked him and I took an interest in him. As messed-up as he was, there was something about him that made me feel responsible for him. He was eighteen and I was just twenty-one, but he followed me around like a puppy. Except for his grandpa, whom he idolized, I guess I was the only Indian he'd ever met that he could look up to—an instant role model. I felt a little like a fraud because I had never thought of myself as being Indian."

"That still bothers you, doesn't it?"

"What? Not thinking of myself as an Indian? I'm not sure. I thought I was happy being who I am. Then I met Ernie, and he seems to think there's an Indian inside me trying to get out. Sometimes I do feel as if something is missing in my life—something spiritual, mystical, magical—I don't know. It's probably no different from what everyone experiences at one time or another, except it seems to draw me toward primitivism instead of Christianity, Satanism, soap operas, LSD, or whatever most other people try to satisfy that yearning with. Think of the irony. With their languages, their culture, their beliefs all but lost, how many American Indians—aboriginal peoples all around the world, for that matter—are trying very hard to be modernists? And here I am, the quintessential modern man, contemplating a reversion to primitivism."

Maybe I had become a little too intense, or maybe I had given Beth more of a glimpse into the murky interior of my mind than she was prepared for, whatever the reason, she seemed to want to change the subject.

"Tell me some more about Wally.

"Wally had dropped out of high school when he was fifteen or sixteen and he was very impressed that I had a degree from the U. His dad was a longshoreman in Longview, when he was sober enough to work."

"They didn't live on Indian land? I thought all Indians had the option of living on a reservation and drawing a federal subsidy."

"Apparently the Cowlitz Indians never signed a treaty and consequently never got any land or benefits from the federal government or the state, at least not as a tribe. Wally used to tell me the most dismal, depressing stories about his parents getting drunk every weekend as far back as he could remember."

"What ever became of him?"

"A few days before I was sent to LRP training, Charlie lobbed a single mortar shell into our camp in the middle of the night. It landed between two sandbagged barracks tents. We didn't think anyone was hurt at first. Then we found Wally, dead in his cot with a piece of shrapnel in the back of his head. The sandbags had absorbed most of the blast but a fragment had ricocheted off an E-tool someone had left sticking into the top row of sandbags on Wally's side of the tent, which was next to the impact area. When I got back to Washington, I looked up Ernie just to pay my respects. I've been down to see him at least once a month ever since I moved back here."

Wally's story disturbed Beth. "That is the saddest, most bizarre thing I have ever heard. How in the world do you cope with the tragedy of something like that?"

"I don't know. You just do. But you never forget."

"Ernie must have heard us bumping and splashing up the road, because he was standing outside the cabin waiting for us when we pulled into the clearing. He stood in the cold drizzle, grinning from ear to ear in a new plaid shirt and sporting new red

-CAIN

suspenders to hold up his ragged highwaters. As glad as he was to see me, he was absolutely delighted to see that Beth had come with me. Ernie danced up to the car and gleefully opened Beth's door. Before she could say anything he took charge of her right hand and shook it long and rigorously. That amused Beth and she seemed to fall instantly under the spell of the old Indian's charm and enthusiasm.

Solicitously helping her out of the mud-splattered VW, Ernie stood back and looked her over approvingly.

"You're a good-looking woman, Beth. In that regard John is a very lucky man. But of course you would be just as welcome even if you were ugly. Rain is always good for the skin, but it's warmer inside."

Having said that, he ushered us toward the sagging door of the cabin and gave me a bear hug when I got close enough.

"It's good to see you, John," he said with unusual warmth and depth. "I was beginning to miss you, and there are few people I can say that about."

He hugged me so hard I had to wait until he let me go before I could speak.

"There isn't anyone I'd rather visit than you, Ernie. It's good to see you, too."

Ernie must have had the wood-burning range stoked up for hours to get the cabin so toasty and to permeate the place so completely with the not unpleasant pungence of boiled coffee that steamed out of the big pot atop the stove. Knowing how frugal Ernie was with firewood, having spent days shivering and chattering my teeth in the well-ventilated cabin, I made a mental note to inform Beth just how honored a guest she was.

Except for a patch of dingy gray seeping in through the small window, the cabin was nearly dark. Ernie lifted the blackened chimney of the kerosene lamp on the table, flared a wooden match with a flick of his broad, yellowed thumbnail, and touched the flame to the charred wick. The smoky lamp produced a wavering orb of yellow light that hovered dimly over the table. The sweet smell of kerosene mingled with the burnt aroma of the bitter coffee that he poured into three battered enamel cups in front of us, and we sat around the table and talked in low voices.

Despite the points and slits of daylight peeking through the cabin's metal roof, it did not leak. The drizzle became a steady downpour, drumming the parts of the roof where the pine needles had washed off, dripping and splashing from the gutterless eaves, gathering into gurgling rivulets and pensive puddles. The already gloomy morning grew even darker and enveloped the cabin like a wet blanket. The sound of the rain blended into a soft concatenation of indistinct babbles and wet whispers, barely audible above the unmuffled gush and rumble of the torrential stream nearby.

There was something almost atavistic about the three of us huddled around the table like three children with a dim flashlight under the covers. Insulated against a cold, wet world by the warmth of our womblike privacy, we could have been three Neanderthals huddled around a smoky fire in a dark cave a hundred thousand years earlier, or a trio of Taitnapams squatting in a reed mat lodge a mere two hundred years ago.

The inexorableness of rain and cold had not changed since the first Homo had developed the ability to reflect upon it. Nor had fire lost its magical power to warm the body and heat up the imagination. The yellow flame of the lamp swayed and fluttered hypnotically. For no discernible reason other than the setting, I had a sensation, a feeling that the mystery of existence had deepened, had intensified at that moment, in that place. In some unclear way I had become a participant in that deepness and intensity. There had been earlier, uncertain intimations, but this was the first time I had truly felt the seductiveness of mysticism. From the raptness of her expression in the wavering light as she listened to Ernie talk, I believed Beth must have felt it, too.

The feeling haunted me for only few minutes, but it did not pass entirely. It lingered, still potent but quiescent, and I knew it would resurface and reassert itself now that I had become more susceptible to its influence.

Meanwhile, Beth was asking Ernie how he had been able to preserve his beliefs against the onslaught of science and skepticism during his many years as a member of modern society.

"My grandfather taught me to set my beliefs aside and keep them to myself whenever I was among nonbelievers," Ernie replied. "That way my beliefs were not open to challenge and no one could mock me for having them. Grandfather said, 'No one can take your beliefs from you. You can lose them only if you stop believing.'"

"It must have been very hard for you as young man," Beth said.

Ernie got up and placed a piece of wood in the stove and refilled our cups, smiling all the while.

"At first I was seduced by the pleasures of alcohol and women," he answered at last," but after four or five bad years, I finally got my head on straight and gave up alcohol on my eighteenth birthday. I'm thinking about giving up women one of these days, too." He shook his head sadly. "They cost so much nowadays, you know."

Beth looked a little shocked for a second. "Oh, yes, I suppose they do," she said, giving me an uneasy glance and gulping her coffee self-consciously.

Ernie continued. "My beliefs only require me to act in certain ways in certain places at certain times. The ways of my ancestors never required men and women to be free from impure thoughts and actions as a way of life. They only require that we observe the rites that make us pure for special occasions."

"That sounds like a very realistic philosophy, given the propensities of human nature," Beth said with amusement.

I had been listening to the two of them talk and I hadn't said much. I decided it was time to present my theory about the hidden lava tube and to ask Ernie if he would help me find it.

He listened attentively, nodding ostensibly in approval, as I explained my theory about the lava tube, and proposed that he and I go out to search for it. Thinking he was favorably impressed with my idea, I was completely surprised at his reply.

"I talk too much, John, and I have told you more than you are ready to hear. I am the guardian of secrets that I cannot share even with you, John, until you have earned the privilege of knowing. The Tah-tah kle'-ah are spirits that have taken the form of an animal. They can live anywhere and do anything they want. They can make themselves invisible. That's why no one can find them. To seek them out, you must be able to walk among the spirits. This is not an easy thing. It can only be accomplished according to the old ways, and the preparation is difficult. I can help you prepare, but even then, the spirits might not cooperate. They might become angry that I have brought you too soon and then both of us will suffer because I have grown too fond of you and too foolish."

"I'd never ask you to violate your conscience for any reason. You should know that by now. I don't want to harm the Tah-tah kle'-ah, or capture them, or give away any of their secrets, but I need to know that they are really there, Ernie. Whatever they are, animal, spirit, myth, I need to know for sure, for myself. I need to see them, smell them, touch them if possible. Just tell me what I have to do, Ernie, and I'll do it. Just tell me what I have to do."

Beth's expression conveyed her dumbfounded disbelief that Ernie and I could be having such an exchange. I'm certain she could have allowed Ernie just about any eccentricity, but she was looking at me as if I had gone stark raving bananas.

Ernie's gaze focused on something out past the dark cabin wall, past the hills on the other side of the river, past the cloud-shrouded slopes of Mt. St. Helens. His point of focus existed not anywhere in the present but somewhere or sometime far in the past. That is where he was searching for the answer he would give me.

Somehow my kidneys had managed to sort out the several cups of boiled coffee I had ingested in the past hour and a half, and a trip to Ernie's outhouse was unavoidable. I excused myself and made a dash along the puddled pathway to the facility the Benedictines would have known as the *necessarium*. In keeping with the architectural motif of the cabin, the outhouse door sagged

CAIN

and dragged. The rain streamed off the roof above the entry and ran unerringly down my neck as I tugged on the rope handle to free the rain-swollen door. Once inside, an occupant had an almost unobstructed view of the clearing through the gaps between the vertical cedar boards that formed the sides of the outhouse. My best guess was that they represented a compromise between walls and a picket fence.

The hand-split shakes covering the outhouse roof allowed no rain to come in through the top, but enough came in everywhere else to soak the bench and drip through the cracks in the spongy floor. A rusty coffee can inverted over the roll of toilet paper failed to keep it from absorbing moisture from the wet bench, and the roll had fused into a soggy lump. A few wet newspapers dissolving on the bench next to the rough-cut hole served as backup. The rotted floorboards shifted and creaked ominously under my weight, giving rise to disgusting fantasies of falling through and floundering chin-deep in the contents of the underlying pit. When I came out, I got another jolt of icy water down my neck. I did make use of the roof runoff to rinse my hands, however. No wonder Ernie just urinated off the bank at the edge of the clearing in front of the cabin.

On my way back to the cabin, I went to the car and took out the box of sandwiches, chips, and pop I had brought for lunch. The heavy rain had fallen relentlessly all morning, and by the time I had made the round trip to the outhouse I was drenched. Beth was next in line for the *necessarium* and she wisely put on her plastic raincoat before going out. Ernie must have had a brass-valved bladder the size of a basketball, because he did not have to relieve himself.

When Beth returned, we all attacked the limp sandwiches and dug into the bag of potato chips. Ernie was still meditative, but he had come to look forward to the sandwiches and chips and pop I had been providing for our lunch whenever I visited, and he indulged himself appreciatively. Beth had become quiet, either because she was still trying to make sense out of the situation or because she had been traumatized by her trip to the outhouse.

My mood had turned to silliness. Maybe I needed a defense mechanism, or maybe it was just the strong coffee. Whatever the explanation, I began to babble nonsense and laugh inanely at my own asinine humor. Beth and Ernie proved to be a tough audience, and there was no question but that my fatuous attempts to be funny would have been more warmly applauded by two bodies in a morgue. Eventually they chilled me back into sobriety, and we sat silently, except for the multiple munching of chips.

Ernie broke the tension finally by belching loudly and excusing himself profusely, which made Beth laugh in spite of herself and in turn caused Ernie to laugh, too. Of course, by then I wasn't able to appreciate the humor in it and I just sort of sulked as the two of them had a good laugh together.

Beth and Ernie recovered from their laughter and my pout gradually subsided as we polished off the remaining food. The three of us then managed to get the magic bean of conversation to take root, sprout, mature, and reach fruition in the two hours following lunch. The topics harvested included Ernie's insights into the institution of the berdache—the culturally accepted practice of transvestism among American Indian men—and a hard-won consensus on the distinction between a grave robber and an archeologist.

Ernie said nothing further about my proposal, or about my prospects for getting an answer anytime in the near future, but I knew he would give me an answer when he was ready and that his decision would be unequivocal and irrevocable. I regretted having posed a dilemma for him by asking for his help in finding the lava tube. It was thoughtless and stupid. I, of all people, should have known better. It was his prerogative to offer help, not mine to ask for it.

I had no idea what his answer might be. Ernie was a strict traditionalist, but he was too wise to be a blind literalist. Ernie could separate black and white with a morality as keen-edged as his carefully honed hunting knife—I had heard enough of his opinions and pronouncements to believe that. But I was no less certain of his intimate familiarity with the grayness that often engulfs Right and Wrong, a grayness like dense fog that makes it difficult, if not impossible at times, to distinguish one from the other. Ernie's decision would be well-weighed and worth waiting for.

By late afternoon the rain had stopped, and the overcast had brightened. It was time to go. I think Beth was even more reluctant to leave than I was. Although never maudlin about it, Ernie hated to see me leave and his sadness seemed to increase with each departure. He had seemed so completely self-sufficient when I first met him. Now I had the feeling that my visits and my company had fostered something akin to an emotional dependency. I was a loner, too, but I still needed friends—and a family, if everything worked out the way I wanted it to. Was there a law against an old man needing a friend? Maybe I was becoming a surrogate son or grandson to Ernie, but there was nothing wrong with that either, as long as I didn't let him down. I cared for him, too, and I had no intention of ever letting him down. The bad part was that the leave-takings were getting harder for me, too.

When the good-byes were finally said and the handshakes and hugs reprised, I turned the VW around and drove slowly out of the clearing. Beth and I waved and I caught a last glimpse of Ernie in my mirror as we splashed up the narrow drive into the trees. Solitary and straight in his new plaid shirt and red suspenders, he waved slowly, watching us with misty eyes.

Beth took my hand in hers and held it tightly. Looking into her eyes, I saw that she had guessed what I was trying not to think of. She could imagine that I was dreading that terrible visit—perhaps not soon, but inevitably—when I would drive into the clearing, and Ernie would not be there to greet me—would never again be there to greet me. She felt it as I did, and she probably understood about Ernie and me even more clearly than I did. Her understanding was in her eyes and in her smile. It flowed from the warmth and strength of her reassuring hands into mine, and knowing that she understood helped me banish the morbid thought I was trying not to think.

"Thanks, Kid," I said, suddenly feeling older and more vulnerable than I cared to. "I guess even a loner needs someone, sometime."

"Ernie needs you, John. He couldn't be more proud of you if you were his own grandson. You have a wonderful relationship with that old man."

"That's true, but I wasn't talking about Ernie. I was talking about how much I need you."

"You're not as tough as you'd like for people to think, are you?" she replied, smiling. "I think I'm beginning to like being needed." Beth gave me a sultry look. "Being wanted wouldn't make me mad, either." She ran her hands seductively around the curves of her breasts. I'm not sure what kind of look I gave her.

I thought about it for a minute and decided I needed to impress upon her just how frustratingly difficult it was for me to be a gentleman—and how bizarrely impossible it was for me not to be. I was . . . what? . . . embarrassed? Afraid of getting physical with her? I wasn't sure.

I wanted her so much it scared the hell out of me, but I wanted it to be right. I was reluctant to get started because I wasn't sure I'd want to stop, or be able to stop, or even if I would know exactly at what point I was supposed to stop. I had too many ridiculous notions of ideal love getting in the way, even though I suspected there might be some middle ground between taking frequent cold showers or fornicating at the drop of a hat.

Leering at her like a drunken sailor, I swerved the surprised VW off the main road onto a brushy side road and came to a sliding stop. Ripping off my jacket, I started to unbutton my shirt.

"John, what are you doing?" The sudden veering into the bushes had startled her. I could see she was wondering what the hell I was doing.

Maintaining the most lurid and lustful expression I could create, I grabbed her knee with one hand and continued to unbutton

-CAIN

my shirt with the other. "I am going to make you feel wanted, perhaps several times," I growled villainously. Come over here and kiss me as hard as you can." That sounded ludicrous and I thought she might not take me seriously.

I was right. She started to laugh.

"Oh John, stop it, it's way out of character for you. You don't do this sort of thing very well, do you?"

"What do you mean?" I asked defensively, suddenly realizing why I was also such a sorry poker player.

"I don't know what you think you're doing, but it's not what I had in mind. Even if it was what I had in mind, I'm afraid your bedside manner needs a lot of work. That's pathetic, John."

I shook my head and self-consciously began buttoning up my shirt. "Beth, you know what an animal I am. You've got to stop teasing me like that." I was trying to look serious, but I felt pretty foolish. She could have at least acted as if she took me seriously.

"Sorry, maybe it wasn't the best way to make a point, Beth, but I don't think you realize how provocative you are sometimes—most of the time. I think you just say and do things because you aren't worried that I'm going to take advantage of you. I'll have to say, I find it more than a little difficult to cope with. Maybe I'm out of sync here, I don't know, but I want to have a respectful relationship with you. That doesn't mean I don't have a bad case of the hots for you, because I do. Jesus! If you only knew. But that's not the way I was brought up to treat women." I was getting pretty wound up when Beth interrupted me.

"John, hold it a minute. Stop! You're right. I didn't realize I was tormenting you. It's just that I was feeling a little insecure because you didn't seem to be that interested in me, you know, sexually. I've never had that experience with boys and men before. It's always been a problem the other way—everyone I went out with turned out to be more glandular than gallant. You are the first and only man who has seemed more interested in my brain than my behind. But you know, John, you're not all that demonstrative. I was beginning to wonder if you were uh, well, if you were functional." Her frankness nearly bowled me over.

"You should have just asked me. Yes, I'm functional, and I'll be ecstatic as hell to demonstrate that for you at the appropriate time. I apologize for acting like a eunuch. I'll try to be more demonstrative. As you said, I'm just not very good at that sort of thing—not yet anyway—but I will try harder. That is, if you still want me."

"Of course I still want you, you dope. Why don't you come over here and give me an innocent little smooch or two. Heaven knows, you need the practice."

"Ok, I guess that wouldn't hurt. But just a couple. Let me finish buttoning up my shirt first."

"John, I love you, but you're such a little boy in some ways. You do realize you're thirty years old going on twelve don't you?"

"Yes, I guess so. At least that's the way I've felt ever since I was eleven and a half."

CHAPTER 13

Love's Alchemy

Monday morning I was trying hard to recover the wonderfully erotic dream my alarm clock had shattered ten minutes earlier, when the damned phone jangled me into giving up and resigning myself to another sixteen-hour attempt at reality. No one ever called me before I got up in the morning and I vacillated between curiosity and irritation as I picked up the phone. "Yeah?" I grunted.

"I had a dream, John," a male voice declared. It took me a few seconds to realize it was Ernie's voice.

"Ernie? Is that you?" I think I was more surprised he was using the telephone than at the fact he was calling me before six thirty in the morning.

"Sure it is, John. I hope you don't know anybody else who would call you this early.

"No, Ernie, I think you're about the only one. I had a dream, too, but it wasn't one I was planning to call you about. What can I do for you?"

"Those dreams are also important, John. A young man should awaken in the morning with his organ holding up the blanket like a tent pole. It's a sign his body is healthy and his spirit is strong."

I laughed. "Does that apply to old men, too?"

"Can't say, John. I'll get back to you on that when I'm old enough to find out." He sounded completely serious.

"Where are you calling from, Ernie?"

"From the cafe in Cougar. I come down here about once a week for breakfast. I think the new waitress has a thing for me.

She's been giving me an extra piece of toast with my scrambled eggs."

"Sounds like a pretty torrid affair to me. I hope she's not married." The operator interrupted Ernie's reply and asked him to deposit another fifty cents. I heard the quarters registering in the payphone and then Ernie continued.

"Guess I'll have to hurry, John. That was the last of my change. I called to tell you I have come to a decision about things. It was made clear to me in my dream. You must seek the enlightenment and protection of a guardian spirit according to the old way."

"Go on a vision quest? I thought that was an experience for children."

"Yes, but since you didn't have the experience as a child it will be all right to do it now. The only problem is that it will be much harder for you as a grown man to find a spirit. Children are more open to the spirits. That you have lived as a white man all your life makes it even harder. It may be that you will not find a spirit, but I cannot take you to the cave of the Tah-tah Kle'-Ah unless you do. I hope you understand, John."

"I do understand, Ernie. When do I start this vision quest?"

"Whenever you want to. You need to visit the sweat lodge every day for five days for purification. Then I will take you to a place where you must stay until you find a spirit, or get too cold and hungry to continue. Can you do that, John?"

"Sounds a lot like the Ranger course I took at Ft. Benning. You bet I can do it and I will do it. I have a long weekend coming up and I'll get someone to cover my quiz sections next week. I'll be down Thursday night, ok?"

"That's good, John, I'll see you then."

On my way to the university I stopped by Beth's dorm and walked with her to her first class of the day. She couldn't hide her skepticism when I told her about the vision quest, but she was curious about it and she listened with interest to what I knew from reading and talking to Ernie about the practice.

"How long will this take?" she asked.

CAIN

"I should be back a week from Sunday, maybe sooner. Ten days should be enough time." I explained about the five days of purification preceding the vigil and pointed out the obvious limits as to how long one could stay out in the woods without food or shelter in the middle of winter. Bringing up the subject of hypothermia was a mistake, however, because I then had to reassure her that there was little risk involved; that Ernie would be monitoring me and wouldn't let me stay out too long—which I assumed was true, but didn't know for sure. I reminded her I had successfully shivered and starved through the winter cycle of Ranger School at Ft. Benning and in the Utah desert. I also pointed out I had managed not to succumb to days and nights of wading chest-deep in the swamps at Eglin Air Force Base, where the 50-degree water sucked my body heat as relentlessly as the sluggish leeches sucked out my lukewarm blood.

Beth's comments, although restrained, suggested she was not completely confident my veneer of civilized behavior could contain my latent feral tendencies.

"I can understand how an anthropologist might want to experience this to get a sense of what it was like for the people who believed in it," she said, trying to sound detached, "but surely you aren't expecting to have any sort of epiphany or mystical encounter out there, are you? Even if you do come back believing you've seen something supernatural, it will only be because you were hallucinating from exposure, or hunger, or isolation, right? I mean, it's true you have a few fanciful notions about chivalry, and sometimes your romantic idealism makes you seem a little weird, but you are basically a rational person, and rational people don't believe in spirits."

"'There are more things in heaven and earth, Beth, than are dreamt of in our philosophy,'" I responded, wondering if she would recognize the statement.

"That's a quotation, right? Who said that?"

"Shakespeare's Hamlet."

"You know, John, sometimes it's a little exasperating when you respond with a quotation instead of just saying what you think."

"That is what I think. Don't tell me you think science has all the answers. I have always been fascinated with the implications of one of empiricism's central tenets: that knowledge can only be acquired through the senses—one of the philosophical seeds from which behaviorist psychology evolved. The thing that intrigues me is the idea that we can never know reality directly because our only access to it is through our senses. What we call reality is nothing but perceptions based on sensory input. Not only is reality edited and interpreted to us by our senses and perceptions, we are continually finding out there are things everywhere around us that we can't see, hear, smell, taste, or feel. But the fact that we can't see x-rays, hear microwaves, feel viruses, or smell carbon monoxide molecules doesn't prevent them from having an effect upon us any less real. Who is to say there aren't some other things out there beyond the range of our senses that we don't have the technology to detect? Maybe our lives are influenced by things we'll never know except through ESP, or faith, or as the result of a vision in the wilderness. I don't know. And because I don't know, I can't reasonably discount the possibility.

Scientists only think they are the smartest beings in the universe. If you want reality, the reality is that we know less than a new turd steaming in April compared to whatever created the universe."

"So you're saying you do believe in spirits?" Beth sounded confused.

"I'm saying I don't have enough information and experience to believe or disbelieve, ok? You don't think keeping an open mind is too absurdly irrational, do you?" I hadn't meant to be sarcastic and yet the question bristled with nasty little thorns. I put my arm around her shoulders as we walked.

"Sorry, Beth, I didn't mean to bare my teeth at you. We're not heading toward an epistemological schism here are we?"

-CAIN

She gave me a canny smile. "Actually all that philosophy stuff turns me on something fierce."

I threw up my hands in mock despair. "You and Ernie are incorrigible, you know that? You're both obsessed with sex. It's a damned good thing you don't believe in spirits, or the incubi would be lined up outside your door every night waiting for their turn."

"What are incubi?" she asked warily.

"Demons who ravage you in your sleep."

A teasing twinkle lit up her eyes. "And what makes you so sure I wouldn't enjoy being ravaged?"

I could see I was being outbantered. "Shameless wench. If you had any decency, you'd want to save yourself for intellectual intercourse with some long-bearded philosopher."

"Johnny,"—I think it was the first time she had ever called me Johnny—"you hardly have a hair on your chin. Think again if you think I'm going to wait until you grow a long beard. Besides, you've already deflowered my mind. The logic of the next step should be obvious."

"God! What a brazen hussy you've become!" I said, trying not to laugh.

"Gotcha. You're starting to blush, John." She danced around me gleefully, pointing at my cheeks. Not entirely confident my skin was dark enough to hide a blush, I grimaced and stuck my tongue out at her.

I'm too old for this, I thought. What the hell am I doing? Maybe it was time to just let it happen, time to bed Beth before I regressed any further. Whatever reasons I might have had for avoiding intimacy with Beth seemed no longer compelling. Now it seemed unnatural to resist, wrong even. She was old enough to know what she wanted, even if I didn't. If I waited much longer, not even Beth would be horny enough to consider sleeping with the priapic adolescent I felt I was rapidly becoming. Aroused by our conversation, I sensed I was precipitously close to knowing at last the joy of sexual union with a woman whom I cared for deeply.

I made up my mind it would happen that night or the next, certainly before I left on Thursday for ten days of ritual purification and spirit seeking. I wanted the lovemaking to give us equal pleasure and for each one's pleasure to give the other joy. That was the way it was supposed to be. However, my lack of expertise in sexual matters worried me, and believing Beth to be unpracticed as well, I could imagine our first sexual encounter as an awkward, painful, less than satisfying phenomenon. But for better or worse it was going to happen, of that I was certain. It was no longer a decision either of us had any control over.

There was also the other thing, the wondering about life after orgasm—assuming, of course, at least one of us got that far. In some remote part of my brain that was still thirty years old, I knew the force of the erotic tension pulling us together like two powerful magnets of opposite polarity would not remain irresistible continually or forever. Nor could the heart-pounding heat with which we would embrace and merge in an ecstasy of sensual fulfillment endure very long or sustain us thereafter.

There would be a time after the passion had cooled, before the next passion erupted, a slow, uneventful time that would be eclipsed by the pyrotechnics and pulsating purpose of passion, a time in which to wonder if the passion were everything and if the long, slow times in between were to be tolerated because of the passion that had come before and because of the promise of the passions to come after.

Would Beth and I find joy also in the long, slow times between the passions? My desire for her was too great for me to believe otherwise, and yet I understood the risk well enough, even if I didn't want to admit it. Was Beth aware of the risk? Did we share the risk equally or might one of us be condemned not to find joy and condemn the other to losing it as well?

Upon first consideration, love would seem to be a simple enough emotion, but reflected upon for two minutes, it reveals itself to be more profoundly convoluted and fraught with hazard than all the rest of the emotions lumped together. Love between a man and a woman is not a product, it is a process. It flows from an unfathomable wellspring of human energy and unfolds in a cavalcade of design and chance, passivity and passion, opportunity and inevitability. You don't know where it's going or how it will turn out. It cannot be evaluated in terms of assets and liabilities, because rapture and despair cannot be added and subtracted like numerical values; doubt and certainty cannot be averaged; joy and fear cannot be expressed by rational integers. Love compels and we carry out its demands. If we are lucky, we may even find out whether what we do is good or right or wise, but only in retrospect and not for a very long time.

Sex between lovers is arguably a necessary, but by no means a sufficient condition by which love flourishes. I assumed true love might possibly survive inept sex, but I wasn't so sure sexual satisfaction, even of mythic magnitude, would survive long without true love. Fantasizing about mythic sex felt a little presumptuous. On the other hand, I found it reassuring to believe ineptness might not be automatic grounds for the termination of a budding relationship.

My yearning expectation for the warmth and eagerness of Beth's body was not going to be an insignificant part of the attraction I felt for this beautiful young woman. I hoped the remainder would not pale by comparison. Well, maybe just a little paleness would be ok.

When we reached Balmer Hall, Beth toed up to me to give me the usual peck on the cheek that had become her compromise in lieu of a sloppy French kiss, and mine in lieu of a handshake. As usual, she made sure her flat belly and buoyant breasts got to say their good-byes by leaning heavily against me. This time, to her surprise, I took her by the waist and kissed her firmly on the mouth, our cold noses squashing together. She returned my embrace as if she had been waiting for that particular kiss all her life.

Our eyes were enmeshed by the time our lips separated. There was no mistaking her desire in those hazel embers, and mine had to be just as evident to her in the smoldering coals staring back at her. I felt calm, bold—almost like someone who actually knew what the hell he was doing.

"How a about a late dinner at my place tonight?" I said it without stuttering and without having to clear my throat. I had pulled the pin, released the handle, and now Willy Pete was free to do its thing. To consume us in its explosion of white hot phosphorus, or melt us together forever. Jesus! What if it turned out to be a dud?

The calmness lasted two seconds before the shakes set in and the boldness suddenly found itself way out there by itself.

Beth whispered her answer before I had a chance to dive for cover with my hands over my ears. "I'd like that very much, John." She was smiling, but scrutinizing me intently, as if to make certain there was no mistake about what we had tacitly agreed to.

And then the boldness, still way out there by itself, took it upon itself to add, "And an early breakfast?"

She pulled away bright-faced and girlish, laughing the way clear water laughs as it bubbles over smooth pebbles. Backing away, she bumped into a student hurrying to class.

"Two eggs over easy, dark toast, and orange juice," she called out, then she blew me a kiss and bounded as gracefully and effortlessly as a doe up the stairs and into the building.

It would be a long day, but fortunately, I had many things to do before dinner. First, I would have to minister unto the needs of my quiz-section flock after the nasty test Dr. Jackson had zapped them with the previous Friday. After that, I would head for the jewelry store on the Ave, where I had been surreptitiously window shopping for some time. While I was over there, I could pick up a few things from the surplus store just down the street.

I was ok. I could function despite the excitement and boiling anticipation that threatened to commandeer my common sense. My only real problem was that I could not stop humming "Oh What a Beautiful Morning." Gordon MacRAE, eat your heart out buddy!

-CAIN

I planned and carried out my preparations as if for a combat mission. By the time I left to pick up Beth shortly after seven, I had attended to every last detail on my list and double checked it. There were twelve roses in a new vase on the table and the apartment was neat and clean enough to pass any inspection. Luigi had made a special take-out dinner for us that I was keeping warm in the oven. Earlier in the evening, I had borrowed some good china and glassware from Mrs. Cunningham, who got all tittery and insisted I take a full setting of her silverware, a linen tablecloth, napkins, and silver candlesticks as well.

Dr. Cunningham hadn't been home fifteen minutes before he was knocking on my door with a bottle of elegant old red wine in his hands and a wink in his eye. Since there was more than just dinner at stake, I was a little uncomfortable about having the Cunninghams upstairs wondering what was going on in my apartment. But whatever they imagined was going to take place, they were cheering me on as if they had been waiting for it to happen for quite a long time. All that was missing was a call from Beth's parents wishing me well. That thought gave me a moment's chill as I envisioned the inevitable meeting with Beth's stern father, standing before him wearing the guilt of having already slept with his daughter.

I had shaved, showered, and at the last minute, scented myself with the aftershave and cologne the Cunninghams had given me for Christmas. I put on my best shirt and my only tie, and brushed off my little-used sports jacket and slacks. Going out the door of my apartment reminded me of the first time I went out the door of a C-130 at 800 feet on the end of a static line.

From the lobby of the women's dorm, I called Beth's room and waited for her to come down. I felt silly as hell with a hand full of carnations and a belly full of butterflies, and all the young women coming and going, smiling at me knowingly and looking amused.

I watched her descend the stairs: svelte, radiant, and lovely in a low-cut, black dress, wearing a strand of pearls and matching earrings. Walking over to meet her, I gave her the flowers and helped her on with her coat. Beaming and bubbling over the bouquet, she took my arm and clung to it tightly. As we walked out, she exchanged greetings and comments with several of the women in the lobby. I wondered if they noticed the hint of smugness about her, as if she knew she had something they didn't and she wasn't feeling the least bit apologetic about it.

We exchanged small talk during the few minutes it took to drive over to the Cunninghams' house. I told her how terrific she looked. She told me how great I looked in a coat and tie, since that was the first time she had seen me wear one. She said she was sorry she never got to see me in my army uniform. I told her I might be persuaded to try it on again just for her sometime.

When we got to the house, I opened the car door for her, and she took my hand, as if we were going into the gym for a high school prom. We walked around the house, and I opened the door to my apartment. The lamp I had left on gleamed across the tile floor I had carefully waxed earlier that evening, and Beth's shoes squeaked slightly as she walked ahead of me onto the glazed surface. It was her first visit to my apartment, and she looked around as if noting every detail of the small abode. I took her coat, and she was drawn immediately to the table, resplendent with Mrs. Cunningham's finest setting, and with the long-stemmed roses arching their ruby buds over the tall vase among the branching clusters of baby's breath.

My small radio on the counter in the kitchen was set on 880 AM, the oldies station, and Dean Martin was singing 'That's Amore' when I turned it on. It seemed like a good omen, so I left it low on KIXI and lighted the long white candles that Mrs. Cunningham had included with the silver candlesticks. Beth sniffed and mmmed over the roses, felt them, and rearranged them.

"I love the roses, John. They smell heavenly." She hugged me and rested her head against my chest.

"I'm glad you like them," I said, holding her to me. "They smell almost as good as you do." I put my cheek against her head and breathed in the strawberry scent of her freshly washed hair.

CAIN

My lips felt her strong, rapid pulse under the smooth skin of her throat and I kissed her softly there and on her mouth. Then the awkwardness set in and we reluctantly released each other. There was no need to rush anything.

"Something smells good in here besides the roses," she said, as if to smooth the transition.

I went over and checked the food in the oven. "Luigi's specialty: lasagna, Italian green beans, and bread sticks. And here we have a most elegant Chianti, compliments of the Cunninghams. Shall we dine and drink? Or perhaps you would rather drink to me only with thine eyes."

Beth smiled. "I like that song."

"'A Song to Celia.' The words are from a poem written by Ben Johnson, a friend of Shakespeare's and darned near as good a playwright." I uncorked the wine and took the food out of the oven.

Beth looked impressed. "How do you know all these things? I thought you were studying anthropology?"

"One of the benefits of a classical education and a classy mom," I said, as I seated her and served up the lasagna and green beans and poured the wine. I held up my glass and she touched it gingerly with hers. "Here's looking at you, kid," I lisped in my best Bogartese, which wasn't very good, and I didn't know, of all the things I might have said, why I had said that.

"My mother loved poetry and she made sure I learned a whole bunch of it. You'd think a kid would be bored out of his skull by poetry, but I liked it, and it was easy for me to learn. My eighth grade teacher gave us an assignment to learn a poem of our choice and recite it in class. I memorized Poe's *The Raven*, but the teacher wouldn't let me recite more than the first twenty lines or so because he said I was just showing off and using up too much time. When my mom found out about it, she had a fit. She gave the principal and the teacher such a bad time they finally let me recite the entire poem in class—I think it's a little over a hundred lines—just to get her out of their hair."

"You must have been close to your mother."

"Yeah, we were close. She was a beautiful, exceptional person, and no, there was nothing oedipal about it, although come to think of it you do remind me of her in some ways."

"And which ways would those be?" She held up her empty wineglass and I refilled it.

"Oh, you're beautiful, and smart, and just a little feisty."

"Only a little?" She looked somewhat disappointed.

"Let's just say that you're feisty enough to suit me. A little feisty goes a long way, you know. Are you going to want a second helping of Luigi's lasagna?"

"It's delicious, but no thank you. Another pound of Luigi's lasagna and I'll be too fat to be feisty."

"Then how about a spoonful of spumoni?"

"Maybe I can handle that, but just a spoonful."

I took another sip of wine before going to the refrigerator to get the spumoni. I brought back two small dishes of it.

I watched, spellbound, as she deliberately licked the spumoni off her spoon with sensual sweeps of her extended tongue, and she watched me watching her. The flicker of the candles played the shadows defining the roundness of her breasts above her low-cut dress. They shifted the deep shadow of her cleavage in a way that made it appear as if her breasts were throbbing, and my eyes would look at nothing else. I felt an overwhelming compulsion to run my hands over her breasts, to explore and absorb every stunning curve of her body.

"You seem to like my chest, John." Beth giggled. The idea seemed to amuse her a good deal more than it should have, and I suspected two glasses of wine were her limit.

I think I was sitting on the edge of my chair, I'm not sure. All I could say was, "My God, Beth, I adore your chest!"

Already half out of my chair, I got up and moved around the table behind her and began kissing her neck, her shoulders. My hands moved down to her narrow waist, and their sudden encounter with her hips thrilled me. Eagerly, but ever so gently, my hands traced the electric contours of her breasts. Shaking with exhilaration, I bent over her and she reached up, pulling me to her.

I don't know which one of us was trembling more as I scooped her out of her chair and carried her to my bed. Setting her on the edge, I touched her eyelids and earlobes with my lips and nose. We kissed, open-mouthed, our tongues caressing, clutching; the tip of mine circling her wet lips, falling like a petal along the invisible downy hairs of her perfect skin to her throat and fluttering softly again into the warm crevice between her breasts.

My fingers tingled along her flanks and hips to the hem of her dress and under. I knelt, turned back the edge of her dress, and kissed the inside of her thighs, her knees, her ankles. Removing her shoes, I stroked her feet while she moaned softly.

Rising, I watched, goggle-eyed and tumescent, as she stood up, removed her necklace and earrings, and set them on the night stand. She seemed almost transformed somehow, calmer, more purposeful, but still unmistakably seething with passion. Slowly, tantalizingly, she unzipped her dress, stepped out of it, and placed it neatly over the back of the chair by the bed. I observed with fascination as she deftly removed her stockings and underpants. I could see that she felt her power to excite me, and that she was excited by that power.

The black whisper of a slip she was wearing clung to every nuance of her shape and licked her sleekness with the sensual lambency of a lover's tongue. When the black film collapsed into nothingness around her feet and the black lace bra followed, I gasped audibly. Beth laughed a tinkling, bubbly little laugh, like the sound of Chianti filling a crystal goblet.

I pulled my tie off over my head and peeled off my jacket, dropping it to the floor with one sleeve inside out. Finally fumbling myself out of my shirt, I dropped my pants, nearly tripping as I danced on one foot trying to pull my pantleg over my shoe, which I eventually managed to kick off.

Stripping off my socks and shorts, I stood naked before her. I wanted her more than I wanted to go on living at that moment. I wanted her beauty, her softness, her warmth. I wanted to encompass her, to be encompassed by her; I wanted to be a part of her and for her to be a part of me. I wanted to merge completely with her in an exaltation of flesh and feeling so powerful, so meaningful, that this single act would bond us together for an eternity.

She stepped toward me, and I caught her up in my arms so eagerly I was afraid for an instant she might break. I wanted to be gentle, to be slow, to be patient; but the drive to merge with her overwhelmed me, reduced my whole existence to a single, frantic purpose as I effortlessly lifted her back onto the bed.

"I've wanted you for so long, my love," she whispered. She writhed and undulated beneath me, yielding, vulnerable, her long legs wrapped around my waist.

We coupled—slowly at first. As our movements gathered momentum, I felt the throes of her impending climax matching mine. I kissed her feverishly, and she moaned her exhortation:

"Oh, God, Johnny, I love you so much!"

All that mattered in the entire universe for the next few transfiguring moments were my desperate thrusts into the abyss of ecstasy; the arching urgency of her lean body as she moved beneath me; the final, consummating eruption of the whole intent and essence of my being deep inside her as we melted together in multiple, shuddering orgasms. And then it was over, too soon, and Beth was crying softly with joy, and smothering me with kisses as we held each other.

We lay together, still coupled, for a long time after, exhausted and happy and filled with awe that the force that had driven us so wildly, so inexorably, had been so utterly and magnificently appeased.

As I held Beth and drifted toward sleep, I wondered if this had been her first time. I decided that if it had not been, I preferred not to know. This was our first time together. That fact was all there was to know.

Even if I were not the first, that was her business, not mine. If I were to know, I would feel disappointment that I was not the

-CAIN

first one, the only one. Disappointment would be bad enough; the jealousy I would also feel would be intolerable for both of us. I tried to put it out of my mind. She didn't ask if she were my first woman. She didn't want to know, either. What mattered was that we could find in each other the only lovers we would ever need or want from this moment on.

Just before I fell asleep with Beth still blissfully entwined around me, I thought of the small box in my coat pocket. Its contents would be on Beth's plate tomorrow. She would find it there beside the two eggs over easy, the dark toast, and the orange juice. When she discovered it, I would humbly, reverently, joyfully ask her to marry me. I would ask her to bear our children; to share my love and my life all the rest of our days.

CHAPTER 14

Nature: Metaphor of the Mind

It was eleven thirty by the time I got to Ernie's cabin Thursday night. The clearing lay in a pit of blackness under a lunar crescent, which hung in a partially clear sky like a dirty toenail clipping caught on a linty, black bath towel. It had already begun to freeze. The crystalized droplets of rainwater hanging on everything sparkled in the movement of the headlights as the Volkswagen thumped and rattled up the familiar ruts. My lights caught Ernie nonchalantly scratching his ass as he stood barefooted in the doorway of the dark cabin, waiting for me. He wore only his dingy longjohns, and his thick, gray hair hung loosely about his face and flowed over his shoulders to the middle of his chest.

"Good to see you, John," he called out as soon as I opened the car door. "I thought you might get here earlier, but I'm glad to see you anyway."

I waved at him as I got out and pulled my duffle bag from the back of the car. The smell of wood smoke hovering in the clearing was strong but pleasant. Ernie held the cabin door open for me, grasping my hand and crushing it in his big bony grip as if he hadn't seen me for months.

"Sorry I'm so late, Ernie. It took me longer to say goodbye to Beth than I figured it would." Ernie nodded understandingly.

My eyes had quickly adjusted to the darkness outside, but when Ernie closed the cabin door, the totality of the absence of light would have impressed a psychiatrist, or a proctologist—members of the two professions concerned with examining the darkest places on earth. I set my bag down. A few seconds later a match spurted yellow flame on the other side of the room, waking up the oil lamp and the resident shadows, which took up their eerie activities in the wavering dimness. Ernie added a piece of wood to the damped stove, whose smoldering emanations of warmth did not venture far from their source in the drafty room.

"How is it between you and Beth?" Ernie asked, as he closed up the smoky stove and turned his back to it to warm himself. Something about the way he asked it made me feel he already knew how it was between us.

"I can't begin to describe how good it is," I replied. "She is the most potent stimulant in the world and I'm hopelessly addicted to her. I can't get enough of her. I asked her to marry me and she said yes."

Ernie beamed excitedly at the announcement and slapped his leg. "Hot damn! That's wonderful, John. I knew you two were good for each other. I'm damned happy for both of you and I'm really looking forward to kissing the bride. When's the big event?"

"Hopefully in June at the end of spring quarter. I'm going to try to get my dissertation finished by then so I can start looking for a job. Of course, I haven't even met Beth's family yet, and three months may not be enough time to get everything organized."

Ernie shook his head knowingly. "When I decided to get married, it took me three months just to settle on how much whiskey I would have to give my father-in-law for him to let me have his daughter. Then it was another month before I got together enough money to buy a case of Jack Daniel's. I could have gotten the older daughter for half a case, but I didn't love her as much. Besides, she was just too damned fat and ugly. Yes, I understand how much time these arrangements can take and how complicated they can get."

I unpacked my sleeping bag and spread it out on the floor, as I had done on other occasions when I had stayed overnight. Only I had a heavier bag now that I had purchased at the surplus store on the Ave. Removing my clothes, I crawled into the cold bag.

"Do we start tomorrow, Ernie?" I asked, wondering how many hours I was going to have in which to enjoy the hard, cold floor.

"Yes, quite early. Sleep well tonight, John. There will be few comforts for you in the coming week." Ernie blew out the lamp and I heard his cot squeak as he lay down. I took Ernie's comment to be ominously prophetic. Having few comforts was Ernie's way of life, but for me, I was pretty sure it meant an ass-freezing ordeal.

The surplus army bag warmed up in a few minutes and having had a long day, I fell asleep rather quickly. At some point I began to dream—a murky, Kafkaesque dream without a beginning or an ending, a dream that filled my sleep and seemed to run continuously all night. In my dream I searched for something, but I didn't seem to know for what or why. I had the feeling I had been searching for a very long time. I felt a sense of urgency in the dream, yet I seemed to know little about the search. Some quest had compelled me to reluctantly abandon a hauntingly beautiful, but obscure, female and to entered some strange, frightening place fraught with mystery and danger. Threatening shapes moved among the shadows of a cavelike dreamscape. Dark, tumultuous rivers thundered into ominous pits so profoundly black no light could penetrate them. I was possessed by a deep, nameless fear. At any moment I expected to stumble upon something hideous lurking among the shadows. There was something familiar about the strange shapes that I caught glimpses of without really seeing, something almost recognizable, but which I could not quite identify in the uncertain flicker of a torch's flame.

My wakeup call was Ernie building a fire in the stove and banging the big enameled coffeepot into submission. In the predawn promise of light, I could see Ernie at the stove measuring out the coffee grounds. He started to replace the lid on the pot, looked at the unstirring lump in the sleeping bag on the floor for a moment, and added another two scoops of coffee to the pot. Scratching and farting, he then went outside in his longjohns and unlaced boots, presumably to take a steaming piss over the bank. I

-CAIN

needed to go, too, but the warmth of the sleeping bag convinced my bladder it could wait for a few more minutes.

After a short while, I heard Ernie break the ice in the bucket outside the cabin and pour out some water to wash himself. Stiff from sleeping on the floor, I crawled painfully out of the warm bag. Shivering, I dressed quickly, plunged my feet into my frigid boots, and stood as close as possible to the cookstove, which was roaring now and beginning to put out a good deal of welcome heat.

When Ernie came back in, we exchanged grunts, and I tore myself away from the stove and headed for the bank to liquidate an asset or two, i.e., about a pint of urine. An image popped into my head of a crowd of well-dressed stockbrokers at the New York Stock Exchange pissing against a wall like a bunch of bare-assed hippies at an outdoor rock concert. Far out, man. Either I had been breathing the residual fumes of drycleaning solvents in the sleeping bag, or Ernie's nocturnal farts were more potent than LSD. I was embarking on a religious pilgrimage this morning with a mind full of psychedelic silliness. I wondered if anyone else suspected how weird I really was.

As I stood on the frosty bank enjoying the simple sensuousness of draining my bladder, a bright blade of sunlight thrown by the new sun cut between the trees and stuck with all its sharp-edged radiance into the frosted bank at my feet. The arc of my urine sparkled through the shaft of light and pattered against a decaying log resting peacefully on the steep hillside below the bank. The purity of the blueness overhead was transcendental; the only sounds were those of my heart beating and of the thin stream of urine piercing a shaft of light and returning to the earth.

For some inexplicable reason I had a feeling of rightness at that moment, as if I had just figured out something my ancestors had understood instinctively. At that moment, the urine passing through the light and falling to earth seemed the most elegant, powerful metaphor for life I might ever encounter. Would I, too, at my zenith be privileged to pass through the light and scintillate in that one microsecond of glory before returning to the earth? And if there were to be no microsecond of glory, would not the beauty of the arc itself and the long decline according to the natural order of things suffice?

Jesus! I hadn't even begun my initiation yet and already I was able to turn pissing over a bank into a metaphysical experience.

The coffee was beginning to boil, and Ernie had put on his pants and was fixing breakfast when I came back. The morning's menu consisted of dried bread fried in slightly rancid bacon grease, which we flushed down with copious amounts of chewable coffee. If nothing else, the meal was filling. I took some comfort in the likelihood that the massive dose of caffeine would protect me from being taken unawares in my sleep by a sudden and inevitable attack of diarrhea brought on by the bacon grease.

For the most part, we ate in silence directly from the cast iron skillet Ernie had set between us on the scorched tabletop. Ernie seemed preoccupied, perhaps reviewing his plans for the day, and I didn't feel much like talking either. With the last piece of bread, he mopped the remaining grease out of the skillet and set it back on the stove, which had consumed its helping of firewood and was beginning to cool off.

Ernie laced up his boots and pulled his moth-eaten mackinaw off its peg on the wall. "Let's go down to the sweat lodge, John, and see if we can sweat some of that white man's shit out of you that you've been storing up so long."

Burping up equal parts of rancid grease, bitter coffee, and hostile hydrochloric acid, I grabbed my coat and watch cap and followed Ernie out of the cabin—filled with as much anticipation, dread, and wonder as a pubescent boy beginning his rite of passage.

Ernie led me down a narrow trail that switchbacked along the steep hillside through a thick stand of firs, trees that probably had been replanted in the logged-off slash sometime during the early years of Prohibition. It took us about fifteen minutes to snake our way down the half mile of trail to a secluded inlet on the lake.

CAIN

The sweat lodge sat on a ledge, perhaps eight feet above the water. A dense thicket of willows hid it from the view of any passing boaters—not that we had to worry about anyone being out on the lake at that time of the year and at that time of the morning.

The lodge stood four feet high by six feet in diameter. The dome-shaped structure consisted of a supporting framework of willows lashed together and covered by a heavy tarpaulin. In front of the lodge, a fire in a firepit had burned down to a bed of glowing coals, in which a half dozen melon-sized river rocks and a slightly larger chunk of vesicular lava stone had heated up about as much as they were going to. Ernie had obviously come down several hours earlier and built the fire to heat the stones. Near the firepit sat the bottom half of a wooden barrel. Inside the barrel, greenish rainwater lay dark and fuzzy beneath a thin layer of ice.

Ernie pulled up the canvas flap at the front of the lodge and used a rusty pitchfork to transport the hot stones from the firepit to a stone-lined hearth inside on the left side of the entrance. Coming back out, he closed the flap to allow the heat to build up in the lodge. He then took off his clothes, broke the ice covering the slimy water in the barrel, and began dipping out the water with his hand and letting it run over his body. Stripping off my clothes, I joined him, wincing and clenching my teeth as the icy rivulets ran like electric shocks over my skin. After a few freezing minutes of lavation, Ernie turned and intoned a prayer of greeting to the spirit of the lodge, *Pusa*, which I recognized as the Sahaptin word for paternal grandfather. Ernie entered the lodge carrying a wooden bowl of water from the barrel. He sat next to the hearth on the fresh fir boughs strewn about the floor. I followed, pulling the flap down after me and sitting next to him in the darkness.

We meditated in silence. The hot stones turned the lodge into an oven; turned my shivering goosebumps into beads of sweat; turned the fir boughs into a pungent green aroma. Ernie splashed some water from the bowl onto the piece of lava topping the other stones in the hearth. The water fizzed and whistled as it turned to steam in the pores of the stone. Sweat began to run off me like snow melting under a spring chinook. I could feel the heat sucking the toxins out of my system, sucking the venom from every civilized snakebite I had ever suffered or inflicted.

William Empson was right: the waste does remain, and it does kill—but not if the heat sucks it up and spits it out on the greenly fuming fir boughs covering the dirt floor; not if transgression and guilt are washed away by a deluge of sweat, and evil is purged by the pouring forth of perspiration in a dark place.

I don't know how long we sat and sweated—an hour, perhaps two. It was long enough anyway for me to develop a rapid pulse and a ravenous thirst. Then Ernie told me to open the flap, that it was time to get out. My head pounded as I crawled out of the lodge into the brilliant morning light and stood up, naked and steaming like some newborn demon rising out of the underworld.

The March air had not warmed perceptibly since we had entered the sweat lodge. The frost remained pristine and feathery where the sun had not yet found it. Ernie crawled out behind me and chanted to himself as he went over and seated his glistening buttocks on the frosty shadow of the rock ledge above the lake. After a minute, he stood, clamped his nose with his fingers, and jumped feet first from the ledge into the lake, startling into flight a pair of unsuspecting mallards swimming near the shore. When I looked over the ledge, Ernie was backstroking a wide circle in the thirty-five degree water as calmly as if he were lolling in a heated pool.

Before I gave myself time to contemplate the matter, I backed up a few yards and ran as hard as I could for the ledge, diving with perfect form into a spectacular bellyflop that resounded across the water. I don't know which hurt more, the bellyflop or the cold water, but it didn't make any difference after the first ten, breathtaking seconds, when the numbness began to set in.

Ernie climbed out of the water and pointed at me, laughing his head off and saying something in Sahaptin about "*wispus*." Heading for shore as rapidly as possible, I emerged with my belly and chest slapped scarlet, but otherwise nearly blue from the cold.

My teeth chattered uncontrollably as I demanded to know what a "*wispus*" was. Still chuckling, Ernie explained my bellyflop had sounded like a giant beaver slapping its tail on the water; hence, "*wispus*," the Sahaptin name for beaver.

We climbed back up to the ledge and Ernie sat on a log to put his boots on, but instead of putting on his clothes he just tucked them under his arm and took off up the trail dripping, steaming, and buck naked. I pulled my boots on over my freshly frozen feet, wadded up my clothes, and marched up the hill behind him, clicking my teeth together in a way that would have earned me the admiration of a skilled telegrapher—and wondering if my genitals would ever return to their former size and color.

What the sweat lodge didn't purge from my body, the bacon grease took care of. I divided the rest of the morning and part of the afternoon between splitting firewood and dashing to the outhouse. Ernie stacked the wood as I split it and coached my attempts to master the strange phonemes of the Sahaptin language. I had found a few partial lexicons and a couple of useful but incomplete references that provided some insight into the difficult grammar of Sahaptin, but no system of phonetic symbols could adequately represent the actual pronunciation and inflection of the language. As is the case with learning any tongue, there is no substitute for hearing it spoken by a native speaker.

When we had finished splitting and stacking the large pile of firewood, Ernie took me with him to check the snares he had set the previous evening in the old clear-cut that bordered his property at the top of the ridge. He showed me the tunnel-like rabbit run beneath the partially flattened fireweed stalks and matted blades of dead grass. The first snare had been set at a point where the run crossed under a tangle of slash debris. A cold, stiff cottontail lay where it had strangled itself in the invisible loop of piano wire that Ernie had set.

Ernie talked to the dead rabbit in Sahaptin as he removed it from the snare. He detached the wire from the half-buried branch to which it had been anchored, coiled it tightly, and placed it in his pocket. When I asked him what he had said to the dead rabbit, he explained he had apologized for killing it and had thanked it for providing our dinner.

A hundred feet from the first snare, we found a possum caught in a second one. The possum's foreleg was caught in the wire loop around its neck and it was still very much alive and struggling to free itself. When it saw us it bared its nasty little teeth and hissed at us. Ernie picked up a stick and I thought he was going to hit the possum with it, but he used it to pin the animal to the ground instead. As soon as Ernie touched the frightened creature, it stiffened up and fell over as if dead. Ernie removed the snare from around the possum's neck and leg and put the wire into his pocket, along with the other snare. I watched with great interest as Ernie gently examined the ugly little marsupial and grunted with satisfaction when it did not appear to be injured. He addressed the still, hard form of the animal as he had that of the rabbit and then smiling, he patted it softly, stood up, and gestured for me to go with him, leaving the possum curled up rigidly where it lay.

"The possum will stir in a few minutes and run away. It will be all right," Ernie assured me. "I set two snares not to catch two animals but because one snare does not always provide a dinner. I'm thankful the possum was not hurt. I have always regretted the snare could not be a kinder way of providing meat. The snare is a cruel thing because it does not kill quickly. It must be used with the greatest respect and frugality. The killing itself is not cruel if it serves a good purpose. Waste is cruel, though, waste and unnecessary suffering. The spirits of the animals understand and forgive the hunter if he is respectful and does not kill wantonly. It is the natural way of things."

"And what happens if the hunter is disrespectful and kills wantonly?" I asked.

Ernie thought about it for a few seconds and replied, "The spirits will curse a hunter who kills for sport or kills more than is needed. One day when he is very hungry, he will find no game to

CAIN

kill, because the spirits will have made all animals invisible to him. Sometimes the disrespectful hunter has an accident and dies."

As we walked back down the ridge toward the wall of tall firs that marked the edge of Ernie's property, the curious part of me wanted to question him about his understanding of how the spirits could make animals invisible, but the intuitive part of me already comprehended, and I wound up mulling and reflecting instead of asking Ernie another dumb question. Whether he meant it as a metaphor, or meant it to be taken literally, the real mystery was how had he managed to maintain his belief in spirits and magic against the crushing influence of mundane materialism that had surrounded him all his life. I wasn't thinking of materialism in the sense of preoccupation with wealth and possessions, but materialism in the sense of reducing all things to mechanical, chemical, and electrical explanations; explanations in which concepts such as soul, spirit, and magic are excluded, ridiculed, and relegated to the realm of fairy tales, or attributed to chemical imbalances in the brain that stimulate fantasies and hallucinations.

It would be a thin thesis indeed that differentiated primitive and modern cultures solely on the basis of their attitudes toward wealth and possessions. Of course, some primitive cultures were more materialistic in that sense than others. The Algonquians had their wampumpeag, white shell beads used as currency; the Dakotas, who were barterers, placed great value on buffalo robes and horses. One of the most frequently cited examples was the institution of the potlatch among the coastal Indians of the Pacific Northwest, particularly among the Coast Salish and the Southern Kwakiutl, the latter of which from 1849 to 1925 made the potlatch the focus of their whole culture, including developments such as interest-bearing loans and copper pieces that served as negotiable checks for credit and property.

Skeptics would have characterized Ernie's way of seeing his world as a colorful attempt to preserve a quaint but empty tradition, soon to be lost except for a footnote or two in some obscure and probably inaccurate text on primitive practices, buried in a university library. The thousands of years of aboriginal wisdom from which Ernie drew his understanding of life amounted to no more than a meaningless anachronism as far as most non-Indians, and many Indians themselves, were concerned. It was not uncommon to hear the sentiment expressed that it would be better for the Indians to just throw away all of the shabby, outdated baggage of their primitive heritage and move into the twentieth century.

Who said the twentieth century was godless and lacked spirituality? What about the pantheon of Apple, IBM, and McDonalds? What about the daily prayers in public schools addressed to the spirits of progress and change? To the technological white man, it was perfectly obvious the damned Indians needed to stop trying to live in the past and to start living in the future. All they needed to bring them into the new age were degrees in computer science and jobs at fast food franchises. After all, Native American animism had no chance of becoming another Islamism, Hinduism, Buddhism, Judaism, or Christianity. There was no money, no political power, and no future in primitivism. Even Ernie's own son had rejected the old ways.

It was bad enough that primitive cultures were sinking out of sight, leaving not even so much as a ripple on the surface of Time's river. But the greatest tragedy was that Indians who no longer had a culture and religion, who had forgotten the wisdom of their ancestors and had lost their intimate relationship with nature, were no longer Indians. Removed from grace by the loss of the old ways, they joined the rootless ranks of modern people and became preoccupied with paying bills and raising kids in an increasingly troubled society, sustaining themselves with memories of a few good times past and hopes for a few more good times to come, and using up their lives watching bad TV and eating too much junk food. And as modern people, they, too, would not discover the point of it all.

Not that primitive life had been easy or idyllic, consisting for the most part of a struggle just to survive, but my ancestors and Ernie's faced life's hardships with the advantage of a certain knowl-

CAIN

edge of the way things worked and how they as individuals fitted into the order of things. Knowing, accepting, and making the best of the way things were gave them strength and purpose. Living in harmony with their natural environment gave them peace and fulfillment. What better way to live than to find purpose, peace, and fulfillment in the challenge of one's existence? What more was there to know other than that the point of it all was the process itself?—the arc, the zenith, the chance of passing through the light, the slow decline back to the earth, and the comforting assurance that succeeding generations would be able to experience life in the same meaningful way.

It all boiled down to the same old question: have progress and civilization improved the quality of human existence? Are we happier, wiser, more moral? Do we lead more fulfilling lives? Are we closer to achieving some postulated teleological goal of individual and social evolution? Every time I had asked those questions of myself during the past ten years, I had been forced to answer in the same way. The only difference now was that after ten years I was absolutely certain that the answer was correct. The answer had to be an emphatic NO.

When we got back to the cabin, Ernie showed me how to remove the rabbit's skin as easily as peeling a rubber glove off my hand. We talked into the evening about the habits of rabbits and possums, about tracking and setting snares. Then it was time to prepare a fire outside to roast the rabbit and for more talk while the rabbit roasted. Darkness came and we ate the rabbit by the light of the fire, sitting close to the coals to keep warm. When we had finished eating and talking for the night, we went into the dark cabin. Without bothering to light the lamp, Ernie got into his squeaky cot, I squirmed into my sleeping bag, and we said goodnight. Long before dawn I would accompany Ernie down to the sweat lodge and help him build the fire to heat the stones. Thereafter, it would be my responsibility to build the fire each morning so that the stones would be ready by sunrise. The cabin floor was not quite as hard and cold as it had been the night before. and I sank gently into a deep, dreamless sleep.

The tritium dial on my watch showed 0330. I could hear Ernie's cot squeak as he sat on it, pulling on his boots in the darkness. Ernie didn't have a watch or clock to his name, and yet he always knew the hour and seemed able to wake up in the morning at any predetermined time without the assistance of an alarm clock. I was pondering Ernie's uncanny sense of time and was on the verge of giving up the womblike comfort of my sleeping bag, when something scurried up the length of the bag and scampered across my face, digging its tiny claws into my skin—a damned mouse. I swore and sat up abruptly, spitting and wiping my face. A chuckling came from the direction of the cot and moved across the room as Ernie walked over to the door and went outside. I could hear him laughing as he headed for the bank.

I was dressed and had my sleeping bag rolled up by the time Ernie came back in.

"*Lakas,* the mouse, is attracted to you, John," Ernie said, still laughing. "The two of you must have kindred spirits."

"Tell *Lakas* and his spirit I'm deeply honored, but I'd just as soon not wake up with mouse turds stuck between my teeth—no offense, of course."

Mouse turds between my teeth struck Ernie as the funniest thing anyone could imagine and he guffawed so mightily that he farted, which made him laugh even harder. Not inclined to be much amused at first, I quickly succumbed to the absurdity of the whole thing and before long I was laughing, too, and groaning at the foul presence Ernie's butt-thunder had conjured up in the darkness.

On the way down to the sweat lodge, I asked Ernie a question that had been gnawing at me almost since the first time I met him.

"Ernie, how were you able to work as a logger most of your life when logging seems to be so blatantly antithetical to what you believe about the sanctity of nature?"

CAIN

"Sometimes your words are too big to pass through my ears and into my head," he replied. "I remind myself that your many years of schooling have made you ignorant. If you had spent more time studying nature and less time reading books, you would be able to ask a simple question and I would be able to understand you. Still, I know you do not intend to sound like a book and confuse people who understand only ordinary spoken words. Actually, for a person with so much education you make a lot of sense most of the time. I take it you want to know how a follower of the old ways could help spoil the land by cutting down the trees? I'm surprised you didn't ask about that sooner."

"Uh-huh," I grunted as humbly as possible, trying to apply Ernie's constructive criticism about the need for simplicity in communication.

"My grandfather taught me many things when I was a boy, but I was headstrong and I developed a fondness for whores and whiskey. Whores and whiskey were expensive and I had to earn money to pay for them. Logging was about the only employment around and the pay was good, so when I was fifteen I got a job setting chokers. I was strong and nimble and I learned fast enough to keep from getting killed or fired. I liked working in the woods. I got a dollar a day, a place to sleep, and all the food I could eat. Once a month we got to go into town to get drunk and visit the local cathouse. It seemed like paradise to me. Some of the loggers didn't like me and treated me badly because I was an Indian, but most of them didn't care as long as I held up my end of the work and didn't get anyone hurt. All in all, it was a good life. I was so busy thinking I had it made it never occurred to me I was doing anything wrong.

"I continued to take instruction from my grandfather in the winter months when there was no work in the woods. He had taught me the old language from the beginning and we talked it whenever we were together. Gradually, I began to see that logging, like just about everything else the white man had done, was ruining the land. The forests were disappearing, the mountainsides were becoming scarred by ugly logged-off areas, the streams were becoming choked with silt so that the salmon could not spawn. It had always been sad for me to see the forests burn and to see fine old trees fall before the wind, but there had always seemed to be enough forest to allow for that. Fire and wind were as much a part of nature as the trees themselves. I saw I was helping to destroy the land faster than it could heal itself. I thought, what if I stopped cutting down the trees? And then I thought, if I stop cutting down the trees, someone else will take my place and the trees will still be cut. But I knew it was a harmful thing, and to do a harmful thing knowingly was bad."

Ernie fell into a thoughtful silence as we moved down the dark trail toward the sweat lodge and I prompted him to continue. "But you kept on working as a logger even though you felt it was bad?"

"I was weak, John. I was too weak to give up the job and the money and the cathouse. I pretended it would be all right if I just apologized to every tree I cut down and planted a new one for every one I helped destroy. I even gave up whiskey, and began to take my grandfather's instruction seriously. Funny thing . . . if I hadn't felt so guilty, I might have turned out like my father, or like my son, and my grandfather would have died without passing on to me everything he knew of the old ways. I stopped working about fifteen years ago and I've tried to follow the old ways as well as I can since that time. Much has been lost and much of what remains no longer can find a place in this world. It makes my heart glad, John, that you have taken an interest in the things only a few old people still believe to be important. Only now do I know what a wonderful thing it was I did for my grandfather."

I was deeply touched by Ernie's confession and half sorry I had asked the question. But Ernie's explanation had revealed an inner part of him that I felt privileged to see, a fallible, vulnerable part that completed his humanness; a part that made me feel I could not have loved the old man more if he had been my own grandfather.

We came to the edge of the black lake, where invisible ripples softly lapped at the shoreline. Quietly, almost as if not to awaken the sleeping water, Ernie showed me how to build the fire around the heating stones so the tinder didn't burn away before the larger pieces were fully ignited. We added larger pieces of driftwood as the fire slowly grew and we sat without saying anything, searching the thoughts that flickered ephemerally among the dancing flames.

The fire burned down to a bed of coals before there was any color in the gray light of dawn. Ernie handed me the pitchfork and I transferred the stones to the sweat lodge following his instructions. We undressed, bathed, and entered the sweat lodge as before. The fir boughs on the floor were still fresh and fragrant.

Ernie had me repeat in Sahaptin the ritual invocation to the spirit of the sweat lodge. After half an hour of struggling with the explosive popping sounds of the glottalized consonants, the catch-in-the-throat glottal stops, and the preparing-to-spit laterals, my rendition of the short greeting began to sound almost recognizably similar to what Ernie was speaking. He grunted his approval next to me in the darkness and sprinkled water on the hot stones. There was something thrilling in the utterance of those strange sounds and I was pleased with myself. The prospect of actually being able to converse with Ernie in Sahaptin seemed less remote and it excited me in a way that learning new things had not excited me since boyhood.

The heat and meditation cleansed our bodies, cleared and focused our minds. Long golden arrows of sunlight streamed through the trees into the lake by the time we emerged from the sweat lodge. This time I plunged eagerly, deeply into the lake. Shocked into a new consciousness by the chill, I gasped to the surface like a newborn infant dropped from the womb into a pail of ice water. When I waded out onto the gelid shore, I felt unfettered, powerful; as if my consciousness had been magnified and my ability to understand things had been increased threefold. I no longer felt the cold and I followed Ernie back up the trail to the cabin with a new lightness in my step and a tingling exhilaration warming my naked skin.

As I walked into the cabin, I was startled by a tin can rolling and tumbling around the cabin floor by itself as if it were possessed. "Hey, Ernie, look at this. What the hell?"

Smiling, Ernie chased down the haunted can, picked it up, brought it over to me, and held it out for me to examine. The lid of the old pork and beans can was still attached by half an inch of uncut metal and had been pushed part way into the can, from which came a busy scratching sound. Looking closely into the crack around the lid, I could see two little beady eyes looking back at me. It was *Lakas*, the mouse.

"I'll be damned," I said in amazement. "Did he get in there by accident or is this an ancient Indian mousetrap you learned about from your grandfather?"

Ernie laughed. "The principle is quite old, John, but we had to wait until the white man started throwing away his old cans until we could put it into practice." He showed me how he had braced the can against the wall and pushed the lid in just far enough so that the mouse could squeeze in to get at the dab of bacon grease, but couldn't get back out again.

"Ernie, I'm hoping this doesn't mean we're having mouse stew for dinner tonight."

He grinned. "No, it means we're having trout for dinner. You'll see." Leaving me curious as hell about how he was going to turn a mouse into a trout, Ernie stashed the can in the wood box and went back over to the cot, where he had set his clothes, and began to dress.

When we were dressed, I built a fire in the cookstove while Ernie got out the ingredients for our breakfast. He dipped out about a pint of water into a two-quart pan and set it on the stove to boil. As the water began to steam, he added a carefully measured two-fingered gob of bacon grease from an old shortening can, dumped in what appeared to be about a pound of questionable corn meal and a handful of salt, and gave me the wooden spoon to stir it with. After a lot of stirring the mixture turned to a thick glue, which according to Ernie had been cooked to perfection. Being sort of a guest and everything, I got to use the spoon. Ernie dipped the substance out with his fingers, smacking his lips and shaking his head with gustatory delight. I shook my head, too. I was beginning to think of mouse stew with a little less repugnance.

About noon, Ernie set about changing a mouse into a trout. He led me up to the top of the ridge and several miles along its crest to a point where we made a steep descent down a brushy slope to the upper part of the lake. It took us nearly two hours and the return trip with its difficult climb back up to the ridge would take even longer.

Ernie searched along the bank until he found the place he was looking for. He sat down and took out of a pocket of his mackinaw a short stick wound with ten or twenty yards of fishing line, to which was attached a rusty treble hook. He looped several half hitches in the end of the line, pulled the can with the mouse in it from his other pocket, and managed with difficulty to lasso the mouse snugly around the midsection with the hook dangling off to one side. All the while, the mouse was a blur of churning feet, writhing tail, and snapping teeth, which found Ernie's finger more than once and drew blood. When the mouse was secured to the line, Ernie held the stick loosely in his left hand and let the line run through his fingers as he tossed the mouse out into the water about ten feet from the bank. The undaunted rodent paddled a circle and headed for the shore. Before the mouse had swum a yard the water boiled up beneath it and a huge fish erupted out of the water, somersaulting and slapping its tail on the surface as it fell back into the lake. The line zipped between Ernie's fingers as he let the big trout run a short distance before braking it and setting the hook. Realizing that it had been hooked, the old lunker tried to dive down into the stumps and snags that lined the lake bottom, but Ernie had the strong line snubbed around his wrist and the fish found it could go nowhere except up. The fish jumped 30 inches or more out of the water, shaking its big head like a tarpon; then it dived and exploded out of the water even higher than before. But the fish had swallowed the hook along with the mouse. Its valiant struggle was to no avail.

Two more jumps, a last desperate attempt to run, and the old fish was exhausted. Carefully, Ernie pulled the fish up to the bank and lifted it out of the water with both hands. He held it up and talked to it in the old language and then he turned to me.

Lakas died bravely for our supper, John, and this beautiful old fish fought like a great warrior. I am proud of them both and I honor them. We shall eat with much respect this evening."

I agreed. It had never occurred to me to feel sorry for the steer that wound up in my hamburger, or the tuna that had given up its existence so I could be bored by a tuna and noodle casserole. It seemed the least a predator could do was to kill its own prey, look its victim in the eye, and say, "I'm hungry and I'm going to eat you. Thanks for dying so I can live."

The trout—more precisely, the char—was a Dolly Varden nearly two feet long and weighing perhaps eight or ten pounds. There was enough for several meals unless I got any hungrier by dinnertime. Ernie hung the fish over his shoulder and started up the steep slope. I looked around before following him.

Clouds were moving in from the southwest and the air had warmed up considerably. A breeze was beginning to stir, and catspaws gamboled across the smooth surface of the lake. A small boat carrying a single occupant purred up the lake toward us less than half a mile away, and I wondered who would be out on the lake this time of year more than a month before the opening of fishing season. I turned and followed Ernie, who was moving steadily up the slope. I began to imagine how wonderful that fine old valiant fish was going to taste.

CAIN

* * *

My wristwatch beeped me awake at 0400 on the third day of my purification. The fact that Ernie was still snoring softly was a compliment. It meant he was not worried that I would fail to get up in time to get the sweat lodge fire going. His built-in alarm clock would wake him up in about three hours and he would amble down to the sweat lodge, confident that I had taken care of everything. He would not be disappointed.

I got up, dressed, and left the cabin as quietly as I could. It was much warmer beneath the layer of clouds that blanked out the stars and made the darkness even blacker. Without Ernie to follow, I didn't think it was such a good idea to try to feel my way down the steep, narrow trail in absolute darkness, so I got my flashlight out of the car.

Thirty minutes later I had the fire going in the fire pit and I was practicing the invocation Ernie had taught me. When my tongue got tired and I grew hoarse from repeating the difficult Sahaptin sounds, I decided to look along the beach for more firewood.

A short distance from the sweat lodge, the beam of my flashlight locked on to a bit of whiteness in the willows that didn't seem to belong there. Looking closer, I saw that it was a cigarette butt, recently flicked into the willows from its appearance. Apparently, the smoker hadn't bothered to put it out first, because there was half an inch of intact ash still connected to the scorched filter. Trying to figure out where the smoker who flicked the butt might have been standing, I examined the surrounding area on my hands and knees until I found a footprint between two clumps of dead grass, and then another, and another. I soon concluded they were tracks made by one person leading to the sweat lodge and back to the beach again. I hadn't seen them at first among the tracks Ernie and I had made, because I hadn't been looking for them, but once noticed they stood out as if painted red.

The smoker's boots had almost new Panama soles, the same kind I had walked on in Vietnam—the same gouge-out-of-the-edge pattern that reminded me of the tire tread on a military vehicle. Following the tracks along the water, I found the marks in the mud where the smoker had beached his small boat a short distance from where Ernie and I got out of the water after our daily plunge. Most likely, it was the boater I had seen yesterday because I had not seen or heard anyone else on the lake since my arrival.

Looking for the tracks and trying to figure out who had made them, when, and for what reason, brought back memories of Chun and his patient tutelage in the fine art of tracking. He had taught me a great deal, but I had not mastered much more than the smallest part of what he had known. Chun and Ernie would have had enormous respect for each other.

I took an armload of wood back to the fire. As far as I could see, there was nothing sinister about a boater pulling up to a beach and walking around. Still, I couldn't shake a vague feeling of uneasiness.

Ernie managed to walk up behind me, even though I was listening for footsteps. The way I jumped when I finally discovered his presence gave away the fact I was not at ease about everything. Ernie looked at the tracks and the cigarette butt and shook his head. He didn't know who it was or why the person might have been snooping around.

The rain came just as we entered the sweat lodge, pecking noisily at the stiff canvas covering. I recited the invocation, which drew a comment from Ernie in Sahaptin, followed by what I assumed would have been the same affirmative grunt in either Sahaptin or English.

"I actually could recognize what you said, John. I am impressed," he added.

For some reason, I couldn't clear my mind as I had the previous day. I kept thinking about Chun. I kept seeing him on the

CAIN

floor of the cave, with black blood gurgling out of the hole in his throat, and Sonny's blackened face above me.

I crawled out of the sweat lodge into the driving rain, my eyes blurred with sweat, and my mind blurred with thoughts of other times and places. I felt the stranger's presence before I looked up and saw him standing there on the other side of the fire pit.

Water beaded and ran off what was left of the shine on his muddy new combat boots with Panama soles, but the rain had not yet softened the razor-sharp creases of his gray-green pants. From the valley of the plastic rain cover on his wide-brimmed Stetson hat, a stream of water poured off, just missing the end of the unlighted cigarette between his thin lips. He was young, not more than twenty-five, with short sideburns and gray eyes glaring sternly beneath yellow eyebrows. About my height, he stood rigidly erect with his chin tucked in and his shoulders back like a second lieutenant straight out of OCS taking command of his first platoon. His long raincoat was open and pulled back and his left hand gripped the butt of the holstered .357 revolver on his belt. A patch on his raincoat declared him to be an officer of the Washington State Fish and Game Department.

I stood up. Seeing that I was completely naked, he moved closer and looked me over with obvious contempt.

"Goddamned crazy Indians," he muttered to himself. "Anybody else in there, Chief?" He nodded toward the sweat lodge. "If there is, you tell him to come out 'cause I saw you bastards catch that fish yesterday and I'm haulin your sorry asses into court for fishin outta season."

I stared at him sullenly. I had already developed an instant and intense dislike for this prick and I realized right away that one of us was headed for a lot of trouble. With all of the execrative intonation I could muster, I looked straight at him and recited the invocation Ernie had taught me, complete with grimaces and denunciatory gestures. As a final touch, I managed to hit the toe of one of his boots with a big gob of spit. The wildlife agent stepped back, pulled his gun half out of the holster, and shook his finger at me with his other hand. I was certain he thought I had called him every kind of dipshit known to the Great Spirit.

"Don't get smart with me you son-of-a-bitch! I'm an officer of the law and I'm authorized to use deadly force if necessary!"

Sweet Jesus, what an asshole! Then, before we had a chance to get to know each other better, Ernie crawled out of the sweat lodge talking Sahaptin and carrying the pitchfork in his hand, unaware of what was going on, our talk drowned out by the rain pelting against the canvas lodge. As soon as the pitchfork came into view, the revolver came the rest of the way out of the agent's holster with his nervous finger already on the trigger.

I could see what was going to happen unless I stopped it.

Taking a step toward the agent, I grabbed the revolver and kept the cylinder from turning and the gun from firing while I twisted it quickly out of his hand. From the look on his face and the popping sound in his hand, I guessed I had probably broken his trigger finger, but I didn't care.

I emptied the cylinder into my hand and threw the shells out into the lake. Finding a willow branch handy, I pulled it off, jammed it tightly into the pistol's barrel and down into the empty cylinder, broke it off at the muzzle, and stuck the gun back into the idiot's holster. Then I spun him around so he was facing the beach and motioned for him to go.

With Ernie and me right behind him, he stumbled off toward the beach, clutching his disappointed trigger finger with his other hand and not saying a word. When we got to his boat, I started the outboard for him, gestured for him to get in, and pushed him off the beach. He turned the boat around and headed out into the rain-dimpled lake without looking back.

We watched the boat disappear around the edge of the lake toward the dam. Ernie said something in Sahaptin that had an appropriately vituperative quality about it, and I replied with the same affirmative grunt he had been giving me. Then wondering what he had said, I looked at him.

CAIN

"Loosely translated, John, I said the white man has shit for brains. I've lived here on this river most of my life, since before the dams when there used to be big runs of salmon, before the arrogant bastards decided when I could fish and how much I had to pay for the privilege." He spat bitterly into the lake. He waded chest deep into the water and submerged. I joined him. In a few minutes we came out of the water and walked back up the trail.

"He's going to be back, you know," I said.

"I know, but don't worry about it, John. I'll take care of it." He didn't seem the least bit concerned.

I thought it odd Ernie seemed so casual about the matter, because I was starting to think about the possible repercussions. Having to face charges of assaulting an officer, resisting arrest, and whatever else they might accuse me of was less than appealing to me. The game warden didn't have any proof we were poaching. He didn't even know who we were. But even a dumb-ass like him might find out an Indian lived in a cabin above the lake and assume the sweat lodge was used by that Indian.

When we got back to the cabin, Ernie built a fire and boiled some coffee. When it was ready we sat at the table and Ernie explained what he was going to do.

"Now would be a good time for you to seek out a guardian spirit, John. You have had three days in the sweat lodge and I can see you are ready. Besides, we won't be able to use the sweat lodge for a while with the game warden looking for us." He drew a map on the back of a bean can label and gave it to me. "Go to this place. There is good water there to drink and you can make a fire, but eat nothing. Take only the clothes you wear, a knife, and matches. In two days I'll join you and bring food."

"I have a friend who lives down the river a few miles. He will come and stay here. When the game warden comes looking for us, he will believe someone else lives here and he will look elsewhere for the two Indians he's after."

"Is your friend an Indian?"

"Yes."

"Is there any chance the game warden might mistake your friend for one of us?"

Ernie grinned. "No way. My friend is short, fat, and he only has one arm."

I laughed. "Sounds like it could work. But what about later? You have to live here. You could run into this asshole by accident sometime."

"Haven't figured that one out yet. I might decide just to scalp the son of a bitch."

I waited for him to smile, but he didn't.

"What are you going to do for the next two days?" I asked.

"The spirits will make me invisible," he replied, grinning this time.

"Since the spirits are going to take care of you, do you think we might help them out and make the rest of that trout disappear for breakfast?"

He laughed. "I've got some more of that cornmeal left, too, John."

CAIN

CHAPTER 15

Because His Heart Is Pure

Ernie fried hush puppies to go with the leftover trout, which we devoured down to the last inedible bone. Stuffing myself with the fried cornmeal fritters was like taking a sack lunch for the next two days, since it would probably take that long for the grease-sodden lumps to digest.

We cleaned up the cabin, buried the telltale remnants of the trout, and Ernie stuffed his accumulated rabbit skins into a garbage bag to be stashed up on the ridge where only he could find it. Everything of mine went into my duffle bag and into the Volkswagen. Ernie packed everything he needed into a small canvas rucksack and tossed it along with his old Winchester into the cab of his pickup. I waited for him to get his truck started, dubious as to whether the rusty old hulk would actually run. Seeing my surprise at how easily it started and how well it ran, Ernie rolled down the dirty window and stuck his head out, looking pleased with himself.

"I gave it a tune-up and a new battery for Christmas. Runs like a clock," he said proudly. He gave me his hand through the window and gripped mine with a strength that would have been impressive even in a much younger man. Growing serious, he said, "I have a feeling you will be successful in your quest, John. The spirits will know you are a good man."

"Thanks. You take care of yourself, Ernie. I'll see you in a couple of days."

He nodded, ground the transmission into reverse, and turned the truck around. He waved out the window as he rattled down the driveway. I got into my car and followed him out to the road, where we exchanged final waves and he turned left up the hill.

I turned down the hill and headed for the highway. The bean can label with Ernie's map neatly penciled on the back lay in the passenger's seat beside me. According to the map I would be spending the next two days on the west side of Mt. Adams, in a place revealed to Ernie by his grandfather nearly three quarters of a century ago. It was the place where Ernie as a small boy had kept his own vigil and had found his own guardian spirit.

* * *

Trees grew where detritus, volcanic ash, and organic matter had accumulated in the crevices in the lava and had, over centuries, turned to plain old dirt. A finger of a newer flow lay on top of the old and stood eight feet or more above it in a thick basaltic slab. Walking uphill along the wall of the lava flow, I came to an alcove where the stone had split and separated, forming a blind channel about ten feet wide at the entrance, and perhaps seventy-five feet long. The uphill side of the ten-foot-high lava wall was undercut about five feet, and the sharp-edged overhang formed a natural shelter. A fire-blackened block of lava that had split cleanly off the main wall sat in front of the overhang in the rift. Fortunately, the area was not high enough to retain the snow that must have covered it at various times during the last few months. But another thousand feet up the mountain there was plenty of snow left.

I wondered how many frightened children had huddled here, sitting in front of the fire, with the heat reflecting off the stone, waiting for some sign from the spirit world—an omen, an epiphany, a realization, something out of the ordinary. But then, just being in the lava field at night with the mountain towering above you would make everything seem out of the ordinary.

CAIN

Night, fire, isolation—each has the power to stimulate the imagination, to trigger the complex autonomic exchanges between the body and the brain. In concert, they synergistically break down the bounds of perception and the barriers between mind and matter. They awaken genetic memories of archetypal human experience going all the way back to the beginnings of consciousness: fear, wonder, loneliness. They provide the stage and the atmosphere for a psychological drama that begins in the subconscious, expands into conscious awareness, and finally becomes a solipsistic dream, creating the fabric of each person's universe—subtly, powerfully, absolutely, irrevocably.

The final reality of spirits, extraterrestrials, and chimera of every conceivable and inconceivable type, of every possible and impossible nature, lay in the mind. The question of objectivity becomes irrelevant because what we experience as real is, at the psychological level, real. Whether or not something exists independently of the mind raises legitimate questions with practical implications, but it is not a question germane to the experience of the mind itself.

There had been no rain in the afternoon. The sun had even found its way through the dark clouds scudding beneath the dirty gray overcast. But now the clouds were thicker, blacker, causing daylight to fade early and promising a long, wet night.

Dead trees lay everywhere along the lava flow in every stage of decomposition, and gathering firewood was an easy task. In half an hour, I had enough wood stacked by the rock and under the overhang for an all-night vigil. With the fire's crackle echoing off the surfaces of the lava alcove, I sat cross-legged under the ledge on a bed of dead branches, and rested my head against the cold, hard lava.

The rain started sometime during the uncertain period in which premature dusk was transformed into Cimerian night. I awoke with a start. The raindrops hissed against the heated rock like a shower of tiny vipers. Looking into the fire deprived me of night vision, and I could see nothing beyond the pale of the fire's wavering light except shadows dancing like black ghosts.

I had stacked some of the wood under the overhang to keep it dry and I added a piece to the fire. No one knew where I was except Ernie. It was a place next to impossible to find without instructions, and not that easy to find with a good map. No one from a distance could see the fire hidden in the lava fissure. No one was going to stumble onto this place by accident. I told myself there was nothing here that I had not brought with me in my own mind. Somehow, that provided little comfort.

I thought about Beth and guiltily realized that it was one of the few times I had thought about her in several days. I reviewed the events of the past three days, trying to put them into perspective. In the process, I fell asleep again. I was violently blasted awake by a brilliant, sizzling flash of lightning striking something, probably a tree, followed almost instantaneously by a deafening, explosive crack of thunder that sent shock waves through the lava and continued its rumbling reverberations for several seconds afterwards. A few minutes later a second bolt arced crookedly into the hillside, lighting up the low, ragged clouds dragging their heavy tentacles of rain across the lava flow. Another teeth-rattling boom bludgeoned my eardrums.

Torrents of rain mixed with snow hosed down the alcove for several minutes, as if bent on extinguishing my fire. I retrieved some of the still-burning wood and started another small fire under the overhang. Trees toppled and snapped off with loud cracks and pops before the sudden onslaught of wind that roared and crashed through the timber like an invisible avalanche. Gusts howled through the alcove and I had to shield with my body the smoky, nascent flames under the overhang to keep them from being blown out.

Within ten minutes the disturbance had flashed, rumbled, blasted, and deluged its way farther up the valley, taking its violent entourage with it. Only a dark drizzle, stunned into a murmur by the storm, continued to come down. The wind-driven

CAIN

rain had found its way under the overhang and everything was wet, including me. The new fire was sickly, reluctant to feed on the damp wood I offered it. I curled myself around the tiny fire to nurture it and to absorb what little warmth it produced. My eyes burned and watered and I was fighting the urge to cough the acrid smoke out of my lungs.

I hated to cough. On a recon mission, coughing meant revealing your presence and position. It could mean capture or death for you and for those who depended upon your silence, and upon whose silence you depended. And so I had come to hate coughs, sneezes, and hiccups. Not that there was any reason to conceal my presence now, but I still hated to cough. Burying my face in my coat, I tried to expel the irritating phlegm from my chest as softly as I could. My attempts were not very effective, and I lay on the wet ground, wrapped around the fuming, faltering fire, painfully struggling to avoid a fit of involuntary hacking.

So where was the vision, the sign? I had no idea what I was supposed to see, hear, or feel. Maybe it had already come and gone and I hadn't recognized it. Maybe I was just too impatient or too uncomfortable to be receptive. Maybe there was nothing to be receptive to. I nursed the sulking, smoldering excuse for a fire until finally I dozed off, despite my intention to stay awake in order to keep the fire going.

The next time I woke up, I thought at first I was dreaming. Everything was dead silent and pitch black. With a rush of disappointment, I felt the hardness of the ground beneath my aching bones, and the cold gnawing at me. Other than my own snuffling breath, there was not another sound. I didn't move. There was a hint of warmth beneath me where my body heat had warmed the ground, and I debated whether I should continue to lie there or get up and try to build another fire. As I lay there, I discovered I was also hungry and thirsty. Finally, however, it was the pressure on my bladder that forced me to try to unlock my stiff joints and get up. Almost at the precise moment I began to stir, something more persuasive than a full bladder caused me to lie quietly a while longer. I thought I heard footsteps.

Being afraid of the dark had never been one of the great bugaboos of my childhood. But neither did I have any older siblings to take charge of systematically scaring the crap out me with ghost stories and eyewitness accounts of monsters in the closet and goblins under the bed. Like any child however, I did have a healthy respect for the possibilities inherent in darkness. I always found it best not to tempt fate by being too complacent in the absence of light.

Now, lying in a strange place on a black night, straining to identify a strange sound, I still would not admit to being scared. To be scared was to show fear; ergo, not showing fear implied not being scared.

Bullshit! Everyone is afraid of the unknown. It's just that not everyone becomes irrational enough about it to let it adversely affect his behavior and judgment.

I could stop the sound of my breathing, but I was having trouble hearing over the noisy thump of my heartbeat. There it was again, a scraping sound and several soft thuds.

Was it Ernie? I didn't believe even Ernie could walk across a lava field in total darkness, and I didn't see any light anywhere. For that matter, I doubted any large wild animal would venture into the natural pitfall of the lava field without at least the benefit of moonlight. So what the hell was making that noise? I felt around and found a stick of firewood that made a suitable club, and quietly got to my feet. Feeling my way along the wall of lava, I worked my way out to the opening of the alcove, from where I would be able to see any light within fifty yards. I gripped the wet piece of wood tightly, peering into the depthless black curtain of night, waiting. No light, no sound.

After a few minutes, my bladder reminded me it had been on hold long enough, and I had to relieve myself. It was so dark, for all I knew I could have been urinating on whatever it was that had made the noise. I felt extremely vulnerable. All my senses were on full alert as I stood expectantly with my back pressed against the cold face of the lava wall. After ten minutes or so, I had heard nothing more and I was beginning to shiver uncontrollably. I had to start another fire and get warmed up. When it got light, I could check out the area and generate a little body heat by moving around.

I felt my way back into the alcove and lit a match to find tinder for a new fire. Alternately working by feel and lighting matches to check my progress, I managed to pare enough dry shavings from the remnants of the second fire to make a third attempt. When I finally got a good-sized blaze going beneath the overhang, I transferred part of it to the original fire site in front of the block of lava. In thirty minutes my wet clothes were beginning to steam and my shivering was beginning to subside, as I sat between the two fires and waited for morning. With the darkness held at bay by the firelight, I could tell myself I had no reason to be concerned about some mysterious sound I may or may not have heard.

Morning was a bleak, soggy affair ushered in by a cold mist. Even so, I was glad to see it come. When it was light enough, I set out to find water and to check the area for an explanation of the sound that had been the source of so much adrenaline during the night. I quickly saw what Ernie had meant when he said water would be available. Every depression in the lava rock, from the size of a thimble to the size of a bathtub, held a pool of fresh rainwater, and I quenched my thirst with the cold, sweet water from a basin just outside the alcove.

Criss-crossing the area within a fifty-yard radius around the entrance to the alcove, I looked long and hard for a trace of a footprint, or any other sign. There was nothing to see except wet rock, patches of wet moss, and a few stunted junipers. Farther over in the timber, there was a wide swath of splintered tree trunks, sheared off as if by a low flying airplane. The scorched halves of a solitary dead tree lay where it had been smitten by the lightning bolt the night before.

I climbed onto the elevated finger of the newer lava and walked over to the ledge above the alcove, where the woodsmoke was hanging in the mist. I could look down into the fire in front of the lava block. It was burning low and I would have to add more wood soon if I wanted to keep it going. Even from my vantage point, I could see little of the surrounding landscape. The valley below faded into a pearlescent mist, as did the top half of Mt. Adams rising above me. Having seen all there was to see, I turned to go gather more firewood. Six feet back from the edge of the rift lay a piece of rock about the size and roughly the shape of a small book. Most of the horizontal surfaces of the lava were covered with thick moss, as was the small, rectangular piece I was looking at, but something about it caught my eye, and I walked over for a closer inspection. I realized the piece had been moved quite recently. Kneeling down, I examined the sharp-edged impression where the moss had grown around the rock, and from which the rock had been displaced by an inch or more.

Stumbled over in the dark perhaps? But by what? Was this where the sound had come from, from someone or something prowling around on the ledge above the overhang? I scoured the area thoroughly and didn't find another hint as to what had moved the rock. I couldn't decide which bothered me more, that I could so easily be sneaked up on and observed, or that there was someone or something out there with an interest in observing me, and possessing the stealth to do it. All I could think of was that Ernie must be sneaking around keeping tabs on me. Nothing else made any sense. Actually, that didn't make any sense, either, unless Ernie had been serious when he said the spirits would make him invisible. Whoever or whatever it was, if it came back tonight it would find a few things that weren't on the regular menu.

The first order of business was to gather enough firewood to keep a small fire burning all day and a big fire burning all night. I spent the rest of the morning carrying and dragging dead wood until I had collected enough to form a pile taller than I was and nearly as wide as the alcove.

More cold water helped temporarily fill the growing void in my stomach. I could stand being hungry for another day, but

CAIN

without food, I would become more and more susceptible to the cold. The chilly water I was drinking, although necessary, made it even more difficult to keep warm as the temperature hovered at what I guessed to be around forty degrees.

Although I was sweating after the exertion of gathering wood, I built up the fire and warmed myself. The continuous fire had dried and warmed the area directly in front of it beneath the overhang. I was able to bask in the reflected heat and doze almost comfortably into the afternoon, stirring only to add more wood to the fire. I had to do several more things before dark, but there would be plenty of time.

There was also plenty of time to think. If I satisfied Ernie's criteria for having acquired a guardian spirit, he would show me the secret lava tube, the dwelling place of the Sasquatch, an entity he called the Tah-tah kle'-ah.

Then what? What did I expect to find there? More importantly, what did I plan to do with what I found or didn't find there? Even if I found a whole colony of Sasquatches who where willing to make the talk show circuit and sign autographs, I wouldn't, I couldn't betray Ernie's trust.

So what was the point of all this? I had set out to vindicate to the scientific community my father's belief in the existence of the Sasquatch. Somewhere along the way, my quest had taken a path that was leading in a different direction, to an uncertain destination.

Spread throughout the community of scientists, academicians, and other professional intellectuals, who generally believed themselves to be the finders and keepers of the truth to begin with, were the defenders of dogma. These were the new inquisitors, who had zealously assumed the responsibility of preserving an intellectual status quo. Certain influential individuals, powerful cliques, controlling committees, and omnipotent organizations patrolled the borders of scientific thought to keep out new ideas and undesirable theories; dealt harshly with internal unrest; and carefully managed the flow of scientific propaganda.

I knew, of course, that my feeling of disgust distorted my view of things, but I also knew that no institution could exist for very long without a reactionary core of traditionalists to provide coherence and to resist schism. Religions, governments, cultures, economies, and sciences existed only so long as they could control and manage change, and represent it as the natural and inevitable growth of preexisting ideas. Otherwise, they were subject to painful reformation or replacement by new institutions, which in turn would eventually have to circle the wagons against the encroachment of even more modern thinking, ad infinitum.

Whether in a council of bishops or in a senate of university faculty members, one would always find a current of narrow mindedness, snobbishness, a readiness to cry witch at the first rumor of heresy, an eagerness to burn any dissenter at the stake or to slowly crush a heretic beneath a heap of obloquy. And along with the willingness to persecute, one would find the unwritten obligation for the inner circle to shield its members against accusations of incompetent, unethical, or illegal behavior—as long as there was no insurmountable threat to the rest of the group or to the institution they served.

Mother had believed him, so had the Cunninghams, and Dad knew that I knew the truth. Did he need to be vindicated to those who didn't care and who didn't deserve to know the truth? Not that they would recognize the truth or acknowledge it, even if I rubbed their noses in it.

My father, a brilliant, decent man, had been vilified and ridiculed for expressing and maintaining an unacceptable opinion based on what he believed to be the truth. Danner, on the other hand, was permitted to commit unconscionable acts of depravity, not only with impunity, but with academic accolades from at least some colleagues and administrators who must have known full well the depths of his degeneracy. Here I was, soon to have a doctorate and probably headed for a seat in the same academic society that tolerated, even fostered, such heinous hypocrisy. Sid Cunningham had somehow managed to keep his academic career

CAIN

in the no man's land between the good old boys of the university and the hunted underground of freethinkers. I didn't know if I would be able to do that.

Jesus, how I hated conundrums. What the hell was I supposed to do? What could I do? I decided right then and there, if I asked another question I couldn't answer I was going to club myself into unconsciousness with a piece of firewood.

Abandoning my unsettling contemplations, I took up the tasks remaining to be accomplished before dark. Two at a time, I carried a dozen rocks weighing fifteen pounds or so each back to the fire from the edge of the timber, where I had spotted them while gathering wood. I set the rocks around the edge of the fire to serve later as portable heaters. My plans included being away from the fire during the night, and I intended to stay warm with the heat stored in the rocks.

I then used a piece of bark to scoop up a few pounds of ash and dry dirt from the burned-out second fire beneath the overhang. Climbing to the top of the ledge, I carefully sprinkled a thin coat of the fine powder all along the ledge and back about four feet. Anything walking around up there tonight was going to leave some footprints. I liked the idea so well, I decided to dust the other side of the rift and the entrance to the alcove. The afternoon had been dry and I was counting on it to stay that way so the powder wouldn't be washed away. That the powder would turn into a thin paste from the ubiquitous dampness would not impair its function.

While I was gathering firewood earlier, I had come across a nifty two-handed club thirty inches long, two inches in diameter, with a heavy knot on one end. I knew the puny piece of wood wouldn't impress a prowling bear, but it was more than adequate for getting the attention of a human prowler, should the need arise.

By the time it got really dark, the fire was flaming above the ledge and sending a column of sparks another thirty feet higher. It had occurred to me such a big fire might keep whatever it was from coming around, but it was the only way I would have the light I needed to see anything that did come around.

The rocks around the fire had heated more quickly than I had anticipated and they were too hot to carry when I tried to pick them up. I wrapped my coat around one and carried it up to a niche in the ledge about fifty feet from the overhang, where I could surround myself with the hot rocks and keep the area under surveillance by the light of the fire. The niche was easily accessible from the alcove, and I would be able to quickly climb up and down to keep the fire burning brightly and to exchange cool rocks for hot ones all night if necessary. Hopefully, I wouldn't get caught moving rocks back and forth if something showed up. Moving the rest of the rocks away from the fire a little so they wouldn't get too hot to handle, I finished carrying some more up to the observation post and settled in for another long night. With any luck—ok, with a lot of luck—maybe I would find the answer to at least one question by morning.

An aura of ambient light hovered dimly over the lava flow immediately surrounding the alcove, as the fire blazed into the night. The niche was well suited to my purpose, and I was able to keep the ledge in view without being blinded by the fire itself. At the same time, I could see the fire when I wanted to. The hot rocks worked better after they had cooled down, and I was able to stuff one inside my coat against my stomach and place another one between my legs. For the first part of the night, I slipped down into the alcove every few hours, exchanging a rock or two and adding wood to the fire. Fortunately it did not rain. The cold, damp air remained still, as if holding its breath in expectation.

My eyelids grew heavy, and the dark outline of the ledge above the firelit alcove kept going out of focus. Barely able to stay awake, I nodded, catching myself and jerking back, but gradually nodding farther and farther, until I startled myself awake by banging my forehead against the ledge.

So far I had seen nothing, heard nothing. Maybe the fire had been too big after all. Maybe there had never been anything to see

CAIN

in the first place. Finally, the desire to sleep subverted my waning interest in continuing the watch. The next thing I was aware of was waking up with a feeling that I was not alone.

The perimeter of blackness had closed in as the fire had burned down while I was asleep. I could hardly distinguish anything above the ledge against the faint glow rising out of the alcove and evaporating into the surrounding blackness. I squinted, trying to focus in the absence of anything distinct on which to focus.

As I stared into the blur of darkness, a piece of the night assumed a form and moved soundlessly toward the ledge. I looked at it obliquely, letting the uncertain image fall on the light-sensitive rods around the periphery of my retinas, clearly detecting movement without detail. The form flowed into the lesser darkness along the ledge with the liquid movement of an animal, but with a shape and stance suggestive of a man.

The fire popped, sending a momentary flicker of light flaring up out of the alcove. Eyes straining, pulse hammering, I beheld clearly, for an instant, a massive, hairy hulk poised warily above the alcove. It looked at me without alarm as the light faltered and faded, stood erect for a few seconds, and then slowly dissolved back into the darkness and was gone.

I rubbed my eyes and took a deep breath. Only the soft sizzle and occasional pop of the fire broke the silence. The only movement was the smoke ascending and disappearing into the canopy of the night. I smelled the smoke, felt the weight of the rocks against my empty stomach and stiff legs as I sat scrunched into the niche, my heart still hammering with excitement. I wasn't dreaming and I wasn't hallucinating. What I had seen was real. I was sure of it, but the objective confirmation that would come with the tracks I knew I'd find would be welcome and deeply satisfying just the same.

The creature hadn't talked to me. It hadn't taught me a power song or given me any special powers, but the mere fact that it had been there and I had seen it was an omen, the sign I had been looking for. I could not imagine the magnitude of the mystical influence such an experience might have exerted over the mind of an Indian child.

Everything seemed clear to me now. Obviously, I was too old, too civilized for such an experience to open my mind completely to the mystery and power of animism. I was as close to the perceptions of my ancestors as I was likely to get. What I had seen was a natural phenomenon, and I was never going to experience it as anything else. I did not have the necessary cultural preparation for my mind to merge with it or for it to merge with me in any way that I would know or understand. Not knowing the language of the spirits, I could not comprehend them, but I believed I might have been privileged to overhear the unintelligible whisperings of their strange utterances. Perhaps that is why finding the Sasquatch was so important to my dad. He desperately wanted a glimpse of what primitive man had once known: a spiritual oneness with nature.

I knew I couldn't enter paradise, but at least I had seen enough of it from a distance to know for certain that it existed. That was closer than most civilized people ever got.

"Thank you, Ernie," I said aloud. "Thank you."

I climbed down from the niche, stiff and tired, my tailbone aching from hours of sitting on the rock shelf with my knees up and a rock in my lap. The big fire had heated up the whole alcove, and the area beneath the overhang was as warm as an incubator. I consolidated the remains of the fire, added more wood, and lay down. It felt good to stretch out and absorb the heat, and I fell asleep quickly.

A dream came in which I found myself following the large, deep footprints of a Sasquatch. In dream time, I tracked the creature for many days, but came to a point where the tracks ended abruptly. I could not understand how the creature could have vanished along with its tracks. Then I saw the creature in the distance, looking back at me over its shoulder as it strode across a clearing and disappeared into a dark forest.

CAIN

Leaping and bounding toward the place where t had appeared, I came to another set of tracks that should have belonged to the creature. Instead, they turned out to be the footprints of a man wearing boots—footprints vaguely familiar, although I didn't know why. I followed the seemingly endless tracks of the man. After many days, I finally gave up. When I turned and looked at my own tracks, I saw the footprints of the Sasquatch over the bootprints and I realized that I had changed places with the creature. The familiar bootprints I had been following had been my own.

It was daylight when I woke up. The details and impressions of the dream were immediate, remarkably vivid, fascinating. I should have felt intellectually manic, but the juices just weren't flowing. I had a hard time concentrating. I felt weak, listless, disoriented. All I really wanted to think about was food. I could barely force myself to build up the fire. I wanted to go check for footprints, but I lay down again instead, unwilling to leave the comfort of the fire. All morning I lay by the fire, thinking any minute I would get up and go look for footprints, and yet I just continued to lie there.

I recognized the symptoms as the same ones food deprivation had caused during several phases of the Army Ranger course I had struggled through after coming back from Vietnam. I had gone for weeks on minimum rations during that grueling experience and had been expected to perform my assignments flawlessly while suffering from near starvation and a lack of sleep. It had been a long time since I had gone without any food at all for so long. Energy for my mental and physical functioning was running low. Thinking was hard; turning thoughts into actions even harder. Good God! It hadn't even been two days. I wondered if I would still have what it took to make it through the Ranger course again.

Eventually I forced myself to get up and go get a drink, and then to climb up onto the lava flow to look for tracks. They were there by the ledge, as I had not doubted they would be: half again as long as my foot-long bootprints and a third wider. The impressions of the five toes in the wet powder were quite clear, showing big toes that splayed out considerably. The footprints looked as if they might have been made by a very large, flat-footed human, except the toes were disproportionately shorter and more nearly of the same length than those of a typical human foot.

I didn' find any tracks where I had dusted at the entrance to the alcove, nor did I find any on the other side of the rift. Apparently, the creature I had seen had been by itself. Unfortunately, I hadn't seen it well enough to determine its sex or its precise color. All I knew was that it was big and covered with hair or fur, that it was very agile, and that it had an extraordinary ability to move about easily in the dark.

I waited for Ernie to show up well into the afternoon. I stared into the fire and slept, at times unable to distinguish staring from sleeping. If Ernie didn't come soon, I'd have to leave. I didn't want to spend another night without food, and I had to give myself enough time to walk the two miles back to my car before dark. But he said he'd come and I'd wait as long as possible.

Ernie arrived a short time later. I looked up and he was standing by the fire with his rucksack slung over one shoulder, watching me. I sat up and stretched, a big smile on my face.

"Man, am I glad to see you," I said.

"You look like shit, John." He grinned. Good thing I brought some pizza with me." He set the rucksack down in front of me. "Want to heat it up?" he asked.

I already had the greasy box out of the rucksack and was tearing it open. "Nope," I replied as I stuffed a piece into my mouth. I didn't know where or when he had obtained the pizza, but I had never tasted anything as satisfying in my entire life.

"There's some pop in there, too," Ernie said. "Thought you could use some good food for a change."

"It's wonderful," I tried to say with my mouth full, "damned near as good as your hush puppies."

After wolfing down the first few pieces half chewed, I slowed down and savored the remaining wedges of rubbery cheese and leathery pepperoni. Between bites of pizza and gulps of foamy

CAIN

pop, I described the events of the past two days to Ernie, who nodded and grunted, but did not comment. I picked off the melted cheese and tossed the box into the fire. A long, booming belch signaled a satisfactory breaking of my two-day fast.

Feeling as if I had swallowed one of the twelve-pound rocks that had rested on the outside of my stomach during most of the previous night, I showed Ernie the tracks by the ledge. He knelt and traced them reverently with his finger, chanting softly in Sahaptin. There was no mistaking the fact that Ernie was deeply impressed. After a few minutes, he methodically wiped out the footprints with his hand. Rising, he addressed each of the four cardinal points of the compass in Sahaptin and then turned to me.

"This is more than I expected, John, much more. The man-bear has taken an interest in you. He has allowed you to see him, and has appeared to you in a dream. In time, he will make himself known to you in other ways. It is important that you do not talk of this experience, not even to Beth. I'm sorry. I know it will be hard, but it is the way it must be. There will come a time for these things to be known by others. I know that before I die I will see you dance in the winter ceremony and hear you sing the song of your spirit power. This has turned out well for you, John. I could not be more pleased."

"But Ernie, I don't know a power song and I don't know how to do a power dance."

He smiled. "Trust me. You will."

I couldn't help feeling that Ernie was reading more into my experience than was actually there, but it certainly had been an extraordinary experience and I was thankful the old man had not been disappointed. Whatever the experience meant, I did have a powerful feeling of its portentousness. Buried beneath the cold ashes of skeptical rationalism, there still smoldered a fervent ember of hope that what Ernie believed to be true might possibly be.

Back in the alcove, we removed the larger pieces of wood from the fire and left the rest to burn itself out. During the hike back to the road, Ernie told me he was driving over to Toppenish to stay with friends until the one-armed neighbor at Ernie's place had been visited by the game warden and it was safe to go home. I asked him if he had talked to the neighbor. He said he hadn't, but a prearranged visual signal had informed him it still wasn't safe when he had checked it earlier in the day.

It was nearly dark when we reached the road and the vehicles. I said I was heading back to Seattle and asked Ernie if he were headed south to take Highway 14 up the Columbia to Highway 97, which ran northeast over Satus Pass directly to Toppenish. He said he liked the country better to the north and he always went over Highway 12 through Randle and Packwood, and over White Pass to Yakima, and then on down to Toppenish.

"It gives me a chance to see the Tieton River country where my people, the Taitnapam, came from," he explained.

Ernie gave me one of his powerful hugs when we said goodbye. He didn't object to my suggestion that I follow him back down to Woodland and up I-5 to the Toledo cutoff, where he would turn off to intersect Highway 12. Before he got into his pickup, he said, "We'll go to the place of the man-bear in a month or two. I'll let you know when the time is right."

Ernie never exceeded a sedate fifty miles-per-hour during the hour and a half it took to reach his turnoff at Toledo. When he turned off the freeway, I flashed my lights and honked as I passed him, and he did the same. It would be a while before I saw him again and I missed the old man already. A short distance up the freeway at Chehalis would be a good place to get some coffee and to call Beth and the Cunninghams.

I felt a little strange, like a time traveler. However, I wasn't sure whether I felt as if I had just returned to the present from an expedition into the prehistoric past, or as if I had somehow been thrust into a remote future from a prehistoric present. The lights, the noise, the movement of vehicles, and the proximity to other people in other vehicles on the freeway were a little overwhelming. I had stepped from a sanctuary of quietude and darkness into the accelerated, confusing bustle of an alien world.

Still, it wasn't so alien that I couldn't look forward to holding Beth close to me—especially after I'd had a long shower and a good cup of coffee.

CHAPTER 16

She with Profound and Fragile Lips

I pulled into the Cunningham's driveway a few minutes after nine. I had talked to Maxine from Chehalis, and they were expecting me. I had also called Beth. She was expecting me to pick her up around ten. Maxine was looking out the window by the time I got out of the car, and both she and Dr. Cunningham were standing at the front door when I reached it. Dr. Cunningham latched on to my hand as if he had thought he would never see me again, and Maxine gave me her full smothering-hug greeting. I became a little self-conscious because it occurred to me how dirty, smelly, and disheveled I had become.

"Sorry I'm so filthy," I apologized. "I just came straight here without stopping to clean up. I should really go take a shower and change my clothes."

"Nonsense," Maxine objected, "you're fine. Come in and have a bowl of soup and a glass of milk. You must be starved. I know you'll be anxious to go see Beth, so we won't make you stay very long. Come along, now, and have some nice hot soup and tell us how it went." Maxine hooked her arm in mine and pulled me toward the kitchen, mud-caked boots, and all.

The Cunninghams respected my promise to Ernie not to disclose the privileged parts of my experience, but they were greatly interested in my adventure and wanted to know everything I was free to tell them. They were appalled at the incident with the game warden and fascinated by my description of the storm on my first night in the wilderness. I'm convinced that the fact I

CAIN

couldn't tell them everything made them certain something mysterious and wonderful had taken place. I had the feeling they were probably as excited by the mystery of it all as they would have been by the parts I couldn't talk about.

Maxine's homemade pea soup was heavenly. After slurping down three bowls of it, I declined another refill out of embarrassment at my piggishness. She was delighted to have rescued me from starvation. Somewhat reassured I would not drop dead of malnutrition, she gave me a bag of freshly baked cookies and herded me toward the door, telling me I shouldn't keep Beth waiting. I thanked her for the soup and cookies as she pushed me out the door. As I hurried down the front steps, Dr. Cunningham called after me.

"Stop by my office tomorrow, John. I have something I know you'll want to see."

"Ok, I'll see you tomorrow. Goodnight."

A quick shower and change of clothes made me feel almost presentable. At ten minutes to ten, I bounded up the steps to the front door of Beth's dorm, bursting with ardor and anticipation, and the three bowls of pea soup sloshing heavily in my stomach.

I called Beth on the visitor's phone in the waiting room, and she said she'd be right down. An excited piquancy colored her voice, the sound of which aroused a sweaty, sweet sensation in me—like a transfusion of hot maple syrup and couple of wraps in a steaming blanket of buckwheat cakes. I thought I had missed her, but hearing her voice, I found it impossible to imagine how I could have existed five days without her. Eroticism, affection, admiration, and other feelings I couldn't begin to name or describe commandeered my composure. If Beth didn't hurry, she was going to find nothing but a heap of swirling ashes in my place—the remains of one consumed by an inferno of impatience and desire.

I heard her running down the stairs. There was hardly anyone else around, and I knew it had to be her. When she saw me waiting at the foot of the stairs, she lit up the lobby with her thousand-watt smile. We embraced with the intensity and complexity of two octopi: touching, squeezing, kissing. I'm certain if I had seen another couple in such a public display, I would have been thoroughly disgusted, but at that moment she and I were the only two people in the world and we could not get close enough to each other.

"You can't imagine how good you feel to me, Beth."

"Hold me, John. God, you feel so good to me, too."

After a few minutes the hugging, kissing, purring, and sighing tapered off. We walked over to a couch and sat down, still holding hands.

A wistful, expectant expression informed her beautiful bright eyes and sensual mouth. Everything about her overwhelmed me. Her beauty lay far, far deeper than just in her appearance. There was a sentience, a presence, about her that imbued her with pulchritude, substance, depth. As I lost myself in her eyes, I knew that from the other side of that lovely face the complementary half of our mutual soul recognized its counterpart in me. Neither of us could ever be whole without the other. My feeling for Beth transcended anything physical, yet it could find its immediate expression only in inadequate, unsatisfying words, or in the fulfillment of sexual intimacy.

"Shall we go to my place," I asked.

"Yes," she replied softly, eagerly.

Shortly after ten the following day, I went to Dr. Cunningham's office in Guthrie Hall. He was with a student, and another one was waiting to see him. Taking a book out of my briefcase, I leaned against the wall outside his door and read for half an hour until he was free.

Dr. Cunningham pushed the manila envelope across his desk toward me with unrestrained satisfaction. "Take a look, John. I believe we have Danner . . . have the scrofulous bastard by the balls, as a matter of fact."

It was not the kind of comment I would have expected from Dr. Cunningham, and I looked at him in surprise.

CAIN

"Oh don't be such a prude, John. Surely, you can grant an old man an occasional crudity. I'm the last English-speaking person on this earth whose conversation is not replete with filthy language and you know it. But do open it up." He gestured impatiently.

"I'm sorry to hear Maxine has succumbed to the influences of foul language. I rather thought she might have held out even longer than you."

"Oh, very well, the next to the last person on this earth. Just open the envelope and repress the repartee if you will."

I unfolded the clasp and opened the envelope, peeking inside first and then dumping the contents out on the desk. A strip of negatives and a dozen five by seven photographs slid out. The photos were dim and grainy, but there was no mistaking what was going on in them, or, for the most part, who was doing it.

Half of the photos clearly showed Danner enjoying the sexual favors of Janice Rawlings atop his desk. At least two pictures showed Ms. Rawling's face well enough to suggest she was not a reluctant bestower of those favors. The remainder of the photos revealed a well-endowed, undressed female on her hands and knees in Danner's office, and Danner, wearing a different pair of pants around his ankles this time, vigorously addressing her shapely posterior. None of the photos showed her face completely. All of the pictures showed enough of Danner's office and the view out of his second story window to identify where they had been taken. The calendar on his desk was even visible in several of the shots.

"How in the world did you get these?"

"Well, I'm afraid I had to borrow some equipment from the experimental psych lab and employ the services of a couple of grad students. They put a camera in Danner's office and got together a team to monitor it. This is what they came up with over a period of about six weeks."

"Pretty devious."

"Yes, and unethical, illegal, underhanded, etc., etc. Certainly less than poetic, but rich in irony, and essential for any kind of justice to prevail. The end justifies the means in this case, don't you think?"

"You won't get any moral objections from me. But how did you convince your students to undertake this? They must have known that if they got caught all of you would be in over your heads. They could be kicked out, you could be fired, and all of you could face criminal charges."

"Yes, don't remind me. Actually, it wasn't my idea. After you and Beth came to me, I talked to a doctoral student of my mine who is a former FBI agent. He's the one who suggested placing Danner under surveillance to get incriminating evidence against him."

"Is he the one who rigged the camera?"

"Yes. He has a niece who is in her first year here at the university. When I told him about Danner, he insisted on helping us. Apparently, he got a lot of experience gathering this kind of information in his work with the FBI.

"I know you wouldn't have consulted this guy if you didn't trust him, but how well do you know him?"

"Don't worry. I've known Bryan for nearly twenty years—a nice man, very intelligent. He was a student of mine back in the early sixties. After he graduated and got into the FBI, he used to write me and come around to see me occasionally when he was in town. He worked out of the Seattle office for years. Now he wants to start a second career as a psychologist."

"Did he have any recommendations about how to use this evidence?"

"Extortion is one option. Danner gets a copy with a suggestion to resign and a hint about how the University president, the newspapers—including the campus newspaper—the board of regents, and his wife might appreciate having copies as well."

"I'd hate for Mrs. Danner to have to go through that," I said, "She's a nice lady."

"Yes, I know, I've met her. I believe they also have two daughters. I certainly have no desire to hurt his family, but if they don't know about him already, it's probably only a matter of time before they find out anyway. I'm betting, though, he'd find it easier just to leave. I'm afraid, however, we won't accomplish much more than inconveniencing him, because he'll just get a job somewhere else and pick up where he left off.

"I think a second option, John, would be to go public with the evidence straight away. It might be better to ruin him with a public scandal. If this got out, he wouldn't even be able to get a job teaching in an obedience school for dogs. Of course, it's up to you and Beth. Do you just want to get rid of him and let him prey on young women somewhere else, or do you want to expose him, with a good chance of making sure he never gets another position as a teacher to abuse?"

"What if we force him to stay here and clean up his act?" I asked.

"What do you mean?"

"We have the goods on him—sort of. We can threaten to expose him if he doesn't stay away from his students. If he stays here, somebody can keep an eye on him. That way his family doesn't get hurt; the problem is solved. There's no retribution involved, I know, but at least no innocent parties are hurt. If some of his victims decide to complain about him, well, *c'est la vie*."

"That's very civilized, John, but I wouldn't count on its working quite that way. What makes you think Danner can change his ways so easily? He's a smart bugger. Maybe he'd just be a little more discrete about his activities. It might even prove enough of a challenge to interest him in coming up with something of his own."

"Such as?"

"That's just it. Who knows what his Machiavellian mind might come up with. We might just wind up getting burned with our own torch. He won't be grateful, you know. Besides, who is going to monitor him? Do you want to take on that responsibility? I know I don't."

"He would be madder if we exposed him."

"Undoubtedly, but he'd no longer have the position or credibility to support any manipulations of the system. You have to bear in mind, John, that the people who are going to be hurt in this matter are going to be hurt because of what Danner has done, not because of what we might do. The blame is his, not ours."

"You're right, of course, but it doesn't make it feel any better."

"No it doesn't, but how would it feel to know you had the power to stop him but let him continue doing what he's doing? Talk to Beth. Let's see what she says about it. She's the first one who has had the fortitude to come forward and complain about Danner. I think she is the one who should decide on his punishment, don't you?"

"Absolutely. You know, a few months ago I was ready to skin Danner alive. I wanted to hurt him any way I could. Now, I don't know. I'm not any less interested in putting a stop to his abuses, but I keep thinking about the consequences for his poor family. I think I dislike Danner as much for what he's doing to his family as for his perversity. I've suspected Danner of being cozy with Janice Rawlings for a long time, but I think she's as much a predator as he is. For that matter, any student who has allowed herself to be coerced into trading sex for Danner's patronage is not entirely without culpability as far as I'm concerned. Of course, I have no doubt Danner has bullied more than a few young women into submission and forced himself on others, as he tried to do with Beth. I suppose the longer he goes unchecked, the more despicable his behavior will be become, if that's possible. It's a shame that a man like Danner with so much going for him could allow himself to sink so low."

"Power corrupts . . ."

" . . . and absolute power corrupts absolutely," I said, finishing the aphorism. "Maybe Lord Acton was right. Maybe there is something about having power over others that can corrupt a person. On the other hand, maybe the same attributes that make a person capable of attaining power can also make that person susceptible to corruption."

CAIN

"Well, John, I have no doubt you could find a plethora of examples, especially among politicians, to support that thesis. However, I find the implications a bit chilling. Are you sure you want to believe that power equals corruption? Personally, I'd like to think there might be at least a few decent, incorruptible people in positions of power."

"So would I. I just wish it were a little easier to know which ones they are."

After leaving Dr. Cunningham's office, I walked across campus to the Hub, where, if he got the note I had left for him in the anthro office, Max was supposed to meet me around eleven. The lunch crowd had already filled the cafeteria and I wandered around, carrying a sandwich and cup of coffee, for several minutes before I spotted Max at a table with some other people. He saw me and waved.

"Hi, John. *Que pasa hombre*?"

"*Nada* Max, *y usted*?"

"*Siempre demasiado*—as usual, there are always too many things to deal with and too little time. Sit, John, and let us share commiserations."

"Thank you for taking my quiz sections. I owe you a bunch."

"*De nada*, John. It was worth it to find out your section is even more vacuous than mine. Makes me appreciate how well off I am."

"Vacuous, indeed. I think you give them too much credit, Max. Shall I pass on your compliment?"

"Tell them I fart in their general direction, for all I care. I'm sure they are all too witless to take offense. They might even take it as a compliment."

"I'm glad to see you had such a good time. It makes me feel somewhat less guilty about imposing on your generosity."

Max grinned. "Happy to help out, pilgrim. Hey, you want to hear about my good fortune?"

"Of course."

"Get this. The Spanish Ambassador wants me to come and work for him as a cultural attaché. Can you believe it? Max the diplomat. What do you think?"

"Congratulations, Max. Did you apply for the job or what?"

"That's the thing, John. I didn't know anything about it. I know my father has been dumping a lot of money into the political arena for years, but I didn't realize the extent to which some important people are in his debt. The position is a minor one, but the perks are outrageous: diplomatic immunity, an expense account, parties, and women. I think I could die young but happy in that job."

"So when do you leave for Washington D.C.?"

"As soon as my dissertation committee has accepted my dissertation and I've sat for the final exam—six weeks at most. I'll be back for the graduation ceremony in June of course. You're going to be there aren't you? How's your dissertation coming?"

"I have one more section to finish. I think I'll get it in just under the wire. I want to get it out of the way because I want to get married in June."

"Married? Good grief, John, why don't I know anything about this? To whom? You sly devil, you. And here I was feeling so sad for you because you seemed to have no lady friends. When do I get to meet her? I am delighted for you, my friend."

My announcement put Max into a gleeful and munificent mood, as if he weren't already wound up by the prospect of his new job in the diplomatic corps. He insisted on taking Beth and me out to dinner, and I accepted. I knew Beth would be pleased to meet Max, and Max would be completely enchanted by Beth. As for me, I was looking forward to a hell of a fancy meal at a very expensive restaurant. Damn! I might even have to rent a tux for the occasion.

Max had to go monitor a test for somebody, and so about a quarter to twelve he floated off on a froth of merriment, buoyant as hell about his prospects and mine, and about the forthcoming dinner to celebrate both our good fortunes. Several more students

CAIN

lunched at my table and left as I guarded an empty chair for Beth and tried to work on a draft of the last section of my dissertation.

I had requested a change in my dissertation committee, which Danner, as department head, had apparently approved without prejudice, removing himself as chairman and designating Dr. Bennett, whom I had requested. Dr. Bennett was a congenial, easy-going man, who was enthusiastic about the finished parts of my dissertation. I just needed to complete the damned thing, take care of all the fees and forms, and schedule the final exam.

In a few months so many things would be behind me, and so many more would lie ahead. Marriage, responsibility, a profession, a family—soon all would be a beginning. Was I prudent to look so far into the future, to expect so much? Why not? I had my head, my health, prospects for a decent living, good friends, and above all, I had Beth. No reasonable man could ask for more out of life. I didn't feel I deserved to be so fortunate, but I wasn't going to decline life's generous offer out of humility, either. I'd take it with thanks, knowing how damned lucky I was, and try as hard as I could to make the most out of it. By limitation, I could do no more than that; by obligation, I could do no less.

Lost in my ruminations, I had become completely unaware of everything around me. Not until Beth sat down beside me did I fade back into cognizance of where I was.

"Boy, you were really way out there," she said. Her comment triggered a flash of recollection and I thought of sitting by the bay window in my mother's shiny kitchen, daydreaming about the big yellow leaves on the maple trees outside, and waking up to my mother's same comment. Across the street from the cafeteria stood a thick-limbed old maple, its tiny clusters of yellow-green flowers already boldly beginning to emerge. Tightly-wrapped, lime-green leaf buds, more reticent than the flowers, still clung to their parent branches and refused to open into the cold March air.

"John? Everything all right?"

I smiled at her. "All right? It's wonderful! I love you so much I can't stand it!" I kissed her ardently. She was surprised and pleased by my intensity.

The bubbly chime of her laughter found a resonance somewhere in the vicinity of my solar plexus and sent a tingling sensation radiating all through my body. The delicate scent of her skin aroused me so deeply I ached for her. The memory of the burning crescendo of last night's long, slow lovemaking throbbed in my brain, almost perfectly balanced by a whispered remembrance of the impassioned serenity that had come afterward.

"Beth do you have the slightest notion of how profoundly you affect me? Look at me. You haven't been here two minutes and already I'm sweating, panting, and I want to make love to you right here on this table."

"Might I finish my coffee first?" she asked playfully.

"By all means, my dear. As I have the feeling that I may be able to carry on far into the evening without cessation, I should encourage you to seek refreshment while you may."

"You are all solicitation and kindness, dear sir."

"A gentleman must deport himself properly in these matters, my dear. Lust is categorically no excuse for ill manners, I always say."

We both laughed. Although farcical, the idea of having sex on a table in a crowded cafeteria had a certain titillating appeal—kinky, but titillating. I realized it would be wise to change the topic before I developed a more serious case of priapism than I already had. I finally understood why I saw so much unadulterated foreplay almost everywhere I went, and why clandestine erotica had such a following among the Victorians.

"You know, Beth, I was thinking about marriage and parenthood and living happily ever after."

"Starting to get cold feet are we?" she said with a mock pout.

"Hell no, I can't wait to get started."

She smiled coyly and fluttered her lashes. "I think you've made an extraordinary start in at least one area already."

Seriously, Beth, are you comfortable with the way things are going? I mean, you're not sorry we didn't wait are you?"

She took my hand and squeezed it. "Why would you ask that? I've never been happier, John, and I'm not sorry about anything."

"Well, I was thinking, if you'd like, we could make it legal right away and then have the big wedding later."

"I trust you, John." A frown began to darken her expression.

"I know that. I trust you, too. I just feel a little awkward about our situation. There is always the possibility of an unexpected pregnancy you know, especially since we are so, uh, *en rapport.*"

It seemed to me I was being very sensitive and sensible about the issue, magnanimous even. I was sure Beth would appreciate my bringing it up, even if it were not something that caused her undue concern.

She removed her hand from mine. "Are you worried about what other people are going to think?" I saw something in her eyes, heard something in her voice, the significance of which completely escaped me as my appreciation of my own frankness and humble wisdom continued to swell.

"I hate to admit it, but yes, I guess I am, a little. What would really bother me would be for anyone to think ill of you. Let's face it. We're not fooling anybody. Your roommate has to know what's going on between us; so do the Cunninghams. How would your family feel about this if they were to somehow find out? Your parents would be hurt no matter how understanding they are. What we feel for each other is too wonderful, too wholesome to have any stigma attached to it."

I beamed benevolently at Beth, satisfied with the eminent sapience and judiciousness of my words.

This time when Beth spoke, her crisp reproach almost reached out and slapped me in the face.

"Do you really think my family will be any less hurt to find out I've secretly married a man they've never even met? My marriage is something they are entitled to know about, to plan for, to enjoy, to be a part of. But my sex life is my business, not theirs. I respect their values, their expectations, even their wishes in most things. They have to respect my right to exercise my own judgment, whether they agree with my choices or not. If my parents have to accept my judgment, why shouldn't everyone else have to as well?

"John, you're running around with your nineteenth-century knickers unbuttoned and your chauvinistic notions hanging out. If you're not worried about your reputation, why should you be worried about mine? What makes it all right for men to have sex before marriage, but not all right for women? As much as we've argued and discussed this in the past, I would have thought you, of all people, would be able to allow me the same privileges you enjoy. I'm disappointed, John. As much as I love you, I think you need to take your head out of your ass and look around. You might be surprised at the changes that have taken place in the last two hundred years. I flatly refuse to be a character out of a Jane Austen novel, so don't try to treat me like one."

"Beth, why are you getting so upset? I'm not even sure what you're talking about. What did I say that rubbed you the wrong way?"

"You see, John? You don't even know you're doing it." She got up from the table huffily. "I've got to go to class."

The barrier with which Beth surrounded herself was half fire, half ice. Presumably, resulting from some combination of ire and estrogen, the formula for which had been passed from mother to daughter for untold generations, and which no man had ever succeeded in breaching.

"Doing what? Don't leave, Beth, we need to get this straightened out—whatever it is."

"No, you need to get it straightened out." Impaling me with an angry glare, she picked up her book bag and stomped off without looking back, leaving me to wonder what the hell I had done to upset her so.

Somehow, I had gone from a state of erection to a state of rejection, with only a few ostensibly innocuous words providing the transition. Maybe she didn't like my offer to make an honest woman out of her, but . . . oh, shit! That was it. How could I possibly have been so stupid not to know how that was going to sound? And I hadn't even said it, I had only implied it. So there it was. Now she was profoundly pissed at me, and I probably had the dubious distinction of being one of the few people in the world who could put my foot in my mouth while my head was in my ass.

We hadn't discussed what to do about Danner and I hadn't even had a chance to tell her about Max's invitation. Dammit all! I took back everything I had thought about being so fortunate in life. There could be no doubt: the universe had it in for me.

It took me an hour to compose a satisfactory apology to Beth. I sincerely desired her forgiveness—that wasn't the problem, although I couldn't help feeling she was a little too sensitive and intolerant, on the whole. As it turned out, the hard part lay in achieving the proper tone. "I'm sorry, I didn't mean it . . . I'm sorry, but you'll have to admit . . . I'm sorry, you misunderstood me . . ." I couldn't seem to get it right. Finally, I went for the abject, unconditional surrender, I-deserve-to-be-shot-please-give-me-another-chance approach:

> My most beloved Beth, whom I do not deserve, I humbly beg your forgiveness. I would not offend you for all the world. That I have so carelessly disappointed you brings me to the brink of despair and beyond. I love you so much I would gladly kill myself and consider it too small a punishment for having hurt you in any way. I fear I suffer from that repugnant testicularity of outlook peculiar to males, and so regrettably offensive to females. I abhor my reprehensible lack of sensitivity. Strive as I may to overcome the burden of miscreancy that plagues my maleness, I fear I am doomed to failure. And in failing, I fear even more terribly I shall lose that affection with which you have so graciously honored me. Unworthy though I am, I ask your pardon.

> Though I be held eternally accountable for my heinousness in Hell, might I taste your sweet lips one last time, I happily could endure an eternity of damnation.
> Your grieving, pining, humble servant,
> John, the Remorseful

The Hub bookstore didn't have what I wanted, so I jogged over to the University Bookstore on the Ave, where I bought several sheets of vellum, a calligraphy pen and ink, and a length of red satin ribbon. Down the street, I rented the use of a restaurant table by purchasing a cup of coffee, and laboriously scribed my apology onto the vellum. When the ink was dry, I carefully rolled the vellum and tied it with a red satin bow. From the restaurant, I hurried back up the street to the flower shop, where I ordered a dozen red roses to be delivered, along with the beribboned scroll, to Beth's room. All that remained was to go home and wait for a call.

Waiting for the phone to ring and working on my dissertation proved to be incompatible tasks, but I kept trying to concentrate on writing anyway. The end of the quarter was fast approaching, and I had not made much progress since before Christmas, having devoted more time than I had realized to Ernie and to Beth.

I was getting credit for five hours of dissertation research, which fortunately entailed no commitment to do anything or be anywhere at any specified time. My teaching assistantship nominally required twenty hours of work per week. I seldom spent more than fifteen hours each week conducting quiz sections, grading papers, monitoring tests, and taking my turn filling in for professors who were sick or out of town attending a conference or giving a lecture.

I might have considered trying for a predoctoral lectureship if I had remained on speaking terms with Danner. In view of how little I had accomplished in the past few months, however, it was probably just as well I had no additional demands on my time.

Ten o'clock, and still the phone had not rung. I lifted the receiver and listened for a dial tone. Yes, it was working. Maybe the flower shop screwed up and didn't deliver the flowers and the apology. Maybe Beth wasn't mollified by my apology. Maybe I should have appeared in person to quench the fire and melt the ice.

Already agitated, I set about compounding the problem with caffeine. I began to pace, carrying a cup of coffee in one hand and gesticulating with the other as I talked to myself. I told myself I was a silly fool for worrying, that she would call, and even if she didn't, all would be forgotten in a day, or two at most.

I continued to pace. It seemed safe to assume that if reason were not the antidote for my own foolish disquietude, it would not be one for Beth's, either. If only she would call.

Pondering the imponderable always seemed to neutralize a lot of my nervous energy. Around ten thirty I stopped pacing, sat down, and tried staring at the ceiling. Some time later, half asleep and floundering somewhere between self flagellation and self pity, my thoughts wandered into Mr. Poe's neighborhood and kept stumbling over lines from *The Raven.*

I don't know whether I was dreaming, or in that state of uninhibited imagination that comes just before sleep, but suddenly I thought I heard a tapping, as of someone gently rapping, rapping at my chamber door. 'Tis a figment of Poe's imagination, I thought—only this and nothing more. There it was again, a tapping somewhat louder than before. I opened my eyes. Someone really was rapping at my door. I walked over and pulled the blind apart to see what late visitor entreated entrance at my chamber door—half expecting to see a big black bird. Instead, there stood the rare and radiant Beth.

I opened the door with a rush of relief and excitement, but, as we faced each other, there was a moment of hesitation, self-consciousness, uncertainty. All I could utter was, "Come in."

I wanted to hold her, to kiss her, but something held me back. I needed a sign from her that it was all right, some subtle assurance that I would not be turned away. I suppose she did, too.

"How did you get here? I didn't hear a car."

"I walked. Couldn't sleep." She looked at me as if trying to decide what to say and how to say it. "The roses are beautiful . . . and the note . . . I liked the note very much—a little sappy and melodramatic, but sweet. It made me cry." The tears welled up in her eyes and I put my arms around her. "I'm sorry, John," she sniffled. "You didn't deserve what I said to you today. I don't know why I'm such a bitch sometimes." She lifted her wet face and I wiped away the tears. "Forgive me?"

I kissed her tear-salted lips. "Always, my love," I whispered. "Always."

Oh God! how exquisite the joy of making up!

We were late and rushed the next morning. Beth wanted to stop by her room before going to class, and, of all mornings, Dr. Bennett called and asked if I could monitor a test for him. He said he had to take his wife to the hospital and no other assistant was available. I barely had time to mention Max's invitation to Beth and to tell her briefly about the evidence against Danner. After I dropped her off at the dorm, I sped over to Denny Hall and parked in a loading zone, hoping my car wouldn't be ticketed or impounded before I had a chance to move it in an hour.

I dashed into the anthro office to pick up the test questions, took the stairs two at a time up to the second floor, and spilled into Dr. Bennett's classroom along with three students who were arriving two minutes late. I recognized half a dozen of the thirty or forty faces in the room as current or former members of my quiz sections.

One other face was also familiar. Stuffed into an undersized chair in the back row, head and shoulders above nearly everyone else in the room, sat the illustrious Mr. Brent Woody. I looked at him long enough for him to know that I saw him and for him to glare back at me; then I counted out the tests for each row and passed on Dr. Bennett's instructions.

When everyone had begun to work on the five-page test, I went to the front of the room, perched myself on the edge of a table, and started taking notes on a book I was reading, glancing up from time to time to make sure no one was on a ladder outside, holding up cue cards with the answers on them. But of course, that wasn't likely. Because Dr. Bennett had been using the same test for the past two years, I assumed every fraternity and sorority had a copy of it in their files, and that it was probably available for a fee from other sources. After forty-five minutes, the test papers began to accumulate on the table beside me as the faster students finished and left.

I happened to be looking down at my book when a copy of the test fluttered through the air, missed the table, and landed on the floor. I would have known to whom the paper belonged without looking, but I looked anyway. Woody stood by the door, ten feet away from the table, glowering menacingly, waiting to see me pick up his test from the floor. I leaned over and looked at his test papers lying on the floor and then back at him.

"I hope the janitor finds your test and turns it in, Mr. Woody. It would be a shame if you had to retake it."

He almost lost it, taking a step toward me, then looking around and checking himself. He turned as if to leave. Suddenly the remaining test takers who were not already watching him were startled by the crash of his big fist against the wall. Walking over to the table, he snatched the test up from the floor and slammed it down as hard as he could on the table.

I watched him coolly. A word, a smile, a gesture; that is all it would have taken to set him off. Too bad. I would have enjoyed flipping his big bad ass out the second story window, but I knew it wouldn't be worth the shit storm it would create.

He stood by the table for a few seconds, huffing and growling, waiting for me to say or do something. Finally, when he saw he could neither intimidate nor provoke me, he left.

The dozen or so students in the room sat bug-eyed and catatonic with astonishment.

"I understand there is no other class in this room next period, is that right?" I managed to sound completely unperturbed. Some heads nodded. "In view of the unfortunate distraction, I'll give you a little extra time to finish up, say until ten after. Ok?" I picked up my book and started to read again. The only sound in the room was that of furiously scribbling pencils.

CHAPTER 17

In the Shadow of the Pleasure Dome

I left the tests in the anthro office and went out to see if I still had a car. Amazingly, it was still sitting there in the loading zone in front of the "Unauthorized Vehicles Will Be Towed" sign. Even more surprisingly, it had not been ticketed. The campus police sought out parking violators with the same patriotic zeal with which the FBI rooted out subversives, except the campus police were much more ruthless and efficient within their tiny purview. I took the fact that they had somehow overlooked my car as a hopeful sign that Big Brother had not yet achieved a state of omniscience and infallibility.

At our ritual coffee tryst that afternoon, Beth told me that, despite her misgivings about Danner's family, she felt he should be exposed. She believed the evidence of his misdeeds should be sent first to the university president and to the regents, and then made public only if the university refused to act on the information. I agreed.

There was no trace of meanness in Beth, I already knew that and loved her for it. That her sense of justice bore no stain of vindictiveness did not surprise me. I was proud of her. I wondered if she would be proud of me if she knew how pleasurable the thought of throwing Brent Woody out the window had been for me—and continued to be.

The rest of the week passed quickly. Beth had projects to complete, exams to prepare for; and we agreed to see each other only for coffee at the Hub each day until Saturday night, when Max was taking us out to dinner. I dug into my work and the final section of my dissertation began to come together. By Saturday afternoon, I felt I had earned a break. I was looking forward to an evening of high society and conspicuous consumption, courtesy of Max Alavedra and the generous allowance he received monthly from his affluent father in Madrid.

Limited by a middle-class imagination, I assumed a fancy meal in an expensive restaurant meant eating lobster thermidor at a window table in the Space Needle and having two kinds of sherbet for dessert. I even contemplated the thrill of being able to leave a crisp twenty on the table for an appreciative waiter. That's probably what Beth expected, too. Max had diplomatically suggested that we might feel more comfortable in formal attire, and so, not having any other suit anyway, I cheerfully rented a conservative tuxedo and planned to enjoy being overdressed and ostentatious. Beth was borrowing an evening gown from a friend, which amounted to overkill in my estimation. With her looks and figure, she'd be a knockout in anything from a pantsuit to pajamas. But it would be fun and festive to be dressed to the nines and out on the town in a town where nobody noticed or cared if you wore a sweatshirt and jeans to the opera.

The first inkling I got as to the paltriness of my humble expectations was the long, black limousine Max had rented for the evening. He and his date showed up in the limousine at the Cunningham's about seven. Max's tailored tux looked a lot better on him than mine did on me, but at least he hadn't shown up wearing tails and a top hat.

Max's date, whom he introduced simply as Michelle, was a Brigitte Bardot look-alike with an impressive set of feminine credentials playing peekaboo through a curtain of waist-long, blond hair. Her dark blue skirt was long and full. She wore a short, dark blue sequined jacket over a form-fitting, precariously-laced lavender bodice. I suppose Beth might have insisted it was forget-me-not taupe, or periwinkle mauve, or perceived it as some other arcane combination of hue and saturation that only women can discern. To me it looked lavender.

This was no bimbo. Being a circumspect chauvinist, I didn't let on that I was surprised by her pleasant poise and intelligent conversation during the short ride over to Beth's dorm. She was probably in her early twenties, although her obvious refinement made her seem older. A Vassar girl perhaps? Then again, maybe I gave Vassar too much credit as the principal producer of genteel females in the United States. I could certainly see why Max might be interested in Michelle. Why Michelle might be interested in Max was a matter for conjecture.

Getting out of a limousine and entering the women's dorm dressed in a tux was a good confidence builder, and I didn't really mind the stares and titters that my presence in the waiting room elicited. Beth was prompt—another of her virtues—and within two or three minutes of my call she descended the stairs like a princess. I didn't know the friend from whom she had borrowed the gown, but I guessed it was expensive and it fit Beth as if it had been made for her. The tight, low-cut, black velvet gown was strikingly elegant and provocative. A tear-shaped onyx pendant hung sensually from her graceful neck by a gold chain and dangled gracefully in miniature reprise from her earlobes. Her only other jewelry was the engagement ring flashing on her finger. A black lace shawl draped around her bare shoulders and she carried a small, black velvet purse. Every time I saw her, I thought she could not be more beautiful, but every time I saw her, she was.

A faint flush of excitement glowed in her cheeks and her big smile betrayed just a hint of girlish self-consciousness that imbued her with a youthful sweetness. There was an endearing naturalness about Beth, a casual grace and genuineness that gave her elegance without studied refinement; poise without a hint of Vassarian hauteur. Perhaps, part of what I saw in Beth was an illusion created by my intense feelings for her. Illusion or not, as far as I was concerned, Beth was the fairest of them all in every respect I could imagine.

Watching her come down the stairs, I could not help wondering what she saw in me. I dared to conclude only that I had real attributes of which I was not aware. Otherwise, I would have been forced to contemplate the degree to which I existed in Beth's perception as an illusion.

I saw nothing inherently wrong with illusions, other than they were about as transparent as the Emperor's new clothes to anyone who didn't share them. So far, though, no one had challenged Beth and me about being naked in public. Possibly, what we thought we saw in each other was really there, or at least there with a presence sufficient to preserve our modesty against the prying eyes of those who had no illusions.

I escorted Beth to the waiting limousine, where the middle-aged chauffeur opened the door for us with a wry, but polite comment. I introduced Beth to Michelle and Max, who uncorked a chilled bottle of champagne and embarked on a lengthy toast to just about everything, including Beth's and my engagement, Beth's and Michelle's beauty, his and my good fortunes, and to his father's wealth and generosity. Beth was appropriately flabbergasted and delighted at Max's good-natured, unpretentious flamboyance, and Max was equally flabbergasted that I even knew a woman of Beth's charm and beauty, not to mention that one had actually consented to marry me.

Meanwhile, the limousine headed toward a destination unknown to everyone except Max and the chauffeur. The excellent stereo system provided us with Handel's *Water Music* as we sank comfortably into plush seats behind darkly tinted windows, sipping champagne, talking and laughing ebulliently, and thoroughly enjoying each other's company.

Twenty minutes later, the limousine stopped under the portico of a building in downtown Seattle and the car door was opened by the concierge. Inside, the women excused themselves to the powder room. The maitre d' greeted Max as if he knew him.

"*Bonsoir, Monsieur* Alavedra, your table is waiting. Good to see you again, sir."

"Thank you, Jacque. My friends and I are celebrating this evening. I would be so pleased if they were made to feel just a little special. Do you think that might be possible?" As he spoke, Max discretely placed a folded bill into the maitre d's hand.

The maitre d' glanced at the bill in his hand and lit up appreciatively. "Ah, *mais oui, monsieur.* I'm certain your friends will be most favorably impressed with both the cuisine and the service."

"Thank you, Jacque. I knew I could depend on you."

Max, seeing I was watching him, smiled and shrugged.

"Aren't you laying it on a bit thick, Max?" I chided. "This little shindig is going to cost you a fortune."

"Loosen up, John. It's going to cost my father a fortune, and he can well afford it. Besides, he would approve; no, he would insist on it. Enjoy, my friend."

"Well I certainly wouldn't want to disappoint your father, Max. Lead on."

In a few minutes, Jacque led Beth and Michelle to our table, where Max and I were discussing the menu. Max finally persuaded everyone to have the escargot and we settled on several vegetable dishes. No sooner had we decided, than a platoon of waiters descended upon us bearing everything from pate de foie gras and truffles to cheeses and hors d'oeurves I'd never heard of and couldn't even identify.

For two hours, we were the final destination of a continuous caravan of waiters bearing food and drink. We began with an aperitif of dry Madeira to complement the hors d'oeurves. Then came the dry champagne with the main course, followed by a Marsala and coffee with dessert, which turned out be a magnificent flaming dish of glazed fruit and brandied cream reinforced by a platter of napoleons. By the time we had finished dessert, we were pleasantly bloated and slightly tipsy.

Max must have signed away a substantial portion of his inheritance with his credit card payment for the meal. He produced an alarming wad of bills and personally rewarded each of the waiters and the chef. The maitre d' received an additional token of Max's appreciation as well. On the way out the concierge got his share from my expansively pecunious friend.

I had never seen Max throw his money around so freely before. I knew his father was well off, but I had never suspected Max of being filthy rich. That was probably because, although rich, Max was not the least bit filthy about it. I had a hard time believing he would try to impress anyone with his extravagance, least of all me, and probably not Beth. For all I knew, Michelle's father might have been wealthier than Max's. In any event, Michelle did not strike me as a young woman who could be impressed by tasteless profligacy. Surely Max had figured that out for himself. After what he had told me about his being rejected by a blue-nosed debutante and her aristocratic family, I would have thought he would eschew appearing as a parvenu. Still, no one appeared to be offended by his prodigal impulse to please his friends. It seemed that neither Beth nor Michelle found anything particularly vulgar or insecure in Max's beneficence. I wasn't offended, but I wasn't completely comfortable with it, either. Maybe I was too conservative; maybe, deep down, I was a little envious.

Our next stop was a dance club just off Pioneer Square, where we stood in line, conspicuously out of place, for twenty minutes; paid a hefty cover charge; and squeezed into a smoky, dark, deafening pit of a place, which, had it been larger, less crowded, better lighted, and less smelly, might have been mistaken for the interior of a tin of sardines that had gone bad. Disappointed, we squeezed out again past the swelling queue of restives waiting impatiently to get in. They seemed so young and hyper, with an unpleasant current of crudeness running through their language, looks, and gestures as they milled about, blocking the sidewalk. Stigmatized by our formal attire, the four of us immediately drew remarks that quickly became raucous jeers as we jostled through the beer-breathed crowd. Without any ostensible explanation, other than the synergism of individual hostility and group anonymity, crudeness was fast turning into ugliness as the crowd scuffled and coalesced into a mob.

·CAIN

The alert chauffeur, parked down the block, saw us and pulled up to the curb beside us right away. Just as he got out and started around the front of the car, an empty beer bottle bounced off the side of the limousine and broke on the sidewalk. Another one whizzed over our heads and shattered in the street.

Yanking the car door open, I yelled at the driver and pushed Beth inside. "Get us out of here, right now!"

I held the door open as Max pushed Michelle into the car behind Beth and dived in after her. A third bottle glanced off the windshield, just missing the driver as he scrambled behind the wheel. Before I could pull the door shut behind me, the chauffeur had punched the long Lincoln into a screeching getaway under a smoke screen of burning rubber.

The window separating the driver from the passenger compartment retracted. "You folks all right back there?" the driver asked.

"I think so," I replied. "Thanks for getting us away so quickly. "I'm afraid you might have a few dents in your car, though."

"Insurance'll take care of that," the driver said philosophically. "Boy, I'd like to get my hands on those yahoos."

"I know what you mean. So would I."

"Where would you like to go now?" the driver asked.

I looked at Max, who shook his head and shrugged. "I think we'll have to discuss it for a minute," I told the driver.

"That's fine. I'll just cruise up the waterfront while you're thinking about it." The window went up again and we all looked at each other. Beth was the first to speak.

"I don't think we ought to let this ruin our evening, do you? Is there somewhere else we can go? What do you think, Michelle?"

"That was a little more excitement than I had expected, but I'm game for another try." Michelle looked at Max.

"I apologize for having chosen that place," Max said. It wasn't quite that bad the last time I was there. Why don't we go over to the Edgewater and have a few quiet dances with the old-timers for a change of pace?" They smiled at each other and nodded their approval. There seemed to be a natural affinity between Beth and Michelle, and I was pleased to see how easily they had warmed to each other's company.

"Good," I said. "I should be in my element there—with the rest of the old-timers. They'll probably all wonder why I brought my three kids with me."

"Don't be silly, John," Max said. "I would be surprised if more than a dozen people thought we were your kids."

Max laughed as he pushed the intercom button. "Driver, we'd like to go to the Edgewater."

"Good choice, sir," the driver replied over the intercom. "It's just up the street and I think they're all too old there to throw beer bottles."

Beth and Michelle looked at each other and burst out laughing. Max joined in. I smiled, but for some reason it didn't really seem that funny to me.

After we got into the Edgewater and settled at a table by the dance floor, Beth and Michelle set out on a powder room patrol. They were gone a long time and I began to wonder what was keeping them. Finally, Beth returned by herself, showing enough distress to cause both Max and me to become alarmed.

"What's wrong, Beth? I asked. Are you all right?"

"And Michelle? Where is Michelle?" Max asked with concern.

"She's still in the ladies' room. She's all right, she's just terribly upset. I'm afraid it's my fault. I had no idea. I opened my big mouth. How was I supposed to know?"

"Beth, take it easy. Know what? What are you talking about?" Max and I were giving her our undivided attention.

"There was this woman in the ladies' room. She was crying and her dress was ripped. Apparently her blind date turned out to be a pretty serious groper and got carried away. Michelle and I helped her pin her dress up and gave her a little moral support. The thing made me angry and I happened to make a comment about what happened to me." Max raised an eyebrow and looked at me.

"Yes, and then what?"

"I got a little wound up about it and the whole business about Danner came out. I shouldn't have said anything. All evening, and I didn't even know." She turned to Max. "I'm sorry, Max. I like Michelle. I wouldn't do anything to hurt her. I just didn't know."

"For God's sake, Beth, know what!" I demanded.

Beth gestured helplessly. "Danner is Michelle's father."

Max was completely confused. "John, what is going on? What is this thing about Professor Danner that has upset Michelle?"

"Max, I feel like an idiot. It never occurred to me that Michelle might be Danner's daughter. I should have recognized her name, but I just didn't make the connection. I thought she was going to school in New York."

"She's on spring break," Max explained. "She's the one who asked me not to mention that Professor Danner is her father. That's why I introduced her only as Michelle. She said we could get around to last names later. Now that I think about it, it does seem somewhat strange. But you still haven't told me what she is upset about."

"Beth, do you want to explain to Max about Danner?"

She took a deep breath, sighed, and hesitantly embarked on an explanation. She described the situation to Max and I described the photos we had. Max was stunned.

"You'll have to forgive me," Max said, "but this is hard to believe. Poor Michelle must have thought you were crazy to say such a thing about her father."

"That's the odd part. Instead of being outraged and calling me a liar, which is probably how I would have reacted, she seemed more upset that I had found out about her father. She didn't even try to defend him. She must have known about him, or at least suspected something." Beth got up from the table. "I'm going to go check on her."

I caught her hand as she started to leave. "Are you all right?"

"Yes, I'm fine. I'm not the one whose father is a dirty old man."

I could see Beth's sympathy for Michelle had rekindled her anger at Danner. She had undoubtedly already imagined herself in Michelle's circumstances and had contemplated the shame, the disappointment, the hurt. It would not have surprised me that Beth was now angrier at Danner's betrayal of his family than at his attempted assault on her.

Although Danner's behavior toward Beth had come as a rude and frightening revelation, it had not resulted in any irrevocable harm to her, but the effects of Danner's vile prurience on Michelle and on the rest of his family could not be other than terrible, tragic. His betrayal of trust and responsibility was a fait accompli, the consequences of which were likely to continue to unfold in unpredictable ways, but with effects upon those involved that were all too predictable. Having met Michelle and having seen some of those effects first hand, Beth would, by her very nature, be compelled to despise Danner more for Michelle's sake than for her own.

As soon as Beth left, Max ordered a stiff drink. I ordered a glass of orange juice. The news about Michelle had been sobering and I was not in the mood for any more alcohol.

"Max, how long have you been dating Michelle?"

"I met her several times at the Danners' house last summer—at some of those barbecues you never attended. The first and only other time we dated was during the Christmas break, when I took her to a symphony concert at the Opera House. I like her very much, who wouldn't? But it's just a social thing between us—nothing serious. I assume that is what you are asking about?"

"Yes, I suppose it is. I wouldn't want any of this nasty business to affect you. I'm damned sorry Michelle has to go through this. I like her."

"I'm curious, John. Why didn't you tell me about Danner sooner?"

"It wasn't because I didn't trust you, Max. Danner threatened to cause problems for Beth if she told anyone, and so we were trying to keep it a secret until we figured out how to proceed. I thought telling you about it might prejudice you and unnecessarily complicate your dealings with Danner. Besides, we didn't have any proof of what he was doing until just a few days ago. Perhaps I should have told you."

"No, you were right, John. I didn't need to know. You were also right in assuming that such knowledge would affect my attitude toward the man. I can no longer allow him to serve as my advisor or to chair my dissertation committee."

"Take care, Max. If you ask for a new chairperson, as I did, Danner will probably figure out you know about him. He granted my request without saying anything about it. I hope he doesn't suddenly decide to cause any problems for you. I'm not certain what he will do when the shit hits the fan. You might want to make sure you're some place where you won't get splattered."

"Thanks for your concern, my friend, but I have no sympathy or tolerance for a man who abuses a position of trust and behaves dishonorably toward women. I may be disdained by some in my own country as little more than a nouveau riche, but my family has always respected honor, and I know how a gentleman should behave. Danner is not a gentleman, and he has no honor. I won't hesitate to tell him that to his face if he wants to know why I want a different advisor."

"I'd think twice about challenging Danner to a duel, my friend, metaphorically or otherwise. Of course, he wouldn't accept your challenge; he's too smart, too cunning. But he would get even, and you can bet his revenge would be sophisticated. You're almost out of here. Play it cool and don't cross swords with Danner if you can avoid it."

"No duel? After all that money my father spent on my fencing lessons? More's the pity. Someone like that could use a few good runnings through."

"Max?"

"*Touché*, John, *touché*. Of course I understand what you are saying. Just because I have a little money, it does not necessarily follow that I am also a fool."

"I didn't mean it like that, Max, and you know it. You are one of the least foolish persons I know. I respect your intellect and judgment as much as I respect your sense of honor."

"I apologize—a lame attempt at misplaced humor. I value your respect, John, because I respect your values. You are an honorable man, John, and for such a capable person, you are exceedingly modest—perhaps too modest at times. Like me, you have very little to be modest about. I admire you and I value your friendship—and yes, even your opinions and advice."

"Thank you, Max. I feel the same way about you, except I would never accuse you of being too modest." Max tossed off the rest of his drink and grinned.

"The other thing I so much admire in you, John, is your delightfully twisted sense of humor."

Beth and Michelle reappeared: Beth as solicitous, as protective as a loving older sister; Michelle red-eyed, waifish, but with her pretty chin up and still able to look us, or anyone, for that matter, straight in the eye. As if moved by a single impulse, both Max and I sprang to seat them. When she was in her chair, Max gently took Michelle's hand and kissed it so tenderly, so expressively that nothing he might have said could have conveyed his feelings more completely, more elegantly. Michelle sat with impeccable carriage, bravely struggling to hold back the tears, and managed a fleeting smile of gratitude. Obviously what Michelle saw in Max was the same thing I saw in him: he was a hell of a nice guy.

"Would you like something, Michelle?" Max asked.

"No thank you, I think I'd like to go home. I'm sorry, I don't want to spoil things." She looked at Beth and me apologetically.

I wasn't sure what to say that wouldn't sound oafish. "You are not going to spoil anything. We are all sorry that your evening has been spoiled."

"Especially me," Beth said, full of self-reproach.

"Beth, you didn't do anything. I should be apologizing to you for what my father did. I'm so ashamed of him." Tears that would not be restrained any longer burst forth, carrying away in a flood of emotion all words, thoughts, and pretenses of poise, leaving behind a heartbroken little girl sobbing on Beth's comforting shoulder.

We left the Edgewater with Max and Beth on either side of Michelle, supporting her. Possibly, all the wine we had consumed during dinner had primed Michelle for this breakdown, but even so, for someone like Michelle to come apart so completely in the company of strangers suggested the tumult had been seething just beneath her lovely, cultivated surface for some time.

Perhaps she clung to Beth now as she was accustomed to clinging to her mother for solace. Perhaps Michelle and her mother solaced each other. And what of her younger sister? How long had the father's villainy festered among them? How long had the hurt and humiliation abscessed in the hidden corners of their hearts? I wondered if the lancet of truth poised for the critical incision would allow their suffering to drain away, or if it would simply release a gush of accumulated misery and toxin, poisoning everything and everyone it touched.

I could tell the chauffeur was dying to find out what was going on, but he minded his own business. Seeing that he was genuinely concerned, I attempted to assuage his curiosity with the explanation that Michelle had received some bad news about her father. That seemed to satisfy him. As soon as the limousine began to move out of the parking lot, the chauffeur's voice came over the intercom.

"Sorry about your father, Miss. Hope he gets better real soon."

The chauffeur's sincere, albeit misguided, well-wishes released a new flood of tears and sobs from Michelle. Max and Beth both nailed me to my seat with their glared reprimands. Cursing myself, I scrunched down into the soft seat and tried to make myself as inconspicuous as possible.

Needless to say, there was not a lot of conversation on the way home. I closed my eyes and let my thoughts wander, not that I could have kept them from wandering if I had tried.

I don't know what obscure, free association brought the *Rime of the Ancient Mariner* to mind and saturated my thoughts with it. Whatever Danner's weakness or compulsion, his offense was greater than laying low a harmless albatross with his cruel bow. I suspected many a bird had felt the prick of Danner's arrow, yet thus far he had avoided any curse whatsoever. Now, it seemed, the maker of all things great and small had decided punishment and penance might be in order after all.

I had a hard time, though, imagining Danner as penitent. More likely, he would see to it as many people as possible wound up with something foul hanging around their necks. I wondered how many of us, like the wedding guest in Coleridge's poem, having been fixed by Danner's glittering eye, would wake up sadder but wiser in the morning.

Justice is often a murky, closureless process. If young Samuel Taylor Coleridge had been able to set his laudanum aside long enough, he might have commented on the plight of Danner's wife and daughters in the following manner:

> These women have anguish felt
> And anguish more will feel.

John, oh John, when the going gets tough, you get all weird and dredge up some dead poet to hide behind.

The limousine stopped first at Beth's dorm. Beth gave Michelle a hug and a piece of paper with her phone number on it and thanked Max effusively for the royal dinner. Max naturally apologized for the evening's shortcomings and promised her we'd do it right next time. She also thanked the chauffeur, and I escorted her up to the front door, since male visitors were not allowed inside after ten thirty. I kissed her goodnight and she held on to me as if she didn't want to go in.

"You were magnificent tonight, Beth, the way you took Michelle under your wing like that. I'm proud of you. You know

-CAIN

that, don't you?" For the first time since dinner she gave me a little smile that quickly faded to a troubled look.

"I like her, John, and I feel so sorry for her. This whole thing is really beginning to stink. I wish I could just make it go away."

"I know exactly how you feel. Don't worry about it, Beth. I'm sure everything will work out—somehow. Get some rest; you look tired."

She gave me another fleeting half-smile as she went into the building. She didn't think everything was going to turn out for the best any more than I did.

The limousine's next stop was in front of the Cunningham's house. I had tried to come up with something meaningful and appropriate to say to Michelle all the way over from Beth's dorm. As I prepared to get out of the car, I still didn't know what to say to her.

Finally, I just took her hand and squeezed it between both of mine. "Hang tough, Michelle. Time will sort everything out, I promise. In the meantime, if there's anything I can do for you, please let me know. Max and Beth have my number. Give my regards to your mother."

Michelle mustered a weak, teary smile and placed her other hand on top of mine in a double clasp.

"Thanks, John, you're very kind."

I got out of the limousine, thanked the driver, and Max walked part way up the drive with me.

"That was the most extraordinary dinner I've ever eaten, Max. I'll never forget it, because I'll probably never be able to afford another one like it. Thanks for the evening, especially for the sentiment behind it. I know Beth feels the same way."

"It was my pleasure, John. It was worth it just to meet your Beth. You lucky bastard, you don't deserve her, you know."

"Don't remind me, and please don't tell her that. I'm hoping she won't discover it until we're married. I think she was pretty impressed with you, too, Max."

"I hope so, John. I would be depressed if she didn't like me. Take care, my friend. I'll talk to you next week."

"Right, Max. Thanks again."

The sweaty patent leather shoes came off first, then the tux, as I left a trail of rented finery between the apartment door and the shower. Ten minutes under a hard stream of hot water softened me up for sleep. I brushed my teeth, pulled on a clean tee shirt and shorts, and flopped onto my bed. The next thing I knew, the phone was ringing and it was ten o'clock Sunday morning.

CAIN

CHAPTER 18

House of the Father

"Hello?" The garlicky little green fur coat my tongue was wearing must have made me sound like Jimmy Stewart with a mouth full of mush, because Beth didn't recognize my voice.

"John?"

"Just barely, Beth. Top o' the morning to you, Sweet Lips. Did you call to tell me how much you missed me last night?"

"Missed you? I had wild, erotic dreams about you all night long. I woke up this morning hot, horny, and wet with sweat. Will that do?"

"Just about. I take it your roommate is somewhere else?"

"She left yesterday to spend spring vacation with her parents up in Blaine. It's just you and me, Baby. Would you like to go out for breakfast? What time is it, anyway? I suppose it's brunch by now. I'd like to talk to you about something."

"Of course I would. I'll be over to pick you up as soon as I shave my tongue and put on my pants. I trust I'll find you panting in front of the dorm, naked and sweaty, with lathered loins and a wild, lascivious look in your eye? Hell, maybe I won't waste time putting on my pants after all."

"Sorry, John. I've already taken a long, cold shower. We'll have to save the sweat and lather for later."

"Jesus, Beth. You really know how to bring a guy down. What the hell, I guess I'll come over anyway. I'll see you in about fifteen minutes."

"Don't forget your pants, John. Bye."

Beth was wearing jeans and a sweatshirt when I picked her up. I found it very hard to think about anything but the tantalizingly firm, naked curves flowing beneath the thinness of her clothing. I don't know whether it was the look or the drool that gave me away, but Beth was impressed.

"You realize, of course, you're giving me goosebumps everywhere your eyeballs reach out and caress my bare body. I'd better be the only woman you use that X-ray vision on."

"I have X-ray eyes only for you, my love. It's about to drive me crazy, too. I'm sorry I didn't take the time for a cold shower myself this morning." Her musical laugh was all pleasure and sensuality.

Over coffee and bagels, we reviewed our impressions of the previous evening; then Beth got around to what she had wanted to talk to me about.

"You know my parents are expecting me home tomorrow."

"Yes, I assumed you'd be going home for the break. Why?"

"I wondered if you'd like to come home with me and meet my family?" There was a hint of uncertainty in her voice and in her eyes, which I took for her unsureness about how I would respond; as if I might have changed my mind since she had first asked me, weeks ago.

"I can't wait to meet your family. But isn't it rather short notice? . . . for your folks, I mean."

She looked relieved. "Oh, it will be fine, John. I'll call my mom and it'll be just fine. I know the prospect of meeting my family must be a little daunting, but you'll like them and I know they'll like you, so don't worry about it. Ok?"

"I'm not worried. I've had people shoot at me before."

"Oh, John, nobody's going to shoot at you. You're going to impress the crap out of them. They're going to think you've got the nicest butt they've ever seen."

"Yeah, especially your father. I hope he doesn't decide to plant his boot in my nice butt."

It was a bright, warm day, unusually so for the end of March. Beth suggested we take a stroll around Green Lake, along with the thousand other walkers, joggers, bicyclists, and skaters who had the same idea. Since I had Beth with me, I didn't care how crowded it was. The day was beautiful, and so was she, and I liked the thought of everyone on the busy path seeing her hang on my arm.

After a couple of turns around the lake, which were pleasant despite the tightly-packed parade of path users, I dropped Beth off at the dorm with a promise to show up later in the evening to buy her a hamburger. We both had preparations to make in order to leave by seven the next morning. Beth was eager to call her folks and spring the good news on them. I suggested that because she, instead of her parents, had invited me, maybe I should plan to stay only a day or two. Beth insisted, however, I stay the entire week. They needed that long to get to know me, she said. I couldn't help feeling apprehensive about how I was going to be received. I was beginning to get butterflies like the ones I used to get before a recon mission in Nam. As I recalled, however, those butterflies had seemed smaller and fewer than the ones I was now feeling.

The Cunninghams were very enthusiastic and supportive when I told them I was about to meet Beth's family. I guess my butterflies showed, because Maxine and Dr. Cunningham made a special effort to reassure me that everything would turn out all right, even if I did experience a few awkward moments.

They regaled me with an anecdote about the first time their daughter, Isolda, had brought her husband-to-be home to meet them. Marvin, the future husband, who apparently was a little clumsy and a lot nervous, managed to break a wineglass and spill red wine all over one of Maxine's lace tablecloths at dinner.

"Sid thought the unfortunate young man was a complete idiot," Maxine said. "He just couldn't understand how Isolda could be interested in such a dope."

"And Maxine was certain he had a neurological impairment that caused him to keep bumping into things and tripping over his own feet," Dr. Cunningham added, shaking his head. "Isolda talked Maxine and me into going out with her and Marvin for dinner and dancing the following weekend. We couldn't think of an excuse to get out of it so we went, hoping and praying Marvin wouldn't fall on the dance floor and injure himself or someone else."

"I was scared to death I was going to have to dance with him," Maxine exclaimed.

"He actually did pretty well during dinner," Dr. Cunningham explained. "He spilled his water only once and dropped his fork on the floor only two or three times. Of course, there was the piece of meat he flipped across the table, but that could have happened to anyone. The crisis came when Marvin asked Maxine to dance the first dance. Now, Maxine has always been an excellent dancer—much better than I ever was . . .

"Oh, Sid, "Maxine interrupted, "that's not true. You've always been a darn good dancer, too."

"No I haven't," he objected. "What about that dance contest we entered right after we were married, where we were the first ones eliminated? The judge told you it was a shame you didn't have a partner who could dance a little better."

"He didn't say that. He said it was a shame he couldn't have been my partner."

The conclusion of the anecdote was placed on hold while they argued for a few minutes about what the dance judge had said. Finally, without coming to an agreement, Maxine let Dr. Cunningham get back to the story.

"Anyway, I thought Maxine was a good enough dancer to keep out of Marvin's way, at least for one dance."

"What happened?" I asked, wondering how poor Marvin had ever redeemed himself.

"It's a funny thing about some people, John. The harder they try to please, the more mistakes they make, until they decide to just be themselves. I was never so amazed in my life as I was to see Marvin dance with Maxine. Out on the dance floor, Marvin was a different person, just as graceful and smooth as you please—a regular Fred Astaire. Isolda had failed to tell us Marvin had put himself through accounting school by working as a dance instructor. His

CAIN

clumsiness was due to his nervousness around Maxine and me—mostly around me, I think. But when he was out on that dance floor, he was in his element, and there was nothing clumsy about him at all. Maxine enjoyed dancing with Marvin so much, Isolda had to go pry her away from him in order to dance with him herself. How many times did you cut in, Maxine?"

"Sid, I didn't cut in exactly. I just didn't want Isolda to tire herself by dancing too long at one time. Lord, that young man could dance, though, and he still can."

The Cunninghams were trying to put me at ease, but I realized that if the Hansens were waiting to be impressed by a good dancer, I was in big trouble. Possibly Beth's father would like to learn some judo? Maybe Beth's mother would be impressed if I recited some poetry? At least I knew better than to belch, fart, pick my nose, and scratch my ass in the presence of polite company. I could only hope Beth's family would be impressed with my good manners.

About eight o'clock, I drove over to the dorm to get Beth. When I asked her if she would come to my place after we ate, she suggested we take her things so we wouldn't have to pick them up in the morning. Three bags, four boxes, and a mound of loose miscellanea later, the back of the VW was jammed to the headliner and half the space under the hood had disappeared. I suspected the only reason Beth wanted me to remain in Cheney all week was so she'd have a way to get all of her stuff back to Seattle.

We got burgers at Dick's Drive-In and ate them in the car, enjoying the cozy ambience created by the tightly-packed suitcases and boxes blocking the back windows.

The prematurely warm spring day had persisted into the evening. Some stars stood out in the clear sky above the glow of city lights. Our front row seats on Crown Hill at the top of Holman Road gave us first glimpse of a nearly full moon rising majestically out of the darkly silhouetted Cascades.

The bucket seats in the VW had not been designed to encourage intimacy between driver and passenger. Beth and I succeeded in establishing a fair amount of body contact nonetheless, not the least of which were my lips against her warm throat and my hand celebrating the resiliency of her breasts, the erectness of her nipples.

By the time we got back to my apartment, we were both desperately aroused. We barely made it inside the door before we started tearing off each other's clothes, while at the same time trying to climb into each other's mouth. Having stripped each other completely, we stood by the door in a frenzied, writhing embrace, kissing and feeling each other until we could delay no longer. She wrapped one leg around my waist and then the other as I lifted her buttocks and felt her hot wetness surrounding me, massaging me.

Turning and pressing her against the door, I thrust myself into her with all my strength, and she moved with me, crushing me against her with her legs, forcing me so deeply inside her I thought I would never find my way out, or ever want to. We rode the quickening cadence with gasps and moans and meaningless exclamations of gratification through the last shock and shudder of spewing sperm, through the last convulsive twitch of her orgasm.

We remained there, welded to each other: interlocked, intermingled, heavily breathing the same air, tasting the same taste, tingling with the same emotion. During one infinitesimal segment of infinity, our intertwining strands had reached the goal of evolution, had fulfilled the purpose of all existence—for one brief moment, our libidos had been one with the energy of the universe, the infinite power of the Creator. Too intense to be experienced for more than an instant, it had gathered its charge slowly, like a bolt of lightning, and then it had discharged in a blinding, searing flash.

Even the mighty Zeus, in the form of a swan, had felt a power greater than himself in sexual union, as he forced the hapless Leda to his feathered breast and beat his great white wings in rapture.

What Zeus, the rapist, could never have experienced, was the sense of fulfillment brought by that brief, shuddering meld of a man and a woman who love each other both physically and spiritually. It was not just the sex; it was the sex between true lovers that was the portal to exaltation. I felt it. I believed it. I knew I could never get enough of that kind of sex, just as I knew I would die eternally grateful for the intimacy I had already been privileged to share with Beth. It was not only that wonderful; it was that important.

Coventry Patmore was an eminent Victorian whose biography did not make it into Lytton Strachey's book. He counted Alfred Tennyson among his friends and was champion and advisor to the Pre Raphaelites, the most notable literary representatives of which were Dante Gabriel Rossetti, Christina Rossetti, Algernon Charles Swinburne, and William Morris. Morris and Swinburne were noted for their vivid images of medieval sex and violence. I suspect, however, Christina Rossetti's religious poetry held more appeal for Patmore.

I had read the essays and poetry of Coventry Patmore while I was still in high school. That was when I still thought the only thing mystical about sex was how you ever got a girl to agree to have it with you; or more precisely, how you ever got up the nerve to ask. My lack of experience had made it impossible for me to comprehend Patmore's concept of married love as a reified metaphor for Christ's love of the soul. Even with my still-limited capacity to comprehend mysticism at age thirty, I now understood Patmore had been trying to make a case for something more ethereal than coitus interruptus as a means of birth control. No, he knew something of the transcendental potential of sexual love, as esoteric and uncertain as that knowledge may have been.

My apologies, Coventry Patmore. In my ignorance, I mistook you for the one who was the fool. I now understood that sexual ecstasy—the apotheosis of the Id—need not evoke the selfish lust of Pan or Dionysus, or be restricted to the erotic passion of Eros. For the initiated, sexual love was the ritual, and its cries of ecstasy the incantation by which Anteros, brother to Eros and the god of mutual love, might be summoned.

* * *

Beth and I crossed the Columbia River at Vantage shortly before ten the next morning. A patina of new green covered the bare wheat fields and vernal stirrings livened the patches of otherwise somber, gray sagebrush. The dry road stretched out to the northeast under the glare of a bright overcast. A few miles up the road, Interstate 90 would turn due east and unroll in a straight line for twenty-five miles, all the way to Moses Lake. Tranquilized by the husky thrum of the VW's engine, I drove steadily, effortlessly, my thoughts and emotions serenely inert in an inner Elysian garden.

Beth had been sleeping most of the way, snuggled into her pillow against the window with her jacket over her. She sat up and looked around, yawning and stretching. She gave me her waking-up smile, leaned over, and kissed my cheek.

"Where are we?"

"Just a few miles from George. Have a good sleep?"

"Boy, did I. I don't know what it is about riding in a car, but it makes me sleep like a baby." She found the Thermos bottle on the floor and opened it. "Like some coffee?"

"I thought you were never going to wake up and pour me some. That's one of the copilot's most important jobs, you know."

She handed me a cup of coffee. "But Captain, if that's true, why did God create stewardesses?"

"To serve the Captain in other, more important ways, my dear." I cackled lecherously, and she pretended to be put off.

I decided to the change the tone of the conversation. We were going to spend a week together at her home, in the company of her parents and her sister. Getting ourselves all worked up with suggestive banter was foolhardy. I was not going to risk alienating her family by having someone discover us in a midnight rendezvous behind the garage, or chance getting caught by Beth's father as I tried to sneak into her bedroom. With my luck, I'd probably mistakenly get into bed with her sister and then there would be all

CAIN

hell to pay. The very idea of such a disastrous fiasco gave me the shivers.

"Beth, now please don't take offense at this, but would you think it too duplicitous of us to give your parents the impression our relationship is still—how should I say—chaste? You know, loving but chaste?" It was not without trepidation that I brought up the subject, remembering how she had reacted to my concerns about the appearance of our relationship on another occasion.

"John, I don't think they're going to ask us to sign affidavits that we've never had intercourse with each other."

"No, of course not. I just wondered if it would be better if we weren't too, uh, demonstrative around them."

"You mean no cunnilingus in the kitchen?"

I was shocked. "Jesus, Beth, where did you pick up that term?"

"It's in the dictionary."

"Yeah, so?"

"My sister and I used to look through the unabridged dictionary for naughty words. That was one of them. I see you know what it means."

"That's different. I took Latin in high school."

"Hmm, I always wondered what the kids in Latin Club talked about," she teased.

"You and your sister aren't going to spring a bunch of naughty words on me just to embarrass me, are you?"

"I wouldn't do that to you, John. I don't know about my sister, though. She isn't nearly as inhibited as I am."

"Good God! What have I gotten myself into! If your parents don't skin me alive, your sister'll probably embarrass me to death. How about if I just say hello and leave?"

"You can't."

"Why not?"

"You have to stick around and haul all my stuff back to Seattle." She laughed. She was getting a kick out of teasing me. I hoped Beth's sister was more reticent than she had led me to believe.

At Moses Lake we stopped at a roadside restaurant for a snack. Over apple Danish that was just short of being coprolitic, our talk changed from seriously salacious to just plain serious.

"Beth, can we get married in June? We haven't really talked about setting a date. I think maybe we should, before your parents bring it up."

She studied the iridescent sheen on the bitter coffee in her chipped cup as if trying to decide what to say. After a long pause, she asked, "Will you be able to get your dissertation finished next quarter?"

"Absolutely," I said with confidence, even though I was a little disappointed she seemed to be avoiding my question. "Obviously I won't get much done on it this week, but I should have a final draft completed by the end of next week. The week after that I have two interviews for teaching jobs, at Wazzu and at Western. If I have a choice, which job should I choose? Where would you like to live?" I hoped she would respond to that tack.

Still she avoided answering. "You know I want to get a doctorate, too."

"Of course."

"And you also know the UW is the only place in this state I can get a doctorate in physical anthropology."

"And you know there are no teaching jobs available at the UW," I replied. "Not to mention that if there were, I probably wouldn't be able to get one. What do you want me to do? Just tell me."

Disappointment was becoming frustration. Was she beginning to have second thoughts about marriage? That couldn't be it. What could be so hard about deciding on a date?—not a specific hour, not a particular day, just a certain month in a designated year.

"Any fellowships, grants, research assistantships you might be able to get at the UW?" she asked.

"I don't know. Since I haven't been talking to Danner, I haven't been getting any inside information about the anthro department.

CAIN

Most of the information about money for research jobs and grants is not publicized to any extent. As department head, Danner is one of the few people in the department who know what money is available for what. Whenever possible, he makes sure the students he likes or owes a favor get first crack at any opportunity. But then, everyone else in the department does the same thing. It's a version of the spoils system like you'd find anywhere. The ass-kissers shall inherit the earth." My bitterness surprised even me.

"So you think Danner is going to keep you from landing any kind of job through the anthro department?"

"He's not going to bend over backwards to help me, that's for sure. Not now. I don't think he has enough reason yet to go out of his way to sabotage me, but I've definitely lost his support and the benefit of his influence. Both of the interviews I have came out of applications I made last November that included a recommendation from Danner. Since then, with Dr. Bennett's recommendation replacing Danner's, a half dozen applications have not produced a single interview. Danner knows people at Wazzu, Western, and other places. Bennett's recommendation just doesn't carry as much weight."

Beth frowned. "If Danner gets wind of our little expose, he may make sure you don't get hired at Wazzu or Western or anywhere else, for that matter. You got the interviews, but what happens when it gets down to the final selection and somebody calls Danner to ask about you?"

"It will suddenly have come to Danner's attention that I may have cheated on an exam, plagiarized somebody else's work, or paid somebody to write my dissertation. The slightest intimation of something like that would turn me into an instant academic pariah, and no one would ever tell me the real reason they didn't want to hire me. I'm sure he'd enjoy arranging that. Whether he has a chance to or not depends on how fast and how far his influence and credibility decline."

"I suppose he could get me tossed out of the doctoral program, too."

"Maybe, but I doubt it, at least not for any legitimate reason. Your qualifications are too good. Besides, you've already put in a successful year's work at the UW. Danner would have a hard time making a case for the department to drop you. He might be able to create some problems for you, but I don't think even he can get you kicked out. You're already set up for next fall aren't you? Danner should be gone before then."

"For all the good it will do me. Danner's here now and he's going to do something, I just know it."

Beth wasn't exactly glumfounded and wringing her hands, but neither was she elated over the dismal prospects she had conjured up for both of us. Although I should have been, for some reason I wasn't bothered by what Danner might be capable of, or willing to do to me. I was not about to tell Beth how little it mattered to me whether I ever got a teaching job, as far as being interested in teaching was concerned anyway. Writing and research appealed to me, but I knew that without an assistant professorship I would have a hard time getting published and an even harder time getting recognized by academicians.

I was willing to tolerate having to teach in exchange for the opportunity to do other things. I could be a good teacher if I had to, but if at some point I didn't decide I loved to teach, I would surely come to hate it. Perhaps my feelings explained why indifferent teaching was the rule rather than the exception in so many universities, where the laurels went to the researchers, not to the teachers. Research brought fame and fortune to an institution; teaching did not. Some researchers were also great teachers; many were not.

Unfortunately, I would have to get some kind of job, sooner or later. If we were frugal, the money I had in the bank would keep us going for a year, and selling Isolda and Marvin's mortgage on the house would probably provide enough for us to live on for a few more. Then what?

What about the cottage with the white picket fence? The patter of little feet? I could see how the enormity of the commitment we were making might daunt Beth without reflecting on her love for me. We were about to hold hands and jump off a cliff into a raging sea of conjugal responsibility. She was entitled to be hesitant. One of us needed to show a little common-sense apprehension. The idea of jumping off a cliff was less terrifying to me, however, than the prospect of meeting Beth's family. Besides, all that conjugal responsibility churning around down there at the bottom of the cliff looked more to me like a sea of love.

Neither of us drank more than a few sips of the caustic coffee or ate more than a few bites of the stale pastry. The quality of the cuisine, along with the waitress's persistent scratching of something that itched under her dirty apron, dissuaded us from lingering any longer.

When we got out to the car, I gave Beth a long hug. "Everything is going to work out, you'll see. You can let me know about the wedding date when you're ready. Whatever you decide is fine with me. Have I told you in the last half hour how I love you?"

"No."

"Get into the car and let me count the ways."

We arrived in Cheney a little before one that afternoon. I parked on the quiet street in front of the Hansen residence. The large, old, two-story frame house had been restored and remodeled to retain most of its original features and all of its 1930's solidness and charm. A new brick walk led across a well-kept yard up to a large front porch, which was supported by four brick pillars and extended the width of the house. Three dormers with shuttered French windows and lace curtains sat above the sloping porch roof. A new concrete drive ran past a large bay window on the east side of the house to a separate four-car garage set back about fifty feet from the street. The two-floored garage was a newer building, but its design matched the style and character of the old house. Everything about the place was new and fresh. The roof of the house had been newly shaked. The white paint was fresh. Even the old brickwork had been recently cleaned and treated, so that it looked almost new.

The front door was unlocked. Beth opened it and walked in ahead of me, past the staircase and into the living room.

"Mom? It's Beth. I'm here. Yoo-hoo, where are you?"

We walked through the living room toward the back of the house.

A woman's voice came from upstairs. "Beth, is that you down there? I'll be right down, honey." A door closed above us, followed by rapid footsteps. Beth led me back through the living room to the foot of the stairs, where her mother was hurrying down to greet us.

In her early fifties, tall and willowy, Beth's mother was an attractive woman with short, gray-streaked sandy hair and big brown eyes set in a warmly expressive face. Her movements were graceful and energetic, and her slender form looked good in the dark gray skirt and white turtleneck sweater she wore. Had it not been for her gray hair, I could easily have mistaken her for an older sister rather than the mother.

They hugged, and then Mrs. Hansen noticed the ring on Beth's finger and threw up her hands in astonishment.

"Oh, my God! Beth, is that what I think it is?"

Beth smiled and nodded excitedly as she held her hand up for her mother to examine.

Mrs. Hansen gave me a sidelong glance, smiling at me uncertainly, and then she hugged Beth again. Trying hard not to reveal how sheepish and guilty I felt at that moment, I smiled pleasantly and made sure I maintained eye contact whenever Mrs. Hansen looked at me.

"Mother, I want you to meet John Brockman, my future husband. John, this is my mother, Joan."

I stepped forward and shook her hand firmly. "It's a pleasure to meet you, Mrs. Hansen. I see a strong, and may I say a pleasing, family resemblance between you and Beth.

Mrs. Hansen smiled, flattered, but politely reserved. "How kind of you to say that, John. Well, this certainly is a surprise. I'm just overwhelmed, as I'm sure your father will be."

"Mrs. Hansen, I realize Beth invited me here on short notice. I hope I'm not imposing."

"No, of course not, John. Beth called me yesterday and we're expecting you to stay the week and make yourself at home. We have lots of room. We knew you had to be special for Beth to bring you home with her. Of course, we had no idea that the two of you were engaged—no idea at all." A hint of reproach found its way into Mrs. Hansen's comment, but it seemed to carry more disappointment about not having been informed sooner, than any disapproval of the engagement itself. I decided if I didn't break any of her good china or throw up on her shoes, I might just have a chance of winning her over.

"Have you had lunch? I was about to fix myself a sandwich. Would you care for a ham on rye?"

"I don't know about John, but I'm starved, Mom. We stopped at Moses Lake for a snack, but it was so bad we hardly ate any of it."

"Ham on rye sounds good. I'm a bit hungry, too," I said.

"Beth, why don't you get John settled into the guestroom while I whip up some sandwiches."

"The empty bedroom next to mine?"

"Well, uh, actually, I think John would be more comfortable in the guestroom over the garage. The bedroom upstairs is too frilly and feminine for a man, don't you think?"

"Oh, you're right about that, Mom. Come on, John, let's bring in all my stuff and I'll show you where you'll be staying."

Sleeping in the room above the detached garage would be good—less stressful than sleeping in the room next to Beth's. This way I wouldn't have to worry about Mr. and Mrs. Hansen staying up all night listening for the sound of doors opening and closing and for furtive footsteps creaking up and down the hall.

We packed the baggage upstairs to Beth's room, a spacious boudoir busily flounced and ruffled in pink and white organdy—the kind of ovarian decor that causes a man's testicles to slowly shrivel.

"Nice room," I said as appreciatively as I could.

Beth smiled knowingly. "You think it's too feminine, don't you."

"For me, perhaps, but not for you. I am a little surprised, though, to find so much traditional femininity in a feminist's lair. I guess I expected barbells, dirty sweats strewn around, maybe some model airplanes hanging from the ceiling—I don't know."

"I never said I didn't want to be a woman. I just don't want to be treated as an inferior because of it."

"Amen. I can't tell you how happy it makes me that you're not just another one of the boys with a nice set of tits. You are the most womanly of women, Beth, and there is nothing about you that is inferior to anyone—man or woman."

"You're not so bad yourself—for a man. Come over here and look in my closet. I want to show you something."

She led me over to her closet and dug out a big box buried beneath a dozen pairs of shoes. She removed the lid from the box and stood back. Carefully stacked inside, painstakingly assembled and painted, were at least a dozen plastic models of World War II fighter planes.

"Do you have a P-40 in there?" I asked.

"Yeah, there's one in here someplace." She got down on her knees and began setting the models out on the floor. We were comparing a P-51 to a Spitfire when Mrs. Hansen called up from the foot of the stairs that the sandwiches were ready.

Beth, oh Beth, if only we could have been ten years old together, what buddies we would have been!

We ate lunch at the kitchen table. The sandwiches were thick, and lightly relished with small talk and a pinch of local gossip. Mrs. Hansen was careful not to ply me with too many questions, tactfully inquiring about my studies and interests, but avoiding anything more personal. She was undoubtedly curious as hell about my family, my age, and what I had been doing for a life before I met her daughter, but she restrained herself admirably and kept the conversation politely informal and low key.

"Where's Lisa?" Beth asked her mother.

"She went to work with your father today. He has some work for her for a few days this week while she's on vacation. They should be here around five or so. We'll have dinner as soon as they get home. I hope you like meatloaf, John."

"It's one of my favorites. My mother used to make meatloaf at least once a week when I was a boy. I've missed it ever since I left home. I think the last meal she fixed for me was meatloaf."

"John's mother was killed in a car accident nearly eight years ago," Beth volunteered.

"I'm very sorry, John." Mrs. Hansen said.

"It was a long time ago, but I still miss her . . . Well, that was an excellent sandwich, Mrs. Hansen. Thank you."

"I'm glad you liked it. Maybe you can get Beth to show you your room now."

"We did get sidetracked with Beth's model airplanes. I have most of those same models packed away in storage."

"Beth used to be such a tomboy. My goodness, we thought she'd never grow out of it."

Beth gave her mother a tolerant smile. "I still haven't, Mom. John likes me because I'm just one of the boys with a nice set of model airplanes." Beth gave me a teasing glance.

"Actually, Mrs. Hansen, I like your daughter because she's bright and beautiful. I love her because she is who she is."

"My, my, John, you do know exactly what to say, don't you. Beth, you'd better take this eloquent young man to his room and lock him up before you have to fight your sister for him."

"He is sort of a golden-tongued gallant, isn't he? I guess that's why I like him. Of course, I love him because he is so highly intelligent and handsome—that and the fact he admires my model airplanes so much."

Beth led me out to the garage and up the stairs at the end of the building. I set my battered, half-full duffle bag by the bed and she showed me the guest quarters. There were two bedrooms separated by a bathroom.

Making sure we weren't standing in front of a window, Beth gave me a lingering kiss before leaving me.

"My mom likes you, John."

"Hey, what's not to like? I like her, too. I hope your father and sister like me."

"They will."

"I guess I'll take a shower before I go back to the house. All this anxiety is causing a lot of perspiration."

"Are you going to take a hot shower, or a cold one?"

"Both. Now get out of here before your mother starts to wonder if I'm over here twirling the propellers on your P-38 with my golden tongue."

Back at the house after my shower, I took Mrs. Hansen up on an offer of a glass of sherry. Beth was upstairs performing her predinner toilette. We sat on the sofa, and taking advantage of Beth's absence, Mrs. Hansen addressed me ominously.

"John, I find this extremely awkward, but I feel I would be remiss if I didn't say something to you about it."

I had a sinking feeling and I had to fight the compulsion to check my pants zipper.

"I don't know what Beth has told you to expect about her father. He's a decent man who loves his family. He has worked very hard for twenty years building and managing a business, only to have it sold out from under him after it had finally begun to grow and become lucrative."

"Yes, Beth told me he was being forced out. I'm sorry. Does he know what he'll do yet?"

"He's looking for another job and thinking about a franchise investment. He'll be back on his feet before long, doing something and working just as hard at it as he always has. I'm not worried about that, but he is feeling the frustration and disappointment of having to start all over."

"That's completely understandable. It can't be easy for you either."

"You must be wondering why I'm telling you all this. I hardly know you."

"It looks as if you may get to know me better as your son-in-law."

"Yes, it does. You seem like a nice man, John, and I can see that Beth is very taken with you. I respect her judgment. But her father . . . her father has always been very protective of both the girls. Sometimes that has caused problems for their social lives. I'm sorry. I'm not doing this very well."

"Let me help you Mrs. Hansen. You are trying to prepare me for a cool reception by Mr. Hansen, who may resent a stranger showing up and announcing he's going to marry one of daddy's little girls. You also suspect his attitude may be exacerbated by the fact of my race."

"Yes, I guess that pretty well covers it. You have to understand, John. Frank is not a bigot in the worst sense of the term, but he can be intolerant and insensitive. Unfortunately, he has always had strong opinions against interracial marriages. I forget the term for mixed marriages . . ."

"Miscegenation."

"Yes, thank you. I know, once he gets to know you, he'll accept you as a person, but it may take a while. Please, try not to be offended. When he sees how much Beth cares, he'll come around. Her expressive eyes deepened as she studied me with candid concern.

"Mrs. Hansen, I appreciate your trying to spare my feelings, but I assure you I'm not easily offended and I'm certainly not sensitive about being an Indian. I was adopted and raised by white parents. I probably have the same prejudices your husband has. If I am ever fortunate enough to have a daughter, I am certain her suitors will find me every bit as vigilant and formidable as Beth's father could ever be. Don't worry, Mrs. Hansen, I won't let him scare me off. He'll have to accept me." I hoped I sounded more confident to Mrs. Hansen than I sounded to myself. Of course he wasn't going to scare me off, but I was not convinced he had no choice but to accept me.

Mrs. Hansen patted my hand and gave me a hopeful, but troubled, smile. "Yes he will, I don't know how he could not accept you, John. Well, I suppose I should start preparing dinner." She rose and picked up her sherry glass from the coffee table.

"Is there anything I can help you with?" I asked.

"Oh, goodness no. Thank you, anyway. You just sit here and relax, and have another sherry. I have a feeling you're going to need it. If you'll excuse me, I'll go get dinner started." She smiled appreciatively and went into the kitchen, leaving me with a decanter of sherry and a sense of uncertainty to savor.

* * *

Frank Hansen stood well over six feet and projected himself even larger. He looked as if he might have once been athletic, but had been overtaken by encroaching corpulence brought on by too many responsibilities behind a desk. His salt and pepper hair was thick and short. Severe, steel-framed glasses and determined creases divided his intelligent countenance into craggy dominions that converged beneath bushy gray brows into intensely blue eyes. He was an energetic man, with quick, decisive movements and a natural air of authority—a man who gave the impression of being quick to make up his mind and slow to change it.

He and Lisa had come in while Beth and her mother worked and talked in the kitchen; while I sipped sherry and looked at a magazine in the living room.

I got up when they entered the room, trying to look pleasant, but not fatuous. Beth's father stopped when he saw me, his eyes squinting down to the thickness of a scalpel blade and dissecting me in short, deft strokes. Having anatomized me to his satisfaction, he approached. I walked up to him and extended my hand.

"Mr. Hansen, I'm John Brockman. Nice to meet you, sir." He raised his hand slowly and took my hand firmly, but without enthusiasm. His eyes never left mine.

"Uh huh, Beth's . . . friend?"

"Yes, sir."

"Hmmmm."

He continued to try to stare me down, and I continued to smile at him, to the point where not to look away could only have been taken as a gesture of defiance. I turned to Beth's sister, who was quietly wide-eyed and seemingly fascinated by the palpable aura of tension between her father and me. Lisa was a little taller than Beth, but more slender, with dark brown hair falling around her shoulders, and dark eyebrows arched over deep brown eyes. Her full lips tended to pout like her sister's, but with an engaging girlishness that lacked sensuality.

"Hi. You must be Lisa. I've been looking forward to meeting you." I held out my hand, and she shook it, smiling and looking away for an instant with a genuine and charming touch of self-consciousness.

"Hi, it's nice to meet you, John," she replied pleasantly.

Beth hurried into the room, followed closely by her mother, thinking, perhaps, I n needed to be rescued. Mr. Hansen's demeanor changed from dour to delighted when he saw Beth. She threw her arms around his neck, and he picked her up and swung her around the room like a bear dancing with a doll.

"Hey, it's nice to have you home, Kitten."

"It's nice to be home, Daddy. Did you get to meet John?"

"Yes, your friend introduced himself."

I was waiting for Beth's father to notice her engagement ring, wondering how he was going to react. So far, Beth hadn't exactly waved it in his face. He set her down, and she hugged him and then turned to hug her sister. I looked at her hand, expecting to see the ring flash and draw everyone's attention, but it did not flash and it drew only my attention because I saw that it was not on her finger.

Mrs. Hansen dispersed the crowd by announcing dinner was ready. Ok, so Beth didn't want her father to see her ring just yet. Maybe that was well advised. It would have been nice if she had let me in on the plan, though. I was beginning to see that breaking the news to her father was more difficult for her than she let on. As for me, round two was coming up, and so far Beth's father had hardly laid a glove on me.

When we were seated around the dining room table, Mr. Hansen sat at one end of the table opposite Mrs. Hansen, and I wound up sitting between Lisa and her father, across the table from Beth. The strategy behind the seating arrangement was not clear to me, but I was pretty sure Mrs. Hansen had one, judging by the care with which she had prepared and presented dinner.

A vase of jonquils and two tall, saffron candles sat on a crisp tablecloth of pastel yellow. Matching napkins rolled in saffron rings lay in the heavy crockery plates. The flatware was unusual, with porcelain handles and broad, heavy surfaces. The food was served in matching crockery bowls and platters: a large meatloaf garnished with stuffed green olives and pineapple rings, baby lima beans and carrots julienne, freshly baked croissants, potatoes au gratin, garden salad, and a tray of sliced apples and oranges. A bottle of burgundy stood uncorked and ready to pour.

The meal started off innocuously enough, with Lisa talking about her day with her dad and Mrs. Hansen talking about the neighbor's children getting into mischief. Then, the preliminaries over, Mr. Hansen and I squared off in the middle of the ring.

"Had any military service, Mr. Brockman?"

"Yes sir, I was in the army for eight years."

"What did you do in the army?"

"I was in Special Forces."

"I suppose you were too young to have been in Vietnam."

"No sir, I was there from 1969 until 1972."

"How old are you anyway?"

"I'll be thirty-one in August."

"Kind of old to be going to college, aren't you."

CAIN

"Yes sir, I've had the same thought myself."

"What are you going to have when you finish school?"

"I'll have a doctorate in anthropology."

"And what kind of job will that get you?"

"A college teaching job."

"A professor, huh? What does a job like that pay these days?"

"An assistant professorship at the University of Washington starts at about twenty thousand."

"That's all? Twenty thousand? What does a full professor make?"

"In the anthropology department, it's around thirty-five thousand."

"You're not going to get rich, are you?"

"Probably not."

"You know, I have two Ph.D's working for me and I never even finished college. One of them works in shipping and the other one is on the maintenance staff."

"It happens."

"What sort of work does your father do?"

"My mother and father died when I was a baby. The parents who adopted me and raised me are also dead. My adoptive father was a physicist at the University of Washington."

"Ever involved in any sports?"

"High school track and cross country. I didn't go out for any sports in college."

"How did you and Beth meet?"

"We had some classes together."

"I see, so are you two just friends, dating, what?"

"Actually, Mr. Hansen, we're planning to get married."

He ignored me, acting as if I had said nothing at all. Pausing to take a deep drink of wine, he addressed Beth.

"Hey, Beth, I saw an article in the paper about Brent Woody— "" He paused, looking at me with calculating eyes from behind a cold smile. "—that big football player you dated a while back. He just got drafted by the Bears. That boy will be making some big bucks, and he's only twenty-one years old." His comments had been for me all along, but now he addressed me directly: "I bet you wish you'd been big enough to play football, huh?"

"No sir, I never cared much for the game." I took my napkin off my lap and placed it carefully on the table beside my plate. "I don't care much for this game, either. You know, Mr. Hansen, no matter how much I might dislike you at this moment, I would not treat you as rudely as you have treated me.

"Mrs. Hansen, the dinner is really exquisite, thank you so much, but I'll have to ask you to please excuse me." No one said anything as I got up and walked away. I got to the door before Beth caught up with me.

"Oh, John, I'm sorry. I didn't think he'd go that far."

"Neither did I. I thought I could handle it, but I couldn't. Jesus, Beth, is it true you actually dated Brent Woody? How could you possibly have had anything at all to do with that Neanderthal asshole? I don't understand. I thought I knew you, Beth. How in the hell could you do that?"

"John, it's not what you think. It was all a stupid mistake. I can explain."

"No you can't, Beth. I'm not taking any explanations right now. Maybe later—maybe not. Just leave me alone, please. I need to be alone." I pushed past her and out the door. I needed to walk and so I set off down the sidewalk, trying to get away from the hurt and the anger, knowing they were an inescapable part of me.

I walked for hours, trying hard but unable to sort it all out. Forewarned and thinking I was prepared, I had let Beth's father get to me. I had gone down in the second round, and my ego had immediately thrown in the towel. Some contender I was. It was that damned low blow about Beth and Brent Woody that had put me on the canvas. I might have danced and ducked my way through the whole fifteen rounds if not for that. Maybe if I had been able to go the distance, I might have earned his respect. The irony of it was that he couldn't have known how much the Brent Woody punch would hurt me.

CAIN

I couldn't get past the image of Woody's leering face and the thought of Beth submitting to his defiling touch. I ached and burned to beat him back into the excremental paste that was his true essence; to flush him once and for all time down the toilet of oblivion. It was easy to hate Brent Woody, to blame him, to make him the reason for the way I was feeling. Yes, God help me, I was smitten with stupid, jealous rage, and even angrier with myself that I could be made jealous by a piece of shit like Brent Woody.

I had once conceded to myself that the boyfriends Beth may have had before me were none of my business. It was a sound principle. Unfortunately, I had failed to see how pettiness, possessiveness, and jealousy might qualify that principle. Apparently, Beth's former boyfriends were none of my business only as long as I didn't know anything about them.

I knew I was not being fair to Beth, but the pain in my gut was not listening to the advice of my brain. Even if she had gone out with him—as inexplicable as that seemed—it didn't mean they were lovers. It didn't even mean she liked going out with him. Maybe it just took her a while to discover what a giant, jerking turd he was—as inconceivable as it was that it could have taken more than thirty seconds to make that discovery. Clearly, she not been happy to have him paw her and press her to the column in front of the library that day I had intervened. Why hadn't I let her explain, instead of pushing her aside and running off like a twelve-year-old twit? I hadn't lost my temper, but I had lost something else. The Hansens got to see a side of me I would have preferred to keep hidden, especially from Beth. I didn't feel good about any of it, except maybe for the delicious fantasy about tearing off Brent Woody's arm and clubbing him to a pulp with it. When it came right down to it, I guess I didn't feel very good about that either.

It was nearly ten o'clock before I found my way back to the Hansens' and climbed the stairs to the rooms over the garage. I had made up my mind I would go back to Seattle in the morning. My leaving would resolve nothing, but I was convinced the only way I could make things worse, other than to go now, was to stay. I'd go over and make my apologies to Mrs. Hansen after her husband left for work.

I wasn't sure how I stood with Beth. I wanted to tell her I was sorry for not listening to her, for not loving her enough not to be jealous. Disturbingly, a part of me—some sick, self-serving, self-destructive, jealous part of me—was feeding on the pain and anger. That ugly part was urging me to punish Beth, to make her feel as miserable as I felt, as if she might not already feel that way. As much as I hated the feeling, its power was almost irresistible, and I realized it was by no means certain I would be able to apologize to her.

Now was a hell of a time to be learning about relationships and jealousy and sexual politics. I should have taken care of all that in my teens and twenties and been done with it. Having to cope with these things now for the first time was like getting the measles or the mumps at my age—they were likely to be a lot more serious and painful.

A small lamp by the bed was on when I opened the door to the guestroom. I saw Beth curled up on the end of the bed asleep, apparently having been waiting for me for some time. I closed the door quietly and she didn't wake up. Standing by the bed, I watched her as she slept: the rise and fall of her breathing, the trace of a frown that not even sleep could erase from her pretty face, the teardrop still trembling in the corner of her eye.

I knelt by the bed, kissed her forehead, and stroked her hair without waking her. I knelt there for a long time; then I got up and moved to sit in an easy chair across the room. As I continued to watch her, my turmoil subsided and my love for her welled up and overflowed. Marveling that my love for her could leave room for any other feelings at all, I fell asleep, too.

It was daylight when the door crashed open. Beth's father towered darkly, bellowing and lurching into the room with all the fury of an affronted grizzly.

Beth bolted upright, frightened and confused.

Seeing me in the chair and Beth fully clothed took the momentum out of his charge. He stopped in the middle of the room with a startled look.

Mrs. Hansen was running up the stairs behind him yelling "Frank! For God's sake, Frank!" Lisa's anxious calls chased after her mother from the house, "Will someone tell me what's happening? Where is everybody?"

"Daddy, what are you doing?" Beth asked, anger displacing her confusion.

"You be quiet! Just don't say anything," he snapped at her. He looked wildly at Beth and then at me. Things were not as he obviously had expected to find them, and now he could not decide what to do.

I stayed in my chair and said nothing. To have risen or to have spoken might have helped him decide what to do, might have allowed his wrath to vent on me even though he had to know the circumstances did not warrant it.

Mrs. Hansen fluttered through the door in a panic, probably expecting mayhem, but finding it still tenuously in check, as her husband's rage groped blindly for its proper object.

Beth got off the bed. "I won't be quiet, Daddy, not this time. How dare you break in here like this."

He paid no attention to her, focusing his ire entirely on me. "This is my house, dammit, and I'm not going to let some goddammed Indian come here and screw my daughter in my own house! Get out of here! Get out of here right now!"

"Frank! You should be ashamed of yourself! Leave them alone!" Mrs. Hansen pulled on his arm, but he shook her off.

I stood up. Beth's father was big and he was angry. If he came at me, I wouldn't be able to stop him without hurting him seriously, assuming he didn't break me in half first. I wasn't big enough, or strong enough, or skilled enough to subdue him without disabling him, and I didn't want to have to do that. As out-of-line as he was, he still had some rights in the matter: it was his daughter, his house. He was Beth's father, for Christ's sake.

Beth moved between her father and me and faced him. "All right, if that's the way you want it, we're going, Daddy. We're going away from here, we're going to get married, and we're not coming back. Not until you decide you love me enough to let me be a woman and live my own life; not until you apologize to John and accept him for the man he is and as the man I want to spend my life with. I never thought I'd ever be ashamed of you, Daddy, but I am. I'm so terribly, terribly ashamed of you." She turned and came to me, crying, and I held her tightly, defiantly.

Lisa entered just then with her hairbrush still in her hand. "What's going on? What's all the shouting . . ."

Mrs. Hansen shook her head at her. "Shhh. Not now, Lisa. Not now."

Somewhat deflated, but still angry, Mr. Hansen shoved roughly past Lisa and rushed bitterly out the door and down the stairs. A few seconds later, his car squealed out of the driveway and roared off down the street.

By this time, Lisa was crying on her mother's shoulder, whether out of empathy or because she saw herself in Beth's shoes a few years hence, I didn't know. Women cried; so did men, sometimes.

Mrs. Hansen and I stood there comforting Lisa and Beth, looking at each other apologetically.

The morning sun streamed through the window with dispassionate brilliance. Through the open door, a meadowlark had its musical say from somewhere out in the wet grass in the still of a clear morning, knowing nothing of human emotions, nor wanting to.

The trip back to Seattle was long and dreary, made longer and drearier by the silence—not a sullen silence, just a sad, despondent quiet we tacitly agreed to share with each other. Beth sat looking out the window, two sniffs away from a sob the whole way back. Every so often, she would reach over and clutch my hand as if she were afraid the door would suddenly fly off and she would be sucked out of the car.

CAIN

Whatever there was to talk about would wait until some of the emotional swelling had gone down. Less than twenty-four hours ago, we had been going in the opposite direction. Beth had been happy, sassy, excited about going home and about bringing me with her. I wondered how long it would be before Beth could take those feelings home with her again.

I hurt for her. She had given up a great deal for me, perhaps more than she had really meant to. I hoped she believed I was worth it, because I wasn't sure I was. I was sure, however, that never again would I fail to beware the green-eyed monster. It was a promise I made to Beth, and to myself.

Othello and Desdemona had a different story, but it still revolved around jealousy. I had never understood how Othello could love Desdemona so much and yet doubt her so easily—Iago notwithstanding. Now the story made sense.

Excellent Beth! Perdition catch my soul,
But I do love thee! and when I love thee not,
Chaos is come again.

Sweet Beth, Love conquers Chaos; and I will conquer Jealousy. I hope your father will one day bless our union and say better of you than did Desdemona's father to Othello.

CHAPTER 19

Communing

Taking Beth's things out of her bedroom and packing them back into the car had been an ordeal. Leaving her mother and sister would have been difficult enough for Beth, under the circumstances, without having had to gather up her things out of the room she had occupied in the house since she was in elementary school.

"Your father will relent, just give him a little time," Beth's mother had reassured her. "He'll miss you too much not to."

Mrs. Hansen had become tearful at the last moment when we were ready to depart. Lisa had clung to her sister as if she would never let her go. But heavy hearted and hurting, Beth had left with me in a shower of tears, trailing behind her the ragged ends of a hard goodbye.

Now, after one of the world's less lenient turns, we were back in front of Beth's dorm, and all of the stuff crammed into the overburdened Beetle had to be rehandled and rehashed.

After we emptied the car, Beth needed something to do besides cling to me and sigh heavily; I needed to do something besides watch her mope. I suggested we go camping for a few days up past Granite Falls on the Mountain Loop Highway, little more than an hour's drive north of Seattle.

"Won't there still be snow up there?"

"With the light snowfall we've had this year, it'll be mostly gone in the valley. We'll stay in one of the campgrounds and maybe take a few hikes.

"What do I need to bring?"

"Warm clothes, walking shoes or boots if you have some, a tooth brush, a couple of good books. I'll bring everything else. What do you say? I don't even think we're supposed to get any rain for a few days. We can drink wine in front of the campfire, sleep as late as we want to, and we won't have to think about anything. Ok?"

"I think I'd like that."

Beth got her things together, and we stopped by a grocery store for provisions. The Cunninghams were not at home when we got to my apartment, where I changed my clothes and picked up my sleeping bags, my small tent, and the rest of the camping paraphernalia we'd need. On the way out, I grabbed a handful of thin volumes of essays by Loren Eiseley and Lewis Thomas I had been rereading.

One more stop for gas and a quart of engine oil, and then we were northbound on I-5. Once past the stench of the pulp mill in Everett, we drove northeast on 204, crossing the muddy Snohomish river and climbing up the other side of the valley to Highway 9 at Frontier Village. Two miles north on Highway 9, we turned northeast again on 92. We passed the Lake Stevens turnoff and drove by the berry and dairy farms, then past the row of motorcycles parked in front of the tavern in Granite Falls. From Granite Falls, we drove east along the Mountain Loop highway through the Robe Valley in the shadow of Mt. Pilchuck, up the slate-green Stillaguamish river, past the ranger station at Verlot, through the old mining town of Silverton, and finally, into the empty campground at Big Four, where patches of dirty snow still decorated the shady areas.

According to my odometer we had traveled exactly 74.7 miles from the Cunninghams' house. In a straight line, we were probably no more than forty miles from the northern city limits of Seattle, and yet we were in a setting that in many ways might have rivaled any scenic wilderness in the world.

Gold, silver, and copper had brought mining to the area in the early 1890's. The Big Four campground had once been a station and summer resort on the Hartford & Eastern Railway. The tracks had snaked laboriously up switchbacks with as much as 6% grades another nine miles southeast of Big Four to its terminus at the mining community of Monte Cristo. The spot where a two-story hotel and numerous summer cottages had once nestled at the foot of mile-high Big Four Mountain was now marked by a U.S Forest Service campground: a toilet, a turnaround and parking area, wooden picnic tables, trees. Nothing except a relic piece of a foundation remained to remind anyone of the history of Big Four.

The old lodge at Monte Cristo was still standing, but unused. When the mining had petered out, the place had become a resort and hunter's lodge, until that enterprise also had petered out. The railroad tracks had long since been torn up, and one had to look carefully to find the few overgrown vestiges of the railway grade where it diverged from the highway.

The Stillaguamish river valley at Big Four lay about 1600 feet above sea level and spread out a mile wide. At 6135 feet, Big Four Mountain harbored snow year round in the pockets beneath its granite crags rising above the southwest side of the valley. Hall Peak, only a few hundred feet shorter, stood to the right of Big Four Mountain when viewed from Big Four Campground, and also was laden with snow most of the year. Less than half a mile from the campground, in the hollow between the two peaks, ice caves formed beneath the glacial accumulations of snow and were a popular, although somewhat dangerous, attraction for hikers.

Dad and I had hiked the dozens of trails leading up into the mountains on both sides of the valley many times while I was growing up. We had found abandoned mine shafts and rusty artifacts nearly everywhere we had searched for them. Dad had told me of his readings in the history of the glory days; of the claims named the Bonanza Queen, the Bornite, and the Helena near Silverton; the Pride, the Mystery, and the Justice above Monte Cristo; of miners poisoned by arsenic water and buried by rockslides; of places once booming and buzzing, long since quiet

CAIN

and empty, or having vanished as completely as the era that had created them.

Farther down in the Robe valley, named after T. K. Robe, who had opened a post office and station on the railway nine miles east of Granite Falls, the lumber industry had boomed. Loggers had planted their five-foot springboards in ten-foot-diameter red cedars and hundred-foot-tall Douglas Firs. Double bitted axes had scarfed, and long crosscut saws had toppled the stoic giants. Trees fell; lumber and shake mills rose. But like the mining operations, logging and lumbering had dried up. The teamsters, fallers, barkers, skid greasers, hook tenders—all gone. Now it was as if the place had forgotten its own history in order to accommodate another few generations of visitors from a different era. It was an accommodation the valleys and mountains had made many times since the first human eyes had beheld them and the first human feet had trodden them. There was much more to Big Four Campground than just scenery; there was the history: the loggers, the miners, and before them, the Indians.

Most of the villages of the Stillaguamish Indians, the "river people," had grown up along the north fork of the river bearing their name. They had stayed in temporary summer camps along the upper south fork of the river, hunting for blacktail deer, elk, mountain goats, beaver, and marmot. They had caught rainbow, cutthroat, and Dolly Varden in reed traps set in the river, and had picked thimbleberries and salmonberries during the warm months, blackberries in late summer, and huckleberries and blueberries in the fall before the snows came. They had spoken the North Lushootseed dialect of Salish, along with the Swinomish, the Skagit, the Snohomish, and the Skykomish groups. They had lived, loved, fought, and died for hundreds of generations before the white man came with his gifts of civilization and disease. Now they were few, their blood intermingled with that of the white man and with that of the other tribes gathered together on the Tulalip reservation, their native customs and language all but forgotten.

And before the Indians? Eagles shrieked, grizzlies roared, rutting elk bugled. Wolves and coyotes choired the bright-mooned nights with yips and howls. Glaciers groaned, cracked, toppled into the sea, while thunder rumbled in the distance. Earthquakes shook the earth like a wolf shaking a rabbit in its jaws. Volcanoes blasted, spewed, and oozed out the secrets of earth's innards, to be shuffled over by the giant sloth, trampled by the wooly mammoth, flowered by a vagabond seed scudding vast oceans on a restless wind. Cycles of crushing ice and rushing water swayed imperceptibly to the millennial cadence of one eonic dance in the cosmic cotillion.

* * *

Beth began having her monthly female affliction, a phenomenon I had successfully avoided contemplating up to that time, and indeed not a subject for general conversation among the people with whom I had grown up. Of course, I had been forced to note in my readings the recorded observations of anthropologists and other observers describing the taboos and practices associated with menstruation in various cultures around the world. The Coastal Salish Indians, and other groups as well, believed menstrual blood to have powerful properties, and required menstruating women to stay in a separate hut designated for that purpose. Although primitive cultures had interpreted the significance of menstruation in a variety of ways, they seemed mostly to agree that the subject belonged to the domain of women, and that it was not a topic suitable for the male forum.

According to ancient Hebrew law, on the eighth day after a week of uncleanness, Beth would have had to take two turtle doves or two young pigeons to the tabernacle to be offered up by the priest. That provision in Hebrew law must have kept the suppliers of turtle doves and young pigeons very busy. It would also have kept both the priests and the suppliers of birds well-informed as to the menstrual activity of every woman in town. It's my guess,

CAIN

however, that even among those men unfamiliar with Hebrew practices, the symbolism of being served a dinner of baked squab once a month by their mates, after a week of involuntary sexual abstinence, would not long have remained a mystery.

The intimacies of camping and sharing a small tent have a tendency to break down the barriers of civilized privacy and to compromise modesty. Silly as it was, I suppose, neither of us was comfortable even with undressing in front of the other, yet alone in acknowledging or, heaven forbid, having to discuss anything as intimate as "the curse." As yet, we were some distance from complete familiarity with each other in all things physical and personal; but, as was to be expected, the more we were together, the more familiar we became.

And so, observing the Hebrew holiday of abstinence, it was a passive, platonic time we shared at Big Four. Sleeping, watching the river, gazing into the fire, staring at the mountains during the day and at the brilliant array of stars during the night, eating, cuddling; reading together without talking, feeling the closeness of each other in small ways that also had a subtle power to bond, comfort, and satisfy. This was part of the slow time between passions—slow but deep; by no means emotionally fallow, but filled with a spiritual warmth that did not consume itself, as did the fire of passion.

Beth was not an avid reader of fiction, having been baptized in the clearer shallows of expository prose, rather than in the murky depths of poetry and creative literature. I didn't expect to make a convert of her overnight, but she was beginning to show both interest and appreciation.

She was reading D.H. Lawrence's *The Rainbow*, which I had recommended to her, and which we talked about. Perhaps I saw a little of Lawrence's Ursula Brangwen in Beth and wanted her to know the character in order better to know me. Even if such a connection were too esoteric to hope for, his writing was worth reading for its own sake.

Notwithstanding his preoccupation with matters of the flesh, I considered D. H. Lawrence to be one of the most powerful and evocative masters of English prose—curiously more poetic in some of his prose than in most of his poetry. I had often thought it unfortunate that Lawrence's adult subject matter prevented his consummate writing from being introduced to aspiring readers and writers during their formative years in high school.

But what did I know? For all my precocious reading in high school, I had managed to reach the age of thirty with a fair proficiency in reading and writing, but with hardly a clue about how to relate to the opposite sex. Maybe my time would have been better spent unfastening bras and exploring young female body parts in the back seat of a car, as apparently most of the guys I knew did—or claimed they did, anyway—instead of sitting up until the wee hours, pondering image and cadence in D. H. Lawrence's prose. I narrowly avoided becoming a complete introvert by virtue of the occasional titillating passage that led me to suspect something mysterious and wonderful existed completely outside the realm of books, something that words alone, no matter how eloquent and evocative, could at best only suggest, but not allow one to fully experience.

* * *

PUNT, COUNTER PUNT

I guess I was ready for Brent Woody. Not as ready as I had been right after Mr. Hansen's backhanded disclosure about Beth and Woody, but ready enough. I had dealt with the idea of Beth and Woody together by burying my feelings. But I hadn't forgotten where those feelings were buried, and they weren't buried as deeply as they should have been. The rest of what I felt about Brent Woody I had been wearing around my neck like some grotesque garland. When Brent Woody came up behind me in the narrow aisle between the stacks of shelved books on the third floor of Suzzallo library, he could not have guessed just how ready I was.

Why he was there, in that part of the library, at that moment, is still unclear. Maybe it doesn't matter. My impression was that Brent Woody seldom used the library for much of anything except as a place to take a nap, and he wouldn't have bothered to go up to the third floor to do that. I assumed he had followed me to that unfrequented, secluded section of the nearly deserted library on some half-baked, nefarious impulse.

Engrossed in the evolutionary naturalism of Herbert Spencer as I leaned against the steel shelf rack, I didn't hear Woody sneak up on me. Presumably, Spencer might have predicted my temporary state of equilibrium would have to be destroyed in order for me to achieve a higher form of reality. I'm not sure what he would have said about Woody's bashing the back of my head with something hard and heavy.

My equilibrium disappeared at the same instant the universe contracted to a bright point of light and then winked out. The next reality I experienced was lower, rather than higher. The universe came painfully back into existence as Woody's big foot kicked me back into consciousness, and I found myself clinging to the floor with all the intensity of an unroped rock climber hugging the sheer face of El Capitan.

Fortunately, the aisle between the bookracks was so narrow Woody didn't have enough room to get in a really good kick, otherwise I might have been seeking a higher reality somewhere in the spirit world among my ancestors.

I lashed out with a kick of my own and felt the satisfying crunch of a testicle between my toe and his pubic bone.

Not surprisingly, Woody stopped kicking me and staggered back, doubled over and clutching his tormented testicle with both hands.

Using the rack for support, I clawed my way back up to a standing position, spilling onto the floor several volumes of a 1925 edition of the *Gesammelte Werke* of Nietzsche, multiple volumes of an 1887 edition of Hegel's *Werke*, and every book on three shelves from Schopenhauer and Feurbach, to J.F. Herbart in the process. Everything was getting dark and fuzzy as I lurched dizzily toward him, raking another dozen books from the shelf and stumbling rubber-legged over them.

Still bent over, groaning and retching, Woody's head was no higher than my waist. I shoved down hard on the back of his head and battered my knee up into his face as hard and as fast I could, feeling his teeth gouge into my knee, and then again, harder, and again—until the blood gushing from his nose soaked my pantleg and splattered across the jumble of books littering the aisle; until I was too weak to lift my leg anymore.

My head pounded and everything spun around me as I hung on to the bookrack to keep from collapsing.

Brent Woody should have given up at that point for both our sakes, but he didn't. Instead, gasping unintelligible obscenities and choking on the blood pouring down his throat from his smashed nose, he grabbed my legs, lunged me backwards onto the pile of books behind me, straddled me, and began beating my face with his huge fists.

Trying to fend off the blows with my left arm, I desperately reached out with my right. My hand closed on the hard cover of one of the books lying on the floor next to me.

I picked up the book and jabbed it into Woody's bloody face, corner first, into his eye, gouging and twisting until it was too slick with blood to hold onto and Woody knocked it out of my hand.

Woody's hands went to his face and he began to whimper. Then he started screaming.

"My eye! Oh, fuck, my eye! You motherfucker, you tore out my eye!"

I'm not too clear about what happened after that. I seem to remember Woody with one hand over his eye, trying to choke me with the other hand, and some people pulling him off me, and then I was lying in the ambulance.

I woke up at Harborview twelve hours later in intensive care with tubes running into and out of nearly every natural body orifice and into some that were unnatural. An ungodly pain throbbed in my head and I couldn't get my eyes to focus worth shit. Eventually a doctor came in, checked my chart, waved a penlight in my eyes, and had me squeeze his hands. The doctor appeared to be in his mid-forties, thin, kinky-haired, wore thick glasses, and talked with an r-dropping East Coast accent. He said there was hardly anything wrong with me except for a cracked skull, severe concussion, a broken cheek bone, a lacerated knee, and a bruised, bleeding spleen.

"I'm sahry, Mr. Brockman, you've gotta be hurting, but you wah unconscious fah quite a while and I can't give you anything fah the pain just yet. You've got a little bleeding from yah spleen, but I don't think weah going to have to go in and work on it. Weah going to watch you fah a while to make sure theah ah no complications from the blow you took to the back of yah head. Did you hit the back of yah head on the flah?"

"No, he hit me with something from behind."

"Just a little hahda, and right now you probably would be lying on a slab in the mahg feeling no pain at all."

"The way my head feels right now, lying in the morgue doesn't sound all that bad. What about the other guy, Brent Woody?" I asked.

"He had extensive facial injuries: broken teeth, nose, facial bones. Weah still trying to save his left eye. Oh, yeah, he also had a ruptured testis. I'm curious," the doctor said, "Did you do all that to him by yahself?"

"I guess so," I answered.

"You know, Mr. Brockman, I've watched Brent Woody play football. I've seen him put 250 lb. linemen in the hospital. Yah what, about five-nine? One-sixty? Yah lucky he didn't rip you apaht."

"You're right, Doc. I'm one lucky son of a bitch. Let me know if you need any help hammering the bastard's eyeball back into place."

"I think the ophthalmologist has already taken care of that, but I'll let him know you offered to help. You've got some people waiting to see you. I'll send them in, but they can only stay fah a few minutes, ok? I'll be around latah."

"Thanks, Doc."

I was pretty sure that short of actually attacking me, Brent Woody would not have been able to provoke me into a confrontation with him, even though on more than one occasion, I had imagined deriving tremendous satisfaction from beating him to a pulp. Since I hadn't exactly kicked his ass while composing a sonnet, the outcome was less than conclusive. The only satisfaction I was entitled to was the knowledge that I'd been able to prevent him from killing me.

The step from pissed-off bully to back-of-the-head-bashing assassin was a big one, even for Brent Woody. There was no doubt he wanted to hurt me, and hurt me badly, but I was reasonably confident he hadn't actually planned to do me in. He would have wanted me around afterwards to show him some fear and cowering respect—the kind of relationship he seemed to prefer. It probably never occurred to him that he might bludgeon my brains out by hitting me in the back of the head with whatever he hit me with. Nobody seemed to know what that might have been, although it had felt like a two by four, or a baseball bat. Hell, for all I knew, he had cracked my skull by whapping me in the back of the head with his huge, hard cock.

I wasn't proud of having gouged out his eye, but on the other hand, I also wasn't all that thrilled with the broken head and the abominable pain I had gotten out of the exchange.

Intentionally or by miscalculation, he had come close to killing me. It was only because I had lacked the means that I hadn't come even closer to killing him. I might have killed him in self-defense and been well justified in so doing, but now I was relieved I hadn't been able to kill the stupid bastard. However, I did allow myself to take comfort in the thought of Mr. balls-for-brains Woody awakening sadder but half as wise after the lobotomy I had performed with my trusty toe on his lowest-hanging frontal lobe.

Beth came in first. She had put on a smile for me, but even with my blurred vision, I could see she was worried and frazzled. I felt the warmth of her touch on my hand and her fervent lips against my forehead.

"Oh, my poor, poor John, you feel so cold. Why aren't they keeping you warm?"

"Maybe the cold pack on my stomach has something to do with it. I feel a lot warmer now with you here beside me. Don't worry. I'll be fine. We Indians have thick skulls. I think it's a Lamarckian adaptation to being thumped on the head with war clubs over the millennia." My throat was sore from having tubes shoved down it, and my tongue felt about as wieldy as a sand dune in my dry mouth. I was hoping my breath was not as foul as the horrible taste that had crawled into my mouth and died.

"Don't talk, John. The doctor says you need to rest. The Cunninghams are waiting to see you and I'm only supposed to stay for a minute. I'll be back as soon as they'll let me. I love you," she said, as she squeezed my hand and kissed me again.

I gripped her hand as hard as I could and the effort incited the unruly throb in my brain to a full-scale riot. I tried to suppress the wince and grimace, but I don't think I hid from Beth the fact I was hurting pretty good—just as she didn't manage to hide from me the fact she was crying as she hurried out of the room.

The Cunninghams came in wearing a transparent cheerfulness over their concern.

"Good grief, John, you look as if you could take a *summo cum dolore* hands down. I'm sorry this is such a nasty business for you." Dr. Cunningham was smiling, but I could see he hadn't been prepared to find me lying there with tubes sprouting out of me everywhere.

"You should see the other guy," I tried to quip, "He's the candidate for *summo cum dolore*. I have to settle for *magno cum dolore*. "My humor was hurting along with the rest of me.

"Well, I imagine you won't mind letting him take first honors this time, will you?"

"Being number two is about as intense as I can handle."

Maxine held my hand and patted it the way my mother would have. "Sid, don't make the poor boy talk. Now John, you just rest and get well. We're going to leave now, but we'll be back when you are feeling a little better."

"Thanks, I appreciate it. I'll try to be better company next time."

The Cunninghams were barely out the door before the cold sweat and dry heaves hit me. Whether from the loss of blood oozing out of my spleen or the hematoma pressing the back of my brain, I don't know, but a shadow closed in on me, and the pain went away, as did everything else.

* * *

I was propped up in my hospital bed, reading a book, when I looked up and saw him standing in the doorway. He was a big man, mid-fifties—both in age and style—with a receding gray crewcut and an advancing paunch. As he approached, I could see on his wide, flowered tie a record of several encounters with dripping food. After he got closer and introduced himself, I guessed the stains on his tie were probably indicative of a fondness for jelly donuts and heavily creamed coffee. His wrinkled tweed jacket sported a small tear on the upper part of the right sleeve, and the cuffs were beginning to fray.

"Sergeant Worthin, Seattle police. You John Brockman?"

"Yes, yes I am. I was just on the phone with someone from your department less than an hour ago, and she said someone would come by to talk to me."

"I had some other business here so I'm the one who gets to talk to you. So you have a complaint against Brent Woody, huh?"

The Seattle police detective had an advanced case of sarcasm, with full-blown symptoms and a less than hopeful prognosis. It

CAIN

contorted his features, controlled his body language, and trickled out of one corner of his sneering countenance like acid out of a cracked battery.

"That's right," I answered. Another snotty cop, I told myself.

"You realize the UW campus police have jurisdiction over this and are conducting the investigation? You should be talking to them. It's not our problem unless they ask us to help, and so far they haven't."

"Then you won't accept a complaint?"

"Nope."

"The campus police wouldn't accept one either."

The detective looked mildly interested. "Is that so? Why not?"

"All I know is that a Lt. Jesperson told me over the phone they would decide if a crime had been committed, and by whom, and they would take any steps that were warranted."

He shook his head and snorted with disdain. "Typical. My advice to you is to get yourself a good lawyer, mister. If I had to guess, I'd say they're either going to drop the whole thing or go after you."

"Me? I was just minding my own business when Woody came up behind me and nearly caved in my skull. They can't charge me with anything."

"Anybody see it happen?"

"I don't know, probably not."

"Yeah, well I'd definitely get a lawyer if I was you. Sorry, I can't do nothing for you." He walked to the door, paused, and came back to the bed. "You ever had trouble with this guy before?"

"Yes, on two occasions. The first time was last fall at the beginning of fall quarter. We had a disagreement outside the main library. A few weeks later he and three of his friends jumped me over by the Northlake tavern."

"And?"

"Nothing came of the first incident. The second time the cops came and hauled off Woody and his friends, but when my friend and I went to the Wallingford precinct the next day, nobody seemed to know anything about them. Then the prosecutor calls me in and tells me she ought to charge me instead but she's not going to. I wasn't happy that she thought I was the villain, but it was a good thing she didn't charge Woody and his friends either."

"Why's that?" He pulled a chair up to the side of the bed and sat down. He was definitely interested.

"Because the day before I was supposed to talk to the prosecutor, a lawyer representing Woody and his friends came around and threatened to hit me with a civil suit for inflicting injury upon his clients if they were charged with anything. He also threatened to have my friend's student visa revoked."

"What about the first time, the disagreement at the library? What was that about?"

"Woody was giving a young woman a bad time and I intervened."

"What do you mean, 'you intervened'? What happened?"

"He grabbed me and I took him down with a wrist lock and told him to leave her alone. Then I left."

"Wait just a goddamned minute. Brent Woody is six-three, two hundred and twenty pounds, and built like a brick shithouse. You want me to believe you took him down with a wrist lock and then walked away, just like that?"

"Well, I guess maybe I twisted a little harder than I should have. It's something I learned in the army."

"I was in the Marine Corps during the Korean War. They taught us some judo, but I wouldn't want to try any of it on Brent Woody. What did you do in the army?"

"I was in a special forces unit."

"One of them green berets, huh? Officer?"

"No, sergeant first class."

"That's good. Never met many officers who weren't pricks."

"I know what you mean."

"I thought you guys were all supposed to look like John Wayne."

-CAIN

"Don't believe everything you see in the movies."

"So you humiliated the prick in public and he was out to get even?"

"I guess that pretty well sums it up. Apparently he has some influential friends who don't want to see him get into any trouble and don't care how much trouble they cause me."

"I'd say you're probably right about that. Maybe I can do something for you after all. I've had a couple of run-ins with the mortarboard patrol over the years and I sure as hell don't owe 'em any favors. So you took down Brent Woody with a wrist lock. Damn! I wish I could have seen that. Let me check around. I'll get back to you. If you don't already have a lawyer, give Aarron Greenbaum a call. Tell him Bud Worthin referred you. He took a dog-eared card out of his jacket pocket, wrote a phone number on it, and handed it to me."

"Thanks, Sergeant. I'm going to be right here in this damned bed for the next few days."

"So what all's the matter with you?"

"A cracked head and a spleen that wants to bleed. The doctor says I should be all right in few weeks, though."

"Sounds pretty bad to me. Get well soon. I'll be talking to you, John." His sourness had softened noticeably, which seemed to be about as amicable as he could make himself appear. The caustic mask was back in place, however, as he ambled out the door.

The detective was ok after all. So much for first impressions.

CHAPTER 20

Worth a Thousand Words

Ernie's letter came the day before I got out of the hospital. The Cunninghams brought it with the rest of my mail when they came to visit me Thursday evening. The envelope was postmarked Cougar, WA, and the letter was neatly printed in pencil on a single sheet of lined paper:

> Hi John
>
> I am back home now and everything is good. Jimmy said the game warden came one night with some deputy sheriffs and broke open the cabin door which was kinda stupid because it does not even have a lock on it. Jimmy said they scared the crap out of him when the game warden jumped through the door and shot my raincoat hanging on the wall with a shotgun. I guess he thought it was somebody standing there. Jimmy said the game warden looked pretty foolish when he found him instead of me or you. Yesterday Mike Ozawa came by and brought me a new raincoat and apologized for the game warden who was a prick. Mike is the regular game warden for this area. I have known him for many years. He said he had been off work for a month because he had to have an operation. The young prick was a temporary replacement. Mike said the young prick got transferred up north to Omak. I told Mike the young prick was likely to wind up getting a serious circumcising by one of them mean-assed Sinkaietks up by the rez.

> Mike said the young prick needed to change his religion anyway. The mountain is waking up again after its long sleep. I think we should go to the cave of the man-bear very soon. I will be here. Come see me soon.
> Your very good friend. Ernie

I was expecting Beth to walk through the open door of my hospital room about three o'clock, as she had every day I had been there. I was not expecting her to charge into the room, flared and furious, and throw a manila envelope on the bed.

She paced angrily as I opened the envelope and at first I thought she was mad at me. The contents, however, explained why she was angry and at whom. Inside the envelope were two enlargements of pictures taken in low light, probably with high speed film. They had been taken through a window—the window of my apartment—and they showed Beth and me unclothed on my bed. For their kind they were very good pictures, showing graphically what was going on and who was doing it.

"Do you see that? Do you see that, John? Damn that dirty bastard! Look at the note on the other side."

A typed note taped to the back of one of the photos read:

> You are not the only one who has a camera. You told on me, but I won't tell on you if you drop this thing right now and bury it permanently. After all, I think we have already established the fact you're a slut. I also think you'll find most people don't have a lot of sympathy for sluts who make accusations. Don't disappoint me, or your parents will be thrilled to see how your education is progressing. Of course, there is also the matter of that exam you cheated on. It certainly raises the issue of whether you should be allowed to continue your enrollment as a doctoral student, does it not?. Need I say more? Oh, yes, I almost forgot. I understand your boyfriend could be charged with assaulting one of the university's finest young athletes. Your cooperation

> may help to avert that eventuality as well. It also would be extremely ill-advised for your boyfriend to make any accusations against anyone, anyone whomsoever.

Beth was still livid and obviously planned to stay that way until someone was able to do something about Danner. "We sent the pictures of Danner and my affidavit to the Provost, right? Then how did Danner find out, huh? Tell me how."

"Unless Danner regularly reads the Provost's mail, either the Provost or someone in the Provost's office gave Danner the information. We sent it by certified mail, we should check and see who signed for it. Let's call the Provost and ask him if he got the stuff and, if he did, what he's doing about it. You were right, Beth, we should have taken it to him in person. Wouldn't you know? I was worried Danner might find out if we went to the Provost in person. It's my fault. Dr. Cunningham warned us about Danner, but I had no idea how cunning he could be, and how extensive his intelligence network is. The CIA would like him a lot. Maybe he already works for them."

I called the Provost's office, but his secretary said he was not there. She also said she knew nothing about the certified letter.

Beth and I discussed our options and mutually concluded we didn't have many, and that the ones we had were hardly better than having none at all. If we gambled and lost, besides having her reputation flushed down the toilet, Beth might be denied further enrollment in the doctoral program. Because the accusation of cheating would follow her, she might not be able to get into any doctoral program anywhere. As for me, there was an unsettling possibility I might wind up taking a long vacation at one of the state correctional facilities at Monroe, Walla Walla, or Shelton.

What had happened? Beth and I were the good guys, the victims, and it was beginning to look as if we wouldn't even be able to keep our places on square one.

Danner and the University, or at least some cabal within the University, had made the option of doing nothing exceedingly attractive. They seemed to be awfully good at this sort of thing, as if this were not the first time they had done it.

It was pretty obvious that Beth and I were rank amateurs. She was supposed to be one, but I had seen enough of spooky special operations and butt-saving bureaucracy to have been better prepared. Professional spooks and bureaucrats take it for granted that the system will screw them "for the greater good" and so they are prepared to screw everyone else as long as they can before they get theirs. They trust no one; use everyone; coerce when they can't negotiate, trick, or bribe; protect themselves by cleverly transferring responsibility to others; they lie, deny, scheme, contrive. Cover-up is SOP, whatever it takes. And when the stakes are high enough, they don't mind adding kidnap, murder, or terrorism as a means to an end.

Paranoia is the only possible protection against conspiracy, corruption, and criminality. Only if one is vigilant enough, wary enough, distrustful enough, and warped enough to see conspiratorial danger everywhere, is there a chance to avoid being screwed by the system, by the takers, by those who individually or as part of a system live out their personal or political agenda of screwing the unsuspecting.

The only problem was that I didn't want to have to live my life suspecting everyone and everything. I didn't want to have to walk down the street looking over my shoulder. I didn't want to have to see a conspiracy in every institution, agency, program, and group of people I met. I didn't want to feel that I had to check my phone and lampshades for bugs every night before I went to bed.

Not knowing how things work, not wanting to believe how they might work, and not wanting to live out the paranoia that such knowledge and belief would bring are the reasons most people are not prepared for the Danners and the other individual and institutional conspirators who screw first and don't bother to ask any questions later. Sometimes the unsuspecting wise up, get lucky, and manage either to thwart the screwers or bring them to justice.

More often, they don't catch on soon enough, they aren't lucky, and the screwers not only escape unscathed, but flourish.

However, for Beth and me this was not, after all, the classic dilemma of Odysseus, who was faced with navigating the narrow passage between the monstrous Scylla and the personified whirlpool, Charybdis. There was real danger here on one side only. The other side held only disappointment, frustration, psychological thralldom—galling to have to choose, painful to have to live with, but in this case perhaps the better part of valor.

Sergeant Worthin was a stranger. I couldn't guess what he might come up with, what he might be willing to confront, or why he should put himself out in any way for me or Beth. As for the lawyer Worthin had recommended, I hadn't yet decided to call him, but I was beginning to think I should.

For better or worse, Beth wasn't ready to capitulate and I despised the idea of surrender. I had promised her that Danner would get his comeuppance. I didn't know how I was going to keep that promise, and I was beginning to think maybe it was unkeepable. As a last resort, I could always rip off my clothes, paint my face, and scalp the son of a bitch. Ernie might appreciate a good scalp-lifting; Beth probably wouldn't—not unless she got to do it herself.

I checked out of the hospital just before noon the following Thursday, after waiting all morning for the doctor to come around and make up his mind to let me go home. Beth had my car but she had classes all day Thursday, so I asked Maxine to pick me up at the hospital. She invited me to lunch, during which she managed to pry out of me all of the unpleasant details of my visit with Beth's family and some of the details of more recent developments. I told her Danner had threatened to accuse Beth of cheating on an exam and that he was also somehow a part of what seemed to be an attempt by the university to prevent charges being brought against Brent Woody. Maxine probably would not have been surprised or shocked that Beth and I had been sleeping together, but I couldn't bring myself to tell her about Danner's photos of us.

CAIN

Maxine bristled with outrage. She had assumed the responsibilities of a maternal surrogate toward me and she was deeply concerned, angry, protective.

"If I weren't afraid it would get you into trouble, John, I'd tell you to go punch Danner right in the nose."

"If I thought it would solve anything, I'd go punch him in the nose no matter how much trouble I got into. Unfortunately, punching Danner in the nose would just make it easy for him to have me taken out of the equation, and leave him free to carry on as before. As much as I want to, I can't."

"I know that, John. I'm glad you're the kind of man who can use his head and not do anything stupid."

So far, I hadn't done anything at all, and Danner had still made me look stupid—and feel stupid. It had become painfully clear nothing was going to come out right unless someone made it come out right—unless I made it come out right. Danner had succeeded in taking the initiative and putting Beth and me on the defensive, making us feel beleaguered, preventing us from putting together an offensive. Screw that. We were the ones beset and it was time to implement the best defense. Instead of falling back, we'd attack.

As soon as Maxine brought me back to the house, I made some calls. Aarron Greenbaum's secretary took my name and number and asked if he could call me back. I said I would rather talk to him in person, so she told me I could come in Friday afternoon at one.

Meanwhile, I had decided to visit the provost and try to ascertain whether he or someone else was responsible for the contents of the certified letter falling into Danner's hands. I took with me copies of the pictures and a copy of Beth's affidavit that we had sent to his office. I also had a copy of the postal receipt that showed a Julie Aagaard had signed for the letter nearly two weeks ago.

The provost's secretary hadn't been able to give me a specific appointment time for Friday morning, but she said I would probably be able to see him between nine and ten thirty, if I were willing to wait. I had agreed to wait.

The next morning at five to nine, I walked into the provost's outer office on the second floor of the administration building. In her early thirties, blond and attractive, the secretary behind the desk asked very pleasantly if she could help me and I gave her my name and reminded her she had said I might wait to see the provost. The nameplate on the desk said "Julie Aagaard." I had the feeling I had seen her somewhere before, but it was a vague, general kind of nudging that could have come from having passed her on my way to class or in the Hub. It could have been only that she reminded me of someone else. At any rate, I couldn't figure out why she seemed familiar and dismissed the sensation as being unimportant.

About half an hour later, the provost's office door opened and a man and a woman emerged carrying coats and briefcases. They talked briefly with a second man who had followed them out, shook the second man's hand, and said goodbye. The second man was obviously Norman Barkley, University provost: the person nominally second in charge after the president of the university.

He was a man in his middle forties, about my size. His hair was still dark brown, and he still had all of it. He wore a tailored white shirt with a blue tie and sharp gray slacks, but no jacket. An expensive-looking gold watch stood out against his tan wrist, and he wore a gold wedding band on one hand and a some sort of college or fraternity ring on the other. He looked fit and trim and he moved smoothly, full of energy and self-assurance. My impression was that the provost was neat, businesslike, courteous, even genial. I couldn't help wondering if he were also honest.

When the people who had come out of his office had gone, he turned to me with a smile.

"Are you waiting to see me?"

"Yes sir. Your secretary told me I might be able to have a few minutes of your time if I waited."

The provost glanced at his gold watch, strode across the outer office to where I was standing, and extended his hand. "I'm Norm Barkley, and you are . . . ?"

"John Brockman. I'm a doctoral candidate in anthropology." He shook my hand crisply and looked me in the eyes with the kind of flattering sincerity and attentiveness that car salesmen dream about mastering.

"Mr. Brockman, I can give you fifteen minutes. Please come into my office."

Plush carpet, a massive walnut desk, paneled ceiling, and stately drapes greeted my curiosity upon entering his office. Numerous pictures of Barkley with his wife and several children sat and hung around the room. Good. He was a family man.

He closed the door behind us and motioned toward the four comfortable-looking armchairs arrayed across from his desk.

"What can I do for you, Mr. Brockman?" He sat in his leather chair behind the desk and leaned back casually, his elbows on the arms of the chair, the tips of his fingers lightly pressed together beneath his chin.

"Mr. Barkley, about two weeks ago a friend of mine, a young female graduate student, sent you a certified letter containing several photographs and an affidavit in which she accuses a male faculty member of making unwanted sexual advances toward her. Did you receive that letter?"

"I'm sorry Mr. Brockman, but I didn't get the letter."

I took the postal receipt out of my shirt pocket and handed it to him across the desk. "Apparently your secretary signed for the letter, as you can see from the postal receipt."

"Yes, I see that. Just a minute. I'll ask her about it." He pressed a button on his intercom. "Julie? Could you come in for a second?" A few seconds later the door opened and she came in.

"Julie, it seems we received a certified letter a few weeks ago, but somehow it never got to me. Do you know anything about it?"

"Two weeks ago? No, I don't think so . . . oh, wait a minute, there was a nine by twelve envelope I had to sign for. It should have been in your basket with the rest of your mail. That's odd. I wonder what could have happened to it."

Barkley shuffled methodically through a neat stack of papers on his tidy desk and then went through several drawers of his desk.

"This is very embarrassing, Mr. Brockman. I can't imagine how something like that might have been misplaced. I surely would remember it if I had opened it. I don't know what to tell you. I apologize. Julie, could you double check to make sure it's not still in the outer office somewhere?"

"Of course." She returned to the outer office.

"I doubt you'll find it," I said. "Unfortunately, it has already found its way into the hands of the faculty member who is accused in the affidavit." I took another paper out of my coat and gave it to Barkley. "This is a copy of the affidavit." He skimmed through it, raising his eyebrows.

"What makes you think the letter got into the hands of Professor Danner?"

"Because he sent her a note saying so. And because he referred to these." I handed Barkley the photos of Danner and Janice Rawlings and the one with the other woman.

Barkley stared at them for a few seconds and then threw his head back and sighed deeply.

"Oh boy, this is unbelievable. Do you realize who this is?"

"Yes, it's professor Danner and one of his teaching assistants. I don't know who the other woman is."

"You don't recognize the blond? Dammit man! It's my secretary!"

He handed the photo back to me and I looked at it closely. Her face was only partly visible, but it was enough for me to tell that it was the same person who had just walked out of Barkley's office, now that I thought about it. Barkley had recognized her right away because he knew her, saw her every day, although the thought crossed my mind he might also have recognized her bare hips and pendulant breasts. Quickly rejecting that possibility, I handed the picture back to Barkley. So that was where I had seen her.

"I guess that might explain why you never got the letter, mightn't it."

He punched the intercom again, angrily this time. "Julie, would you come back in."

She came into the room and stopped just inside the door. She must have already guessed that she had been caught, even before she saw the way we both were staring at her.

Undressing her with my eyes, I saw the same voluptuousness the camera had seen. There was no doubt in my mind she was the one in the photo, except standing there, expectantly, she seemed too pretty, too wholesome, too nice to be Danner's whore, or anyone else's. I felt sorry for her. I wondered if she had seen the picture of Danner and Janice Rawlings and had read Beth's affidavit. Had she been naive enough to think she was the only one helping Danner create the beast with two backs? If she had seen them, why had she so dutifully given them to Danner?

Barkley held up the photo. "I know what was in the letter, Julie. You gave it to professor Danner, didn't you."

She glanced guiltily at me and then looked away in embarrassment. From her reaction, I guessed she hadn't seen the contents of the letter. Most likely, Danner had just asked her to intercept any correspondence from Beth or me on some pretext or other.

Without saying a word, she wheeled and ran out of Barkley's office, through the outer office, and down the hall, with Barkley calling after her.

"Julie! We need to talk about this. Julie?"

He rushed to the door, but Julie had already disappeared. He threw up his hands and shook his head.

"I really don't know what to say about all of this, Mr. Brockman. She's really a good person. I'm sorry."

"Mr. Barkley, I'm sorry, too. We don't want to cause problems for anyone except Danner. We have no interest in your secretary's relations with him. Given the circumstances, it's not surprising she intercepted the letter. If we had known she wasn't a student, the photo would have been destroyed. We were trying to document the fact that Danner is coercing young women students into having sex with him. These pictures were all we could come up with. Although they don't prove coercion, they certainly raise questions about his ethics and morals. Danner is very clever and he has booby-trapped Beth Hansen's complaint. Before he even came on to her, he had sent a report to the dean recommending Beth be disciplined for offering to trade sex for a better grade."

"Did she?"

"No, of course not. After he saw the letter Beth sent you, he threatened to report she had cheated on a test if she didn't drop her accusations."

"Did she cheat?"

"Hell no. She doesn't have to cheat and she wouldn't. He made some other threats as well. Danner has to be nailed. Can you do it, Mr. Barkley? Can you nail him?"

He came over and sat on the edge of his desk in front of my chair. "Before I answer, I have some questions."

"Fair enough."

"You said he had made other threats. What kind of threats?"

"Two kinds. First, he had someone take pictures of Beth and me through the window of my bedroom and he has threatened to send them to her parents. Second, he seems to think he has some influence as to whether I'm charged with assaulting Brent Woody. He implied I wouldn't be charged if Beth didn't pursue her complaint against him."

"I heard about Brent Woody. You're the one who put him in the hospital?" He looked at me incredulously. "According to the university police, the man who beat him up was some psycho, jealous ex-commando who used a heavy flashlight to smash Brent's face. How could Danner have anything to say about whether or not you're charged?"

CAIN

"I don't know, but someone has already made sure no charges were brought against Woody in an earlier incident." I told Barkley of my earlier run-ins with Brent Woody, including the fact that the first one had been over Beth.

"Another question" Barkley continued. "If Danner has been forcing all of these students to have sex with him, why hasn't anyone complained about him. I came to this university as provost nearly four years ago and during that time I've not heard a single whisper against Danner."

"As I said, Danner is very clever and he has friends. Obviously, there are people in this university who either don't give a damn about what he does or who don't want his or their own dirty laundry hung out for everyone to see. The reason none of his other victims have complained is that Danner has convinced them that they are the ones who'll get into trouble if they say anything. I think he always gives them something in exchange for their 'cooperation' so they feel guilty about their complicity. He's good at it and he thinks he's so good at it that he can get away with it."

"One more question. Did you assault Brent Woody?"

"Yes, I most assuredly did. Right after he coldcocked me from behind and I came to on the floor with him kicking the shit out of me. If a flashlight was involved, that must be what he hit me on the back of the head with. If you want, I'll have the doctor send you the x-rays of my fractured skull."

"That won't be necessary, Mr. Brockman, I believe you."

"You do?"

"Mr. Brockman, there are some things here that make me want to believe you, but you must understand that I'll have to look into this some more. Your version of the Brent Woody thing seems more plausible to me. And the fact Julie is obviously involved with Danner certainly does raise a question or two. Whether it lends credence to your friend's accusation is debatable. It seems a little farfetched to think the campus police would have anything to gain either by protecting Brent Woody or by helping Danner. I tell you what I'll do. First, I'll ask the campus police to turn the investigation of the Brent Woody thing over to the Seattle police. Would that satisfy you on that issue?"

"Yes. Would you request a sergeant Worthin be assigned to the case?"

He went to his desk and wrote down the name. "With an 'e' or an 'i'?"

"With an 'i,' Sergeant Bud Worthin."

"We can ask for him. However, the Seattle police department doesn't exactly jump when the university snaps its fingers. I wouldn't be able to make any promises about who is assigned the case."

"I understand."

"The second thing I'll do is turn Miss Hansen's complaint over to the chair of the faculty ethics committee, which is where the complaint would have ended up no matter whom you gave it to."

"Do you think the faculty ethics committee will have the balls to stand up to Danner?"

"They may be shy on balls, Mr. Brockman, but they certainly will stand up to him. Two of the three committee members are women."

"And the chair?"

"Also a woman, Angela Gutierrez. I know her. Believe me, she's tough enough to stand up to anyone and frequently does."

"Isn't she the head of the Women's Studies Program?"

"That's right."

"Aha! Beth will be delighted to have Dr. Gutierrez read her affidavit."

"Other than that, the only thing I can do is to keep informed of what's going on. There is something you and Miss Hansen can do, however."

"What's that?"

"Get at least one other student to come forward and accuse Danner. It could make all the difference. The ethics committee may have sympathy for Miss Hansen's complaint, but they can't do much without some kind of corroboration. Just a minute, I've got to do something about that damned phone."

I followed him as he dashed out to the secretary's desk and picked up the incessantly ringing phone. He apologized, asked the caller to call back in a few minutes, and then called someone and said his secretary had taken ill and he needed someone to come up and fill in for her.

I looked at my watch. I'd had my fifteen minutes and then some and I was more than satisfied with what had transpired in that time.

"Thank you, Mr. Barkley. Frankly, I hadn't expected to get much from you. I was wrong. Beth and I appreciate your help."

"Not everyone who works for this university is indifferent, corrupt, or incompetent. I apologize for the few who make it seem that way." I offered my hand and he shook it.

"I'm sorry about your secretary. I hope you're not going to fire her."

"Well, if I ever find her, we're going to have a serious talk, but I'm not going to fire her. Good secretaries are too damned hard to find."

"That's great. I'm glad to hear that. You can tell her I'll burn all the pictures and negatives of her and Danner."

"That would be appropriate, thank you . . . and good luck to you and Miss Hansen."

"Thanks." The phone started ringing again as I left.

* * *

Beth had an hour between classes beginning at ten, and I had told her I would see her in the Hub if I got out of Barkley's office in time. As I hurried over to the Hub from the administration building, I knew Beth would be encouraged when I told her about my meeting with Barkley. I knew I was.

Finding some of Danner's victims would be easier than getting any of them to come forward, but that was going to have to be

Beth's responsibility. If anyone could do it, she could. None of them would want to talk to me, except one, maybe, and she was a special case with whom I'd deal in my own way, since I really didn't think of her as a victim.

Beth was pleased to find out what Barkley had promised to do. Her eyes lit up when I told her about Dr. Gutierrez and the women on the ethics committee. She wasn't quite as joyful about having to beat the bushes to scare out some of Danner's toys and then having to persuade them to join her in making a complaint against him. She accepted the responsibility, however, as something that had to be done, and had to be done by her. Frankly, I was glad she was the one who was going to do it and not I.

After discussing it over coffee and muffins, we agreed she should begin with the female TA's and research assistants who were still working in the anthro department, and therefore easily accessible. She also wanted to try to contact the TA who was rumored to have quit because of pregnancy. I suggested it would probably be a waste of time for her to talk with Janice Rawlings, and she concurred. I had noticed the mention of Janice Rawlings universally met with high-hackled hisses and extended claws among her female peers. Beth was no exception. She didn't try to conceal her feline disdain and disapproval of Janice.

When Beth had to go to class, I gave her a kiss and wished her luck. I didn't mention the assignment I had given myself, because I wasn't entirely certain she'd approve, nor exactly on what grounds she might disapprove. I wasn't sure I approved of what I was about to do. I wasn't even sure why I wasn't sure about it. Maybe it was that I didn't much like having to use the same sleazy tactics Danner used.

I checked the TA schedule in the anthro office and went over to Johnson Hall to wait for the class to let out. Janice Rawlings, the instructor, was surprised to see me waiting for her outside the classroom door. She knew who I was, although she had never been all that friendly toward me. I guess I just wasn't her type, i.e., I

CAIN

didn't have anything she wanted badly enough for her to offer to screw me for it.

I told her I had something important I'd like to talk to her about and asked her if she'd let me buy her lunch. She declined at first, but her curiosity, probably more than anything I said, finally persuaded her to come with me.

I had my car in the underground parking garage, three levels beneath "Red Square," so I drove her over to the Salmon House on Northlake Way at the north end of Lake Union. We ordered fish and chips and lemonade from the sidewalk fish bar, taking it around back to the outside dining area by the lake to share it with the flies and the assortment of bold, thieving birds. The peckish sparrows, raucous crows, and surly seagulls scoured the area of any edible crumb and defecated on everything else. I'd eaten there often, and I knew enough to buy a newspaper while we were waiting for our orders.

Perhaps twenty people were sitting in the sun at the tables along the water. I spread the papers out on an empty table that someone had wiped off in the past few days and on the bench, where at least there was nothing too fresh to cover adequately with a double layer of newsprint. My dad had always said the newspapers could gloss over anything. Neither of us was wearing clothing light-colored enough to be noticeably smudged by the ink from the newsprint—another characteristic of newspapers my dad had commented on more than once, although always in the context of smudged character and reputation. He had once told me that if I could learn to flaunt the inane, trivialize the profound, sensationalize the disgusting, and learn to write diagonally on yellow paper, I might aspire to becoming a prizewinning reporter.

"How are you and Danner getting along?" I asked her.

"What's that supposed to mean?" She was suspicious.

"Look, I have nothing against you, Janice, believe me. Beth Hansen and I are having a problem with Danner and I wondered if you might consider helping us."

"What makes you think I could help? . . . or would?"

"Let me put my cards out on the table—in this case my photos." I laid the photos of her and Danner on the table between us. She looked at them indifferently and then at me, calmly dipping a big stick of potato into her tartar sauce and sucking it noisily.

"So? I'm over twenty-one. There's no law against getting a little . . . private tutoring, you know? What's this got to do with you? How'd you get those pictures anyway?"

I ignored her question. "Are you screwing Danner because you like him, or because you're getting something else from him in exchange?"

"I guess that would be none of your goddamned business, John."

"Did it ever occur to you he might be banging half the student body?"

She tore off a piece of deep fried cod and pushed it slowly between her lips, smiling.

"Which half?"

"The female half, the bottom half . . . whatever.

"He's not."

"Oh, really?"

"Shit, I guess it doesn't make any difference now anyway. The only student body he's banging belongs to me. He's divorcing his wife. We're going to get married." She took several gulps of lemonade and her greasy lips left bright red smears of lipstick on the plastic cup.

"That's odd. I just met somebody else who told me Danner had promised to marry her, too," I lied.

"You are full of shit, John. What are you up to?"

I took out one of the pictures of Danner and Julie and tossed it out on the table. "It looks like all those private tutoring sessions really keep Danner humping. You can see the March 1980 calendar in the picture. It was taken one week after the one of you and Danner. I'd say he was sowing the seed of wisdom pretty damned deep, wouldn't you?"

She looked at it with surprise at first and then with rage.

"That lowdown, fucking bastard!" she yelled, startling the birds into flight and causing everyone sitting on the dock to look at us.

Now that I had her attention I could proceed. First you insert and then you twist.

"Of course, we weren't able to get pictures of Danner in action with all of the other TA's, research assistants, secretaries, passers-by, poodles in heat . . ."

"That goddamned, lying, cheating son of a bitch. I suppose you're pissed because he's been fucking your little Beth, too?"

"No, but he tried. Now he's threatening to accuse her of cheating on exams if she raises a stink about it. She needs someone else to point the finger at him, too, in order to have a case. You could do it. You could get him fired, pay him back for being such a prick. Come on, what do you say? He deserves to be brought down."

"He said we'd get married as soon as his divorce was final, the lying prick."

"As far as I know, he hasn't asked his wife for a divorce, but I'll bet he'll be getting one soon enough when she finds out about him. Janice, don't let him use you like that and get away with it. Castrate the son of a bitch."

"The funny thing is, I came on to him to make sure I got the TA job. And then I started thinking he really liked me. All the bastard really liked was jamming his dick up my snatch. Shit!"

Janice said it with enough vehemence and volume that the diners at the next table, older people, grumbled and glared disapprovingly at us as they got up and moved to a table farther away. She downed her lemonade and threw the cup and the rest of her fish and chips over the railing into the lake, setting off a noisy commotion among the ducks and geese waiting in the water for a handout, and setting off a round of reproachful stares from some of the other diners for throwing her garbage into the water. The unabashed bawdiness of her loud comments took me by surprise, too, and if I had been a bird, I gladly would have taken flight.

Fortunately, I had no time to be overwhelmed with embarrassment by Janice's display of crudeness. Beth needed her statement, her name. The fact he had promised to marry Janice was a bonus. It showed Danner had turned the tables on her, letting her think she had seduced him when in fact he was the ultimate seducer. For all her experience in intimate intrigue, Janice had failed to keep straight who was screwing whom. Janice was plenty mad at Danner, but was she mad enough to put her relationship with him into writing and sign it?

Janice's statement wasn't all that Beth needed, but it would go a long way toward exposing Danner for the wanton libertine he was. Besides, getting Janice to turn on Danner was going to be my contribution to his tarred and feathered ride out of town on a rail.

Janice got up from the table and walked away, while I gathered up the papers and my garbage off the table and bench and stuffed everything into a trash can. She was halfway to the car before I caught up with her. I walked with her, not saying anything, and opened the door for her when we got to the car. Her short skirt covered little of her shapely thighs as she slid into the seat.

"Shit! Look at that! I just ruined another pair of panty hose! Come on, let's go," she said impatiently, "I've got to get back to the anthro office and pick up some papers."

I drove up 15th avenue and entered the campus through the north gate on 45th street to drop Janice off at Denny Hall. As we approached Denny, I made my closing pitch.

"You're picking up your Ph.D. this quarter aren't you?"

"You bet I am."

"Got any job prospects lined up?"

"Arizona State offered me an assistant professorship, and I have a chance to work as a part-time instructor at the University of Hawaii if I want to."

"I see. I wish I had a job offer."

"Don't whine, John, I deserve those offers—and I didn't have to fuck anybody for them either, if that's what you're thinking."

"So you're not going to have anything to lose by sticking it to Danner, right?"

-CAIN

"I suppose not."

"Will you do it then? All it will take is an affidavit to fry Danner's ass." I stopped behind Denny Hall to let her out. She gave me a long look as she opened the car door, and I thought I saw a momentary glimmer of genuine sadness behind her tough, sensual mask.

"I'll think about it. Thanks for lunch."

I watched her herd her sexy parts up the stairs and into the building. She wasn't my type, either, but she was something to behold. Maybe she didn't have to lie down to get those job offers, but I was absolutely positive the offers had been made by men, not by women.

* * *

Aarron Greenbaum had an office on the tenth floor of the Merchandise Mart and Terminal Sales Building on 1st Avenue, just a few blocks north of the Federal Army Navy surplus store on 1st and Madison. Family-owned Federal Army Navy Surplus, Inc. Est. 1917 had been around longer than any other surplus store I knew of. Inside its display window were mannequins decked out in fatigues and web gear, and a fifty caliber Browning machine gun with a long belt of ammo feeding out of a steel ammo box.

I had often wondered if any passing agent of the Bureau of Alcohol Tobacco and Firearms had ever had an impulse to check the machine gun to see if had been deactivated. The holes in the shell casings were visible. It was easy to see they had been rendered inert. But just looking at it you couldn't tell whether the gun was functional or not. It was a stupid idea, I know. After all, the thing was right out there for everyone to see and had been part of their display for as long as I could remember, and I could remember going through the store with my dad when I was seven years old.

Several times a year on a Saturday afternoon, he'd take me down to the surplus store, and we'd browse through the fascinating collection of brass and canvas accouterments of two wars: bins of ancient C-rations, olive drab cans of sun burn cream and foot powder; swords and rifles hanging on the wall, medals and ribbons in a long, glass case; helmets, gas masks, rucksacks, sleeping bags, receptacles and interesting-looking bits and pieces of gear and apparatus—the function of which was known only to those who had actually used them for something. I always suspected that some of the stuff never even had a function.

History and mystery filled that dark, cluttered store. It smelled of musty canvas and preservative, rust and cosmoline, of leather, rubber, and powdery green brass, of painted wood and moth-eaten wool. I loved it.

Surplus was the history of war from the supply depot perspective—no bombs exploding, no ricocheting bullets, no fire, no sweat, no fear, no blood. Just empty boxes, empty uniforms, empty shells. A museum of the obsolete materials and artifacts of war without reference to the horror of the thing itself. When I was a kid, that was all I saw, just the fascination of the stuff. I didn't know about the rest of it—the horror, the suffering, the boredom, the stupidity, the waste. For me the surplus stuff had been just a bonanza of unusual toys.

I didn't make the connection between all of that surplus and the real essence of war until much later, when I saw some of those olive green accouterments being soaked with human blood. I had quickly and painfully discovered that war was not an assortment of deactivated equipment and obsolete paraphernalia displayed in the quiet clutter of a surplus store.

Greenbaum's secretary was a middle-aged woman, with reading glasses on a chain and long gray hair pulled back tightly into a ponytail. She was typing when I came in. Without missing a stroke, she looked up at me with the kind of detachment developed by one who is reconciled to having more work to do than can be done.

"Are you Mr. Brockman?" she asked in a neutral tone. The electric typewriter maintained its steady, rapid staccato even while she spoke.

-CAIN

"Yes, Ma'am, I answered, having already received all of her attention I had been allocated.

When she had finished the page she was typing, she stripped the paper out of the machine with one hand and buzzed Greenbaum with the other.

"Mr. Brockman is here."

"Thank you, Rachel, I'll be out in just a second."

She inserted new paper into the typewriter and resumed her tattoo on the keyboard without wasting any further words on me.

The office, like the secretary, was business-like and short on amenities: no pictures, no plants, no magazines. It did have a decent view over the rooftops of the waterfront, across whitecapped Elliott Bay to Bainbridge Island, and beyond to the snowcapped Olympic Mountains glistening on the western horizon.

I heard a door open in the back of the office and then someone clomping up the short hallway behind the secretary.

Aarron Greenbaum, tall, gangly, with angular features and clown-sized feet, emerged from the hallway, crossed the room in three long strides, and offered me a hand the size of a third baseman's glove. With my hand engulfed in his, I stood looking up at him, feeling somewhat as a Lilliputian meeting Gulliver for the first time might have felt.

Despite the analogy, I was counting on my concerns seeming more important to Mr. Greenbaum than the concerns of the Lilliputians had seemed to Gulliver.

"Hi. I'm Aarron Greenbaum."

"John Brockman."

"Let's go into my office and talk, John."

There was little in his manner and appearance on which to form an impression. My first impression of sergeant Worthin had been wrong, and I was determined not to come to any conclusions about Greenbaum until I knew more about him.

He was about my age, maybe a few years older. Coarse, dark, unruly hair thatched his big head and brows like sheaves of dark brown straw. The sleeves of his crisp white shirt were too short for his long arms. A gold clasp with a peace sign on it restrained his loosened tie.

Possibly he had been an anti-war protester. A flag-burning liberal, chanting in front of the ROTC building at the UW, or wherever he had gone to school. I could allow him that, now, even though I had to make sure the door was closed to the room in my mind where the resentment still brooded. I wouldn't have liked him much ten or twelve years earlier if he had been a protester, but that was another age, a different reality. There had to be something worthy of respect about Aarron Greenbaum or a former jarhead grunt like sergeant Worthin, who had had his ass fried, frozen, and shot at in Korea, would not have recommended him to me.

His private office was as plain and practical as his secretary's hairdo, with the exception of a small cluster of family pictures on his desk, which I guessed were of his wife and small daughter, and his mother. Among the pictures, stood a faded snapshot of two marines leaning against a Korean war vintage jeep.

I sat down in a chair by his desk. He walked over to the window and watched a seagull hovering into a stiff breeze a few yards from the building.

"Tell me why you think you need my services, John," he asked, turning toward me, but staying by the window.

"Bud Worthin said you might be able to help me."

He raised his shaggy eyebrows.

"Bud sent you, huh. Are you a friend of his?"

"I met the man for the first time a few days ago when I was in the hospital. I thought he was a little crusty at first, but he seemed to be interested in my problem."

"Crusty? That's Bud all right. Hell of a good-hearted guy, though, and a damned fine cop. Like a bulldog, you know?"

"Sounds as if you know him pretty well." I was curious about their relationship.

"My father and Bud were in Korea together. Best friends. There's a picture of them on my desk. My father was killed over there. When Bud came home, he took it upon himself to help out my mother and me. He's always been like an uncle to me. Even after my mother remarried, he used to take me to ball games and on fishing trips. I guess you could say we know each other pretty well. But it looks like I'm doing all the talking. Next thing I know, you'll be sending me a bill. What is this problem Bud thinks I can help you with?"

I explained the situation to him in considerable detail, including my talk with Eileen Duggins after my last run-in with Woody. He listened attentively, interrupting frequently to ask questions. When I was finished, he paced around the room with his long arms folded across his chest, scowling at the floor. After about a minute of pacing he went to his desk and sat down.

"Do you feel there is a racial issue here, John?"

"No, race has nothing to do with it. Why? Is that good or bad?"

"I'm not sure. I just need to know how you feel about it."

"I don't feel anything about it."

"Ok, if you say so. I can't really advise you until I've gone over the police reports and made a few inquiries of my own. It sounds as if you might have a problem, though, if Duggins gets hold of this thing. I've gone up against her a few times and I can tell you she's not someone you want to get on the wrong side of. On the other hand, the county prosecutor's office, not the city prosecutor, would handle a felony assault case. If, as you say, there were no witnesses in the library, it's just Woody's word against yours. From what you've told me, your doctor's statement and the absence of your fingerprints on the flashlight ought to keep you in the clear. But you'd better keep your fingers crossed that Woody doesn't suffer any permanent damage to his eye."

"You may have seen the article in the *Times* about the incident," I said. "Oh boy, what a piece that was! 'Husky Star Hurt in Library Attack.' Apparently, the campus police and the press both got all of their information from Woody and his lawyer. They made me out to be an eight-foot-tall, psychopathic, trained killer."

"John, you seem to be involved in a kind of local *cause célèbre.* Woody is a well-known college ball player, and your military background makes you a convenient itch for anybody who wants to scratch the scabs off old anti-war, anti-government sentiments.

"Do you have any idea how I could get into so much trouble just minding my own business?"

"I know, I know how you feel. One of municipal court's venerable jurists threatened to fine me for sneezing in court last week. Our judicial system at times seems like it was lifted out of a story by Kafka, but considering human nature and the nature of institutions, it works surprisingly well most of the time. Anyway, it's all we've got."

"I suppose, Mr. Greenbaum, the legal system, generally speaking, is more orderly than a lynch mob. But if this had happened during football season, a bunch of wild-eyed prosecutors would have strung me up from a goal post, while a mob of jeering judges stood around with torches."

Greenbaum laughed. "Well, I don't think things are quite that bad, but there are Husky fans in high places. If Bud gets this case, he'll sort out the investigation in no time. You can count on it. After that, you shouldn't have to worry about any charges being made against you. But don't be surprised if no charges are brought against Woody either."

"I'd be surprised if he were charged. Hey, I'll settle for a draw. I don't know if Woody will, though."

Greenbaum glanced at his watch for the third time in as many minutes.

"So you think I should just hang tight until Bud does his job?"

"That's about all you can do for now. I'd like to go over some things with you right now, but I'm due in court in about half an hour and I'm going to be late if I don't hurry. The same judge who doesn't like sneezes is presiding. It wouldn't do for me to show up late."

I grinned. "I imagine the repercussions wouldn't be anything to sneeze at, right?"

-CAIN

"Good one, John. I've got to remember to use that expression in court today. Let's go out and have Rachel explain the paperwork to you. Consider today's visit a free consultation. You don't need to worry about my fee until we see where we're going with this thing, all right?"

"Thank you, Mr. Greenbaum."

"Aarron—call me Aarron."

"Okay, Aarron."

He grabbed his coat and followed me out to the secretary's desk, where Rachel was typing and talking on the phone at the same time. She continued to type and to listen to the caller while nodding at Aarron, who pointed at me and then at his watch.

"I'll talk to you later, John. Rachel will take care of you." With a couple of stilt-like strides, he exited the office in a flurry, his size fourteens loudly slapping the terrazzo as he ran down the hall to the elevators.

I left Greenbaum's office with the all too familiar feeling that nothing had been resolved, but with a feeling that at least the business with Woody was being addressed and that it wasn't just dragging me helplessly along with it. After talking to Barkley, I felt as if we might also be at a turning point in our efforts to bring Danner to justice.

When Beth had told me about her experience in Danner's office, at first, what needed to be done had seemed simple. Ostensibly, all that was needed was for me to beat Danner into repenting, resigning, and retreating out of our lives. Too bad it wasn't actually that simple, but it was good I had seen it wasn't that simple.

Among many of the northwest coastal Indians, such matters would have been resolved rationally according to well-accepted custom. The family of the victim would have approached the wrongdoer and asked for compensation commensurate with the offense against their kinsperson. If the wrongdoer refused to compensate the victim or the victim's family, depending on the seriousness of the offense, he would have been beaten or killed on the spot, and the matter would have been settled.

Things were far more complicated in modern society, although the principle was somewhat the same. Now the negotiations were carried out by lawyers representing both sides and adjudicated by a third party representing the law. Wrongdoers still had the option of making compensation, but the victim's family was no longer at liberty to murder the accused if a satisfactory agreement could not be reached.

In Indian culture, a man's unwanted sexual advances toward an unmarried woman might have been considered an affront to the woman's family or a violation of cultural propriety, in some cases, but it probably would not have been considered a killing offense. However, in primitive societies as well as in modern ones, a lot could happen between the lodge and the loo on a dark night.

Beth had begun her inquiries while I was confabulating with Greenbaum. She had obtained a list of anthropology/archeology TA's and research assistants from the anthro department and had already talked to two of them. One of the TA's had denied any knowledge of Danner's activities.

Beth had talked to the other one over the phone, the girl who had quit the previous quarter. She had admitted to Beth knowing a research assistant who had had an arrangement with Danner, but she had denied having been involved with him herself. Beth said the young woman wouldn't talk about why she had suddenly quit her job as a TA and had dropped out of school. However, she had given Beth the name of the research assistant whom Danner had reportedly seduced. Unfortunately, that person had finished her doctorate the previous summer and was long gone. Beth thought she might be able to trace her either through the Alumni Association or from the biographical data noted on her dissertation.

My news from my meeting with Greenbaum got a mixed reaction. She was disappointed, as I was, that Woody seemed nearly as untouchable as Danner, and that I was weighed down by the onus of having to establish my innocence in the matter. But she was encouraged, as I was, that Greenbaum thought I would not get into trouble—even if it was a sorry substitute for vindication.

Early Monday morning, I was scheduled to hop a flight to Spokane for a job interview at WSU. I had also arranged to talk to Professor Grover Krantz, a WSU anthropologist who was one of the few scientists actively investigating reports of Bigfoot evidence in the Northwest. Wednesday I had an interview at Western Washington University in Bellingham. It was going to be a busy week. I decided I would write Ernie a letter and let him know I would be down to see him the following Saturday.

CHAPTER 21

Professions

In the letter I sent to Ernie, I included a copy of the last page of the conclusion of my dissertation:

"Though they are spirits with powerful magic, they mostly protect us in a spiritual way by bestowing courage in the face of danger, strength of will, strength of character, strength of mind. They guide and they counsel. Nowadays the spirits seem not to intervene much in a physical way in the events of the non-spirit world. I guess there are so few humans left who recognize them and their works that they feel unappreciated.

"The white man has had a hard time understanding that the essence of life is a melding of the physical and the spiritual, not a separation of the two. The missionaries, who promised a life in heaven with God, did not understand that. They tried to teach us life was a prison of evils, and the body was tainted and to be tolerated only until we were shed of it and thus freed to ascend to heaven as spirits. The Indian who had always lived half in the physical world and half in the world of spirits did not comprehend. That is why many of the Indians who were converted to Christianity believed heaven to be a place somewhere nearby, where they would receive earthly rewards and keep on living instead of dying. A desire to separate the spirit from the body made no sense to those who knew how closely spirit and body were intertwined in the fabric of existence.

"The Indian saw the physical world as an extension of the mind and the heart. Why we do what we do, what we think, what

-CAIN

we feel, what we believe—these are the things that bind matter and mind, body and spirit. Yes, we are measured by what we do in the physical world, but what we do is shaped and controlled by what we are in our minds and in our hearts. Good is as good does, but without goodness and understanding in the heart and mind, goodness cannot truly exist. Perhaps, what is seen as good and right is not the same for all peoples. I do not know. But maybe that is why it is best for people to follow the beliefs they have grown up with, to stay close to their own cultures that have given them a deep and sure understanding of what is important. Maybe that is why the world was a better place when there was still room enough for peoples of different cultures to stay clear of one another."

The words belonged to Ernie Wells, something I had recorded during one of our talks. I had decided to conclude my dissertation with them. The statement was cogent, moving—not the prattle of an eighty-year-old logger who left school after the sixth grade. Ernie was the quintessential wise man: philosopher, historian, scholar, storyteller, comprehender of the human condition. I didn't think he'd be much impressed with having his words appear in one of the books he so thoroughly disdained, but I suspected he would be pleased that I had placed so much value on something he had said.

That evening Beth and I had dinner at Luigi's and I told her I had submitted my dissertation. I gave her a copy of the last page and she read it.

She reread it, and when she finally looked up from the page I could see that Ernie's words had struck her as they had struck me when I had first heard them, as they continued to strike me every time I listened to them on the tape or reread them.

"What a remarkable man! He sees things so clearly, so eloquently. I'm glad you included this in your dissertation. I can't wait to read the whole thing. You haven't talked much about your dissertation, you know. I don't even know what it's about."

"I began with a thesis about the myths and stories related to Bigfoot among some of the Pacific Northwest Salish Indians. After I started working with Ernie, I decided to include Sahaptin-speaking Indians and to look at the similarities among the stories as a regional development attributable to contact and intermarriage among the groups. I think it turned out to be more an analysis of their religious beliefs."

"Why Bigfoot? Were you trying to explain how the Bigfoot myth got passed down to modern times?"

I looked at her for a while, trying to decide if I should go into the matter or skirt it, as I had in the past. I had never discussed with Beth my experience with my father or my encounter in Laos. Was this the time? If not now, when?

"There are many Indian stories and myths about creatures you and I would identify as Bigfoot, even though many more have been lost and forgotten. There are also many stories and myths about the bear, crow, coyote, otter, and every other kind of animal known to the Indians. That they talked, had human characteristics, and supernatural powers does not make the animals on which the stories and myths were based any less real. That Indian mythology also synthesized many different chimera should neither surprise us nor convince us that myths are inherently antithetical to truth and reality."

I found myself intellectually up and pumping, adrenaline greasing the semantic skids and letting the words slide out fast and hard.

"Most of us have relegated satyrs, centaurs, minotaurs, unicorns, sea serpents, and fire-breathing dragons to the realm of fable. But even in this presumably enlightened age, not every well-educated person would agree that the big guy with the horns and hooves and pointed tail is nothing but a fable.

"Encoded in myths are both the collective consciousness of a culture and its collective unconscious, as Jung called it, the half-remembered archetypal fears, urges, ambitions, and symbols carried in the psyche by each succeeding generation. Freud saw all

-CAIN

kinds of repressed ideas and emotions in myth—patricide, fratricide, incest, uninhibited lust, unrestrained cruelty. Myths are populated by beings who pursue pleasure and self-satisfaction without the encumbrances of conscience, morality, or law. They are creatures of the id let loose. Maybe cultures address their inhibitions and frustrations collectively through mythology in a way that is analogous to how individuals seem to sort out their psyches through dreams. I don't know. But I do know myths have power and function and meaning, and we oughtn't dismiss any culture's mythology as merely naive, primitive fantasy."

Beth stared at me, grinning incredulously.

"This stuff really turns you on. I think I'm a little jealous."

"Sorry. Must be the wine. I didn't realize I was getting so carried away. Anyway, something I know to be a fact, something I did not put into my dissertation, is that Bigfoot is as real as I am."

"You're serious, aren't you?"

"Yes ma'am, just as serious as I can be."

"This is really weird. I just finished an assignment in which I had to outline the scientific arguments for and against the existence of Bigfoot. I'm sorry, John. I don't know what you saw, but I have to say that I'm totally convinced that not only doesn't Bigfoot exist, but that it couldn't exist."

"Assume for a minute you were to see one and become convinced of its existence. How would you explain it?"

"You know, the part you want me to assume is the part with all the problems. But if such a thing did exist, it would have to be either some species previously thought extinct or previously unknown. I've read Napier's book and the articles by Krantz that theorize about the possibility of some descendant of *Gigantopithecus blacki* having survived. It just seems too farfetched. There are no fossil remains of any large primate in North America. If it had existed from prehistoric times to the present, surely there would be some record along with the other fossils we have found."

"What if it weren't native to this continent? What if it came from Asia over the land bridge along with the humans. There are plenty of primate fossils in Asia, including *Gigantopithecus*."

"Even so, no one has found a trace of any large primate bones anywhere on this continent. You'd think a few of them would have turned up after 15,000 years."

"I don't know exactly what they are or how they got here, but they do exist. All I know is that they're big, and except for being bipedal, they seem more simian than humanoid. Do you want me to tell you about my encounters with them?"

"Why haven't you told me about this before, John?"

"Didn't want to spook you. Just because I know something, it doesn't mean anyone is going to believe me, or even listen to me. At one time, I was dying to tell someone—anyone. After years of not finding anyone who would take me seriously, I just stopped talking about it. Unfortunately, my dad got so obsessed with the idea it indirectly led to his death."

I explained about the sighting my father and I had made back in 1958, his letters to me about the problems his enthusiasm was causing him, how his career suffered, how he had died searching. I told her about my experience in Laos and I told her that my vision quest experience had added to my certainty that Bigfoot did indeed exist. Of course, she was frustrated that I wouldn't tell her more.

"I promised Ernie I'd be down next weekend.

"Do I get to go?" she asked.

"Of course you do, but I have to warn you, Ernie and I have some secret stuff to talk about."

"What kind of secret stuff? You two aren't planning to gang up on another poor game warden are you?" she teased. I had told her about the game warden incident and she had read Ernie's letter.

"You read Ernie's letter. It's about our trip to the secret cave where the Sasquatches live."

"You two talked about that the last time I was there. Why so secretive now?"

-CAIN

"I don't think Ernie was comfortable having you know anything about it. You know, he wouldn't even consider taking me there until I had successfully undertaken a vision quest. Think of it as a religious practice that can be shared only by the initiated."

"I can keep a secret."

"I know, so does Ernie, and I know it bothers him that you can't be included, but you're not Indian and you're not a believer—that's why you can't be included."

"I suppose being female doesn't help either."

"You are probably right about that, but I don't think Ernie would exclude you solely because of your sex. Indian girls also went on vision quests, acquired guardian spirits, even became shamans and leaders. I think the most important reason you can't be a part of this is that you are a nonbeliever. You wouldn't expect to be invited into the sanctum santorum of a Mormon tabernacle, would you?"

"Ok, I get your point. I have no interest in Mormonism, but I am fascinated by what you've told me. Do you think Ernie really knows where to find a Sasquatch?"

"Absolutely. I have no doubt whatsoever."

"You're pretty certain, aren't you?"

"As I said, my vision quest experience left me with no doubt that Ernie knows what he's talking about."

"So you saw one during your vision quest?"

"Beth, you're not going to get me to say any more than I already have. I wish I could say more but I just can't. I gave my word to Ernie. I've probably said more than I should have, so just don't ask, ok? I'm sorry."

"Ok, I won't ask," she said, acknowledging my obligation to Ernie, but obviously still itching to know every detail.

I couldn't blame her. I would have felt the same way. It was worse for her, though, because she had to fight the urgings of the gene that drove women to milk every last nuance out of every conceivable insinuation. Knowing better than to offer my sympathy for any frustration attributable to the peculiarities of her sex, I suggested Ernie might be willing to tell her more than I felt I could. That seemed to satisfy her for the time being.

We went to my place after dinner. I was flushed and keyed up by our discussion, by the wine, by the prospect of bedding Beth after a hiatus of several weeks. Although I had a tender spot on the back of my head, and I was still sore from Brent Woody's kicks, I felt sufficiently recovered to carry out my responsibilities as a lover.

Beth undressed as I ran in to take a quick shower and attempt to gargle away my garlic breath. I loved Italian food, but I always came away from Luigi's with a breath like a carrion-eating monitor lizard. Swishing the astringent green mouthwash around in my mouth, I stood under a hard stream of hot water and let the prickly drops massage my skin, while I floated on a cloud of steam.

The bathroom door opened. Beth turned out the light and squeezed into the small shower stall with me. Finding her next to me in the dark shower was exhilarating, and in my exuberance, I accidentally swallowed the forty-proof mouthwash in one gulp. Like a shot of peppermint schnapps, the mouthwash burned its way down my throat and into my stomach, and for a few moments, threatened to come back up again. But I was already preoccupied with more important matters, and the burning sensation in my gut was lost in the deeper fire I was feeling.

Sensually, we soaped each other in the steamy darkness, kissing and stroking each other's lathered slickness, sputtering and gasping under the jet of hot water from the shower head, entwined, writhing, merged in serpentine ecstasy, suspended in black velvet billows of womb-like wetness . . .

When the hot water ran out, we extricated ourselves from the sodden, hugging jumble of enervated body parts at the bottom of the stall. We dried hastily. With our hair still damp we plunged naked into the bed between cold sheets, where, clinging contentedly to each other, we soon fell asleep.

The Cunninghams were away for the weekend. The weather had turned cool and rainy. Beth and I spent most of the weekend undressed. Loving, lounging, napping, nuzzling, talking, sipping

CAIN

coffee in bed. I hadn't thought I would want to spend much time in bed after a week in the hospital, but then I didn't get to share my hospital bed with Beth, either.

Monday morning came too soon. Beth had gone back to the dorm Sunday night, and I hadn't slept well. O-four-hundred was not my favorite time to get up, but I had to get down to the airport to catch the first Horizon flight to Spokane at 0600.

I wondered if I should have invited Beth to accompany me. I'd be driving my rented car within ten miles of her parents' house on my way to WSU. She said she had talked to her mother over the phone, and so far, her father had refused even to discuss the issue of Beth and me. Beth missed her family, but she was too proud and stubborn to initiate a reconciliation with her father, who likewise was too proud and stubborn to apologize to her. Beth had not indicated in any way that she might want to go with me, to stop by her home. She and her father needed a little more time apart, but not too much time. Inevitably, if they avoided each other long enough, at some point reconciliation would begin to grow more and more difficult. I just needed enough time to figure out what I could do to reestablish a dialogue between them. Sadly, I was the worst possible choice for an intermediary, being the source of the problem. There existed the very real possibility that I could wind up just making things worse.

Decisions would be a lot easier to make if you only knew how they were going to turn out. I suppose you could say the same thing about shooting craps, but then if everybody knew how the dice were going to come up, it would be a rather pointless pastime. As well as I could ascertain, nobody was allowed to use loaded dice in the game of life—except maybe God, and I wasn't at all sure it really made much difference to God how many spots came up.

The hop over the mountains in the twin-engine turboprop was notable mostly for the turbulence, the white knuckles clamped around anything that seemed anchored, and the stains on the clothing of many of the passengers from spilled coffee and juice. The sun was shining and the morning was warming up rapidly when we landed in Spokane, where the eighteen passengers thankfully disembarked.

I picked up a rental car that stank of stale cigarettes and pine-scented air freshener. It would take me about an hour to drive down Highway 195 to WSU at Pullman, which lay only a few miles from the Idaho border and only a few more miles from the University of Idaho at Moscow. My interview was scheduled for ten o'clock, and I wouldn't have a lot of time to wait around after I found the place.

Having to face an interview panel didn't scare me, I told myself. I knew my stuff when it came to anthropology. They couldn't be any tougher than the professors who had conducted my oral exam. Max, who had sat before the same group of professors for his orals, had suggested with exasperation that the procedure might more accurately be called an oral/anal exam.

It was the questions about everything else that worried me. I had no idea what they might be, or how much weight would be placed on my answers. I decided I could do no better than to give my honest opinions and let them see the real me—whoever the hell that was.

Would they know about my problem with Woody? Should I bring it up if they didn't? What was my attitude toward women and minority students? Oh Shit! They're going to look upon me as a minority! What the hell am I going to say?

By the time I got to Colfax, fifteen minutes away from Pullman, I was a nervous wreck.

I found the place after a few wrong turns. The gate attendant directed me to a small, faculty parking lot behind the administration building, where several spaces thoughtfully had been reserved for interviewees. The secretary in the Dean's office greeted me warmly, seated me outside the conference room where the interviews were taking place, and provided me with coffee.

In about ten minutes, I heard voices on the other side of the conference room door. A tall, confident-looking young man with a bushy beard, long hair, and a sharp suit walked out, sized me up, nodded coolly, and continued down the hall. A tall, gray-haired woman stuck her head out the door and smiled at me.

"John Brockman?"

"Yes."

"Oh good. You're here. I'm sorry, we seem to be running over on these interviews. If you would give us another ten minutes or so?"

"Of course." What else could I say?

"Oh good. I'll come out and get you in a few minutes then."

I walked down the hall and found a men's room. When I came back, the secretary offered me some more coffee, which I accepted. It would be good to have coffee during the interview, good to have something to do with my hands, good to give myself time to think by taking a slow, calculated sip of coffee before answering a question.

I thought of the observation someone had made about the function of smoking as an activity to occupy nervous hands and to fill awkward social gaps. I was convinced that fidgeting with a coffee cup, perhaps spilling coffee down my chin, tipping the cup over on the table, dumping it into my lap or into someone else's would be every bit as effective as any ritual involving cigarettes.

Finally the door opened again, and the gray-haired lady came out smiling.

"Oh good, you're still here. I'm Judy Dahlstrom, professor of social anthropology." She extended her hand as I stood up and I shook it. Her hand was warm and her grasp full and firm. She was at least six feet tall, high cheekbones, Nordic blue eyes—an attractive woman even though she must have been pushing sixty.

"Come in and meet the other members of the interview panel."

With my half-empty paper cup in my left hand, I entered the conference room, where three men sat talking at the end of a long table. They rose, and professor Dahlstrom introduced me to the closest one.

"John Brockman, this is professor Moki, whose specialty is Greek civilization. He's just returned from a year's sabbatical at a dig near Corinth."

"Nice to meet you, John."

Professor Moki was a small man, standing maybe six inches over five feet in thick-soled shoes. He was the only member of the interview panel who didn't give me a kink in my neck when I tried to maintain eye contact. I shook his small, quick hand.

"I enjoyed your article about Minoan technology in last fall's *Science*," I said.

"Ok, you're hired," Moki said, laughing, "You're the only one of the candidates we've interviewed who has mentioned that article."

"The man with the big feet is professor Krantz, physical anthropologist," Dahlstrom said dryly. Professor Krantz grinned through his short beard, shrugged, and shook his head. The size of his feet appeared to be proportional to his lean six-foot-three-inch frame. The other two men chuckled good-naturedly.

Professor Moki pointed his finger at Krantz. "She gotcha, Groove, admit it."

"Ok, ok, you guys. I give up. But John already is familiar with my interest in Bigfoot tracks. Isn't that so? It's a pleasure to meet you, John. I never had the privilege of meeting your father, but as you know, we exchanged correspondence for nearly a year before his death. He was a very interesting and intelligent man. I'm sorry for your loss." He turned to the others. "Roger Brockman was a physicist at the University of Washington. He was killed in a hiking accident on Mt. St. Helens in . . . was it '71, John?"

"Yes sir. September 9th, 1971."

"John and I are going to get together for a little talk after the interview."

"Hmm, a candidate with connections." The comment came from the remaining man who smiled and stuck out his hand. "Don Moran, Dean of Arts and Sciences. Nice to meet you, John."

Professor Dahlstrom sat down at the table. "Oh good. I guess we're ready to begin."

She suggested I sit at the end of the table. Krantz and Moki sat on my right, Dahlstrom and Morgan on my left. Dahlstrom was the spokesperson for the panel and she led off.

CAIN

"We'd like to welcome you to Washington State University, John, and thank you for your interest in joining our faculty here. We've received more than two hundred applications for this assistant professorship in anthropology and you are the last to be interviewed among the thirteen prospective candidates we invited here to talk with us. So you can see, you are already in a very select group, among the top six or seven percent of those who applied. From among those prospects we've interviewed, we'll ask the two or three who we feel best exemplify the kind of candidate we had in mind for this position to return for further interviews. We should be able to inform you of your status within two weeks. The final selection will be made in about six weeks. Do you have any questions about what I've said so far?"

"No questions."

"Oh good. First, we'd like for you to tell us about yourself, whatever you think is relevant: events that have shaped your interests, your goals and ambitions, things you excel at, and things you have difficulty with. Take as much time as you need."

I looked around the table. They all seemed like nice people, friendly people, real people. After a dozen interviews, they still had a sense of humor and seemed genuinely interested in getting to know me. I guess I had anticipated something more inquisitional. I can do this, I thought. This will be all right.

I picked up my now cold coffee and took a long, thoughtful sip as I made eye contact with each of the panel members in turn. All at once, I knew what I would say and how I would say it. I set the cup down carefully and pushed it aside. On this occasion, I would not need to fidget with a coffee cup. I knew my hands were going to be busy helping me communicate what I fervently wanted the members of the panel to know and to understand about me. Whatever else they thought about me, whatever they decided, they would have to respect me. Ernie once said that for a man or woman to be worthy of the respect of others, that person must first respect himself or herself.

I had come to believe that taking oneself too seriously was a chief source of arrogance and conceit. I wasn't sure it ever had occurred to me that not taking oneself seriously enough was just as bad. As in the application of so many of life's precepts, just knowing the "what" is insufficient; you have to know the "when" and the "how much" as well. Narcissism wasn't necessarily on a continuum somewhere to the far right of self respect. Even if it were, I had a long way to go before I reached a point halfway between them—so it seemed to me anyway.

I sat at the end of a long table with four pairs of intelligent eyes focused upon me. A job, a career, a lifetime hung in the balance. For the first time in many years, I realized I actually liked who I was. That was what they were going to find out.

Professor Krantz insisted on taking me to lunch after the interview. We talked about my dad, and he said he thought he still might have the letters my dad had sent him, and if he could find them, he'd give them to me. Strangely, we did not talk about Bigfoot, even though he said he had read the copy of my dissertation I had submitted to the panel and had found it well written and weighty, albeit perhaps too literary to be taken seriously as a scientific treatise. He volunteered that the panel had been very impressed with me, but he also had quickly added that the competition was very stiff, and that if he were a betting man he would hesitate to wager fifty cents on who would be among the finalists, yet alone on who would be offered the job.

At about two I said goodbye to Professor Krantz and headed north to Spokane to catch the six o'clock flight back to Seattle. When I got to Spangle, about fifteen miles from Spokane, an impulse hit me and I turned west off 195 onto a secondary road. There was enough time to make a detour through Cheney.

As I parked in front of the Hansen house, I wondered what the hell I was doing there, not having any idea what to say or whether there was anything I could say to help matters.

The driveway was empty and no one answered the doorbell. The discovery left me with mixed feelings: disappointment that I

·CAIN

had got up my courage for nothing; relief that I didn't have to put it to the test. I could have called before dropping by, I suppose, but there was a directness, a concreteness about showing up unexpectedly at the Hansens' that was in keeping with the precipitous notion that had pointed me toward Cheney in the first place.

Besides, I didn't like talking on the phone. It was too easy for the person on the other end to hang up. It seemed a cowardly convention, created to circumvent necessary and beneficial face-to-face confrontations. There was an unsettling artificiality about an age in which people felt comfortable transacting everything from saxophone lessons to sex over the telephone. Not that I was ashamed of the stimulating banter Beth and I had shared numerous times over the telephone, but never once did I ever consider it an adequate substitute for actually being there in the flesh—in a manner of speaking, that is.

I pondered whether to wait for a few minutes in case someone showed up, or to leave immediately and capitalize on my feeling of relief that no one had been home. A warm breeze ruffled the newly leafed trees and swayed the tall tulips along the front of the house. Children's voices came from the neighboring yard to the north of the Hansen house.

As I walked down the porch stairs and out the walk toward the car, the deceptively tranquil afternoon was rent by an unearthly screech, followed by incoherent wailing and excited shouts. At first I thought the ruckus was just part of the children's play, but as it continued and became more intense, I decided I should investigate it.

Hurrying around the end of the Hansens' house, I looked for the children and discovered where they were at the same time a woman came running out of the neighboring house. It quickly became apparent she was the mother of the two boys who were most of the way up a tall cottonwood tree in her yard, one of whom was dangling by one heel from a limb at least fifty feet above us.

The dangler, who appeared to be about six or seven, gave forth a continuous squeal of panic and pain as he bobbed precariously from a fork at the end of a springy branch. A younger boy clung terrified to the main trunk of the big cottonwood tree, not quite as far up, alternately screeching and yelling for help.

I ran over to the distraught mother and got her calmed down enough to agree to go back into the house and call the fire department. Shedding my jacket, I started climbing the tree, with visions of the boy's foot coming out of the branch, and his small, shrieking form plummeting past me into the grass below with hardly a branch between him and the ground to break his fall. He struggled, trying to curl up and grab the branch that held his foot, but he couldn't reach it. He could fall in the next instant.

Breaking branches and nearly falling myself, I scampered up the tree like a chimpanzee that had just been given an electric enema. If I could only get to him before he fell. Dammit! Why did I eat such a big lunch!

It took me only a minute to reach the younger boy, who couldn't have been more than five. Pale and petrified, he hugged the foot-thick trunk with a death grip.

"What's your name, son?" I asked, puffing hard from the exertion, as I pulled off my belt.

"Juh-Juh-Johnny," he finally managed to sob out convulsively.

"Hey, how about that. That's my name, too. Is that your brother up there?" I asked, cinching the boy tightly to the tree with my belt.

"Thuh-thuh-that's my brother, Ryan. He was guh-going to look in that bird's nest up there and then the wind blew the tree and he fell down."

"It's ok, Johnny, I'm going to go get your brother. You hang on tight." He nodded and I started climbing again as fast as I could.

"Please don't let my brother fall anymore!" he called after me as I climbed farther up the tree.

I don't know exactly how far Ryan had fallen, but I could see the bird's nest about ten feet above him when I got to the limb from which he was hanging.

"Ryan, don't move, son. I'm going to get you down. Just don't move, please." He looked over at me, but continued to scream in abject terror.

The limb was a scant three inches in diameter where it branched off the trunk, and it tapered to half that size out where the boy was hanging. Ryan's foot was wedged in a narrow fork about five or six feet from me, just beyond where I could reach while still hanging onto the trunk. The limb was already dangerously bowed with the weight of the child, and I was afraid to add anything to it by using it for support. Surely if the limb drooped any farther it would release the boy's foot before I could reach him.

The hysterical mother below us was crying and yelling at me not to let her son fall. Some other people had gathered around by then, but I was too busy to pay them any attention. A siren wailed in the distance and seemed to be headed toward us, but I was certain that if I didn't reach the boy soon all the help in the world would not keep him from falling.

A puny branch sprouted from the trunk about four feet below me. I carefully lowered my weight on it and it seemed very likely it would either break off or just fold over and allow my foot to slip off. But there was nothing else and no time. Hanging on with my right hand to the creaking branch that held the boy, I inched my way out on the lower branch until I could almost touch his free leg. I got his pants once, touched his shoe, but I couldn't get a good grip around his ankle. Then I had his free ankle firmly in my hand. Feeling my grip, he lunged upward in a panicky attempt to grab my hand.

At that moment his other foot slipped out of the fork, and he dropped with a sickening release. The lower branch broke instantly and I was left swinging by one hand, with fifty pounds of screaming, terrified child thrashing around in my other.

I swung him toward the tree and wrapped my legs around the trunk. With one arm reaching around the trunk, I slid painfully down another three or four feet to the next lower branch that would support the two of us. As soon as the branch came within his reach, Ryan latched onto it, relieving some of the weight that was beginning to pull his leg out of my sweaty hand.

Standing on the branch with one foot and with my other leg hooked around the trunk, I was able to use both hands to turn him right side up. He fastened himself around my neck like a baby monkey, crying, but no longer screaming.

Even fifty feet above the ground, I could hear the collective gasp that preceded the cheers of the people gathered around the base of the tree. I could see the fire truck roaring down the street, lights flashing, siren screaming, horn blaring. I sat down on the branch and waited for help to get the kids out of the tree. Johnny's tear-stained, grimy face beamed up at me from below.

"See, I told you I'd get your brother. You guys aren't planning to do any more climbing this afternoon are you?"

Johnny stared up at me with saucer-sized eyes and shook his head gravely. Ryan just doubled the strength of his hold around my neck.

The firemen took the kids out of the tree first with the ladder truck, and then I came down. Except for a sprained ankle and a few scrapes, Ryan appeared to have suffered no other injuries. The mother dripped tears all over my torn, dirty shirt as she hugged and kissed me effusively. The neighbors shook my hand and patted me on the back. Somebody handed me a cold beer.

I was looking around for my jacket when a voice behind me asked, "Looking for this?"

When I turned around, I saw Beth's father holding out my jacket. We locked eyes for a few seconds, and then he looked away. I took my coat.

"Thanks," I mumbled, at a loss for words.

He didn't smile. Avoiding my eyes, he turned and started walking back toward the house. He gestured for me to follow him.

CAIN

"Better come in and get cleaned up. You're a damned mess," he said without looking back.

* * *

Just before we landed back in Seattle, the lady sitting next to me developed a nosebleed. She left the plane first, and I was next behind her. As we filed out, a nervous-looking man waiting in line to board the plane looked at the woman with blood all over the front of her blouse, holding a compress over her nose, and then he looked at my torn shirt, ripped pants, and scratched face.

"What happened?" he asked worriedly as we passed by him.

"Hell of a ride," I said, shaking my head. "But it wasn't half as bad as the ride over there this morning."

The blood drained from his face and he looked as if he had just experienced a very disturbing premonition. As we moved away, I looked back and saw the man glance around apprehensively. As if having arrived at a decision, he suddenly snatched up his bag and hurried away from the boarding area.

That was a shitty thing to do to that poor guy, I thought—cruel, insensitive, meanspirited. But I couldn't help it. It just seemed so damned funny at the time. I laughed my ass off until I got to my car, where the derisive cackles and shrieks of an evil-looking seagull soaring overhead were about to remind me that to give is funnier than to receive.

Apparently the bird overhead, or some of its buddies, had singled out my car for dive-bombing practice, and the car had taken half a dozen direct hits. The windshield and back window were crusted with splats and gobs of glue-like excrement that had baked solid in the afternoon sun. But the cruelest cut of all came as I took out my keys and started to unlock the door. As if waiting for just the right moment, the big dirty-gray gull swept down and unerringly squirted out a putrid projectile that hit the doorhandle just as I was reaching for it and splattered all over my hand, my sleeve, my shoes.

"You son of a bitch," I yelled, shaking my shitty fist after it. The gull cackled and leisurely flapped off toward another parking lot. Furious, I could have sworn the shifty-eyed little bastard was laughing at me. An omen?

I treated the car to a badly-needed visit to the car wash, stopped by my place to change my clothes, and called Beth to let her know I was coming over to pick her up. It was going on nine o'clock by the time I showed up.

Beth had been waiting by the door of the dorm and she came running out and jumped into the car as soon as she saw me pull up. She greeted me as if I had just turned up after being reported missing in action.

"Guess what, John," she said, excitedly, heaping hugs and kisses on me. "My dad called me this evening! He said he'd talked to you and he wants me to come home—he wants US to come home!"

I'd never seen her happier. Her tears mixed with her effervescent laughter and flowed like spilled champagne, as she headily recounted her conversation with her father.

"He told me what you did, how you rescued those little boys in the tree. I think he was proud of you, John. He really is a decent man, you know, a good, kind man. It's just so hard for him to admit he's wrong. He said Mom and Sis had hardly spoken to him since we were there, and he felt awful about everything. Coming home this afternoon and seeing you save those kids made him decide to try to set things right. Being angry with someone you love, or having them angry with you, is so terribly, terribly painful. I don't know how people live with that feeling for very long without having it turn everything in their lives to bitterness. Promise me you'll never stay angry with me, John. Promise me we'll always work things out right away."

I held her tightly. "We are going to disagree about some things and disappoint each other many times, Beth, we wouldn't be human if we didn't. Nobody ever lives happily ever after who doesn't understand that you can't avoid all the problems, and that the problems you can't avoid have to be dealt with. We can be hurt the

CAIN

most by the people we care for the most. That's the nature of things, and I've never known anyone who hasn't hurt or been hurt by friends, relatives, and lovers. Right now, it seems impossible that I could be capable of deliberately hurting you. I can't imagine that happening. But I know it's possible for anyone to screw up, to be selfish, jealous, to say and do things that hurt people and that are later regretted. You are a part of me, Beth, the best part that ever was or ever will be. I knew before I asked you to marry me that I love you far, far more than I love myself, and I just decided today that I like myself pretty well. You wouldn't love me if I weren't worth something, would you? I promise to love you and to do my best to bring you happiness. I'm hoping you'll be able to forgive me for all those times when my best just won't be good enough."

"You are worth everything to me, John, and your best will always be good enough. I love you so much. We're going to have a good life together no matter what happens, I know it."

*   *   *

Before I knew it, it was Wednesday: the interview at Western.

What a letdown after my experience at WSU. Either the people at Western were bored with the whole process, or they already knew to whom they were going to offer the job and were just going through the motions—probably both. Maybe it was I who was bored and I just projected my attitude onto everybody else, who knows?

The atmosphere had not been quite right at the outset, feeling too formal, too reserved. There had been no spark, no chemistry among the interviewers, and none between them and me. From the first question, "Why do you want to teach at Western?" the interview had bogged down and had deteriorated steadily thereafter. All I knew for certain was that, in the end, I came away from the interview feeling deflated and dissatisfied, perhaps even a little patronized. I suppose the interviewers may have felt the same way.

The only good thing about it was that I wouldn't have to

wait around and wonder whether they were going to offer the job to me. Of course, they hadn't said so, but they were not going to hire me.

I hadn't really wanted to work at Western, but I needed a job. Western had one of the few openings for an anthropology instructor in the state and it was the only other university that had invited me to an interview. It wasn't because I had anything against the place. I had felt the same way about WSU before my interview there. I had good reasons why I didn't want to teach at the University of Washington, but I would have shown up for an interview if I had been invited. I was beginning to understand what someone had told me about how galling it was to be turned down for a job you really hadn't wanted in the first place.

I gave myself the same advice the ranger instructors had given me and every other man who had complained of headache, frostbite, pneumonia, or a broken leg while enduring the ranger course: "Suck it up, and drive on, ranger." That potent prescription also seemed to work for cases of minor disappointment.

After a short week, Saturday popped up out of nowhere and Beth and I pointed the Bug south toward smoldering, rumbling Mt. St. Helens and a weekend at Ernie's estate.

* * *

Ernie listened patiently, attentively as Beth implored him to let her accompany us to the cave of the Tah tah kle'-ah.

"I know I'm not Indian, and up until a few days ago I wouldn't have believed that a creature like a Sasquatch could exist. I don't want to harm it and I swear I will never tell anyone about it. I just want to see it. Sometimes I think of all the mystery and magic I felt as a child and how it somehow all got lost when I grew up. It would mean so much to believe again that there are still wondrous things in nature to be discovered. John and I are about to be married and spend the rest of our lives together. I need to know what

CAIN

John knows. He needs to be able to share this with me. Ernie, may I please, please be allowed to go with you?"

For a few moments Ernie drifted off into the past, or the future, or wherever it was he was able to drift off to. Wherever or whenever it was, his keen old eyes saw things even more clearly there than they did in the dimension in which Beth and I existed. A touch of otherworldliness remained as he brought his focus back to Beth.

"Your roots have begun to merge with John's," he said. "From now on the two of you will grow as one. What one knows, so should the other. Come with us. Understand how John is connected to his past through this experience. Let the Tah-tah kle'-ah know the eternal seed sprouts in your belly to keep alive the ancient blood for at least one more generation. You are white, but your spirit is good even so. The babies you and John make will have the old blood. They will have strong spirits, too."

That Ernie had so easily agreed to let Beth go with us was shocking enough, but the suggestion that Beth was pregnant was a bolt from the blue. Ernie was indeed an extraordinary man, but I doubted even he could know whether Beth had conceived a child within the last few weeks. As far as I was aware, not even Beth could know that. I had to believe it was a only a calculated guess by a shrewd old man with a shaman's flare for the dramatic. He was definitely wrong about one thing, though. Beth was not white, she was absolutely crimson.

* * *

Monday, May 12, I started paying back everyone who had filled in for me during the time I had been in the hospital and the two days I had off for interviews. Max was about to leave for Washington D.C. He had filled in for me more than anyone else had. He had obtained tacit approval for me to fill in for him until the end of the quarter. It was going to be tough to get back into a regimen of having to be somewhere at a certain time, and to actually have to spend most of the day working, but I was glad for the opportunity to do something for Max. He had let me impose on our friendship far more than I had intended, not that he minded doing it at all.

He would be leaving on an early flight to Washington D.C. Wednesday. Tuesday night Beth and I were giving him a sendoff in the form of dinner at Luigi's. We would see Max again in about five weeks when he returned to Seattle for commencement exercises—fully ensconced in the Spanish diplomatic corps.

There was a memorandum in my box at the anthro office before noon Monday reminding me TA's were not supposed to trade assignments and responsibilities without prior permission from the department. My first response was to use it for toilet paper, as an expression of my feelings about bureaucratic butt-covering. But the memorandum was on slick mimeo paper. On second thought, I decided my private protest would probably give me about as much satisfaction as I got out of using the Sear's catalog that Ernie kept in his outhouse for his visitors' reading and wiping enjoyment. So I just stuck it into someone else's box.

Everyone, including me, suddenly got very busy. Beth was finishing her course work and studying for exams. Dr. Cunningham had become involved in committee work for the Psych department, and Maxine was getting ready for their trip to England in July.

I managed to get Bud Worthin on the phone during one of the rare times he was in his office. He said he'd tried to call me several times, but I was never home. His conclusion, as expressed in his official report, was that the evidence supported my version of the incident with Woody and that Woody ought to be the one charged with assault. Apparently, Woody's lawyer had had the effrontery to try to persuade the county prosecutor's office to charge me, but the attempt had only caused the county prosecutor to refuse to have anything to do with the case. The city attorney's office was still considering the matter. Worthin interpreted that to mean that no one would be charged.

"By the way," Worthin asked, "the university didn't send you no bill or nothin, did they?"

"Not yet anyway. Why do you ask?"

"Oh, just curious. Their accounting office called and asked me who they should send a bill to for the books you guys tore up and got blood all over during the fight. Yeah, can you imagine? They were lookin to stick somebody with a bill for almost a thousand bucks."

"And?"

"Oh, no problem. I told 'em to send the bill right to Mr. Brent Woody."

"Good man. I appreciate it, Sgt. Worthin. I know it's your job, but you've gone out of your way to help me. I'd like to pay you back somehow, if I could."

"Naw, glad to do it. You know, though, I wouldn't mind learning that wristlock thing, if you think you could teach it to me."

"It would be my pleasure. Just tell me when and where."

"You know, now that I think of it, I'll bet there are some other guys in the department who might be interested in learning how to do that. You think you'd be interested in a couple of sessions of teaching some of us old farts how to subdue a big-assed suspect without gettin a heart attack from the effort?"

"Sure I would. How soon would you be able to arrange it?"

"Probably by next week sometime. Evening best for you?"

"That would be fine. I'll be around for the next five weeks at least. After that, I'm not sure. Let me give you the anthropology department number: 543-5240. You can always leave a message there for me."

"Thanks, John, I'll be lookin forward to havin you slam my lard ass on the floor." He laughed. "I'll see ya, son."

Right after I talked to Sgt. Worthin, I called Aarron Greenbaum, who also, surprisingly, was in his office and available to talk to me.

"Hello, John. Where have you been? I tried all last week to call you, but you were never home. I'm glad you called."

"Sorry. I guess I should get an answering gadget. I just got off the phone with Bud Worthin, who seems to think I don't have to worry about being charged with anything."

"I know. That's what I wanted to tell you. That's the good news. The bad news is that Woody's lawyer may still go for a civil suit. I don't know how far they would try to take it, but you could always close out your bank account, claim you lost it betting at Longacres, and declare bankrupcy if need be. I could hold a package for you in my office safe if you'd like. It's not that big of a deal, really. Bud convinced me none of this was your fault. I hope you understand that I had to confirm your version of what happened."

"Absolutely. I wouldn't have thought you were a very good lawyer if you hadn't. So I should just wait and see if they sue me?"

"That's about the size of it. I doubt very much if they'll sue. There's not enough at stake for Blackwell and Associates to bother with it, and I can't imagine anyone being connected to this who would want to throw away a lot of good money on a nuisance suit. My guess is that you're out of the woods on this one."

"I didn't realize it was bothering me that much, Aarron, but I'll have to admit it's a welcome relief to hear you say that. I certainly hope you plan to bill me for at least a couple of hours of your time."

"I've hardly spent any time on it, John. I was just planning to call it pro bono."

"Nonsense. Pro bono begins at home. Bill me. I'll enjoy paying you."

"If you insist, how can I refuse? If all my clients were like you, John, I probably could afford a potted plant or two in my office. Thanks, John. Keep in touch."

CAIN

CHAPTER 22

Shadows of Images

Friday evening I got everything together for our pilgrimage to the cave of the Tah-tah kle'-ah. Pilgrimage? Certainly for Ernie. But for me? I wasn't sure what to call it. *Peregrinatio*, *la peregrinacion*, *un Pelerinage*, *eine Wallfahrt*, *hajj*,—in its broadest sense, a pilgrimage implies little more than having a reason to travel to a particular place or to wander in search of something. Still, it is a term probably less well suited to characterizing a journey to the John than a journey to Avila, the birthplace of Saint John of the Cross. It is often used in a secular sense (except by followers of Islam), but its connotation is strongly religious, suggesting worship, a quest for enlightenment and spiritual renewal, exaltation, penance, truth. My journey was definitely a quest, perhaps even in the Arthurian sense. Yes, pilgrimage covered it nicely.

For the first time, I had a feeling of uneasiness about the venture. When I considered each aspect of the thing separately, the reason for the uneasiness eluded me. It was just a vague, nagging sensation, a feeling of apprehensiveness. Because Beth was coming along? Possibly.

There was the uncertain and unsettling condition of the mountain to be considered. There were signs that it was on the verge of erupting, and Ernie's insistence we go that weekend seemed to underscore the imminence of a potentially catastrophic occurrence that might make any later visits impossible. "The mountain is growing impatient and will not wait for us much longer," he had said.

If anyone else had told me he was going up on the mountain that weekend to take pictures, I would have called him foolhardy and reckless. If I had told anyone I was going up on the mountain that weekend with an octogenarian Indian shaman and a damned-fine-looking woman to visit a mythical creature in a legendary cave, he would have called me dumb-assed and demented. I was beginning to suspect that might be an accurate assessment. About the only thing that wasn't threatening was the weather, so far at least.

Cowlitz and Skamania county deputies and the State Patrol were keeping people away from the mountain, which would make it more difficult for us to get to the place. According to Ernie, after parking as closely as we could, we'd have to hike until dark Saturday to get there and then wait for daylight to enter the cave Sunday morning. After spending a few hours in the lava tube, we'd have a long hike back before Sunday night.

Ernie was ready and waiting when Beth and I got to his place about half past ten Saturday morning. His old rucksack sat in the pickup bed, along with a cardboard box containing a lantern and a coil of half-inch hemp rope. The beat-up butt of his antique Winchester carbine protruded from a worn canvas scabbard tied to the rucksack. I was surprised he would take his rifle along and I pulled him aside to ask him about it, while Beth put our stuff into the truck. I saw her looking at it, and I could guess that she, too, was wondering what the rifle was for.

"Powerful medicine against evil spirits," he replied with a wry look. "Don't worry. We have nothing to fear from the Tah-tah kle'-ah." But then a frown consolidated the smaller creases between his bushy brows into a deep, troubled furrow. "I had a dream last night, John. In the dream you and I and Beth were the Tah-tah kle'-ah, and hunters were shooting at us. The outcome was not revealed to me. I feel we might find things we are not looking for—or they might find us."

"Find someone else there?"

"Could be."

"But I don't understand why you feel you need a rifle, even if someone else is there. To protect the Tah-tah kle'-ah? Is that it?"

"If I have to."

"I see. It never occurred to me that kind of situation might arise. You remember what I told you about my experience in the cave in Laos?" He nodded.

"Ernie, if for any reason you have to fire that rifle inside the lava tube, for Christ's sake be careful. I don't want anything or anybody getting hit who isn't supposed to. Promise me, Ernie."

"I promise, John. I don't want any shooting either. I will be much happier if I pack my rifle all that way for no reason, than if I have to use it."

"So will I, Ernie. So will I."

I didn't need anything else to worry about. I hoped Ernie's dream was a false alarm, but added to the feeling I already had, I feared it wasn't. Who besides us would be stupid enough to be out on the mountain? Geologists? Photographers? Ernie said there were hunters in his dream, but were they specifically hunting the Tah-tah kle'-ah, or something else?

It seemed my life was one long search for enough information on which to base an intelligent decision—a quest for certainty. Nonetheless, most of the time I wound up having to make decisions with a dearth of relevant data and a queasy feeling that I probably was making the wrong one.

Perhaps that is why I had tended to seek refuge in books most of my life. A world reduced to black symbols printed on white paper was more comfortably finite and tangible than the real world. Ambiguities, ambivalences, inconsistencies—all seemed somehow more nearly manageable when they appeared in print: less confusing, less intimidating.

A novel can give its author and its readers an omniscience and perspective that no one can ever have in reality. Written poetry is a zoo in which wild and exotic ideas and emotions can be viewed and studied from a safe distance. Essays linger in yellowed pages for us to consider and reconsider as long as we wish, their form and substance frozen in time and space without change in a mortal world where the only inexorable reality is change itself. Old books comforted me against the uncertainties in life. They gave me the illusion that at least some part of the scheme of things in the ephemerality of existence could be grasped and known at a particular point in time, even if only briefly and incompletely.

The glory and the tragedy of being human is how much and how little we learn between birth and death, both as individuals and as a species. Modern man has tried to learn everything about everything, learning more and more about less and less until finally, he has come to know everything about nothing, and nothing about anything important. The Indians strove to learn only that which was necessary for them to survive in their world and to fit into their culture, and in so doing, became certain about a great many things.

But this was no time to wax contemplative. The real, changing, wait-for-nobody world was out there, demanding response and action only, and it didn't give a shit about mine or anyone else's opinions, feelings, or mortality.

Beth was magnificent. As excited as I knew she was about going with us, her demeanor was all business and no nonsense. After exchanging a warm greeting with Ernie, she had put our packs and jackets into the truck while I asked him about the rifle. Now she stood leaning patiently against the truck, as if she were used to making this expedition every morning before breakfast. If she had the discipline to hold back those ten thousand questions I knew were exploding inside her, she had the discipline and determination to do anything.

It had crossed my mind to ask her not to go, to wait for us at the cabin. More and more, the risk seemed too great, and I could not stand the thought of placing her in peril. But I knew she would prefer that I not place myself at risk, either. If we were to be equals, I could not deny her what I would not deny myself. We'd share the adventure and we'd share the risk.

CAIN

Ernie drove us northeast up the Lewis river into Skamania county, east along the border of Swift Creek Reservoir, and north up the main Forest Service road toward St. Helens. He circumvented a roadblock, using an all-but-impassable logging road, eventually coming to another steep, narrow gravel road that snaked up into the southeastern corner of the mountain. After nearly two hours—much of which was jolting; all of which was rattling and dusty from the volcanic ash blanketing everything—Ernie turned the truck around and parked it in a wide turnout, where the road curved eastward to follow the base of the mountain.

"Ape Canyon is just a little way up this trail," Ernie said, pointing at a trail apparently only he could see in the dense, gray-powdered brush along the road.

Ape Canyon rang a bell. A man named Fred Beck had published a story in 1967 entitled, "I fought the Apemen of Mt. St. Helens." It purported to be the account of an attack on a party of miners by an undetermined number of Bigfoots in July 1924. The name of the place where the attack was alleged to have taken place was Ape Canyon. I asked Ernie about it, but he merely grunted in disgust and replied, "Maybe a few white men have a talent for telling stories, but I guess there's no end to the people who have a talent for believing them." I caught Beth trying to suppress a laugh by faking a cough. Ernie didn't bother to elaborate why, but he obviously did not give the story much credence. For some reason, Beth thought it was funny.

The ash was something else I hadn't planned for. The mountain had been belching up plumes of ash and steam periodically since March 27. The most recent eructation had occurred just four days ago. Fortunately, the stuff was mostly solidified and crusted over after numerous light rains and regular soakings with heavy dew. Where it appeared as dust, the ash resembled an obnoxious, choking mixture of gray flour and fine sand. In its solid form, it seemed to have about the same consistency and strength as crusty sugar. Where rivulets of melting snow ran through it, it formed a gray slurry, like watery cement. We tried to brush it off our packs, finding that half of it boiled up into our eyes and nostrils and mouths, and that the remainder clung with magnetic tenacity to everything it touched. Tying our handkerchiefs around our faces as makeshift dust masks, we set out on Ernie's invisible trail. With any luck, we would probably all wind up with some form of pneumoconiosis.

A few months ago the symmetrical mountain had glistened pristinely in the sun like a huge pile of clean white sugar. Now under a high overcast, we walked toward a gray, ash-stained heap. Except for the blending rush and babble of melting snow, there was only the crunch of our footsteps, our breathing, and the sporadic coughing brought on by the residual dust. Birds, rodents, even insects, seemingly had abandoned the place.

The course Ernie chose, still insisting it was a trail, led up a steep, rugged slope and we zigzagged higher and higher toward the dirty snowfields above us, then across the slope and down again. The old man moved slowly but steadily, stopping infrequently. His rucksack, rifle, and the six or seven pounds of rope he carried must have weighed as much or more than the twenty-pound backpacks Beth and I had, and yet he was laboring no harder up the mountainside than we were. I had volunteered to carry the lantern. Swinging it by its wire bale as I brought up the rear, I was confident I would likely drop it or inadvertently smash it against some jutting chunk of broken lava rock before we got to our destination. I had brought flashlights and extra batteries for Beth and me, but Ernie predicted the lantern would prove more useful.

What Ernie had described as a "little way" turned into four hours of hard, steady hiking. Even the old iron man himself appeared weary when he finally dropped his pack and sat down on an ash-frosted block of lava.

"This is the best place to stay the night. Tomorrow at first light we'll go there." Ernie pointed to a broad, gentle slope a few hundred yards away that fanned out from the mountain for nearly a mile and then dropped abruptly into a deep, wooded ravine. We had about two hours of daylight left in which to sink our gritty teeth into some beef stew heated in the can, and to nestle our gritty bodies into the crusty ash for a long and probably restless night.

I spread a nylon tarp out on a relatively smooth patch of rock about the size of a pickup bed. Beth and I rolled out our pads and sleeping bags next to each other on one half of the tarp and folded the other half over us to keep off the moisture. Ernie found a spot a few yards away, where he wrapped himself in a wool blanket and a ragged square of canvas, and reclined against his rucksack, his old rifle cradled against him.

The tattered box of shells he kept in his cabin looked to be nearly as old as the rifle. I wondered if they would still fire if called upon to do so. I had almost asked him when he had shot the rifle last, but it had seemed a condescending kind of thing to ask a man like Ernie. Whether he used it or not, from its appearance he took good care of it, and although old, it looked functional enough.

The dark still hadn't closed in completely when we finally got settled in for the night, twisting and squirming around to find the most propitious combination of lumps and hollows beneath us that hinted at any possibility of comfort. When we had finally exhausted any hope of finding a comfortable position, we lay quietly and listened to the innumerable, tinkling rivulets of melting snow as they combined into a distant, rushing roar of milky water cascading into the Lewis river valley below us.

Despite its earlier threats, the mountain made no sound or movement. Not the slightest tremor came from its troubled bowels. Unsure whether I was awake or dreaming, I thought I heard a cough some distance away in the direction of the pickup. Only that one, uncertain sound; then nothing more. The harder I strained to hear, the more I doubted that I had really heard anything at all. No moon, no stars marked the movement of the night toward morning. Vacillating at the threshold of sleep, I turned often to relieve my aching bones. Beth lay on her back snoring softly, and I could hear Ernie grunt occasionally as he slept. The night seemed interminable.

Eos eventually came, sluggishly, reluctantly, half-heartedly dragging her dull train across the eastern sky. After a while, when the sky grew light enough for me to see, I looked with concern upon the stiffness and unsteadiness of Ernie's movements as he rose and wrestled briefly with his many years for possession of his body. Then, his spirit and brain, having routed the ravages of a long life once more, took charge of his old bones and tired flesh and commanded them to stand straight and to be strong—and they obeyed, as they always had for more than eighty years.

I heated water for instant coffee over hexamine fuel tabs, and we chewed tough English muffins topped with honey for our breakfast. By the time we finished, the overcast had begun to thin. From the west, a pale blue stain spread slowly across an otherwise colorless morning sky.

Our tracks showed clearly in the inch or so of crusted ash, as clearly as footprints in new snow or fresh dirt. As I looked back across the slope to the farthest ridge we had traversed, I could see the broken line of our progress. Now the trail was visible. We could find our way out in pitch darkness by just retracing our steps. Hard on the heels of that thought was the realization that our tracks could be followed just as easily by anyone else. We had drawn a big arrow across the side of the mountain that pointed right at the place we were headed. Rain, wind, and any new deposits of ash would eventually obliterate our tracks, but that might take weeks. Until then? There was no way the fact could have escaped Ernie. What was he thinking?

"What about our tracks?" I asked him, more curious than concerned, thinking he must have planned for such a contingency. When I asked the question, Beth quickly looked back at our path, and I knew she all of a sudden was wondering the same thing.

"I kinda thought you would have asked me about that when we first got into the ash, back on the Forest Service road." His reply was tinged with a mentor's reproof, not only for me because

I was slow to see the obvious, but also for himself for not having succeeded in bringing my awareness up to the level of keenness he had desired.

"I can't explain how I know, but by this time tomorrow the tracks won't matter. We're close to the entrance now. We must move quietly and say nothing."

From the puzzled look on Beth's face, I could tell Ernie's explanation had sounded just as cryptic and ominous to her as it had to me. She had said very little since yesterday morning. For that matter, none of us had said much along the way, and I figured she was just trying to be unobtrusive, but being taciturn for long periods was uncharacteristic of Beth.

"Are you ok," I whispered to her over her shoulder.

She turned around, smiled unconvincingly, and gave me a hug that begged for reassurance.

"I'm fine," she whispered back, "just a little nervous, that's all." I pressed my gritty lips against her upturned mouth and clamped my arms around her as confidently as I could. I wouldn't have admitted it to her, or especially not to Ernie, but she wasn't the only one in need of reassurance.

In a few minutes, Ernie had brought us out on the ancient lava flow to an opening where the lava crust had collapsed, creating a skylight into a deep lava tube. For some reason, possibly during an earthquake, an island of rock ten feet in diameter and eight feet thick had dropped into the tube. Uninviting, dark and deep, but not quite Dantesque, the gaping hole gave no indication of any secrets lurking in the underworld. This was to be the portal to epiphany. If the mountain erupted while we were in the lava tube, it would instantly become the back door to Hell itself.

Thirty feet beneath the hole lay the mound of broken rock that had long ago crashed down from the ceiling of the tube. I tied a double-loop Bowline knot for a sling in the rope Ernie had brought. He sat in one of the loops and the second loop slipped around him under his arms. Beth helped him over the ledge as I belayed the rope and lowered him into the lava tube. I sent down his rifle and lantern and then lowered Beth into the tube. Tying off the rope to the corner of protruding rock I had used for belaying, I slid down the rope into the hole.

Not having rappelled since leaving the army three years ago, I was a little rusty and managed to give myself a few minor burns with the rough hemp rope. We left our packs above and took only our jackets and flashlights. I checked my watch as we prepared to move up the gentle incline of the tube toward the mountain: 0657. I wondered if the Tah-tah kle'-ah were early risers.

The lava tube was very much like the Ape Cave tube my father and I had explored when I was a child. This one seemed smaller, as I compared it with a nine-year-old's impressions from more than twenty years ago. The world had seemed like a bigger place then. My father had been one of the few things in that world that hadn't shrunk as my body and my experience had grown larger. My reflections tapped into the wonder and the excitement that first experience had indelibly imprinted upon the synapses of my child's brain, and it all came rushing back into my consciousness, as vivid and intense as if it had happened only an hour ago.

I remembered being worried that the mountain might suddenly erupt, sending a new river of red-hot lava rushing down the tube. Close on my father's big heels, with my oversized hard hat wobbling on my head, I had listened intently for the distant rumble of the mountain and the roar of impending doom, ready in an instant to turn and run for my life. Along with the other emotions and sensations my memory had touched and had brought back to life, it had nudged awake an old fear.

Ernie led, rifle in one hand, lantern in the other. The scent of burning kerosene spiced the dank air of the tube, and the yellow flame animated in moving relief every flow line in the nearly smooth walls of the tunnel. Here and there, basaltic debris had fallen from ceiling cracks to form sandcastles, fragile pinnacles of detritus rising from the floor like stalagmites. Large drops of water collected above us, shimmered briefly in the unnatural light, and plonked into the pools at our feet. All around us, the concave blackness glistened wetly. Sandy pools, chained together by a trickle of dark water, reflected the probing beams of our flashlights onto the ceiling, creating a confused dance of coruscations overhead.

Thirty minutes into the tube, we found a sandcastle that had been flattened and several footprints in the wet sand, prints as big as the ones I had found at the site of my vision quest. Beth's eyes opened wide and sucked up the huge prints into her astonished brain. Panting with excitement, she traced the outlines of the footprints with her fingers and measured them against her hands. Ernie watched her and nodded inscrutably to himself. As we drew nearer to the mysterious destination he alone knew, we found more tracks going in both directions. Apparently, the creatures took pains to leave as few signs of their comings and goings as possible. That we were beginning to see so many tracks could only mean that we were very close to their lair.

The odor began at the point where the creatures seemed to have lost their concern about leaving tracks. It was pretty much the same sickening stench I had smelled in Laos, and it got stronger as we got closer. Ernie motioned us to turn off our flashlights and he lowered the wick of the lantern until the dim sphere of the wavering flame barely kept the blackness at bay. Even when my eyes had adjusted to the dimness, I could not see much more than a yard or two ahead of the lantern as we crept tensely, expectantly into the waiting darkness.

I felt their presence for at least a minute before Ernie froze and I saw the reflection of the lantern's flame in their eyes. I began to see their outlines, their dusky masses huddled together against the wall in silence, watching us, weighing our presence and purpose, apprehensive, but calmly curious.

Almost inaudibly at first, and then ever so softly, the arcane Sahaptin syllables flowed mystically from Ernie's center of being, soothing, reassuring the Tah-tah-kle'-ah. They leaned forward as if hearing something familiar, something welcome, and I could see two of them more clearly. A large female was closest, a half-grown offspring clinging to her arm almost as tightly as Beth clung to mine.

These creatures, unlike the one's I had discovered in Laos, showed no real fear and no aggression. They seemed almost torpid, as if at some low-functioning level of hibernation. Behind the female and the youth were several more, of which I could make out very little. In the faint flicker of the lantern, I saw that the mother was covered with dull, heavy hair or fur that obscured nearly every feature except her large eyes, the dark crescent of her flat nose, her black lips, and the long black nipples protruding from her breasts. She stood erect on straight, powerfully muscled legs, probably close to seven feet from the top of her distinctive sagital crest, to her enormous, shaggy feet.

I was trying to take it all in, to sear into my mind every detail, every nuance, both of what I was seeing and of what I was feeling. Beth held on to me and looked with raptured awe upon these creatures that a week earlier she would have sworn were only myth and could not exist.

Meanwhile, Ernie continued to chant, and the sounds were all unintelligible to me. The creature seemed almost pleased at the sound of Ernie's chant and she swayed slightly, as if to the ancient rhythm of his sacred song.

Consumed by the power and beauty of the encounter, we heard nothing else, saw nothing else. For the three of us at that moment, nothing else existed. But something else did exist; something that could appreciate the power, but not the beauty.

As I think back, I realize that somehow I must have known, because I comprehended everything in a single, horror-filled instant: the blinding flash of the spotlights; the slow-motion sequence of the ear-shattering blast behind me; the supersonic clap of a 500-grain bullet spinning past my ear; the dust, hair, and blood erupting from the cavitation of the wound in the mother creature's left breast—all in a fraction of a heartbeat, the smallest sliver of a second. After millions of years of evolution, hundreds of generations of survival, decades of devotion

CAIN

to her species, in one second, her ruptured heart ceased to pump, her blood ceased to flow, and her big hominoid brain began to die from lack of oxygen.

She toppled forward without a sound, spinning around and landing heavily on her side as the stunned youth refused to let go of her arm.

Beth screamed and screamed and continued to scream.

The lantern went black, and Ernie became invisible, as the spotlights searched for a new target.

Two more heavy shots exploded—deafening, hammering blows to the eardrums. I could see nothing but the blinding spotlights. Instinctively, I grabbed Beth and pulled her down, futilely trying to shield her with my body.

I didn't know what had become of Ernie. I didn't know what was going to become of Beth and me. All that was clear and certain was the fate of the creatures. Once again, I was helpless to do anything for them.

Then two shots from a lighter rifle cracked in rapid succession from a dozen yards farther up the tube. Two quick spurts of flame sought out the sources of the light and shattered them into nothingness, two shots from an old, but very functional weapon in the hands of someone who knew how to use it.

Someone shouted; swore vehemently in the darkness. A flashlight came on, fell, rolled, and went out again.

More swearing, and then a second voice, groaning.

I wanted to turn on my flashlight, still in my hand, but I knew it would make a perfect target. I couldn't assume they would not shoot at anything that moved or shone or made a sound, and so I lay in the wet sand with Beth, who had stopped screaming and who now seemed too frightened, too much in shock even to whimper. At least two more of the creatures had been shot, mortally wounded if not already dead. Perhaps the rest had escaped. Now it was up to Ernie to sort things out in his own way, and I didn't much care what way that was.

"Call off your friend, John. We didn't come here to hurt anyone." The voice coming out of the darkness twenty or thirty yards away was familiar. It belonged to Tom Danner.

"I'm sure you're wondering how I found this place, how I knew you were coming here. Admit it, John, you're dying to find out, aren't you?" The smugness was still there in his voice, but something else as well. He sounded as if he were in pain. Ernie's bullet could have hit him along with the spotlight, which was probably attached to his rifle.

"The man I hired to keep tabs on you and Beth is quite good. He used to work for the CIA, but now he does private investigative work. You never knew he was reading your mail and recording your telephone conversations, did you John? He found out about Ernie Wells and your plans to visit this place. Of course, it was all nonsense to him, but not to me. He couldn't comprehend the significance of your visit here, but I could. It wasn't hard to follow you from your friend's cabin once we knew when you'd be coming down here. I asked Sonny to fly down from Anchorage and accompany me here to find out if you really were on to something. I've been hunting Bigfoot for more than six years. Surprised, aren't you? Of course it would have been foolish for me to let on I believed it existed—I could have had the same problems your father had. It was Sonny here who really got me started, you know. He told me about the ones he shot in Laos. I've wanted one for my den ever since. Think of it, John, I've made a sensational scientific discovery and taken a magnificent trophy with a single shot. Too bad it was a female, though. Still, it'll look good in my den, standing by the fireplace. What do you think? Don't worry, I intend to donate the others for scientific study. It will make quite a big splash. Come, come, John, they are already dead. There's nothing you can do now except leave. Tell your friend, Ernie, to put down his rifle. It was never our intention to harm any of you. I hope you're not worried about that."

"You've violated a sacred place, Danner; you've desecrated, defiled, and destroyed more than you'll ever comprehend. Ernie believes these creatures are the physical forms of ancient spirits, to whom he has dedicated himself to serve and protect. He's not going to let you get away with it. You had better realize that right now."

"Fuck this shit, Tom!" A different voice came from the dark—familiar only in its impatience and belligerence. "Hey John, remember me? It's Sonny. Don't give us any shit now about spirits, ok? Tell that crazy old Indian if he keeps on fucking with us I'm going to splatter his ass all over this shithole. You know I'll get it done, you just know it, don't you, John? Tell him I want to hear those shells being jacked out and I want to hear him throw that rifle just as fucking far as he can. Tell him he's got ten seconds before I massacre his red ass."

Beth was shivering violently. Wet, freezing, scared out of her mind, she must have been waiting for me to do something and wondering why I just kept shivering there beside her.

What could I do, or say? If only I knew what Ernie was going to do . . . But what if I could tell him what to do without letting Danner or Sonny in on it?

I sorted through the miscellany of Sahaptin words and grammar I could dredge up from memory to construct a command that hopefully would be intelligible to Ernie. I had to get the terms, the inflections, the pronunciation close to right or Ernie wouldn't be able to understand me any better than Sonny or Danner. But I was confident that even if Ernie couldn't understand my misshapen Sahaptin, he would know I was up to something and he would use his head. I could count on that.

This was another situation where I really didn't have enough information to make an informed decision. It didn't seem reasonable that Sonny would shoot anyone he didn't have to. But he could, and he might. If I forced the issue, I could get both Ernie and me killed. Then what would happen to Beth? But what would happen to Ernie if I did nothing? This was a thing that Ernie would be willing to die for. He was not going to throw away his rifle and surrender.

And so it would be one more situation where I had the feeling that I was making the wrong decision, but made it anyway.

"*Wina-as, nam tuchna-ta pyus na . . . aaaww!*" To the best of my meager knowledge, I had shouted, "I am going, you shoot the snake . . . now!"

Nothing.

I repeated it.

Nothing.

Then Sonny spoke again. "You talk English now, John. I can blast your ass just as . . ."

But it was the blast from Ernie's old Winchester that cast the deciding ballot and cut Sonny off. Three quick blasts, to be precise, as I jumped up and sprinted blindly through the black void hoping to get close enough to Danner or Sonny to engage one of them, disable him, get his rifle.

Running desperately in the dark seemed only slightly less thrilling than jumping off a cliff blindfolded, or even without a blindfold. They could hear me coming, stumbling over sand castles, splashing through the shallow water. I waited for the flashes and the bullets coming out to meet me as I ran flat out.

But there were none.

And when I thought I had gone far enough, I held my flashlight away from my body, pointed it down the tube, and pushed it on and off for one brief frame of reference.

I stopped and turned the flashlight back on, holding it on the two figures lying on the floor of the tube ten feet ahead of me. I had seen enough in my first quick flash to tell me that I was not going to get shot by either Sonny or Danner.

Ernie had fired three times at the sound of Sonny's voice, and two of the lumbering, flat-nosed, 170-grain bullets had found their invisible target. One had gone into the top of Sonny's left buttock as he lay prone and had come out behind his left knee. The other one had removed most of the top left quadrant of his big, blond head.

CAIN

Danner sat cross-legged in the water, clutching his bloody left wrist. He looked at me, his handsome face expressionless. Picking up his rifle, I took out the bolt and flung it into the darkness and then swung the rifle by its barrel against the wall of the cave until the walnut stock broke off. I did the same to Sonny's custom .375 Weatherby, but that didn't make me feel any better either. Without saying anything to Danner, I walked back to where I had left Beth in a shivering heap on the floor of the lava tube. Ernie had helped her up by then and had his arm around her as she clung to his waist under the protection of his heavy mackinaw. The beam of my flashlight found the bodies of the Tah-tah-kle'ah. The young one had fallen on top of its mother. A third lay face down a few yards away. There was no sign of any others as far as I could see up the tube.

Ernie handed Beth to me and walked over to the dead animals. His back was to us as he knelt and gently patted the mother's fur. He talked softly to her in Sahaptin, not ritually, but personally. I guessed that he was apologizing.

He had brought Beth and me to this place unaware of the far-trailing strands that connected the mundane webs of our lives back in Seattle to the ethereal threads of his world. He would assume the guilt of this terrible thing, believing his lack of vigilance to be near the beginning of the causal chain. There would be months of fasting, cleansing of the mind and spirit in the sweat lodge, and long journeys to search for answers in that other place and time that only he could visit. I worried that he was very old; that he might journey too far and not make it back in this lifetime.

For me to say I was sorry for my own lack of vigilance, for the links I had forged in the causal chain, seemed inadequate, meaningless to the point of insignificance. Yet I would say it, and having said it, I would know that it meant something at least to me to have said it. Ernie would not blame me, nor even Danner and Sonny, for that matter. He would blame his own lack of prescience, in that he had been unworthy to see into the future, except darkly and without understanding. He would blame himself for having allowed the white man's world to contaminate him and make him spiritually weak. He would blame himself for many things. But most of all, he would blame himself for being nothing more than just a man.

In a few minutes, Ernie came away from the lifeless hulks, stoicism chiseled deeply by the shadows into his handsome old furrowed features. I would have to patch up Danner so we could set out on our trip back to the surface. Ernie escorted Beth past Danner, who must have seen in their grimly shadowed expressions that he was better off saying nothing to them, and they said nothing to him.

Ernie's bullet had punched through Danner's lower left wrist, taking off the end of the ulna and severing the ulnar artery. I should have examined him sooner because although he had stopped most of the flow by direct pressure with his left hand, he had lost a fair amount of blood. The severed end of the artery was exposed and as I had observed in similar wounds in Nam, the severed artery had collapsed and was bleeding less that if it had been only partially severed. Danner held the flashlight while I wrapped his handkerchief and mine around his wrist and tied up the sleeve of his parka to his hood strings to hold his arm up and keep the wound elevated. It must have hurt like hell, but he clenched his perfect teeth and said nothing.

I had him up and walking in five minutes. Although he didn't appear to have any symptoms of shock, I walked beside him and hung on to him, thinking he might pass out at any time from loss of blood. I didn't want to have to carry him all the way back to the truck. I glanced at my watch as we stumbled back toward the skylight. We had been in the tube just a little over an hour. I hated to think how difficult it was going to be to sort out the events of that hour with the sheriff's department. Nor was I comfortable not knowing how Ernie would react to having the police, the press, and the public invade the adytum of his secret, sacred lava tube.

We reached the skylight just before half past eight. I climbed back up the rope and then pulled Beth up in the sling next be-

CAIN

cause she was the lightest. She and I had just started to pull Ernie up out of the lava tube when it happened.

Civilization has encouraged the ridiculous illusion that human beings are the dominant power in the universe; that their weapons, their earthmoving equipment, their airplanes and computers, their vaccinations and medicines, their command of electricity and chemistry and physics, along with their grandiose intentions and pretensions, make them masters of their world. Like a swarm of ants, we brazenly scurry to and fro, building and destroying, all the while believing our ingenuity and organization make us a collective colossus whose proportions and potential verge on the divine. And yet every single day nature demonstrates its utter indifference to man's touted technology and accomplishments, consuming and obliterating with fire, flood, drought, wind, heat, cold, pestilence, earthquakes, tsunamis, volcanoes, gravity. Humankind's most magnificent and most malevolent capacities pale to pettiness in comparison to the unimaginable magnitude of elemental forces.

Suddenly, without any preliminaries; without regard for or acknowledgment of humankind's needs, wants, laws, or claims to dominion; without purpose, pride, or prejudice, Mt. St. Helens erupted.

A roaring, rumbling tremor shook the ancient lava bed so furiously we could hardly stand upright. Almost immediately, visible cracks began to appear in the snowfields a thousand feet above us on the mountainside. Superheated steam and sulfurous gases hissed out of dozens of small vents all around us and above us as the rumble of the quake yielded to the roar of avalanches and rockslides gaining momentum down the crumbling slopes.

Beth and I began to pull Ernie up to the surface as fast as we could. He looked worried, afraid, but not for himself.

The top blew off the mountain with a thunderous, cracking thud. On the other side of the mountain, north of us, the whole bulging northern flank collapsed in a gigantic avalanche. followed by a devastating pyroclastic hurricane of hot gases, ash, and debris. Steaming muddy rivers of ash and melted snow rushed into the Toutle River valley on the west side, and hot pumice flowed eastward from the breach into Spirit Lake, damming off its outlet. Boiling and billowing upward, a black column of ash and volcanic debris quickly ascended miles into the darkening sky.

Breathing became difficult as we began to suck in the hot dust tainted with acrid sulfur dioxide. Now Danner was screaming at us to get him out, and I threw the sling back down to him the instant I had peeled it off Ernie.

Heavier pieces of debris began thudding down around us amidst a thickening rain of ash and pumice. A huge avalanche of snow and mud slid away from the slope a quarter of a mile to the west of us with a great sucking rush and roar.

Danner fumbled with his one good hand to get into the sling, as marble-sized bits of rock pelted us from above, and every few seconds a cannonball-sized projectile crashed close enough to spray us with fragments of shattered pumice and basalt.

Beth yelped as a rock struck her arm. Ernie got hit in the foot, and a chunk of pumice bounced off my back, almost knocking the wind out of me.

Danner was in the sling yelling for us to pull him up fast. We were all coughing and half blind from the fine ash swirling around us. All three of us hauled on the rope and Danner came up. With only one hand, he struggled at the top and tried to hold himself off with his feet where the rope ran over the edge. Ernie and Beth belayed the rope and I ran to help him up over edge. Just as I reached out to grab him, something big whizzed by my nose and ricocheted off the edge of the skylight, spraying me with fragments.

In the time it took me to blink, Danner was falling back into the opening with a surprised look on his face and the neatly clipped end of the rock-severed rope still in his hand. He landed back first on the pile of rubble twenty-five feet or so directly beneath the skylight. His eyes were open but he wasn't moving. Looking down at him I felt the air begin to blow out of the opening and a low,

CAIN

hissing roar filled the lava tube. Several feet of gray, muddy water rose up around the island of rubble on which Danner had fallen, pursued by a raging, ten-foot-deep torrent that sluiced down the tube and swept him away.

We grabbed our packs and held them over our heads to shield us from the debris still dropping out of the sky. There were fewer of the larger pieces falling now, but it still felt as if we were dodging golf balls—most of them at least—on the 50-yard marker of a busy, three-tiered driving range.

The only way out was the way we had come in. We tied ourselves together with the remaining piece of rope and followed Ernie through the dusty gloom, groping, coughing, not knowing whether we'd suffocate before we had a chance to be buried by an avalanche or beaned by a falling boulder.

The rocks stopped hailing down on us after fifteen or twenty minutes. We weren't under the main plume of ash drifting to the east, but a grainy mist continued to settle on us as we gasped, gagged, and coughed our way back toward the truck, sticking our faces inside our coats every few minutes to find a breath of sifted air.

Had the ash been any thicker, I have no doubt we would have choked and perished, but the mountain let us live, if only just barely. Hours later, when we stumbled through the ash-burdened brush and foot-deep gray powder onto the road, our red eyes behind our ashen masks stared at each other with disbelief that we had actually made it back to Ernie's truck.

We scraped most of the ash off the windshield, hood, and grill, got in, and gratefully started down the road. Fine dust fogged into the cab around the doors and through every crack and hole, making the air in the truck as unbreathable as it had been on the slope. But at least we were able to stay on the main road on the way back. As we got farther south the dust thinned, the trees became green again, and at last we were able to draw in breaths of clean air and cough up our lamenting lungs at our leisure.

The Skamania county deputy manning the roadblock we had circumvented on the way up was amazed and excited to see us, having thought no one was in the area we had come from.

"You folks are lucky you weren't over on the other side of the mountain. The dispatcher just told me over the radio the whole north side of the mountain blew up. She said it's a real mess, according to all the reports that have been coming in."

The deputy had a pot of coffee on a campstove, and he gave us each a Styrofoam cup of the hot, strong brew "to help flush some of the grit out of your gullets," as he put it. It did help. So did banging the truck's ash-clogged air filter against a log. It had barely gasped and surged along, trailing a of a cloud of black smoke the last mile and a half to the roadblock.

He noted our names and the time in his daybook and asked us what we had been so interested in that we would want to sneak past the roadblock. I told him Beth and I were graduate students at the university and we had wanted to check out a site of potential anthropological interest before an eruption might destroy it. I told him Ernie was familiar with the area and was acting as our guide. I also told him we had found another vehicle parked next to ours when we got back to the road, and I gave him the license number. All of which was true, except all the truth wasn't there.

I noticed Beth watching me strangely as I talked to the deputy. I didn't know if Sonny's and Danner's bodies would ever be found. I doubted it very much. If by some chance they did eventually turn up, it seemed more than likely their injuries would be attributed to the mountain and not raise any suspicions of foul play. If we tried to explain exactly what happened, we'd be jumping into a bottomless quagmire of incredulity. I had already seen enough weaknesses in the justice system not to believe that being in the right and telling the truth would keep a person out of trouble. If we had to explain, ok. If we didn't, that was preferable, and probably safer as far as I was concerned.

Danner and Sonny would be reported missing. With their vehicle found in the area after a major volcanic eruption, it would

CAIN

be assumed they had been caught in one of the multiple slides or mud flows and had been buried. That would be an appropriate end to it.

The deputy was not the kind of cop who suspected homicide and larceny of everyone he met. He seemed genuinely relieved that we had survived the eruption, and he appeared satisfied with our reasons for having been there. When we left, he thanked us for telling him about the other vehicle, wished us luck, and sent us on our way with refills in our coffee cups.

There had been no opportunity to discuss with Beth and Ernie what we should do or say about Sonny and Danner. I firmly believed Ernie would agree with my decision not to say or do anything about them, but I realized I had acted for the group without the courtesy of asking Beth or Ernie how they felt about it. Even though I didn't think withholding the truth was such a terrible thing in this case, there was a guilty stickiness about it that made me feel conspiratorial. Obviously, Beth was having some problems with it, too, although I think she understood my reasons.

"Is keeping quiet about this the best way, John?" she asked quietly after we left the deputy.

"I hope so. I wish we could just tell the truth, but it would sound so wild and improbable, I don't think anyone would believe it anyway. The thing that worries me is that the part about Ernie's shooting Sonny and Danner would be the only part anyone took seriously. If somehow their bodies were found but the remains of the Tah-tah-kle'-ah weren't, some prancing prosecutor out to make a name for himself or herself might make things pretty ugly. For Christ's sake, Beth, I was almost charged with assaulting Brent Woody! It can happen, believe me."

"I do believe you, John. It's just that it doesn't feel right. It doesn't feel good at all. I guess I'll get used to it. What do you think, Ernie?"

"I think John is right. Telling the truth is always best, but it's not always wise, and being wise doesn't always feel that good. You are an honest person, Beth, and so is John. I respect that with all my heart. Feeling guilty stinks, I know. But you can't feel guilty unless there is good in you. Guilt is a signal, a warning just like pain is. We can withstand pain if we have to. Sometimes we even enter into it willingly because there is no way to do the thing that is right without the pain. Sometimes guilt, like pain, cannot be avoided."

The Lewis river's turquoise color had turned to a milky brown from the ash and mud pouring into it upstream by the time we got to Cougar, where I filled up Ernie's gas tank and replaced the ash-clogged air filter on his truck at the service station there. The wide-spot-in-the-road community was abuzz with colorful commentary and cracker-barrel speculation about the eruption. It had to be a heady topic, where hunting and fishing lies and stale political opinions had recently dominated the forum in the tiny barbershop; and endless rumors of suspicioned romance, and updates on in-laws had provided the ongoing colloquy among waitress, cook, and a handful of regular patrons over at the cafe.

We were too dirty to eat inside—according Beth's and my standards, anyway—so I got hamburgers, fries, and drinks to go at the cafe and we ate them in the parking lot next to the boat ramp just down the road at the upper end of Yale reservoir.

Mt. St. Helens, hidden from our view by the hills lining the river valley, still poured out a plume that grew into the scattered clouds like some dark, billowing beanstalk sprouting from a sinister magic bean. Sheared off by the swift jet stream three or four miles above the mountain, the plume bent over and headed eastward on its way to redecorate a month of sunsets with volcanic dust as it circumnavigated the earth. Lower westerly winds wafted thousands of tons of ash from the tenebrific tower and carried it across the mountains, to be deposited in diminishing amounts on eastern Washington, Idaho, and Montana.

All three of us leaned against the truck, looking up at the ash plume, dripping juicy sauce and pieces of lettuce from the thick, unwieldy burgers down the fronts of our filthy clothes. I, for one, was replaying the events of the morning, that now seemed strangely removed in time although vivid in detail.

"I bet you were surprised when I spoke Sahaptin, weren't you?" I asked Ernie.

"Yes, I was," he replied reflectively. "It took me a while to figure it out, though. At first I couldn't understand why you were telling me you'd pissed your pants and wanted me to shoot myself with a snake."

"That's what I said?"

"Uh huh. Is the university really giving you a degree for writing down what you know about Indians?"

"I'm afraid so, Ernie."

"It's a strange world, John. Very strange."

We left Ernie getting ready to take one of his rare baths in the galvanized tub that for years and possibly decades had hung patiently on the side of the cabin between infrequent clothes washings and even less frequent body washings.

He wouldn't let me apologize or let me take any responsibility for Sonny and Danner, saying everything had happened as it had been ordained to happen and that was the end of it. But he did accept our thanks for having taken us to the lava tube. Whatever else it had been—dangerous, shocking, tragic—part of the experience had also been wonderful and profoundly stimulating. Everything about the experience had felt charged with obscure meaning and veiled purport, as if we had finally been given answers to eternal questions only to discover those answers were tantalizingly encoded. I could almost understand. I was on the verge of knowing something. But the big truths apparently were not that easy to come by, and I, apparently, was not quite ready for them.

Beth had discovered, much to her chagrin I'm sure, that instead of satisfying her curiosity, she had replaced it with an even bigger, more voracious one. For her, the answers had turned out to be just bigger questions. Now she was certain of some things she could not explain and doubtful of other things about which formerly she had been certain. Fortunately, doubt is the beginning of wisdom, and wisdom reveals to us which things, both seen and unseen, we may rightly be certain about.

Danner had spied upon Beth and me because we represented a small, but persistent threat to his power and pleasure—the power to coerce young women into gratifying his insatiable sexual appetite, and the pleasure he derived from both the sex and the power. I think he may have seen himself as a satyr, with license to pursue the maenads and nymphs who frolicked invitingly in the halls of academia. Maybe that actually was his problem—maybe he suffered from satyriasis.

In many other respects, though, he fell short of personifying evil. He could be ruthless, but he wasn't sadistic. He collected trophies, but the hunt—the pursuit, the stalk, the aspect of danger—excited him as much as the kill. His fine intellect both restrained and facilitated his obsessions. He could have been worse, and probably was on a path toward becoming worse. Perhaps he would have become more and more predatory, eventually losing all control and revealing his perversion to the world. I was convinced that he wouldn't have gotten any better. For Danner ever to have repented and reformed was never a possibility. I understood that now. What he did was too much what he was. He never could have separated himself from it and, as far as I could tell, never wanted or intended to.

Sonny? I couldn't decide whether Sonny was a pawn or a bishop. I guess I would at least have to give him credit for being honest. From what I knew of him, he never attempted to hide the fact that he was violent and belligerent—unlike Danner, whose Jekyll-Hyde existence depended entirely on maintaining a respectable facade. As much as I had so fervently desired to see both Sonny and Danner punished for those various acts of predatory selfishness of which I was aware, I could not say they deserved to die. Sonny died as he had lived, because of the way he lived. I suspect it is how he expected to die and would have wanted to die.

Danner's death was more enigmatic. Ernie believed the spirits had wreaked their vengeance on Danner for the killing of the Tah-

CAIN

tah kle'-ah. In his view, justice had been served. For Beth and me, Danner's death did not satisfy our desire for him to be officially censured specifically for those perverse acts by which he had offended us. I suppose we felt cheated that, as Ernie believed, Danner had been brought to justice for more important offenses before having to answer to our charges.

Beth and I didn't get back to my apartment until late Sunday night. I-5 was closed for several hours where it crossed the Toutle river because flood debris stacking up against a beleaguered freeway bridge threatened to take it out. Logs and mud, flushed down the flooded Toutle river, dumped into the Cowlitz, which in turn dumped enough mud and debris into the Columbia to make the ship channel unnavigable. The ants scurried frantically in every direction, flashing their alarm with red and blue lights and wailing their consternation, as they attempted to comprehend nature's inevitable upmanship and adjust their lives accordingly.

The following week would be just another week, except for whatever differences Sunday's events would make. Computing the value of that variable would require too much time and too many complex operations, especially for someone like me, who was better at solving crossword puzzles than differential equations.

CHAPTER 23

Dooms of Love

Beth and I had dinner with the Cunninghams on Wednesday following our pilgrimage to the mountain and our encounter with Danner and Sonny. We were both uncomfortable with the fact that we were covering up, and even more uneasy that we might appear to be covering up some ugly, malevolent secret that was not like our secret at all. I think both of us anticipated a long evening of exchanging discrete glances to find out what to say, and whether we had already said the wrong thing.

Keeping a secret is one thing; being able to keep it a secret that you're keeping a secret is something quite different and far more difficult, if not impossible—especially around someone like Maxine Cunningham. Maxine was a dear, kind, wise woman, whom I had come to regard with filial affection. But she was more adept than a bloodhound at sniffing out the faintest trail of any secret, no matter how deep, dark, or deviously disguised—more adept at it even than my mother had been, and for a long time I had believed my mother to be the eyes-in-the-back-of-the-head, lie-detecting, sixth-sense, Holmesian, detail-gleaning queen of gentle inquisition, casual interrogation, and all-seeing observation.

By dinner time Wednesday, I had managed to wash most of the ash out of my ears, eyes, nose, navel, and other places; and my terminal-sounding cough had subsided to a periodic hack and occasional convulsive hawk. Beth was in similar condition and kept busy hacking, hawking, and self consciously excusing herself and apologizing during dinner.

Maxine, of course, was very concerned about both of us.

"My goodness, I hope you two haven't ruined your lungs. If those coughs don't go away soon, you'd better see a doctor. It might not be a bad idea anyway. You never know what kind of complications could result from something like that."

"I'm sure we'll be fine, Mrs. Cunningham, really," Beth replied, smiling as she tried to repress a stutter of wheezing little hacks behind her napkin.

"John, where exactly were you and Beth when the mountain erupted?" Dr. Cunningham asked.

"We were on the southeast perimeter, just up a little way from the base of the mountain."

"That's a coincidence," Maxine interjected. "That's the area where they found Tom Danner's vehicle. They said on the news that he's still missing. You two didn't see him down there anywhere did you?"

Beth broke out in a paroxysm of coughing, and I must have done a pretty good impression of a sheepherder caught in a compromising situation with an attractive ewe.

What was I supposed to do? Ignore Maxine's question? Take the fifth? Lie?

Not to the Cunninghams; they'd know, and even if they didn't, I would.

The least I could do would be to tell them I couldn't talk about it, which would make Maxine crazy to know what it was I couldn't talk about. I would be better off simply to tell them and trust in their discretion.

I knew Dr. Cunningham could keep a confession to himself at least as well as most priests—probably a lot better than some. Maxine ferreted out secrets, collected them, reveled in them privately, but she was no purveyor or betrayer of confidences. She, too, could be trusted to keep a secret—at least as well as I could be trusted to keep the one that I was about to disclose.

I looked at Beth to see if she objected. She didn't know the Cunninghams as well as I did, but she knew them well enough to like them and respect them as rational, honorable, well-meaning people. She also knew how important they were to me.

She shrugged and nodded yes.

"I guess I have to tell you something I had promised not to disclose. As a matter of fact, it was my idea not to disclose it to anyone. But the two of you are not just anyone. I cannot—will not—lie to you and I won't have you wondering if I've done something that would make you ashamed of me if you knew what it was. After you hear it, I think you'll see why it was not a story that Beth or Ernie or I wanted to try to use to explain what happened Sunday."

I told them how Danner had found out about the trip to the lava cave and had followed us there along with Sonny to find and take the ultimate trophy. I told them from Ernie's point of view what had happened, how and why Sonny and Danner had died.

"They were such strange, detached creatures," Beth joined in. "They let us come within just a few yards of them. Ernie had some kind of connection with them, almost as if they knew him and trusted him. And then there was this awful noise of the shooting and all the confusion in the darkness. I was so completely terrified, and I can't even say exactly what of . . . of the chaos, the violence, the dark . . . I don't know. I don't even want to know exactly what causes fear like that. They were huge and they smelled horrible, but there was something so beautiful, so serene about them; not just in themselves but the fact they were there . . . it's hard to explain."

Finally, I told them how real and immediate the possibility of dying had seemed for us all during and after the eruption. I told them every detail of what I saw, how I felt. I even tried to explain what it meant to me—until I realized I wasn't sure what it meant and I probably couldn't explain it anyway.

Beth was right. So many things about the events and how they affected us were hard to explain.

When I had finished telling them, I took a deep, phlegm-suppressing drink of Cabernet Sauvignon and waited for the Cunninghams to say something . . . anything.

·CAIN

The Cunninghams sat in silence after I finished. Shocked, fascinated, touched, incredulous—I couldn't tell.

My father had confided to Dr. Cunningham about the Sasquatch he and I had seen twenty years ago. Years later, Dr. Cunningham had begged my father not to get carried away with his increasingly desperate search to find and document another one. Dr. Cunningham was too objective to declare that a creature like the Sasquatch could not exist, but, not having personally evaluated any of the evidence offered, he was unwilling to speculate on whether they actually did exist.

The only hint of his personal opinion in the matter was the comment I had heard him make a number of times myself: "The fact that there are so many footprints and so many sightings, many by credible witnesses, warrants at least a competent investigation of the phenomenon if nothing else." If I told him I saw a Sasquatch, I was reasonably sure he would take my word for it. I was nearly as sure about Maxine.

After a tension-gestating minute of hesitation, Maxine, compelled to comfort Beth, got up from the table, walked over to her, and hugged her tenderly, sympathetically.

"I'm so sorry you had to witness those terrible things, Beth," she said softly. "The killing of the animals . . . The deaths of those two men . . . awful, just awful."

Perhaps because Maxine's tender, protective response reminded her how much she missed her mother, or maybe because Beth wasn't quite as tough as she pretended, she suddenly threw her arms around Maxine and began to bawl her head off.

Patting her, soothing her with a mother's consummate strength and affection, Maxine lead Beth out of the dining room and down the hallway, to a room where Beth's inner child could purge herself of anxiety with a flood of tears.

I felt terrible that I had not given a moment's consideration to what effect Sunday's experience might have on Beth's latent well being. On the surface, she had seemed to take it all in stride. Sure, she had been scared in the lava tube, but she had pulled herself together. I thought she was dealing with it in whatever way worked for her. I failed to realize that she didn't have any way to deal with it adequately, because it was something so alien and disturbing to her. I just didn't have any idea that behind the dam of her vulnerable psyche a flood of emotion was rising to the breaking point.

I thought I should go to her, even as late as I was in discovering she needed a shoulder to cry on.

"She'll be fine after a good cry, John," Dr. Cunningham reassured me as I got up to go after her. "Maxine and I raised a daughter, you know. It's a woman thing. Instead of getting drunk, or punching out her best friend, or just locking it all up in a vault inside her, a woman cries—a healthy, well-adjusted woman does, anyway. That's not to say there aren't any female neurotics, of course, but Beth isn't one of them. Crying would work just as well for a man, if doing it didn't make him look and feel like such a sissy. You're an anthropologist; you should know all about gender differences in cultural expectations."

Reluctantly, I sat back down.

"I think I know a little about differences in cultural expectations, but I'm beginning to feel pretty damned ignorant about gender differences. What are these creatures we call women? We don't have the slightest notion as to what makes them tick, and yet we can't live without them. How long does it take to learn how to operate them?"

Dr. Cunningham laughed.

"John, by the time you're as old as I am and have lived with one of those creatures as long as I have, and have raised one, you'll have begun to suspect how profoundly you are never going to understand them. Learning about women is a lot like getting an education—the more you learn, the more you realize how little you know."

Dr. Cunningham's observations were not especially encouraging, and I moped over another glass of wine, while he chuckled to himself over his glass.

-CAIN

Having mused most of the humor out of that topic, he finally got back to Sunday's somber business.

"You don't think their bodies will be recovered?" he asked.

"I suppose it's possible, but I don't think it's very likely. From what I could see, it looked as if the lava tube would fill up with sediment, and the tube could well have been a mile or more in length. I didn't see any other skylights farther down the slope. Besides, it's likely that slides covered the whole plateau. Unless their bodies washed out way down below us somewhere, I'd say they are permanently interred."

"Who was this friend of Danner's?" Dr. Cunningham asked.

"Sonny Larson. He ran a hunting guide business up in Alaska. Danner had been hunting with him for years. Apparently, he and Danner had been going on Sasquatch expeditions together ever since they met." As I answered, I wondered what it all meant.

"It's a strange thing about Sonny," I mused, "I knew him when I was ten years old. After he moved away, I never saw him again until that day in Laos, twelve years later. And then he turns up with Danner at the lava cave Sunday after another nine years. When I was ten, he called me stupid because I told him my dad and I had seen a Sasquatch. In Laos, he appeared out of nowhere and accidentally killed my friend, Chun, who tried to keep him from shooting two Sasquatch-like creatures we discovered in a cave. He came close to killing me, too, when I reacted to what he had done. Sunday he showed up again, helped Danner kill three of the animals that Ernie calls the Tah-tah-kle'-ah, and got shot dead in the dark by Ernie. It stretches the notion of coincidence pretty thin, don't you think?"

"I thought you didn't believe in fate, destiny, predestination, that sort of thing, John. Strictly a naturalistic, *liberum arbitrium* kind of guy—nothing but physical law, random events, coincidental synchronicity, and a free will to sort it all out with."

"I'm starting to think it might be just a little presumptuous of me to pronounce how the universe works or doesn't work. Maybe there are no supernatural forces operating in this world, I can't say for certain, but I am beginning to think that the laws of physics, random events, and free will alone just don't cut it. I think human beings need more than just science, technology, and cynicism to live by. They need beliefs; they need cultural continuity; they need to feel like something out there is paying attention to them, that they aren't just ad hoc collections of atoms being dissolved and recycled as new people every seventy years, more or less. No matter how superstitious and irrational we may think they were, I'd be willing to bet that throughout the existence of humans, the cultures whose people were most at peace with the lives they led were the cultures with the deepest, strongest beliefs. Science and technology may destroy belief, but they are never going to replace it. As far as I'm concerned, the primitive cultures of the American Indians—all of the primitive cultures around the world—represented a level of human existence that will never be improved upon. Not even if humankind survives long enough to explore the farthest reaches of the galaxy will human beings be any closer to justifying their evolutionary purpose, if there is one, than primitive societies have been since the beginning. And do you know what the tragic thing about it is, Sid? Unless we lose science and technology and ninety percent of the world's population, we'll never be able to go back—probably not even then."

"I can't argue humans are any better, or even better off, now than they ever were, John, but there are many who would argue it. I think we are as good and as well off as we can be under the circumstances—some of us are good but not well off, some of us are well off but not good, and a whole passel of the rest of us are somewhere between good and bad, well off and miserable. I don't know if we are capable of being better or doing things differently as a species. It's hard enough for an individual to do better or differently, and an individual doesn't have to get the consent and cooperation of every other individual on the planet to do it. I also can't disagree that we have given up a great deal of wisdom over the millennia in exchange for knowledge of questionable value. However, I don't think too many people would want to go back to

CAIN

a primitive existence if that were possible, and I think you're right—it's probably not possible. On the other hand, it's probably never been possible to do much to prevent change, either for better or worse. We are pretty much stuck with the world we're born into and we'd better accept that it is going to change, because it will; it always has—with or without us. I don't see how wishing one had been born into a different culture or into a different time is going to make things any better for anyone, do you?"

"No, I guess not," I admitted, feeling somewhat unbottled after my outpouring of opinion about humanity's needs. In truth, I had been talking about my own needs, and that had been readily apparent to Dr. Cunningham.

Maxine came back into the dining room without Beth.

"Beth will be along directly," she said sternly, "and I don't want the two of you bringing up anything unpleasant. Is that understood?"

"Of course, dear," Dr. Cunningham replied understandingly, to which I quickly added my obedient "Yes, ma'am."

In a few minutes Beth came back into the dining room and sat down at the table, looking a little sheepish.

"Are you all right, my dear?" Dr. Cunningham asked before I could decide exactly what to say to her.

She mustered a diffident smile and said, "I'm fine, thank you. I don't know what came over me . . ."

He reached across the table and took her hand.

"It's quite all right. I'm glad you're feeling better."

She acknowledged with a much-improved smile.

"We're going to see my parents Memorial Day weekend—John and I," she said, as if to draw the subject of conversation away from herself. "My father invited us."

Maxine had just returned from the kitchen with a custard pie topped with strawberries. Knowing about our problem with Beth's father on my first visit, she was thoroughly pleased to hear the news.

"That's wonderful, Beth," she warbled merrily. "I'm so happy for you. I knew things would work out. They usually do, you know."

"Yes, I think everything is going to be all right now," Beth said, as she dug into the pie, her appetite having returned with the sight and smell of Maxine's dessert, and with the warmth of the Cunningham's kind attentiveness.

Still unable to think of the right thing to say to Beth, I just ate my dessert—enjoying every bite and coughing only once. Maybe I was a selfish, inconsiderate cad, but I knew a damned good dessert when I tasted it—just as I would know the right words when they came to me, eventually.

* * *

I spent the rest of the quarter nursing bruises and sore muscles from letting Bud and his cronies practice judo holds and throws on me that I had demonstrated to them. I was surprised I remembered as much as I did. It wasn't something I had practiced and reviewed very often since the army. Despite the aches and pains and the loud, lingering smell of liniment, I enjoyed the exercise and the camaraderie with Bud and his friends, all men of about the same vintage as Bud. Of course, Bud was delighted to learn the technique that had allowed a "little fart" like me, as he had put it, to bring Brent Woody to his knees.

As I finished out the quarter doing mine and Max's TA work, I gave a great deal of thought to the prospect of a life and profession as a college teacher. Teaching would be a challenge. To be an interesting and effective teacher would require a great deal of continuing effort and practice; to become interested and to stay interested in the students would require a sincere belief that what they were doing and what I was doing were important, meaningful endeavors.

Teaching, taken seriously, is a profession that demands a teacher's best efforts in order to satisfy even the least among the

-CAIN

criteria for success, because the ultimate success of a teacher is not what he or she achieves, but what his or her students achieve.

The hitch is that students vary in ability, whether in kindergarten or in graduate school. Theoretically, the students of a good teacher should achieve at a higher level and appreciate their learning experience more than they would under a teacher of lesser ability. I had no argument with that. Even the slowest learner deserves the opportunity to achieve as much as possible. But just as students may not achieve their full potential under a mediocre teacher, even the most brilliant teacher is limited by the finite potential of mediocre students.

The part that had always baffled and disturbed me was why standards both for entrance and for graduation at public colleges and universities were not high enough to guarantee that graduates were the best in their respective fields. If the goal of education were to produce the most competent, learned graduates in every field of study, the best and the brightest of the teachers needed the best and the brightest of the students to work with. Of course, one could not ask that question or express those sentiments without being accused of elitism. Democracy had asserted "that all men are created equal." Egalitarians were busier now than ever claiming that meant everyone had the same talents and abilities, as well as equal rights and the right to equal opportunities.

My own perversive bent, however, had persuaded me that the right to life, liberty, and the pursuit of happiness did not mean a person could be a brain surgeon, a mathematician, a teacher, or anything else unless the person had the ability required to do those jobs. Not everyone has the ability and the temperament to become a brain surgeon or a barber. Not everyone can be taught to cut hair competently, and not everyone can be taught to do brain surgery competently. As one of Abraham Lincoln's teachers surely must have observed, "You can school all the students in some things, and some of the students in all things, but you just can't school all the students in all things—not if you expect to maintain the highest standards, that is."

From my own experience as a college student and as a TA, I was forced to believe that far too many undergraduates in most areas of study, with the possible exception of some of the sciences, engineering, and psychology, lacked the necessary combination of intellect, basic skills, and discipline to be in college at all. But that was egalitarianism in action, and probably the basis for the snickering among European universities at the low entrance requirements and easy curricula of many, if not the majority, of public institutions of higher learning in the United States of America. Sadly, ironically, I suspected the field of study with the lowest standards and the highest proportion of inept students was education—the training place for public school teachers. Many education graduates became first rate teachers in spite of their training, or lack thereof, but many others did not.

That's why I hadn't been that keen to become a college teacher. The institutions weren't run to suit me, their standards weren't high enough, and there were too many people in college who didn't belong there—both students and professors.

So what had changed? Had the universities changed their requirements and raised their standards? Had students suddenly become smart enough to suit me? Why was I now willing, no, eager to become a college teacher?

I guess I had discovered that the world was not going to change itself to please me. I had tried to find a suitable pouting place in the army, where I could maintain my ideals, attitudes, and opinions, and where I could nurture my intellectual snobbery more or less detached from the real world. But after a while, I discovered I had alienated myself from the people around me because I had felt so damned superior—intellectually, morally, culturally. In fact, I was not superior. I was simply self-involved, isolated, and miserable. Unfortunately, it took me most of a decade to begin to see the light, which was still not as bright as it might be. Dissatisfaction with where I was, who I was, and what I was becoming drove me to try to reenter the fold of humanity, and I had made some progress—hopefully with more to come.

-CAIN

The Cunninghams, Beth, and Ernie had reached out to me in their own ways and had brought me back from the brink of bitterness and cynicism. They had made me think about something beside myself. They had reminded me that there are other people out there who are making the best of what they have to work with, not wasting their lives whining because things aren't the way they used to be or the way they'd like for them to be.

What had changed? I had. I had decided to put my best effort into the world's most difficult, challenging, frustrating, frightening, and ultimately, the most rewarding profession—life. It was only after I had made that decision that I could have wanted to become a teacher; only after that decision could I have any chance at all of becoming a good one.

Teaching would mean becoming a lifelong student who passes what he learns on to his own students. It would mean constantly evaluating and revising both the pedagogy and the content of courses to make and to keep them challenging, cogent, and relevant to the needs of the students, while also meeting or exceeding the requirements of the curriculum.

Research and writing would add to the breadth and depth of my learning. They would provide insights into the hierarchy of significance to be given the vast array of things to be taught. For it seemed to me, one of the teacher's most important functions was to provide a perspective on those things that are most worth learning and what their relationships to everything else are.

To be a competent teacher, I would have to become more patient, more tolerant. I'd have to value and encourage the marginal students as much as the outstanding ones, but I'd have to accept the responsibility of failing those students who couldn't make the grade.

It would be an engaging, rewarding, useful life. It was for the Cunninghams. It would be also for Beth and me.

After three weeks of waiting for a letter from WSU, I had almost given up hope of having made the cut for a final interview. The Friday before Memorial Day weekend the letter came.

I brought the letter in from the mailbox and propped it up on my table, dying to find out what it said and yet afraid to open it. As the water I had put on for instant coffee heated, I paced around the table, superstitiously trying not to be too hopeful. Finally, I sat down at the table. Bolstered by a hot mug steaming at my right hand, I reached for the letter. I held my breath, opening the letter as cautiously as if I were disarming a bomb.

The letter unfolded and I deliberately avoided looking at its contents until I had braced myself with a lip-burning swig of Sanka. My eyes wouldn't avert any longer. They had to know.

> Dear Dr. Brockman:
>
> The members of the Washington State University faculty selection committee are pleased to inform you that you are one of three candidates for the teaching position in the Anthropology department to be invited back for a final interview. We apologize for the delay in informing you, but the large number of extremely well qualified applicants has made the selection process difficult. We also apologize for any inconvenience imposed by the necessity of a second interview.
>
> The committee would like to complete the final round of interviews on Saturday, June 7. Please call the Anthropology Department secretary as soon as possible to confirm your continued interest in the position and to obtain any further details relating to the interview or to the selection process.
>
> Sincerely yours,
> Dr. Judy Dahlstrom

My initial excitement and relief soon yielded to the realization I was far from being home free. Having made it through the first interview was the easy part. Now the chips were down and I was about to win or go broke. Judgment day was at hand.

-CAIN

I dared not contemplate the irony. I had made it into the top three without being certain I really wanted the job. Now that I had decided I was desperate to get it, I suddenly had a disturbing, niggling notion I was ever so ripe for a good shafting by fate's fickle finger. At some point after the next two weeks until the interview, plus however long it took them to make up their minds, I would know whether my wait had been an interminable delay of gratification, or merely a temporary stay of execution. God! the stress of it all!

* * *

Saturday morning, May 24, at exactly thirty-eight minutes past eleven, the Bug sputtered to a stop in front of Beth's parents' house. Only a week ago at almost this same time of day we had arrived at Ernie's cabin to begin our trip to the mountain. The details were still frighteningly fresh, but the event seemed more distant than a mere week ago. I wondered how it might seem to Beth at that moment. I could see from the way she kept her eyes anxiously fixed on the house, more momentous matters occupied her mind. She hadn't wanted to talk about it all morning, but she would bring it up when she was ready.

Nervous, excited, she held my hand tightly as we walked up the sidewalk to the house. The front grass had been freshly cut and the drone of a lawnmower came from the back yard. Instead of climbing the front steps, Beth gave me an inquiring look and tugged me around the house to the back. There, sweating in shorts and tee shirt under the hot sun, her father was walking the mower back and forth across the big yard.

We stood at the corner of the yard and waited for him to see us. He got to the other side of the yard and started back across before he noticed us. He stopped, looked at us for a few seconds, then he shut down the mower.

Slowly, he began walking toward us and then he stopped and held out his arms to Beth.

She ran to him like a little girl—his little girl.

"I missed you Kitten," he said as they embraced. "Can you ever forgive me?"

"I've missed you too, Daddy," she said tearfully. "Yes, I can forgive you. I already have."

I stood at the corner of the yard, feeling like an outsider, but glad to see Beth and her father make up. Mr. Hansen looked up at me and motioned me over.

"Beth, did you know this man of yours can climb a tree like a striped-ass monkey?" He grinned and held out his hand.

"Thanks for bringing her home, son."

CHAPTER 24

Commencements

That weekend with Beth's family could not have been any better. Her father was a different man. It seemed impossible that his first reaction to me and his feelings about Beth's marrying me could have changed so dramatically. It wasn't because I had rescued the boy in the tree. Fundamental attitudes do not change that easily or that profoundly because of tangential occurrences. No, I think he must have reflected long and hard on Beth's willingness to forsake her own father for a stranger. At first, it had to have hurt him terribly, had to make him angry and vindictive, but at some point, he must have realized that he had to choose. He could indulge his monumental pride, cling to his unreasonable prejudices, feed his festering possessiveness, and say goodbye to the love and respect of a daughter on whom he doted. Or, he could love her enough to transcend his selfish propensities and accept her rights, her choices, and her judgment as an adult woman.

Obviously, he had made his choice, not right away and not without agonizing over it, but he had made it. He was the kind of man who, once having arrived at a considered decision, gave himself 100 percent to the implications and consequences of that decision.

Fortunately, when Beth's father decided his love for her was greater than his pride, I no longer appeared to be quite as monstrous and objectionable. I think he saw there was no reason not to like me and accept me, and that maybe there were a few reasons to justify it. And when he offered me courtesy, respect, and friendship, I could see in him the attributes that Beth, her sister, her mother, and his friends admired in him.

That weekend, as I got to know Beth's family better, I was drawn to them as I was drawn to her. We were able to laugh, to play, to be serious, to be at ease with each other to an extent that I found both extraordinary and eminently reassuring, ineffably satisfying.

There was discussion about the wedding. Yes, the wedding—the certain, sanctioned, imminent wedding. I was more surprised than anyone else. Beth had asked her parents if it were too inconsiderate of us to want to get married as soon as possible a week or so after commencement, just a modest ceremony and reception.

I offered to pay for the wedding, for part of the wedding, for something, for anything, but the Hansens would not hear a word of it. Maybe it was because her father felt he needed to make amends for his behavior, or maybe his pride had not been as thoroughly suppressed as he had intended, but he insisted the wedding had to be more than modest, it had to be wonderful, and that he alone would pay for it, whatever the cost. Another considered decision he would implement—even if it meant mortgaging the house. Of course, he was careful to tell Beth's sister not to worry; he'd be able to pay for her wedding, too—as long as she didn't plan to get married for a year, preferably two or three.

Then, after infinitely happier good-byes than the last time, it was back to Seattle to wrap up the quarter, anticipate the wedding, and keep our fingers crossed that I would get the job at WSU.

* * *

Beth flew over to Spokane with me on June 7, and I dropped her off at her home to work on wedding arrangements with her mother. Meanwhile, I took my vorpal sword in hand and, in uffish thought, proceeded to the tulgey wood of Wazzu, there to seek out the elusive Jobberwock (not Jabberwock) hopefully to come galumphing back all beamish and chortling with its head later that self-same frabjous day.

But first, I would have to outsmart and outperform Jubjub and Bandersnatch, the other two candidates. One of us would get the job; the other two would walk. It was simple: get the job or walk. Jobberwock.

This time we were asked to choose a topic from a short list and given an hour in which to write an essay on it. We were asked to present a micro lecture on a topic from another list, with the selection panel playing the part of students and asking questions that ran the gamut from dumb to difficult. The three of us fielded questions and debated issues posed by the panel, by student body representatives, and by the Vice President for student affairs. It was grueling and stressful, but it was fair. It provided the panel with more insight into our knowledge, our writing, thinking, and speaking abilities, and about our personalities in half a day than any other tests could have possibly provided.

The other candidates were good. They looked good and they sounded good. My own impression was that Jubjub came off a little too hawkish and slightly arrogant, whereas Bandersnatch seemed a bit too frumious to suit me. I hoped the panel saw me as somewhere in between. Perhaps it was only bias and wishful thinking that made me feel I had done as well as the others. I hadn't read their essays, but I had seen everything else they had to offer. As far as I could judge, the panel was going to have to decide based on subjective impressions, or by flipping a coin.

I didn't exactly galumph back to Cheney. Maybe I managed a hopeful chortle, I don't remember. I know I was beat, too psychologically exhausted for a one-in-three chance at the brass ring to register one way or the other.

Beth and I stayed overnight and most of Sunday before we tore ourselves away to return to Seattle. She was in high spirits about the wedding, but I was kind of pensive, subdued. The slithy toves were gyring and gimbling in the pit of my stomach, and I felt about as mimsy as Charles Lutwidge Dodgson ever could have imagined.

* * *

Spring quarter's last week of instruction and the beginning of finals left little time for mimsiness. The penultimate week was stuffed with papers to read, tests to write, and students to shrug off who came to me, having suddenly realized they were probably going to fail a course. My best and only advice to those students was to study hard for the final and hope for a miracle. My impression was that none of the students found that advice either helpful or encouraging.

What else could I tell them? I tried to console them by telling them it was too bad they were failing and wishing each of them good luck in finding a miracle. Ok, so this was the first quarter I had turned to mush and said how it was too bad they were failing and wished them luck.

I also had softened a bit the terse, ruthless comments that the students whose papers I read regularly were used to receiving. I was trying to work into the image of the patient, kindly professor just in case I ever got a college teaching job, and especially in the event I got the job at WSU. Suddenly, I was taking way too much time trying to find something good about papers that weren't. Some of the students were going to be wondering how many TA's with the initials "J.B." worked in the department. They were unlikely to believe that I could have become so liberal since their chorus of moans over midterm papers just a few short weeks ago. Still, if some of them had a single, well-formed thought about my comments, it would be one more than they had managed to come up with about anything in their papers. I felt somewhat relieved to know that, although no longer utterly ruthless, I had not yet succumbed to an excess of ruth.

The week gradually gained momentum, then disappeared all at once like a train entering a tunnel. Busyness had consumed it and it had vanished, like all unmemorable time between memorable events that is retrospectively compressed into nothingness, and makes you wonder how the week could have passed so quickly when the days had seemed so long.

On the second Tuesday after the second interview at WSU, I got a call in the evening. Beth and I were sitting at the table contemplatively sharing chicken chow mein out of a box and spacing out after a mind-numbing day of study for her and students for me. I had begun to believe I was neither tough enough nor saintly enough to be a teacher.

I picked up the phone and mumbled something, thinking it was probably another random invitation to attend Billy Graham's revival meeting in the Kingdome.

"Hello, John? This is Judy Dahlstrom."

I'm not sure whether a doctor would have described my autonomic reaction as tachycardia or arrythmia, but I know it would have made a spectacular pattern on a cardiograph.

"Oh, Dr. Dahlstrom, uh, hello . . ."

"I don't want to keep you in suspense, John. Welcome to WSU, you have the job. Congratulations!"

"I do? Well, I . . . I don't know what to say. Thank you. Thank you all very much." I was as tongue-tied as if I had just stepped out of my bathroom naked, and a whole room full of people were standing around yelling "Surprise!" "Surprise!"

"You can be proud of your accomplishment, John. The competition for this position was as stiff as I have ever seen it, and I've sat on at least a dozen selection panels over the years. We're very happy to have you join the faculty here at WSU. We're all looking forward to some impressive work from you, both as a teacher and as a scholar."

"Thanks again. I hope I measure up to your expectations. If I don't, it won't be for want of trying."

"Oh good, that kind of attitude is one of many things that made us pick you for the job. You'll be receiving a formal notification in a few days, along with a contract and a bunch of other forms and other informational kinds of things. I just wanted to inform you of the panel's decision as soon as possible. You might be interested to know it was a unanimous decision, which is not always the case. I'll be talking to you again soon, John. I hope you are planning a celebration. You've earned it."

"Oh yes, absolutely—a celebration . . . Thank you."

Beth was jumping around, squealing, hugging me, and squealing, and hugging me some more.

I had been keeping my feelings locked up: how I felt about the possibility of getting the job or not getting the job and what each of those things would mean. They were too heavy to carry around and took too much mental and emotional energy to contemplate. Now they were out of the box and running amok and I wasn't prepared. It was a little like taking a long swig of 190 proof moonshine on an empty stomach. The elation had gone to my head and weakened my knees before the burning had subsided and my voice had returned.

When it did return I croaked incredulously, "I got the job. Can you believe it? I actually got the job!"

"Yes! Yes! I can believe it! I knew you'd get it! I just knew it!"

And so we celebrated with the opened can of flat pop I found in the refrigerator and a trip upstairs to tell the Cunninghams, right after Beth had called her mom and told her the news. It wasn't news that was going to turn up in any newspaper, probably, but for us, it was definitely front page stuff.

* * *

Max popped in the evening of Friday the 13th, debonair and eager to participate in the next day's commencement pageantry. I had picked up my graduation garb and Max's the previous day at the University Book Store.

Then came the graduation ceremony.

After the introductions, the invocation, the address, the awards; while the wooden bleachers groaned under the weight of thousands of overheated relatives around the perimeter of the auditorium and up above in the sweltering second level; while sneakers hidden under sudorific robes rustled restlessly against the tarped gym floor, and graduates who had been out celebrating all night weaved and creaked on two phalanxes of folding chairs in the center of the floor; before the student who would faint and the ones who would throw up; before the myriad of master's degrees were handed out; it would be our turn.

Max and I wouldn't be separated by too many other Ph.D.'s as we shuffled up the left side of the stage at Hec Edmondson Pavillion wearing our black robes faced with black velvet and bearing three black velvet strips on the bell-shaped sleeves, our long blue and gold-lined hoods with the purple piping draped over our backs, and our mortar boards on straight, of course.

Our names and degrees are droned out, and we march up to the dais, where the university president Dr. Gerberding stands godlike in his murrey robe and black velvet *pileus quadratus* with its gold tassel hanging *a sinistra* and hands us leatherette diploma covers and shakes our hands as if they weren't the twelve hundredth and some he has shaken in two ceremonies that day and while two sweaty photographers blind us at the moment of truth with their perfunctory flashes and we grope our way off stage with purple stars in our eyes clutching the empty diploma covers tightly smiling and feeling a little smug about the whole thing and happy to be done with it.

Then the benediction and most of the Ph.D.'s don't throw their hats into the air because they're smart enough to know they have to return them in good condition next week to get their deposits back and they've already spent a fortune getting the damned degree so why waste any more.

Too bad there hadn't been a way to get the job at WSU without having to go through all the pomp and bullshit of getting a Ph.D. Now Beth had another three or four years of wading through the same bullshit and pomp.

Maybe it was just that I should have gotten some sleep like Beth did the night before and not have stayed up until three in the morning drinking beer and talking to Max.

* * *

Beth and her mother had decided they could just barely get everything together for a wedding on June 28, two weeks after commencement. There were no halls or ballrooms available anywhere, all of them having been reserved for wedding receptions for at least four months. And so the event was to take place outdoors in the Hansen's back yard, complete with portable dance pavilion, a band, and a caterer, who fortuitously had received a short-notice cancellation for that date.

Beth would wear her mother's wedding gown, which fit her perfectly and didn't need any alterations at all. A florist in Spokane was doing the cut flowers, and Mr. Hansen had negotiated with a local nursery to borrow a truckload of potted plants with which to foliate and flower the whole back yard like the garden of paradise itself.

Eight cases of Spanish champagne were delivered to the Hansen house one week after commencement with Max Alavedra's compliments and a confirmation he would be able to serve as best man . . . and that he would be bringing a guest.

We got the marriage license in Cheney, invitations were hastily printed and mailed, and somebody remembered to find a minister who would be available to conduct the service. Things went so smoothly it was terrifying. Something had to go wrong. Nothing this important could escape Murphy's law.

The Cunninghams had had a long-standing invitation to our wedding. They were going to England at the beginning of July and so the timing of the wedding worked out perfectly—another thing gone right to give one pause to listen for the sound of the other shoe dropping.

Isolde and her husband were planning to attend the wedding, and remembering the story my mom had told about Isolde's wedding, and after consulting with Beth, I asked Sid if he would be interested in playing his violin at our wedding. It dawned on me as I asked him that it was one of the few times I had ever addressed him by his first name, and it had felt right. He was surprised and moved by the fact I had called him Sid, but he was overcome by my request for him to play at the wedding.

"Sid, will you play Massenet's *Meditation*?" I asked him.

Tears came to his eyes and he could not have looked more grateful if I had just handed him a pardon from a life sentence in the Walla Walla state pen.

"Yes, I will, John, thank you," he answered, barely able to constrain himself. "I've been practicing . . . just in case you asked me to play."

* * *

"You've missed two periods?" I repeated, surprised but not disturbed by Beth's disclosure.

"Last month and this month," she said, sighing deeply. "I'm pregnant, John."

"And Ernie guessed it," I said, more to myself than to Beth.

"I think he knew somehow," she added. "I don't know how, but he knew before I did." She fidgeted with her engagement ring and looked away as if to keep me from reading her expression.

"What's the matter?" I asked her. "You don't look all that happy about it. How come?"

"Oh, John, I want children," she gushed, wringing her hands. "That's not it, that's not it at all . . . and it doesn't bother me a bit to be pregnant before the wedding, really. It's just that I'm not ready to give up school and be a mother, not yet. I don't want to give up the freedom we have. It's all too soon, John. We were supposed to have more time. I want to do some other things first.

Do you understand? It's all wrong just now." Her face scrunched up and she began to cry.

She was agitated, feeling trapped, disappointed, and maybe a little scared. Her hormones were beginning to go crazy over the tiny embryo growing inside her and they were priming her emotions to go off at the slightest nudge.

At that moment, all I could do was hold her. I didn't know what to say. I didn't have answers and it wasn't the best time for reasons, anyway. Thinking about becoming a father was different, weighty, pleasing to me, but also perplexing. She had obviously been thinking a lot about what she was going to have to give up to become a mother. I agreed. The possibility and prospect of parenthood weren't well-planned in our case. They hadn't been planned at all, but it didn't seem like such an awful consequence, to me at least. But then, I wasn't the one who had to bear the child.

As for getting her doctorate, I'd do whatever it took to make that happen because she was entitled to do it and she deserved the opportunity. Any hardships, any accommodating, any giving up things and struggling to meet obligations would be shared by both of us.

I suspected that I wouldn't fully appreciate the work, the anxiety, the heartaches of parenthood until I had my own kids; just as I couldn't fully imagine and appreciate the joy, the pride, the sense of accomplishment I would come to know as a father. The idea appealed to me just the same. I just needed a little time to make Beth understand that she wasn't going to have to do it all by herself, that she could count on me.

* * *

Glorious weather blessed the day of the wedding. I woke up to a golden sun and a brilliant blue sky and to the sound of a meadowlark that was just as impressed with how the morning had begun as I was.

Ernie had come in on a Greyhound bus the previous day. I had made sure a week earlier that he had his ticket and schedule. He had rented a tuxedo in Woodland or Longview or somewhere and he had proudly worn it over on the bus. I'll have to say, he looked pretty imposing in his tux with his long, gray hair neatly braided, his lean, leathery jaws gleaming and redolent with after shave lotion, and his keen old eyes as bright as sunset glinting off brown water. I even succeeded in pressing out most of the wrinkles in his tux that six hours on a bus had come close to making permanent.

Relatives had been trickling into the Hansens' house for several days, and so I got a room in a motel for Ernie and me. Sunday he'd catch the bus back to Toppenish, where he would stay with friends for while. By the time I awoke, he was already up, standing by the window in his tux and looking out across a field on the other side of the highway in front of the motel.

"You and Beth going to live around here, John?" he asked when he saw I was awake.

"No, I think we'll try to find a house in Pullman, if we can."

"Is Pullman much different than here?"

"It's pretty much the same. Why?"

"Oh, I don't know. I guess it would have to have some mountains and a few more trees for me to want to live here. I imagine there are worse places to live. I hope you and Beth will be happy in your new home, wherever it happens to be."

"Now, Ernie, you are going to be able to stand it long enough to come and visit us aren't you?"

"Hell yes, John. I can probably take someplace like this two, three days, easy. You bet I'll come and visit."

"I'm glad to hear that, Ernie. Let me get some clothes on and we'll go get breakfast. It's going to be a helluva day."

After breakfast I called the Hansens' house. Mrs. Hansen answered and said Beth wasn't feeling too good. Mrs. Hansen assessed the situation as "probably a little case of prenuptial nerves." I told her I was sure that was it.

Beth came to the phone, sounding a little green.

"She knows!" Beth whispered hoarsely. "John, she knows!"

"Calm down, Beth. She doesn't know. Nobody knows except you, me, and Ernie, and we aren't going to tell anyone else. Your mother just thinks you're nervous about the wedding, that's all. Ok?"

"You don't think she knows, then?"

"Trust me. She doesn't know a thing. Nobody is going to figure it out until you have a baby that's two months premature and weighs nine pounds."

"That's not funny, John . . . I have to go. I'm feeling queasy again. Talk to you later. I love you in spite of what you've done to me. Bye."

The wedding was supposed to begin at four and everything appeared to have come together by a quarter to, except Max hadn't shown up yet. He had gone back to D.C. after commencement and he was supposed to land in Spokane at two PM. When I had talked to him over the phone Friday, he was planning to be at the Hansens' before three o'clock. I called the airport and sure enough, his flight was running nearly an hour late.

Mr. Hansen had personally made sure there were no snafus, no omissions, no mistakes in getting everything ready. An excellent organizer and an attentive supervisor, he had gone about whipping everything into shape calmly and efficiently. Mrs. Hansen made a last minute adjustment to his bowtie while he joked ebulliently with one of the guests whom I had met, but whose name and connection to the family I didn't remember.

Max showed up at ten minutes past four with his guest elegantly attached to his arm. The mystery guest turned out to be Michelle Danner. I was delighted to see her, although it felt a little strange to know what had happened to her father, when all she knew was what was assumed by the authorities—that he had been killed in the eruption and that his body had not been recovered.

"Michelle, what a pleasant surprise. I'm very sorry about your father. It must have been a terrible shock for your family. How is your mother doing?"

"Thank you, John. Mom's doing well. We all are . . . but I would rather not talk about my father. I don't want to bring anything unpleasant to this happy occasion."

Michelle stood in the shadow of her father's death—I could see that—but exactly how it had affected her and to what extent were not immediately evident behind that pretty, refined face she wore. In a private moment, she might tell Beth how she felt. Maybe she had talked to Max about it. If I ever found out, it probably would be from one of them, not from Michelle. I could have been mistaken, but for an instant when she looked a certain way, I thought I saw just a hint of the sang froid I had seen so often in her father's eyes, but never in her mother's.

"Beth and I weren't sure you'd be able to come, what with all the last minute plans and the invitations being sent out so late and . . . everything. Max told me he was going to see you in Seattle before he went back to D.C. . . . Well then, I guess we can get started. Beth's going to be so pleased to see you. And so am I. Thank you for coming."

"Max, compadre, I was beginning to think you weren't going to make it."

"Shame on you, John. I would have danced the flamenco all the way across the country on gouty feet to get here, you know that."

"You're beginning to sound like a diplomat, Max, except I didn't know you were a flamenco dancer."

"I'm not, but I would gladly have taken lessons if necessary."

"We can lie to each other later. Let's get Michelle seated up front by the Cunninghams, and get the ceremony started before Beth changes her mind. Oh, before I forget it, here's the ring."

Michelle was seated, Mr. and Mrs. Hansen were notified, the minister was dragged away from the champagne table, and the organist, playing on an electric keyboard, began Bach's motet, "*Jesu, meine Freude.*" Max escorted Beth's mother up to the front row of folding chairs arranged in a semi circle on the lawn in front of the dance pavilion. Beth's sister was maid of honor. Max escorted her up the red carpet runner in the center aisle to the makeshift altar, and then took his place beside me in front of the seventy-five or so people turning around in their seats to see the bride.

A moment of silence . . . then the organist played the introduction and the first eight notes of the wedding march.

Beth's father brought her slowly up the aisle, nodding his big head at various people and grinning from ear to ear, bubbling over with pride and pleasure and several glasses of champagne.

Beth—bright-eyed, blushing, effulgent in the white satin and lace of her mother's gorgeous gown—held onto her father's big arm as proudly as he carried hers.

As I watched them coming toward me, I realized how deeply he loved her—enough to share her happiness, enough to give her away to me because that was what she wanted. He would continue to cherish her as his little girl in his heart, but finally he was ready to let her become a woman, a wife, a mother. He would give her to me, but only because he believed I would cherish and care for the woman she had become, as he had cared for and cherished the little girl she would always be to him.

If Beth and I had a daughter, one day I might find out what it was like to walk up that aisle in his size twelve shoes with my size nine feet of clay.

The formal exchange of vows was traditional—to please Beth's mother. But as Beth dutifully pledged to honor and obey and I promised to cherish and protect, I knew it was going to be a more equitable partnership than that, a partnership without subservience and without dominance.

At some point after the wedding march, the organist had turned down the amplifier and had adjusted the keyboard to sound like a harp for the accompaniment of Sid's solo.

After her introductory arpeggios, the stunningly luscious vibrations of Sid's old violin enveloped the gathering. From the first sonorous note, I doubt if there were a single person present who did not respond to the extraordinary finesse and intensity of Sid's playing and to the appeal of the piece itself.

By the time he had reached the *animando* at the nineteenth measure, there wasn't a dry eye anywhere in that back yard, including mine. Of course, Isolde and Maxine were superlative among the lachrymose. Even Muff was sitting out there crying like a baby, so was Max, and Beth's father—we all were.

Not a sound was made for a full minute after the final, haunting harmonic faded into infinity.

The pastor was so moved that he offered up a tearful paean to God for having exalted the music and the musician with His divine gift of grace and beauty. I think most of the people present would have been susceptible to the suggestion that the rays of golden sunlight reflecting off the neighbor's window behind Sid seemed to give him a kind of aura—yes, a halo. Even if it were not, he had played like an angel all the same.

And then the rings, the blessing, the kiss, the introduction to the gathering as Dr. and Mrs. Brockman, and having been granted only an instant in which to savor the event as it unfolded, we watched everything slowly resume its inexorable slide from the imminent future, through the evanescent present, into the endless reaches of the past.

But it was, after all, a very, very slow slide, no more or less hurried than the imperceptible sweep of the hour hand on a clock. We could occupy that nothing-everything place between future and past as long as we lived, and for the next few hours, we could use it to celebrate the many things we had to celebrate.

Celebrate we did, and if anyone failed to revel sufficiently, it was only because he or she drank too much champagne too quickly and couldn't carry on.

I suspected the champagne must have come from Andalusa, because three glasses assigned a flamenco rhythm to your heartbeat; any more than four glasses and suddenly you got this stomping sensation right behind your eyes. That was true for just about everybody except Max. Apparently he had long since built up an immunity to nearly all of it's potent effects, to all of them that is save the one that made him want to recite poetry to everyone.

Beth drank nothing but pop all evening. Once, I thought I noticed her mother watching her as she passed up the champagne and guiltily sneaked a refill of ginger ale. But so much was going on, I didn't get a chance to worry about any suspicions her mother might be entertaining.

Ernie shook his head at the mountain of food the caterer had provided and dedicated himself to not letting any of it go to waste. The four-piece band arrived in a timely fashion and began to set up while everyone was eating. True, we ate outside and there were a few obnoxious flies, even a few cantankerous yellow jackets, and then there were the honeybees that had discovered all the flowers, but they didn't cause any real problems and no one seemed to mind.

We cut the cake and posed for pictures while Mr. Hansen addressed the gathering, rambling on about Beth's model airplanes and her first day in kindergarten. When he had worked his way back to anecdotes about her potty training, Mrs. Hansen diplomatically sidetracked him and eventually got him to yield the floor to someone else.

It wasn't long, however, before Max had diplomatically commandeered the microphone and was proposing toasts.

"To the bride and groom: May their love be boundless, their joy endless, and their burdens weightless."

"Here, here!" Applause.

"To marriage: A community consisting of a master, a mistress, and two slaves—making in all, two."

A smattering of applause.

I recognized that toast as one attributed to Ambrose Bierce.

"Let me not to the marriage of true minds admit impediments . . ."

I got to the band leader and told him if he didn't strike up a very loud and danceable tune, we were all going to be inundated by a deluge of increasingly poetic and grandiose toasts.

" . . . Love is not love which alters when it alteration finds, or bends . . ."

The band leader gave me a thumbs up and launched the group into a kamikaze set of "Beer Barrel Polka," "Wake Up Little Suzie," a very strange rock rendition of "*Eine Kleine Nacht Musik,*" concluding with "Sentimental Journey."

Max finished the sonnet he was reciting, as if anyone could hear him or was paying any attention to him. The words were lost in the blast of the music, but his lips continued to move for about as long as it should have taken to finish the last twelve lines. When he finished, seeming perfectly content with his oration and totally oblivious to the fact the music had drowned him out, he grabbed Michelle and began to boogie.

Beth and I were surprised to discover that Ernie was a good dancer, a recreational skill he availed himself of with the ladies. He had reserved his first dance for Beth, and everyone stood aside to watch them: the beautiful young bride, who had by then exchanged the fragile wedding gown for a more practical dress, and the straight, tall, agile old gentleman in the slightly wrinkled tuxedo, who would have put Caesar Romero to shame on the dance floor.

I couldn't tell which of them enjoyed the dance more. It actually occurred to me that I should take Ernie aside and have him give me a few pointers, seeing as how I was such a crappy dancer myself.

It looked as if he were systematically trying to dance with each and every one of the women present. Initially, quite a few of the ladies, young and old, politely declined to dance with the old Indian sporting the long braids and wrinkled tux, although I had seen some of them eyeing him favorably while he was dancing with Beth.

That didn't bother him a bit. He'd ask them again after they'd had another glass or two of champagne. In the end, the only one he didn't get to dance with was a woman who had six glasses of champagne and passed out before she could say yes. By nine o'clock they were all asking him to dance.

Of the many women with whom he danced, one definitely caught his eye—a middle-aged widow whose intentions were not clear, although he told me she kept asking him to dance the slow dances. Ernie wasn't having any champagne either, but he did stop by the buffet frequently to snack and to gulp copious quantities of coffee. We bumped into each other there and he was all smiles.

"I think I'm in love, John," he told me. When he pointed out the object of his affections, I nearly had a heart attack—the woman he was enamored of was Beth's aunt, Mr. Hansen's sister. I immediately implored him to move ever so cautiously in case it turned out to be just one of those meaningless flings.

"Please don't ask her to marry you, Ernie. Not until she sobers up. Promise me."

"Ok, John. I'll ask her tomorrow."

And then there was Maxine, who monopolized Isolde's husband, Marvin, for some pretty impressive rug-cutting. Marvin, pie-eyed as he was, wasn't moving too badly himself, but Maxine was the leg shaker. Meanwhile, Sid watched with a slightly sour expression from the edge of the pavilion until Beth got him out onto the crowded floor, too.

Eventually, the band leader cleared the dance floor and I danced a slow waltz with Beth, and then with her mother, and then Beth danced with her dad, and then everyone joined in again and the revelry continued from where it had left off. The Hansens had invited all of the neighbors, so there was no one to complain about the partying that continued unabated into the night.

Tired, but reluctant to leave the festivities, Beth and I finally made our exit about eleven-thirty. We were spending the night in a bridal suite at the Ramada Inn on the outskirts of Spokane and returning for a late brunch of coffee, juice, rolls, and Bromo Seltzer at the Hansens' the following day.

I had made arrangements for someone to take Ernie back to the motel—by himself. Beth and I would drop by and pick him up again the next day on our way back to her parents' house. In a barrage of flying kisses, hugs, handshakes, well wishes, and rice, we left everyone to fend for themselves and drove off, trailing the customary and obligatory cans and boots behind the Bug, which Beth's sweet, innocent little sister had thoughtfully emblazoned with outrageously off-color graffiti.

We reviewed all of the evening's memorable moments during the drive to the Ramada Inn. Of course, every detail of the wedding and the ensuing celebration turned out to be memorable, and so we regaled each other with our impressions and recollections all the way up to the bridal suite, even as we prepared to take a long, luxurious bath together in the suite's enormous tub.

Tired and feeling logy from the four or five glasses of champagne I had carefully metered out to myself during the evening, I had unceremoniously run the tub half full and lowered myself into the hot water while Beth had insisted on modeling her lacey peignoir for me. She came into the bathroom wearing the sheer nightgown with nothing under it, the shadow of her firm breasts and as yet undistended abdomen, the curve of her hips and buttocks even more tantalizing half obscured than unclothed.

I tried to imagine her with swollen abdomen and heavy breasts, as I knew she would appear all too soon. What I viewed as the perfect proportions of her form did not transform easily into anything else, however, and how she might appear in six months wasn't easy to fantasize. I did believe that I would continue to find her beautiful during her pregnancy in spite of the inevitable but temporary transformation she would undergo.

The hot water relaxed me almost to the point of putting me to sleep, and when she shed her gown and slid into the other end of the tub with a moan of relief, I found it only moderately arousing. She hadn't had any champagne, but she looked nearly exhausted. She closed her eyes and we conversed with increasing pauses and decreasing coherence. Finally, we had to get out of the tub to keep from falling asleep and drowning ourselves.

We dried each other with the blanket-sized towels provided. I massaged her graceful neck, her smooth, firm shoulders, kneading and rubbing my hands down her back to her tiny waist, where the flare of her white hips filled and excited my stretching fingers. I was no longer sleepy.

She turned and put her arms around my neck and pulled me to her, and I closed my arms around her. I felt her heart pulsing against me, her warm, sweet breath against my shoulder.

There was more of the smell and feel of her than I could ever take in, no matter how much I wanted it all. There was more of her beauty and sweetness and sexuality than I could know at any given moment or during all the moments of our lives. I wanted to gorge myself with it all: her youth, her beauty, her love, her intelligence. But in my greed, I realized, sadly, I would have to settle for a my privileged portion of the abundance that made her who and what she was. She had given herself, all of that, to me. Though I were to gather and hoard and glut myself on her gift, I never would be able to satiate my need and desire for the sound of her voice and her laughter, her half smile and sideways glance, the way she moved and walked, the way she yielded so willingly and eagerly when I touched her. I regretted that of the treasure offered I could carry away so little.

How I felt, what I felt admitted no ambiguity, but thinking about it, putting it into words—that was another matter altogether. Even if I could have expressed the notion of the thing, the fullness of its meaning was not translatable into any words I knew. What was it Shelley wrote?

> The wingéd words on which my soul would pierce
> Into the height of love's rare Universe,
> Are chains of lead around its flight of fire.

We held each other until our blood boiled with desire, and then we melted into each other, became of one flesh with each other—a union sanctioned and sanctified by our public vows, our private vows, our unspoken vows. It was somehow more than just sensuality, more than the intense pleasure of physical bodies and emotions mutually enthralled that elevated to a higher plane what

4-CAIN

Beth and I shared. I didn't know what it was, whether an intimation of immortality, or the combined archei of a man and a woman reaching out for a sense of connection to the *anima mundi*, the driving force of the universe. But I did know it was something important, something indescribable, something Beth and I were privileged to share together. I had felt it before and I had sensed that Beth felt it, too. On this, our wedding night, the feeling was stronger than ever before.

Maybe the gene of mysticism, passed down from my Neolithic ancestors, had begun to stir. Maybe Ernie was right about the primitive blood that coursed through my civilized brain. I hadn't talked to Beth about it directly, but I was certain she also felt something strange, wonderful, and inexplicable that was part of us, or came from us, or that existed outside us and beckoned us toward a level of consciousness we could only hope some day to discover fully.

Lying contentedly together between satin sheets on a big, round bed, we ruminated ourselves imperceptibly to sleep with equal and interchangeable thoughts of ourselves and of each other.

Thus, the wedding night passed on a different plane, one pregnant with even more promise than what either of us possibly could have imagined in the beginning.

* * *

The previous night's ecstasy, transcendent though it had been, did not transport Beth beyond the pale of more mundane influences, and I awakened in the morning to the sound of her throwing up. I felt sorry for her. Perhaps maternity was the reward of muliebrity, but surely it was also its curse.

We stopped by to pick up Ernie a little after ten and found him out back of the motel in his tuxedo showing two boys how to make a whistle from a willow twig. They were enjoying it almost as much as he was.

Most of the relatives and close friends, many of them squinting painfully in the brightness of daylight and wincing at the loudness of ordinary conversation, had bravely showed up for brunch, where anodynes and antacids turned out to be the most popular items on the menu.

It gave Beth and me the opportunity to thank everyone individually for attending the wedding and to say goodbye to them. Maxine thanked us on behalf of Isolde and Sid for giving him the opportunity to play his violin. Then Isolda thanked us on her behalf, and finally, Sid thanked us on his, her's, and Maxine's behalf. Beth and I thanked Sid on everyone's behalf.

Max was no longer in a recitative mood, in fact he seemed a bit taciturn—for him, that is. Michelle, on the other hand, had become almost garrulous and was acting peculiarly unvassarian. I noticed the way she was acting; I noticed Beth noticing; I noticed Max noticing the two of us noticing. And then Beth noticed the ring that had mysteriously appeared on Michelle's finger since last night and let out a squeal of surprise and delight. Michelle squealed in response and then they hugged. Finally, I figured out what the hell was going on.

"Max, *astuto zorro*! *Felicidades*!

"*Gracias, amigo*. I thought if someone as ugly as you could marry a woman as beautiful as Beth, I could do as well, no?"

"*Si, Compadre*. I had the utmost faith in you, and you didn't let me down."

"Congratulations, Michelle. Any thoughts yet about when?"

"Not yet. So many things have been happening . . . perhaps in a few months. I'm just not sure right now, but you and Beth have to be there. Max thinks we should get married at the Spanish Embassy."

"Oh, Michelle, that sounds so exciting. Don't worry, John and I will be there. Nothing can keep us away." I saw Beth place her hand on her stomach momentarily, as if trying to gage her availability should the invitation be for a date about seven or eight months hence.

With hugs and handshakes equitably distributed, Max and Michelle said goodbye to the Hansens and left to catch a plane back to Seattle, where Michelle would stay on with her mother and sister, and Max would catch a flight back to Washington D.C. I couldn't help wondering how Max's family was going to feel when he told them he was planning to marry an American.

Ernie was next to go after unsuccessfully trying to get Beth's aunt to agree to marry him. Undaunted by her sober rejection, he promised to write, and to ask her again when he came to visit her. He was the only one I overheard mention anything about visiting her, but maybe I missed something. Beth got a special farewell from him. I thought she was going to cry when he gave her a bone bracelet that had belonged to his wife, and which he swore had many powers that she would discover as she wore it.

I took him and his battered satchel of "real clothes" to the bus station. He gave me a long, crushing embrace and said a Sahaptin prayer for Beth and me.

I asked him how long he was going to wear the tuxedo, which was beginning to show considerable distress from having been worn three days already.

"I'm going to send it back to Woodland after I let my friends see how I look in it. I kinda like it, you know, John. Especially that cucumber bun thing—damned good idea! You just pull that down a little and you don't have to worry if your pants are zipped."

I waited until the bus pulled out and Ernie waved to me through the tinted window until I couldn't see him anymore. I missed him even before I got back to the Hansen's house.

EPILOGUE

I had Beth. I had a job. We had a future. We were at some point along the arc of our connected lives. It was probably best not to know exactly where, but I believed the zenith lay somewhere up ahead.

Ernie, the Cunninghams, the Hansens—they were descending the other side of the arc. But then, all arcs were not the same. All life orbited the same center, but each curve was tethered at the end of a different and variable radius, a different and ever-changing distance from the core of things, from the center of existence.

Each individual lived out his own segment of the curve; each family, each species seeking to complete the ambit, to make the concentric journey and return to the beginning. Only when everything had come full compass would the plan of life, the purpose of existence be perfected.

But that was not a matter to concern me now, not what the end result would be, or was intended to be. I wasn't likely to ever know anything about that for certain. The only thing I had any chance at all of knowing was my own infinitesimal segment of the human arc, and at best, I would come to know even that small thing imperfectly. I would touch the arcs of others and they would touch mine, as had Beth, Ernie, and the Cunninghams; as had Max and Michelle; as had the Hansens—even as Danner, Sonny, and Brent Woody had. I would know some arcs better than others, but all of them less well than I would know my own. Next to my own, I would know Beth's arc best. Maybe that was the wonderful thing I sensed with her—our arcs coinciding almost to unity.

It seemed perfectly clear to me now what William Empson might have meant in his villanelle, "Missing Dates," about what does and does not provide the necessary details by which we may live our lives; what does and does not "mill down small to the consequence a life requires."

To truly live requires the greatest attention to the smallest things. Minutes, not millennia, make the difference. If I attended carefully enough to the present, the past and future would take care of themselves. Maybe that was Ernie's secret—how he knew without understanding; how he understood without knowing.

The trick, I decided, is to live every minute of the arc, to waste as few of those minutes as possible on generalities, and grudgingly, to give only the last possible instant to death in any of its many forms.

The End

90000>
9 780738 816869